MW00560892

AFTERSHOCK

FOR:
Nicole & the sweet memory
of Joe P.

D.H.Wolfe

GEORGE H. WOLFE

LIVINGSTON PRESS
THE UNIVERSITY OF WEST ALABAMA

Copyright © 2022 George H. Wolfe
All rights reserved, including electronic text
ISBN 13: trade paper 978-1-60489-313-7
ISBN 13: hardcover 978-1-60489-314-4
ISBN 13: e-book 978-1-60489-315-1

Library of Congress Control Number: 2022931039
Printed on acid-free paper
Printed in the United States of America by
Publishers Graphics

Typesetting and page layout: Joe Taylor
Proofreading: Brooke Barger, Cassidy Pedram,
Savannah F. Beams

Cover Design: McKenna Darley

Front Cover Photo 1: *Kissing the War Goodbye* by Victor Jorgensen
Front Cover Photo 2: Clark Hall at The University of Alabama

Livingston Press is part of The University of West Alabama,
and thereby has non-profit status.
Donations are tax-deductible.

6 5 4 3 2 1

FOR

Captain Ralph E. Graham (USN)
(dec.), my first skipper, nominated
for the Medal of Honor, winner of
the Navy Cross aboard the USS Little
(DD-803), sunk by Japanese kamikazes,
May 3, 1945. A leader, a survivor,
a good man, and a tough S.O.B.

AND FOR
Suzanne

You may be through with war,
but war is not through with you.
——Russian proverb

It is well that war is so horrible,
or we should grow too fond of it.
——Robert E. Lee

He knew that the essence of war is
violence, and that moderation in war
is imbecility.
——Macaulay

What if they gave a war & nobody
came? Life would ring the bells of
Ecstasy and Forever be Itself again.
——Allen Ginsberg

PROLOGUE

I've long been fascinated by actions of the men and women who, in the wake of Pearl Harbor, upped-stakes and went off to war knowing, in most cases, very little about what they were getting into. In mid-1941, my own father was an engineer with a good job, a pregnant wife and a son. He was also 35, and with that profile he could have sat on his behind and urged the younger men: forward, boys, into the breach.

Instead, in August, '41 he joined the Navy as an officer with the SEA-BEES [construction battalions] and spent the duration of the war half in the States and half in the Pacific. Later, I think he reckoned it one of the best things he ever did in his 97 years.

As for myself, during the Vietnam war I served as weapons department head and Nuclear Weapons Officer aboard a destroyer home-ported in Japan. We provided a lot of 5" gunfire support for the Army and Marines fighting in that godforsaken war—and we grew up fast.

There is abroad in the land, I think, a mistaken assumption that the WWII vets went to war, fought, perhaps were wounded, then came home more or less undamaged, and stoically resumed their lives—or in the case of my characters, changed those lives by taking advantage of the new G.I. Bill.

While this narrative fits many of those 1940s vets, it does not apply to all, by any means. Unfortunately, the PTSD travails of the Vietnam and Iraq-era vets have somewhat obscured what those WWII men and women experienced in their readjustment to civilian life.

There was plenty of mental damage to go around; I recall some of my father's golfing buddies (ex-Marines and bomber pilots, for example) who were still held together with baling wire, booze, and pills 10-15 years after the war.

This book is for them.

George Wolfe,

Mt. Pleasant, SC

PART I

Chapter 1

To hell with the war. Sergeant Dante Gabriel Larocca figured he was done. Horn blaring, pedestrians scattering, he sliced through the afternoon traffic in a green surplus Army jeep. Riding shotgun beside him sat an elegant, over-sized, gray Weimaraner, the dog's princely decorum somewhat compromised by the aviator goggles it wore to guard against the slipstream. Larocca, 28, black-haired, battle-scarred, hard-muscled, and lately of the United States Army, was deeply pissed.

"Stinkin' civilians," he muttered, flipping the bird at a yellow cab that cut him off. Dante tailgated the cab to the next red light, then forced his jeep between two traffic lanes, pulling up tight, nearly clipping the cab driver's beefy arm.

"Hey, pal," shouted Larocca, "you ever hear of hand signals?"

The cabby looked at him, looked at the jeep. And spat.

"War's over, hero. Back to work," the cabby said, and drove off.

Although he'd mustered out of the service that morning, Larocca was still in uniform, his unbuttoned tunic open to the early fall air. Pinned on the tunic's left breast were three rows of battle ribbons topped off with two purple hearts and the Silver Star.

Larocca turned to the dog.

"Sir Plus, it appears we ain't in Berlin anymore."

The Weimaraner barked.

Three minutes and ten blocks later, Larocca wheeled into a parking spot in front of a movie theater and right behind a shiny, black 1939

Buick. He eased the jeep forward until its bumper kissed the Buick's, then cut his engine and sat for a moment, staring at the immaculate sedan.

"That's Bruno's. Dead certain."

The dog peered at him through the goggles, hoping this pit stop meant food, water, sex or all three. Larocca reached out and slipped the goggles off Sir Plus.

"Stay here. Anybody approaches, you know what to do."

He eased out of the jeep and looked around, buttoning his tunic and feeling the heat. Passing cars jostled for position with trolleys. Sweaty kids chased each other down the sidewalk, weaving and cursing—and being cursed—through the late afternoon crowd of shoppers heading home. Two drunken sailors drifted by, arm-in-arm—their white uniforms smudged with victory, hats slanted at rakish angles—singing at the top of their voices something that sounded like "Angers Await, My Goys."

Dante didn't see anybody he knew.

"Hey, Sarge, over here. I got just what you need. Tents, tarps, bayonets. You buying or selling?"

A rancid little toadstool with a big paunch, a small mustache, and a failed comb-over beckoned to him from a storefront. Inside, Dante could see mountains of surplus military gear. He glanced back at the Buick, felt his pockets for something that wasn't there, and turned to the toadstool.

"Bayonets you got?"

Inside the store, he fingered the business end of a like-new blade. The fat guy watched, then gestured toward Dante's ribbons.

"Two Purple Hearts. Looks like you got into some real shit over there. Is that the Silver Star or . . ."

"I forget. Let me borrow this a minute."

"Now, wait. . . ."

Outside, Dante worked through the crowd toward the Buick, easing the bayonet out of its sheath. He paused, lit a cigarette, dropped the pack near the car, bent over, and with a lock-picker's skill snicked the long blade into the right rear tire.

With a gentle whoosh, it collapsed.

He sauntered around the car, watching for cops and repeating his game three more times until the Buick had eased onto its rims like a high-paid hooker. The sidewalk throng kept moving. Nobody seemed to notice; however, inside the Army/Navy store, the little fat guy watched. Then he picked up the telephone and began dialing. Before he finished, Dante was standing next to him.

"Calling your wife?"

"Uh, yeah, um, no, I was . . . 'I was calling . . .'" He put the phone down.

"There ya' go. Careful. This thing's sharp."

Dante dropped the bayonet on the counter, wiped his hands on the fat guy's shirt and walked out.

Back on the street, he tied a length of nylon parachute cord around Sir Plus's neck, ordered the dog out of the jeep and led him toward the theater. In the ticket window sat a dour older woman wearing a bad wig, chewing gum, and smoking a cheroot.

"One for the feature," he said, pushing a dollar through the little hole in the glass.

The woman looked at Sir Plus.

"What is that?"

"Weimaraner. It's a highly bred . . ."

"It's a dog, and dogs ain't allowed."

Dante pointed to his head and looked doleful.

"War wound, ma'am. He's my seeing-eye dog."

"I don't care if he's your friggin' brother. No dogs inside."

Dante watched the woman chew and drag on her cigar. He'd never seen anybody do that before, but her smirk reminded him of certain Army MPs he'd confronted in England, Italy, France and Germany, nasty little pissants from places like . . . like Idaho and . . . frigging Iowa. It was the pleasure the ticket woman took in barring him that did it.

"Okay, right, lady. We'll do it your way."

He dropped the ersatz dog lead, told Sir Plus to 'Sit,' turned and walked through the red, padded-leather theater doors to the right of the ticket booth.

"Where the hell are you . . .?" Her voice was muffled.

Once inside, he spun left, spotted the door that led to the booth and saw the key in the lock. Snake-fast, he locked the door and pocketed the key.

"Hey . . . Hey! You bastard!" The woman pounded on the door.

He wheeled, pushed open the front doors and motioned to Sir Plus. The dog leaped forward, and together they entered the darkened theater where Dante could hear Bugs Bunny amusing the crowd. Inside the carpeted lobby, Dante paused to savor the air conditioning.

Jesus, that was nice. How long had it been? Two years? Three? Air conditioning. Jeez.

Jagged memories thrummed through his brain: dead guys; blood; butchery; a dismantling fear; images of his former ringmaster, General Patton, swearing at some hapless lieutenant, those big pearl-handled, Colt .45 single-action revolvers on his hips. Dante flashed on the suffocating heat inside his Sherman tank fighting its way through Sicily and across France. He caught a fleeting sight of Scapoli, of Rosenberg and Fenster, and half a hundred other dead guys.

And particularly of Buddy Fooshee. Old Buddy, who used to say, 'It ain't nothing but luck, boys, and there's only two kinds.'

And then proved it.

Pausing in the lobby was a tactical error. The sergeant and his 110 lb. Weimaraner had attracted the attention of a uniformed usher now hastening toward them. As the man approached, Dante started to lead Sir Plus into the theater proper.

"Hey," a stage whisper from the usher, "you can't bring dogs in here."

"Seeing-eye . . . The ticket lady said it was okay."

Skeptical, the usher hurried nearer, brandishing his flashlight until, at about ten feet, a low growl began leaking from Sir Plus. The sound seemed to originate from some mist-shrouded, Teutonic valley deep in the dog's immemorial Wagnerian past. Sir Plus's purplish lip curled back, revealing what struck the usher as remarkably long ivory tusks. He stopped, flashlight extended in defense.

"Mabel okayed this?" he said.

"Right. Mabel. Lady selling the tickets."

The usher paused, trying to reassemble his dignity.

"Well, all right then, enjoy the show . . . But no barking."

"Thanks. Come on, boy. Let's find our pal, Bruno."

They entered the theater just as the Movietone newsreel was beginning. Inching down the aisle, Dante could see the house was only about a quarter full—snuggling couples and retirees looking to fill the void in a hot afternoon. The newsreel was all about the returning war veterans. Over a patriotic score, Ed Herlihy's voice declared victory in Europe!

The wonderful, dreadful new Atomic Bomb!

Hiroshima! Nagasaki! Tens of Thousands Dead!

The Genius of American Invention.

Victory in Japan!

On the screen, troop ships full of celebrating soldiers steamed beneath Golden Gate Bridge. They hollered. They waved. They kissed the girls. Grinning sailors downed bottles of beer. In New York, Times Square went mad all over again. Ticker tape rained down. Old women wept. Young women laughed and pushed children into the arms of uniformed men the kids didn't recognize. And didn't particularly like the smell of. And maybe never would.

Herlihy continued:

> That's right, folks! Our GIs
> are heading home at last! With
> the war over in the Pacific, these
> boys are returning to a hero's
> welcome in the good old U.S. of A.!
> Well done, fellas. . .!

Dante made Sir Plus sit, then eased into an aisle seat next to a young stud who was chowing down on his date's ear.

"Hey, Vinny, you seen Bruno?"

Vinny whirled, "Dante! You're back! How you doin', man? Hey, Lucille, look who . . ."

Dante clapped his hand over Vinny's mouth.

"I'm good, Vinny. Never better. Bruno around?"

Vinny's eyelids nictated. Dante removed his hand as Vinny's mouth worked nervous little figure-eights. Even in the darkened theatre Dante could see he'd hit pay dirt.

"It's okay, Vinny," Dante said. "I know."

Vinny glanced at Lucille who focused on the screen. Then he too looked at the screen where veterans, loaded down with books, hustled across university campuses, past admiring co-eds and jealous freshmen boys. The vets were intercut with their wives tending babies in cramped apartments and hanging out diapers and sheets on clothes lines strung between knockabout temporary housing. The audience cheered as Herlihy continued his PR assignment:

> . . . Now here're some ambitious
> vets: going to college on the G.I.
> Bill! For most, the first in their
> family to do so. Good luck, men!

For a moment, Dante thought Vinny had forgotten the question. Then he saw that his old stick-ball pal was just assessing the options. Finally, Vinny pointed his chin at a spot several rows ahead, looked at Dante, raised his eyebrows and gave a little shrug—what the American GIs in Europe had called a 'French salute.' The gesture wove together equal parts of loyalty, friendship, sympathy, fear, schadenfreude, and rat fink. Dante nodded his thanks, touched Vinnie on the shoulder, and grabbed the dog lead.

Ten rows ahead, he slipped into a seat behind a courting couple whose heads were nearly touching. The man had his right hand up the woman's dress, while the woman's left hand fumbled with the man's zipper. Both were breathing hard and whispering over each other's lines:

"Can you . . ."

"I can't get it . . . Lean back."

"Wait, let me move my . . ."

"It's stuck or something . . ."

Dante leaned forward: "Can I be of assistance, Bruno? Maria?"

The two lovebirds jumped, then froze.

"Dante?" Bruno's voice came out an octave high.

"The same." Dante said, grabbing a fistful of Bruno's zoot suit jacket. "Get up, fucknuckle. I'm late."

With his scrunched-up coat serving as an ad hoc noose, Bruno couldn't fully turn, but he flailed backward with his left arm trying to strike at Dante. Instead, he had the ill luck to smack the patient Sir Plus on the end of his urbane snout. The startled dog roared to life. A frenzy of barking rose in the cooled air of the theatre. There, it was joined by dueling profanities from the men. Then by a fishmonger screech from Maria.

All in all, it was enough to overcome Mr. Herlihy's filmed paean to Armed Victory. And to bring ushers boiling like cockroaches from every hatch, each armed with a lit flashlight and professional outrage. As five of them converged on the melee, their beams swung crazily in all directions, like tiny versions of the great London searchlights that had recently probed the night sky for Marshall Göring's Heinkels and Junkers during the blitz. Within seconds, the two cursing principals, the roaring dog, the screaming woman and five grunting ushers formed a roiling throng scrabbling toward the nearest emergency exit.

Meanwhile, other audience members fled to opposite sides of the theatre, men buttoning their pants, women their blouses. A few drunks slept through it all. The newsreel had now shifted to President Truman's nasal Missouri twang welcoming two uniformed Medal of Honor winners to the White House in an ecstasy of patriotism.

The young pilot was missing a leg. The dogface, both arms and an eye.

Crashing into the theatre exit door, the two biggest ushers gained a tenuous control over Dante and Bruno, while Maria, following close behind in her bright yellow sun dress, kept reaching past one usher to bang Dante over the head with her matching handbag.

"Get the bitch off me," shouted Big Usher #1.

"Open the door," shouted Big Usher #2.

"Watch the goddamn dog," shouted Usher #3, grabbing Maria's purse in mid-bang.

Usher #4 flung open the exit door.

Usher #5—the original fellow in the lobby—stood by, summoning alibis as to how all this might have begun, with special emphasis on explaining the Weimaraner's presence.

The exit door opened onto a fetid alley separating the theatre from the Army/Navy store. First to spill out was the dog, ears back, at full cry. Following him came Dante, Bruno, and Ushers #1 & #2 locked in a ball of sound and fury. Sweating, their uniforms ripped, the ushers heaved the miscreants as far as they could into the alley, then tried to slam the door, only to be blocked by the body of their bellowing comrade, Usher #3, to whose left ear Maria clung by her teeth like a deranged weasel.

"Somebody kill this cunt," shouted Usher #3.

Usher #4 grabbed Maria by the nose and throat, forcing her mouth open and releasing Usher #3 who, bloodied but unbowed, kicked Maria in the ass, thrust her through the exit door and slammed it behind her. Inside the theatre, management had turned up the house lights to reveal a hundred terrified patrons huddled along the farthest wall.

"It's all right, folks," said Usher #1, his voice hoarse between gasps for breath. "Party's over. Please take your seats." As he straightened his little pill-box usher-hat he nodded to the nice young couple, Vinny and Lucille, hurrying past him to the rear.

Outside in the alley, Dante was completing a brutal whipping of Bruno Kretchmer, while Sir Plus, trembling with anticipation, had Maria pinned against the brick wall, his teeth bared at knee-level, his hackles standing upright in a bristly line from head to stubby tail.

Bruno lay on his back. Dante sat astraddle his chest, one hand gripping Bruno's shirt front, the other slapping either side of his ex-friend's face, emphasizing each blow in a sort of syncopated rhetoric of violence: "That's (slap) for my thirty-seven months (slap), thirteen days (slap) overseas (slap), you slack-assed (slap) draft-dodging (slap) gold-brickin' son-of-a-bitch! (slap) Yo', Kretchmer, you listenin' to me? (two slaps).

"Dante, stop . . . Stop it, you bastard!" Frozen to the wall, Maria was in tears. Mid-stroke, Dante stopped, seeing her and Sir Plus caught in their standoff.

"Sir Plus: Back!" Dante was panting, his face flushed, his knuckles bleeding. The big dog cut his eyes at Dante but didn't move.

"Back! Heel!" Sir Plus released only a milli-erg of tension, but he did back away a couple of steps.

"So, Maria, looking good. How you doin'?"

"You animal!"

"Hey, I'm a war hero."

"Yeah, it was in the papers."

"I'm also your goddamn husband."

Bruno groaned.

"I hate you!" Maria said.

Dante stood up, breathing hard.

"Now you tell me!" he said.

"Whatta you expect? You been gone fuh evah. I was lonely. I didn't think . . ."

The fight had torn Dante's Army tunic at the pocket. His decorations hung by a thread. He ripped them off and thrust them at Maria.

"Lonely? You see these here," he said, "these little colored ribbons? You know what they mean? They mean I just spent the last three years writing you four letters a week and getting my ass shot off while you were back here humping this no-count Kraut motherfucker."

Maria looked away, silent.

"You got nothin' to say about that? No explanations? No 'helpless-war-widow-lost-without-her-man excuses'?"

She turned back toward her husband.

"I love him, Dante."

He stared at her, processing this piece of raw data.

"You love him? That's it? . . . Okay, I get it. I loved you, but you loved him, so screw me. Love!" In his mouth the word sounded filthy.

"Jesus wept," he said, and stuck the ribbons into his pants pocket. Bruno rolled onto his side, blood seeping from his nose and mouth. Dante looked from one to the other, then kicked Bruno's ass.

"I ought to kill the both of yous," he said.

"Bruno . . . darling?" Edging around Sir Plus, Maria knelt by her fallen hero. Dante stepped back.

"So, Maria," he said, "how's old Kretchmer the Kraut in the sack, eh? Good as you and me way back when, before I went overseas like a good Boy Scout to defend liberty and justice for all? Can he go all night with you, like I could, huh, with those long, slow, deep strokes you used to beg for? Or, what about my little thing with the tongue, you know, that drove you nuts that time up on the roof? Made you pass out, as I recall."

Maria didn't answer. Murmuring Bruno's name, she used her skirt to blot the blood beneath his nose.

"Hey, Maria, I'm talkin' to you!"

When she looked up, her face had contorted into a mask of pure malice.

"I hear you, Dante. And let me tell you something, you big jerk . . ." She stopped, uncertain that what she was about to say would not lead to the double homicide earlier threatened. Dante leaned in toward her, making a 'So'? gesture with his eyes. She saw his sweat, the pulsing of that vein in his neck, his thick arms hanging limp.

She knew him totally, and she recognized in his face a more crippling pain than any she had ever inflicted on another human being. At that moment, she was not proud. She did not gloat. She felt no sense of triumph. Still, she may have been a faithless, two-timing bitch, and she was certainly frightened, but she was not, finally, a coward.

"Well?" he said.

"I'm. Pregnant."

* * *

He never saw it coming. For the rest of his life he would replay this moment like a movie scene, trying to see why he hadn't seen what he hadn't seen until she spoke those two words. Yes, he had read the warning letters sent him in Germany by Brooklyn friends, letters hinting of Bruno's black Buick parked near his place.

Aboard the troop ship home, he had stood in the windswept bow, studying the sea and sifting through a range of violent retributions. Even now, he could accuse her of 'humping this no-count Kraut motherfucker,' but somewhere deep in his archaic male core he had not accepted the invasion of his domain, this galling, testosterone rebuke. Instead, like millions before him, he had invented explanations, believing—hoping—that what he'd witnessed back there in the theatre was just . . . just a one-time deal, or, he didn't know—a cosmic aberration of some kind. The war had nearly killed him . . .

Pregnant. The proof.

He'd loved this woman. They'd taken vows. For three years, fighting across half of Europe, he'd kept her picture in his wallet, taking it out every night until it was limp with sweat and handling. He'd told his buddies about her, how she'd never Dear-John his ass, not Maria. At night, alone, terrified under enemy fire, he would weather the worst hours recalling the precise touch and arc of her lovely breasts, her nipples caught between his lips and tongue, the cool, flawless skin on her back and bottom, how her hair smelled in bed on a winter night, exactly how she liked to be made love to, how she'd murmur little begging, animal noises, slipping him inside her, nearly crushing him when she came, groaning, noisy, and wet, demented with sex.

All their secrets. All their promises.

Maria saw what effect her confession had had. Crouched over the groaning Bruno, her eyelids fluttering, she anticipated the blow, believing he would kill her, as he had every right to do.

"Till death do us part."

She heard him half-whisper the phrase and thought it must be the precursor to mayhem, a prophylactic prayer of absolution offered up in extenuation of a crime-to-be. A beheading? Murder-suicide? Who knew? She waited.

But nothing happened, no gunshot, no bayonet through the nape of her neck. After several seconds, she heard footsteps, and when she at last managed to look she saw Dante and the dog trudging down the alley toward the street. He turned the corner without ever looking back. At that moment, it occurred to Maria Costagno Larocca that she may have made a terrible, terrible mistake.

* * *

Back at his jeep, Dante sat exhausted, insentient. Sir Plus bounded into the passenger's seat and whined, licking the drying blood from Dante's hand.

"You okay, Sarge?" It was the fat little toadstool from the Army/Navy store. He stood at curbside, leaning to see around Sir Plus. "You need anything?"

"A tent," Dante whispered. "I need a twelve-by-twelve."

"Got a dozen of 'em. Never used. Come look."

Dante tied the dog to the steering wheel, removed his torn tunic, and limped after the toadstool into the deepest recesses of his store. The place was clotted to the ceiling with gear. Once the war had begun winding down in Europe and everyone—even the German General Staff—could see it was just a matter of time, the U.S. government had begun diverting what would soon become unneeded military materiel from Army and Navy warehouses to the private sector.

In massive, often rigged auctions, Uncle Sugar was selling off—at pennies on the dollar—hundreds of millions of bucks worth of excess inventory. But true to bureaucratic practice everywhere, they were slow to turn off the resource spigot, so the stuff being manufactured on extended contracts kept coming. Trucks and jeeps from Detroit. Airplanes of all kinds from Seattle, Long Island, and Texas. Bulldozers, road graders, and Higgins Boats from Chicago, Cleveland, and New

Orleans. Tens of thousands of weapons, millions of rounds of ammo, plus uncountable tents, C-rations, typewriters, pencils, jock straps, walkie-talkies, gas masks, tooth brushes, horse shoes, pack saddles, cement mixers, nail files, power tools, drill presses, boots, band saws, spare parts, helmets, kotex, uniforms and bits of rain gear from every state in the union. The war may have destroyed 40 million souls around the world, but it had made a lot of Americans filthy, stinking rich.

Followed down the aisles by the proprietor carrying pencil and paper, Dante rattled off a list of things he needed: the tent; a trailer for his jeep; a cot; couple of plates, cups, knives and forks; lantern; typewriter; blankets; sleeping bag; poncho; camera; coffee maker; a big tarp; drafting table; painting supplies . . .

"You an artist or something?" said the Toadstool.

"Architect," said Dante. The Toadstool seemed skeptical. "Or will be. Going to college on the G.I. Bill. Got to catch up with those 4-F bastards who took our jobs and . . ."

"I hear you. Right after Pearl Harbor I tried to sign up myself, but the Army said I was essential to the war effort." Dante cocked an eye. "And, you know, too fat and stuff."

Dante nodded.

"How much for all that?" he said.

"Gotta figure it."

Back at the front counter, the Toadstool consulted his writing pad, sweating out a number while he hummed a tune only he knew. This part was tricky, requiring him to weigh several countervailing vectors of fear and greed: his desire to make as much money as possible; the criminally low cost-basis he actually had invested in the goods; the strong likelihood that if his asking price were too high Dante might use the bayonet on him like he had on the Buick; his own latent patriotism;

the massive inventory excess to which his incompetence had now led; two competing stores in the next block . . .

Being in retail these days was no walk in the park.

"Two hundred and eighty-eight, fifty," he said.

Dante looked at the ceiling while tossing a sinister K-bar knife from hand to hand.

"And I'll throw in this brand-new deck of playing cards."

Dante pursed his lips, then used the K-bar to shave a small patch of hair off his forearm.

"Bastard is sharp," he said.

The Toadstool broke.

"But for you, I mean, hell, you were wounded, after all, and you're buying a lot of stuff here and with the trailer . . ."

"What's your best price, putz?"

"Hundred and ninety . . ."

"Done."

". . . and seventy-five cents."

Dante paid in cash, drove around back, chose a 4 x 4 trailer from among the five available and hitched it up. While Toadstool schlepped items to the loading dock, Dante stored them in the trailer and jeep. Sir Plus looked on, concerned that his place might be usurped by mere goods, but Dante had saved a spot for him and even spread a blanket over the seat to cushion it.

By now, it was late afternoon. The sky had darkened to an ugly blue-purple, and rain was beginning to patter around them. Dante rolled out the jeep's canvas top, snapped the side curtains into place, and thanked the surplus agent, who seemed genuinely pleased to have helped a vet. When they shook hands, the little guy produced a sealed green bucket bearing a host of serial numbers on an Army label.

Dante read the label: "'Rations. Canine. Grade, premium. Gallon, one.'"

"For your pup, there. Official U.S. Government-issue."

"He's German."

"Well, he eats, don't he? Listen, this is great stuff. Guaranteed. Hundred percent." He blushed.

"And, meanwhile, if I get real hungry . . ." Dante said.

"Hey, you never know, you know?"

"Right. Thanks."

The little guy looked at him.

"No, Sarge, thank you."

Dante smiled. The rain was heavier, now, and the surplus merchant's sodden comb-over had disintegrated, the long hair lapsing down over his ear on one side in a fine, disordered mess.

"Better get in outta the rain, pal," Dante said. He snapped off a salute, climbed in the jeep and pulled out into light traffic. When he glanced in the rear view, there was Toadstool standing on the loading dock at what was for him rapt military attention, his hair-do ruined, but his arm raised in a rigid return salute.

* * *

Dante had one stop to make before leaving town, and not at his and Maria's apartment. Whatever stuff he still had there—whatever she hadn't thrown out by tonight—Vinny could pick up later. He headed for the old Greenwood Cemetery where his parents and grandfather were buried side by side beneath a trio of modest limestone slabs.

The Laroccas. Italians by birth. Americans by oath. Immigrants who'd lived in Fiesole, near Florence, for five hundred years before joining the restless hordes heading west around the turn of the century. Dante's parents had been loving but undemonstrative, for Italians—Episcopalian Dagos, he'd called them in jest. One child. One apartment. One job: piano tuners, both of them.

His grandfather, Marco, was the one to whom he had looked for life lessons. The old sculptor who never deigned to learn too much English for fear it would dilute his Italian soul, but who could render a breathtaking still-life or infuse a cast-off piece of walnut or mahogany with a lambent beauty that silenced debate. The old sculptor—a bringer of the genius of Tuscany—linked to his people's creative legacy, hungry to have lived in the time of Michaelangelo, but reduced to giving painting lessons to dilettante neighbor-women—and to Dante.

Dante had admired his grandfather furiously. They'd been odd-couple soul-mates, fifty years apart in age but beneath the skin, clones, the boy adopting values brought to America by the old man. The old man, who had taught the boy secrets about drawing, about shadow and light and composition and color and perspective, about gestural nuance and why art mattered above all else. The old man who had coached him, prodded him, critiqued him, loved him. Who had paid attention. And when Dante had announced with a young man's trepidation that architecture had won his heart, that he would some day build a grand, august building that people would never tear down, it was the old man who'd blessed his grandson's choice.

"Build beautiful but build strong, Dante," he'd said, "to last. Build for the ages, for your grandchildren's great-grandchildren." And Dante had promised.

At the cemetery, in the rain, he stood now with Sir Plus before the graves. He wore an Army poncho and had slipped a K-9 rain protector over the big dog. He didn't bother with a lead. Sir Plus wouldn't stray. In the inexplicable communion between mammals of different species, the dog was quiet, empathic to Dante's sadness—a life's worth crammed into a few hours. He sat upright and compact, leaning ever so slightly against the man's leg, maintaining contact. Alert. Awaiting orders.

No lightning or thunder marred this funereal shower. It was just nature's quiet cleansing of the polluted city air, an ablution that would allow tomorrow to begin afresh. Under his poncho Dante offered a little wave of goodbye to his parents and grandfather, turned, and walked away.

The time had come for him to ship out, to head south into terra incognita.

Chapter 2

On the drive to Alabama, Dante began a slow, painful recovery from Maria, but he knew it would take eons—maybe forever. In the beginning, he went with straight, unbridled willpower, resolving simply not to think about her, to scalpel her cleanly out of his life.

That didn't work.

Driving through Pennsylvania, he'd see a startling cloud formation or a clever series of Burma Shave road signs and instantly recall her laughter. When he clamped down hard on this apparition, Maria would bubble up that night in a dream, freed by a malicious subconscious to dance through the dislocated clamor of sleep.

In the end, he settled on metaphor. Since he couldn't avoid thinking about Maria, he would treat her like a shrapnel wound—something he knew something about. First, he must clean the wound, then work to get over the shock and accept the reality of what had happened. And he must try to avoid self-pity. Someday, he'd learn to live without the slowly receding ache, the memory of her aromas, her voice and touch. Some day the wound would heal, scar tissue would form and harden. Then, she would be alive, but dead to him, and on that distant morning when he waked up and fully understood that, that would be the day he'd be well and could rejoin the general population. He could not hate her, but he could learn to live without her—like his pal, Stephenson, who'd said that getting along without his blown-off leg wasn't so bad, once you got past the damned awkwardness of it.

Dante wondered why they hadn't invented a prosthetic device for the heart.

* * *

Driving west on the new Pennsylvania Turnpike, he realized he'd
only traveled beyond Philadelphia a couple of times—to see the
Frank Lloyd Wright houses, and to attend a Palladio exhibition in '39.
Although he could find his way to any art gallery in the Five Boroughs
and navigate like a native around Paris—and what was left of Berlin—
to him, America west of the Hudson was a mystery.

That fact hadn't proved material before, but now, as he and Sir Plus
motored along the twisting Blue Ridge Parkway, it began to matter.
Or at least to interest him vaguely. Until he'd met Buddy in the
Army, he'd always regarded white Southerners as a species of occult
foreigner: racist; feral; stupid; poor; clannish; rural; backward; and
mean. But in the Army he'd had to rethink that view. For one thing, all
of them he'd known had been tough as whit leather in a fight, and they
were inevitably the best marksmen in the outfit. Further, if you didn't
insult their ancestry or bring up the Civil War—they called it The War
of Northern Aggression—they took orders well, and you couldn't stop
the sonsofbitches from killing Germans—a real plus.

Still, it was that weird politeness thing that had always troubled
him. Unreconstructed New York rudeness didn't bother him. In fact,
he rather admired the moxie implied by ill-mannered urban surliness.
But Southerners, they'd 'honey-child' your ass until you dropped your
guard, and then they'd rob you blind and charge you for it. He'd once
lost an entire paycheck at craps to a smooth-talking, good-looking
kid from Mississippi named Wiley who'd rolled five straight sevens
and cleaned out half the men in the tank squadron—then went around
and shook every victim's hand, apologized for the inconvenience, and
sauntered away counting his money.

Puttering south at 45 m.p.h, pulling the trailer covered with the snugged-down tarp, sleeping in fields, and taking pleasure in not worrying about a column of German Panzers clanking into view over the next hill, Dante wondered what he was getting into—and whether he could even pull it off. College. Christ. Dante Larocca in college. In Alabama. Dante G. Larocca, Architect. Right.

As for Sir Plus, as it turned out, he didn't care much for the Toadstool's generously offered, U.S. government-issue, premium canine rations. When Dante had opened the can that first night in Pennsylvania, Sir Plus took a whiff, then stepped back in patrician contempt.

"What? You expected schnitzel?"

Then he'd copped a smell and understood.

"Hey, there was a war on. What can I tell you?"

When he stopped out in the country to buy gas or ask directions, the local accents astounded him. In the Army he'd heard a cross-section of American Babel, but here, Judas, everybody sounded like . . . well, like Buddy Fooshee.

Late on the third afternoon, he pulled into a decrepit Standard Oil station outside Knoxville. On the seat beside him, Sir Plus peered through the aviator goggles at the approaching attendant who paused when he saw a large, steel-hued dog wearing what looked to him like half a gas mask.

"Fill 'em up, willya," Dante said, "and check the oil. How far to Alabama?"

The attendant remained frozen.

"What?" Dante said.

"Kind of damned dog is that?"

"Weimaraner."

"Never heard of it."

"So, meet Sir Plus, lately of Berlin. I got him off a ritzy German count, a nobleman-like."

"Yeah? What'd you give for him?"

"Well, it turned out the nobleman was in no position to bargain, so I got a good deal."

"Huh." The attendant bent and peered into Sir Plus's unblinking, yellow eyes. "Looks a heap smarter than my young'un. Is he a Nazi?"

"Jewish. He converted."

This news seemed to mollify the attendant, who edged closer to get a better look at the mouse-colored beast sitting up in the passenger seat.

"Me, I'm First Church of the Sanctified Holiness Redeemer of Perpetual Light and Beatitude."

"You don't say."

"Yep, but we usually just call it 'First Church of the Sanctified Holiness,' for short. He don't bite, does he?"

"Not a chance. Say, you got a water hydrant?"

The attendant pointed and moved forward, keeping the red gas pump between himself and Sir Plus. Dante got out, grabbed an Army helmet from the trailer, and filled it with water from the tap. Calling Sir Plus, he stood by as the big dog buried his face in the helmet, the attendant watching them out of the corner of his eye.

"Where in Alabama you headed to?"

"Tuscaloosa."

"Roll Tide, huh?"

"Beg pardon?"

"Roll Tide! Football team. That's what all them Bama peckerwoods holler when they're beating the punkin' out of the other guy. I hate those bastards."

The attendant raised the jeep's hood to check the oil.

"Football's a big deal down there, huh?" Dante said, lighting a cigarette. He had never played football in his life. Had hardly even seen it played.

"Neck-and-neck with poontang and whisky. You're a quart low here."

"Put it in. The good stuff."

Until now Dante had conceived the university as little more than an educational abstraction—Buddy's school, a place to honor his memory and to study architecture. Never having gone to college, he had no working model in his head for what a Southern university was—in the case of Alabama a coddling ground for rich planters' children and aspiring politicians, a lily-white bastion of privilege featuring, deeply ingrained sports traditions, and a baroque social life that would have shamed Caligula.

"You gettin' that G.I. Bill money?" the attendant said.

"Bet your ass. Fifty bucks a month for thirty-six months. Great racket."

"Me, I joined the fifty-two/twenty club. Spent eighteen months seasick on a damned old mine-sweeper in the North Atlantic. Now I'm gonna sit on my ass and cash Uncle Sam's checks s'long as he'll send 'em."

"Good plan. You about done there?"

These were the two chief provisions of the recently enacted G.I. Bill, designed both to reward [mostly] men who'd served their country in the armed forces and to avoid a repeat of the social dislocations that had accompanied demobilization after the First War in 1919. Under the Bill: (A) vets could receive money to go to college and catch up with their non-serving peers; or (B) the government would provide a twenty-dollar-per-month financial cushion for up to a year while they looked for work. Hence, 'fifty-two/twenty.'

The attendant was going with Plan B.

As for Dante, he was the first in his family to give college a try.

Only his mother had finished high school.

That night, near the Alabama state line, Dante set up his lean-to in a fresh-mown hay field 200 meters off the highway. He made a fire and shared some mystery meat and fresh tomatoes with Sir Plus—whose tolerance for outré American repasts had broadened considerably in the wake of the earlier government-rations threat.

Sitting there, leaning against one wheel of the trailer, Dante stares into the fire, and before he can stop her, the fair Maria dances into his head. He sees in the embers the whole jumbled kaleidoscope of their wedding day, February 4, 1942, less than two months after Pearl Harbor, and one week before he will enlist.

They are in the Brooklyn Knights of Columbus hall, surrounded by friends—Bruno and Vinny and Lucille included. Some of the men are in uniform, some not. Everybody is drinking and dancing and flirting. He dances with Maria. He dances with her mother. Bruno dances with Maria. Dante dances with his own mother, who will be dead in a year. His grandfather raises a glass of Chianti to Maria and Dante and makes a little speech in Italian about finding true and lasting happiness with the one you love. Maria is embarrassed. Dante smiles. The old man will expire six months later, to the day.

At sunset, Dante and Maria sneak out to a balcony from which they can see across the East River to a magically lit Manhattan. Black-out curtains for the city are still a few weeks away. It's cold on the balcony but extraordinarily bracing. They hold each other. They say the word 'love' many times. He promises to come back from the war. She promises to wait forever. They both mean all of it.

Later that night, they drive away from the cheering guests in a borrowed car, tin cans and old shoes trailing after them, waving to their friends through the inscription Bruno has hastily soaped onto a side window: 'TRU LOVE.'

* * *

Late the next afternoon, Dante pulled the jeep over to the side of the road and stopped somewhere between Birmingham and Tuscaloosa on U.S. Highway 11, the great arterial route connecting New Orleans to New York. For the past couple of miles he'd been trying to drive, study a map, and read directions written in long-hand. The result had put Sir Plus on edge.

"This must be it, boy," he said, scratching behind the dog's ear. "Let's get it over with."

He wheeled the jeep left, onto an arrow-straight gravel driveway that climbed a hill to its terminus in front of a fine old farmhouse a quarter-mile away. The sere and yellow fields surrounding the house were cleanly cut and strewn with upwards of a thousand hay bales lying in rough rows, trussed and ready for the barn.

Dante had been dreading this stop for days, rehearsing what he would say, what he would omit, what necessary lies he was prepared to swear to. All over America, returning soldiers, sailors, and airmen were performing this sad rite, he knew, but that didn't make it any easier. Where was it written what you were supposed to tell them? What voice to speak with? What face adopt?

As the jeep neared the house, sudden gunfire exploded around him. He ducked, jamming on the brakes, jack-knifing the trailer, and flinging Sir Plus into the windshield. When Dante looked up he could feel his heart pounding in his ears. It was France all over. He grabbed the dog and pulled him back onto the seat, reached under the dash and jerked out an evil-looking German Luger pistol. Working the slide once to chamber a round, he rolled out of the jeep, knelt and peeked over the hood. He felt naked without his helmet.

"Sir Plus, here!" The dog obeyed.

The firing continued, a ragged tattoo of nearby booms. Sweat rolled down Dante's face, his cheek twitched. He was awash in adrenaline and bad dreams.

Then he heard someone shout.

"Nice shot, Milo!"

"Was that a double?"

"Damn right, boy. I only aim for the head."

He saw them now. In the thick, cedar-tree windbreaks lining the field stood 15-20 hunters blasting away at skittering formations of mourning doves fleeing in panic from one shotgun to another. Birds were plummeting everywhere. One second they were trim, feathered torpedoes, aerodynamic beauty designed by nature to cheat the wind, their movements a brilliant blur. Then the shot and a bird would crumple in mid-stroke, some folding their wings tight and arcing toward the ground in a long parabolic trajectory, dead before they hit. Others, whacked by a full-choke twelve, exploded in a cloud of feathers, then pitched straight down. But the cruelest ballet was performed by the lightly wounded which, when struck, twirled down crazily from on high, both wings outstretched like a parasail, spinning slowly, slowly to earth in sustained, macabre pirouettes. He saw a young boy run out into the field and catch a twirling bird in mid-air.

The sight made him sick. What these country bastards needed was a little dose of the real thing—half an hour spent in extremis with a few

Panzers and a platoon of crack Wehrmacht troops, their machine guns' bullets clanging off the tank turret loud enough to extinguish thought, the men inside waiting for the anti-tank round to slam home and stop the clock. . . .

He is in that tank with Simmons, Buffalo, Scapoli—and Buddy Fooshee. He is tank commander now because all officers are dead and he's senior NCO. Sergeant Dante G. Larocca, 675685, United States Army, is responsible for this hot, clanking death-trap, plus the lives of these four men, plus himself. Fine, he knows what he's doing; he's been at this for 20 months or more; but like his men, he's scared rigid. They're not scared because they're cowards, but because they're not stupid. Anybody who says he ain't scared in a tank battle just failed to get the word. Or he's lying through his teeth.

The Krauts have been retreating across France toward Germany for weeks, but they are good rear guard fighters. Booby-trap setters. Snipers. Counter-attackers. Defensive geniuses. Don't try to tell Dante Larocca and his men that the individual German soldier lacks initiative, that he is only effective when led by superior officers, that he's prone to surrender if he sees himself out-gunned. That's what they'd been told in boot camp and in tank school, and that turned out to be a big pants-load.

Dante's crew has located the Kraut machine gunners now and is firing desperately at them with their 75 MM main cannon. Their first round flies high. A second is right on target but explodes prematurely.

Damned civilian munition workers!

Before they can re-aim and re-load, a terrific explosion rocks them. An anti-tank round has blown off the starboard tread. They are dead in the water.

"How you doing, there, fella? Can I help you?"

Somebody was talking to him. Dante glanced down and saw the sleek pistol in his hand but couldn't remember how it came to be there. Beside him, Sir Plus crouched, unafraid apparently, but taut, his eyes wide. At least he wasn't gun shy. Which was more than Dante could say for himself.

He turned and saw about 20 feet away a tall, sun-burned man in his late 30's, dressed in khaki, expensive calf-high boots and sunglasses. Beneath his broad-brimmed hat, he appeared handsome with a prominent nose and slightly sloping shoulders. His large-veined hands cradled a gleaming over-and-under shotgun and a pair of leather shooting gloves. The man stopped moving forward, his posture suggesting something was amiss.

A cocked and loaded Luger, maybe?

Dante stood, motioning Sir Plus into the jeep. His voice betrayed him.

"Umm, no, I was just . . . the gunfire caught me off-guard is all. Sorry."

The man surveyed the pistol, jeep, and trailer.

"What kind of dog you got there?"

"Weimar . . . he's a Weimaraner. German breed."

The man nodded. "Strange color. Never saw a dog that color."

"Right, they're bred for it. The yellow eyes, too."

The man squatted and kissed his lips at the dog. Sir Plus turned his back to him.

"Pretty thing."

"He's probably confused by the firing," Dante said.

"You a vet?"

"Yeah. I am. I was, uh, looking for the house of Buddy Fooshee."

The man's sunglasses gave his face a glacial quality. Dante wanted to see the fellow's eyes as he shifted the shot gun from one hand to the other. Minus the eyes, a face is a mask.

"Buddy's dead."

In that flat accent the bald statement hung in the air between them. The man had pronounced the word 'dead' with two syllables—'Day-ud.'

Dante's stomach clinched. He gazed at the horizon.

"Yeah . . . yeah, I know. I was looking to speak to his, uh, wife and his mother."

The shotguns continued to bark in the field, doves falling, the kid chasing down wounded birds with repellent avidity.

The sun-burned man had the habit of rotating his head a quarter-turn from the person he was addressing. Dante wondered if he were deaf in one ear.

"You in the war with Buddy?" the man said.

Dante was getting a belly-full of this third degree. He'd recovered his equilibrium now, and his Brooklyn genes began to kick in. Instead of replacing the pistol under the dashboard, he thrust it into his pants behind the belt buckle—John Wayne-style.

"Yeah, I was. Dante Larocca. Who're you?"

The man pooched out his lips and nodded his head so many times Dante began to wonder if he was some kind of fruitcake.

"Milo Henderson. Buddy wrote about you a lot in his letters. You go on up to the house there and see the women. They'll be glad you came." An embryonic, not altogether warm smile flickered at the corners of his mouth; he gestured toward the pistol.

"Sort of pistol is that? Looks foreign."

"German. Called a Luger. Their officers carried them."

"You get it on the black market?"

Dante bristled. The question came across as an insult, as though Dante had been a rear-echelon skulker with no combat experience.

"No, Henderson, matter of fact I took it off a Kraut colonel after we ran him over in my tank."

"Well, you won't be needing it here, I don't 'spec."

Milo Henderson chuckled, turned and walked toward the field. Dante watched the man's departing back. Something about this guy spooked him. The sunglasses? The chilliness? Maybe it was just the bird slaughter out in the field. He stashed the pistol in its hiding place and wrestled the jeep and trailer back onto the gravel road, heading for the farm buildings.

Driving up, he stopped before the white picket fence surrounding the house. He'd spied the gold star on the window, signifying a family who had lost a son. His guts tightened, but before he could react, two scruffy Mutt-and-Jeff farm dogs screamed off the porch toward him. Sir Plus, in a display of Teutonic condescension, stood up on the jeep seat, put his front paws on the steering wheel, and stared down mutely on their mad barking like Prince Valiant surveying a pair of unruly Goths.

Dante got out and tried to quiet the dogs, but they were joyfully apoplectic. Up in the jeep, Sir Plus must have looked ten feet tall. The bigger, black dog stood behind the gate roaring, while the little hair-ball raced back and forth from the gate to the porch like a furry yo-yo.

Dante cooed at them. "Gracie . . . Ben . . . shhhh, now; come on, Gracie . . . easy, Ben . . . Sir Plus, damnit, get down here. Sir Plus, here!"

He heard a screen door slap shut on the porch.

"How do you know those dogs' names, Mister?"

The woman was balancing a baby on her forearm. Compact, lean and nicely built, she looked to be in her mid-twenties, with bobbed auburn hair and freckles sprinkled beneath her tan. Dressed in thin cotton paisley, she wasn't pretty in a magazine-ad way, but her lovely barefoot, summer-dressed, casual manner seized in Dante's throat. He recognized her from the photos.

"I've, uh, heard a lot about them . . . I guess."

He could see her appraising him and his: the jeep, the green Army fatigue pants, the tarp-covered trailer.

"You're Dante Larocca," she whispered.

Her voice combined indictment with invitation, suspicion with warmth, fear with love.

"And you're Laney," he said.

She stood there holding the baby, her other hand raised to cover her mouth, stifling that sob vouchsafed uniquely to recent widows and orphans. He could see her eyes water up, tears forming around the iris.

"Come in and meet his mama," she said softly. "Gracie. Ben. You hush, now." They did.

Dante left Sir Plus in the jeep with a long lead, then walked up on the porch. He paused a couple of awkward steps from Laney.

"This is Rafe," she said.

Dante put out his forefinger to the baby who grasped it and hung on like a badger.

"Nice grip," Dante said. "You got a real ball player here."

"Like his daddy," she said.

He shook her extended hand. It was cool.

"Come in."

* * *

The farmhouse was a handsome two-story clapboard affair dating to the last century. It featured a deep porch running across the front, behind which stood high jib windows extending almost from floor to ceiling for air flow. Built by Buddy Fooshee's grandfather, it had begun life as a breezy dog-trot, expanding over the years through several additions so well managed that it would take an architectural historian to identify the seams. Dante spotted them immediately—even while he admired the workmanship.

Inside, the living room was clean and freshly painted. Oval hook rugs and sturdy furniture were placed about, and the walls were hung with water colors, oils, and charcoal sketches whose provenance Dante recognized. Laney Fooshee led him back to the kitchen where a white woman about sixty, her gray hair in a bun, was shelling peas and laughing over a punch line with a black woman, clearly her friend and confidante.

"Mama Lou . . ."

The white woman turned toward them, her face still trapped in a smile.

"Mama, this is Dante Larocca. You remember . . ."

The older woman's smile faded a bit, but her fine hazel eyes retained their affection. She glanced at Dante's clothes: the many-pocketed pants and khaki military shirt.

"Well . . . Mr. Larocca," she said. "I'm Louise Fooshee. Thank you for coming."

"I'm . . . sorry I didn't write. I've been sorta tied up. . . ."

"Oh, that's all right. 'Safely arrived' is what matters." Recovering from the shock of his presence, she met the occasion in true Southern fashion: when in doubt, feed 'em.

"You look thirsty."

She spoke to the black woman: "Olivia, would you get Mr. Larocca some ice water, please? Or, would you prefer mint tea? Olivia just made up a big pitcher while ago. We grow our own mint."

"Tea's great," he said, "But I've got a dog out there that could use some water."

"I'll do it," Laney said, putting little Rafe down on the linoleum-covered floor where he spotted a stray pea next to him and popped it in his mouth before anyone could move.

"Lord, that child is a natural vacuum cleaner. Rafe, come here to Mama Lou before you start in on the linoleum."

She picked up the child, making a little 'ouff' sound as she hefted him onto her hip. "Let's go in here, Mr. Larocca, and visit," she said, leading him toward the living room. Dante followed her, dialing madly through his brain for guidance, for a template. To those who practice it, war requires of friendship a high penance. On the battlefield, aboard ship, under fire, men will demand the most arduous of favors to be undertaken upon their prospective death:

'Write a letter to my wife if I don't make it.'

'Go to Mama and tell her I love her.'

'Drive to where the road ends, find my family and explain everything that happened; they'll want to know.'

And always, contained within the request, the implied promise that, should their positions be reversed, the plaintiff would do the same. The Spartan hoplite lying mortally wounded at Thermopylae. A Centurion of Caesar's in faraway Gaul, dying from spear-thrust and ague in the arms of his comrade. The gassed German storm trooper in '18, sprawled blind, hoarse and fetal in a flooded Flanders trench whispering to his Kamerade: 'Bitte, sprichts du mit mein Frau . . .' In

44

the end, all wars mortgage the survivor's future to another's fate, hold him hostage to a blood covenant, and bend his will to the curve of a promise. As Dante now knew.

In the living room, the women began to nest. Laney put Rafe on the couch and gave him a bottle to quiet him before they turned their attention to Dante standing at the mantel with his iced tea. He felt hot and inadequate.

"Dante, what can you tell us about Buddy?" said Laney, putting on a brave face.

Their tank has ground to a halt in an open barley field, near a tree line. It is canted over to the right, the starboard track blown off, German machine gunners pounding it with heavy fire. Simmons and Buffalo are dead. But the turret still rotates, and Dante and Buddy are working the big gun while Scapoli brings the .50 to bear in a suppressing fire against the Krauts.

He and Buddy get off three shots, one a direct hit that scatters pieces of dead Germans like uniformed mannequin parts. Then another anti-tank round slams home and choking smoke swirls around them. Scapoli makes a single, soft crying sound. When Dante looks down he sees the little corporal slumped over his weapon, his brains spread across the back of his shirt like gray scrambled eggs.

Buddy is screaming that they have to get out!

A fire in the tank now, scalding them, licking toward the remaining spare rounds. He shouts at Buddy to follow him, stands and opens the top escape port. Another heavy round crashes into the tank. The noise deafens him. He and Buddy are both hit. Dante's shirt-front is riddled with shrapnel holes and blood. Buddy's hair is on fire. Dante drops back to the floor of the tank and—like a lover—takes his friend's

head in his arms, smothering the flames. Buddy's contorted face is
smoke-blackened where it isn't running with blood. His front teeth are
fractured stumps; his eyes are wide with pain and surprise. Lisping
through the missing teeth, he tells Dante to get out, to leave him, to
run, for Godssakes . . .

"Buddy died real quiet-like," Dante said. "No pain at all. We were goofing off, eating chow behind the lines, and a stray rifle round caught him in the chest. The docs figured he never felt a thing."

Dante had sold the women the lie he knew they wanted to buy. What's the harm? he thought. It could have been true. It should have been. Anyway, someone who's never been there can never understand, so why bother? The rhetoric of war doesn't translate into any other language. Buddy Fooshee had died in some parallel universe, a barbaric world alien to this lovely old farmhouse, its walls covered with his own paintings and sketches, its rooms suffused with his boyhood dreams, his marriage, his mother, his wife and child.

Having crossed the liar's threshold, Dante fell back on truth. He told the women about the leaves he and Buddy had taken together in London and Paris, about how they had cooked up this scheme to attend the university together on the G.I. Bill, where Dante would study architecture and Buddy continue with his painting. The women chuckled at his rendition of a tipsy night driving around Paris in a general's stolen jeep.

They nodded when he praised Buddy's artistic skills, telling them how his friend could take a piece of charcoal and render battle scenes so life-like that other guys offered him cash for them. At first, Buddy wouldn't take the money, Dante said, but Dante had applied his best Brooklyn street-logic and made his friend see the light. Dante even parodied a thick version of his own accent to show how tough he'd been on Buddy. Next thing he knew, his pal had set up shop, drawing drop-dead perfect caricatures of the guys in the outfit and selling them for outrageous sums.

"So that's where all that money he sent home came from," said Laney, smiling. "I thought he'd robbed the PX or something."

"Nope. It was all from his sketches and stuff. Wait a minute. I've got something to show you."

He ran outside to the jeep, passing Sir Plus curled up asleep on the porch along with his two former antagonists.

"Fraternizing with the enemy, fella; that'll get you the stockade." Sir Plus lifted his regal head just enough to watch through pale ocher eyes as Dante untied the tarp, rustled around in the trailer, and pulled out a hard-backed portfolio. Out in the field, the dove hunters were still at it, shooting and calling out to each other, although fewer birds were falling now.

Back inside the house, Dante knelt on the floor and opened the portfolio. Laney and Mama Lou leaned forward to see. Baby Rafe slept. Dante had brought in two dozen of Buddy's finest watercolors, pastels and charcoal drawings, and now as he laid each one out on the hooked rug the women could see the war and his friends through their hero's eyes.

"Oh, they're wonderful, Dante," Mama Lou said, picking up a finely rendered view of Notre Dame and the Seine seen from Pont Neuf.

"He was good, no doubt about it. And fast, Jesus . . . sorry, but he'd knock those things off before I could get half-started."

Laney stared at the pictures but did not touch them. It occurred to Dante that he'd made a mistake bringing them in. He could almost feel her recoil, but when he copped a glance at her he relaxed. She was sniffling a little, but smiling, too, proud, reminiscent, possessive. She would frame and hang each vestige of her late husband's talent. She would save it all for Baby Rafe. She would honor Buddy's memory. She would never forget.

She touched Dante's shoulder. "Thank you for doing this. You didn't have to, and we appreciate it more than I can say."

Dante was relieved.

And then he went too far.

"Now, this here is kind of a ringer," he said, sliding out a drawing from beneath the others. "It's one I did just before . . . just before I went in the hospital."

It was a stunning portrait of Buddy that Dante had drawn in charcoal a week before his friend died. In it, the reclining, shirtless figure exuded a casual, smiling, young-Rupert-Brooke-gone-to-war quality: simultaneously heroic but fated, the handsome warrior in repose, smoking a cigarette between battles.

It was too much for Laney.

First, her breath caught in her throat, then she broke into wracking sobs that made Dante fear she'd choke. Mama Lou took the girl in her arms, and all pretense at stiff upper lip vanished. The two women cried together as women have since cavemen began slaughtering each other over the rights to a good campsite. In their rhapsodic keening Dante heard the women's loss, incommunicable, bereft. They might not understand war, but they understood personal havoc in a way that Dante Larocca—despite his appalling experiences—didn't, and for the first time he knew it. He had loved Buddy. But they had loved Buddy—and for so much longer. Dante thought that if those who made war were forced to experience this terrible weeping, then all fighting would cease. All weapons be broken, burned and buried. Such depth of women's grief as he heard this day disqualified all pretensions to woe of any mere man—except he too be the parent of a just-dead child.

On the couch, Baby Rafe, startled from slumber by the wailing, waked to add his own.

"What the hell have you done, you jerk!"

It was Milo, the sun-burned man in khaki, back from the hunt. Minus the sunglasses, his eyes seemed strangely colorless and, Dante thought, lawyer-like, empty. He had entered the house through the kitchen and stood now holding his shotgun in the crook of his arm, towering over the carnage that Dante had unwittingly unleashed.

Milo's outrage reordered the molecular structure of misery in the room. Dante leapt to his feet and into a slight crouch, fists cocked, prepared for whatever was coming. Laney scooped up the crying Rafe, whispering to him softly, while Mama Lou, wiping tears with her apron, assessed Henderson over her eyeglasses.

"Milo? Did you knock?"

"No, ma'am, I didn't. I heard y'all hollering bloody murder in here and thought I should come see about it." He glanced darkly at Dante, who had relaxed enough to stand up straight and unclench his fists.

Milo turned to Laney. "Are you all right?" he said, touching, then patting her back.

She nodded.

"We're fine, and grateful to you, Milo," Mama Lou said, "but it's nothing to bother about. Dante was showing us some of Buddy's pictures, and we were a little overcome is all. If you want some mint tea, Olivia has it in the kitchen."

Dante thought he caught a whiff of disapproval in Mama Lou's manner. Something about Henderson rankled her. As for Milo himself, he emitted a mixed scent in this setting, including an almost proprietary claim to Laney's sorrow. The big sunburned man even offered to take and comfort the baby, but Laney shook her head. Smiled, but shook her head.

Dante stooped and pulled together the drawings, replacing them in the portfolio and retying its black strings. He had meant the works as a present but thought now he ought not leave them. He certainly hadn't meant to introduce more pain to this grief-smote family of women. Laney caught his eye and read his mind.

"Thank you, Dante, for bringing these to us. We'll have them framed, and you can fill us in on where they were done and all."

"Sure, I just . . ."

"I hope you'll you stay the night," Mama Lou said to him. "We're having collards, cheese grits and doves." She turned to Milo. "At least, we were promised dove, and after all that shooting . . ."

"Yes, ma'am," said Milo, "We'll have a nice mess of birds." He turned to Dante. "You ever eat dove?"

In Milo's mouth, the question became a challenge, as though Dante were being asked if he'd ever fired a gun or made love to a woman. Dante paused and lit a cigarette with his big Zippo.

"Nope," he said. "Matter of fact, they look like midget pigeons to me, and nobody from Brooklyn eats pigeons."

His unexpected sally tickled the women, but Milo took it ill, as meant to make him look a fool. He scowled and turned toward the kitchen.

"I'll have Olivia clean the birds," he said. "Is there any bacon in the house, Miss Louise?"

* * *

Midget pigeons or not, a dove, Dante discovered, though gamey, was

50

superb.

"Quail's all white meat. Dove's all dark," Mama Lou said. "The trick is keeping them moist. That's what we use the bacon for."

"And red wine, when we have it," said Laney. "Alabama's a dry state, you know."

"Dry?" Dante said, not comprehending.

"Can't buy liquor here, legally," said Milo. "It's the law." He'd been seated at the nominal head of the table, Dante at the foot, like gastronomic adversaries.

"Except at special places," said Laney, "like the veterans' club and such."

Dante was holding the half-eaten remains of a dove over his plate, trying to fathom this idiocy.

"You mean you can't just go to the corner liquor store and buy . . ."

"No such thing as a corner liquor store," said Milo, pleased to serve in the role of instructor.

"So, where do you . . . I mean, how do you get booze?" Dante was beginning to rethink his choice of colleges.

"Bootleggers," said Laney.

Dante laughed out loud.

"Bootleggers? I thought bootlegging went out with Capone and that crowd. I mean, New York makes a mint on liquor sales. Why don't you just pass a law and start charging. . .?"

"Can't. 'Cause of the Baptists," said Mama Lou.

"And, of course, the bootleggers," said Laney.

"Down here, they're making the mint," said Milo.

Dante had been bad wishing for a beer to go with this fine dinner, but he'd hesitated to ask. Now he was glad for his unwonted restraint.

"Well, when in Rome . . ." he said. "Say, does that last midget pigeon have anybody's name on it?"

"Take it," said Laney. "I'm about to pop."

"Thanks," said Dante, spearing another little corpse off the platter. The tension in the room between the two men was palpable, but the women were too polite to try and defuse it, and the Yankee was glad. He felt some contingent need to face down, to beard this man whom he thought of as a poacher on his dead friend's familial territory.

"So, Milo," Dante said, "what do you do for a living?"

"Farm. My own place, and I also lease a thousand acres from Miss Louise, and farm that."

Dante saw the situation more clearly now. He was dealing here with a rustic czar.

"So, would that make you a plantation owner? I mean, what's the difference between a plantation and a farm, anyways?"

"Size, mainly," said Mama Lou, trying to help. "They say 'plantation' down in the Black Belt and in the Mississippi Delta. Here we just say 'farm.'"

"Ahh, Mississippi," Dante said, "I took an awful whipping at craps from an old Mississippi boy, once, right after we liberated Paris . . ."

"Have some more tea, Dante?" Mama Lou said.

"No, thank you . . . So, Milo, were you in the war?" Dante asked, casually. He was pretty sure of the answer, and he realized it was rude to ask, but he was a New Yorker, and this prick irritated him. When the question hung in the air a moment too long, Dante knew he'd struck a vein. Laney inspected a dove carcass on her plate. Mama Lou rang a small crystal bell to summon Olivia.

"No, unfortunately, I wasn't able to serve," said Milo. To Dante this sounded rehearsed. "I was an only child, and my mother wasn't well, plus I was a little old . . ."

"So, how old are you?" Dante bore in, ignoring the muted anxiety rising from the two women like a steam cloud.

Milo's face had reddened, but Dante couldn't tell whether it was from gluttony or embarrassment. He hoped for the latter.

"I'm thirty-eight."

"So," Dante counted on his greasy fingers, "that would have made you, what . . . thirty three-four." He leaned forward, low over the table. "You know, we had a gunny sergeant in my outfit served way back in the first war, if you can believe it. Then, in '42, damn guy went out and bribed his draft board to get re-enlisted . . . Bribed 'em! He was forty-five. Helluva guy, old Gunny Rivers . . . Killed at the Bulge. DSO. Silver Star. Croix de guerre. Gunny Rivers . . . Wife and two kids . . . One helluva guy."

He leaned back and picked at something caught in his teeth.

The ensuing silence was broken by Olivia, bearing dessert.

"Y'all save room for some pie?"

* * *

In the living room, Mama Lou and Laney commandeered the conversation, steering talk away from the war, and instead questioning Dante about his own plans to study architecture. And why architecture? While Milo loomed in the daddy chair, leafing through a farming magazine, Dante—at first reluctantly—began to speak of his love of design, texture, material, structure, efficiency.

"Efficiency?" said Laney.

"Yeah, I'm nuts about making things—a building even—work better than it's supposed to. You see that jeep out there? When I bought it from the surplus agent, it was getting 12 miles to the gallon. I fiddled with the carb and retarded the spark, and now it gets 18. Not bad, huh?"

The women nodded.

Milo snorted. "Gas is going down to nothing a gallon, now the war's over."

"It won't be cheap forever, Henderson. Besides, that's just an example."

Laney seemed interested.

"Isn't there an architecture scholarship or something at the university where you study . . ."

His eyes lit up. "Dalton Fellowship, it's called, one of the best. Set up by some old geezer who made a fortune during World War I cheating the government while he built Army camps all over the country."

"Samuel Dalton. He was from Birmingham," said Milo. "A fine gentleman. Son of a Confederate General. Killed at Shiloh . . . or was it Gettysburg?"

"Whatever . . . anyway, his son was an architect who died at Belleau Wood in the first war. So, when they tagged the old man as a war profiteer in the twenties, he laid down a big pile of guilt money to shut 'em up."

"Typical," said Mama Lou.

"The man knew where he came from," said Milo.

"So, the fellowship pays you to study?" asked Laney.

Dante grinned. "The fellowship pays you to study in Rome," he said. "Rome. For a year. Two, if you're good enough. During the war, they stopped giving 'em out, so this year they're doing double."

"What's all this got to do with you?" Milo said.

Dante stared right through him.

"I'm gonna win one," he said.

Milo looked away.

"Wonderful, Dante," said Mama Lou.

Olivia came to the door and announced she'd finished in the kitchen. Mama Lou asked Milo if he'd mind giving Olivia a ride on his way home. Milo stood, turned to Laney and gave her a little hug, except that Dante thought it actually fell halfway between a little hug and a big one.

"We'll be out haying early tomorrow, Miss Louise," Milo said from the front porch. "Expect us at first light. Come on, Olivia, hope I can find your place down in the quarters."

He put on the big hat and headed for his pick-up, Olivia, two steps behind, in tow.

After the truck had disappeared into its own moon-lit dust trail, Mama Lou said her good-nights, and Laney showed Dante his room. By this time—after the day's drive, the dove hunters, dealing with Milo, lying to the women about Buddy, spilling his guts about the Dalton—Dante was bushed, but he wanted to check on Sir Plus before he turned in. Olivia had fed all the dogs, and Sir Plus seemed contented to be with his new friends on the porch—until Dante turned to leave him for the night, whereupon the big silvery creature stood at the screen door, moaned and cocked his head with a look of infinite melancholy.

It's those damned yellow eyes, Dante thought, and let the dog in, locking the door.

Sir Plus's nails made ticking noises on the floor as they headed for Dante's room, one that shared a bath with Laney's. He made the dog lie in the corner, next to the bed, then took off his shoes and shirt. Looking at himself in the mirror, he grimaced. In soft light the myriad shrapnel wounds on his chest and back glistened as shiny pink slivers of skin, the road map of an afternoon in hell. The scars appeared strangely wet, as though they might soon evaporate—taking with them the memory of their origin. Back in the Army hospital in France, he had lain awake at night wondering if Maria would find them repulsive. If she'd cringe when he held her. Talk about a moot point.

A tattoo on his right shoulder made him sneer. A red heart pierced by an arrow and emblazoned with a pair of tiny putti, it was surmounted with baroque lettering: "Maria Forever."

"Bitch," Dante muttered. "No good, two-timing bitch."

He grabbed his shaving kit and turned toward the bathroom. Laney stood in the doorway, wearing her house coat, face scrubbed, teeth brushed, ready for bed. He stopped, embarrassed at being overheard.

"I didn't know . . ."

"Dante, thank you again for coming."

"Sure . . . I wish it was different, but . . ."

Standing there, soul-inspecting, her dark eyes went all through him, peering into his heart's secret crevices, exploring seams in which he had hidden hurts beneath a flimsy bravado.

"Tell me the truth about Buddy," she said.

They are fighting to get out of the burning tank. At 175 lbs., Buddy is dead weight, though not yet dead. He grabs Dante by the throat and screams at him to leave while he can. Cursing, Dante jerks the hand from his throat, grasps Buddy under the arms and lifts him to his feet. They stand face to face, two drunks dancing a ghastly mazurka. The horrors inside their cramped, metal sarcophagus overwhelm the senses—smoke, cordite, shit, blood, explosions of unknown origin.

His lungs bursting, slipping in his own blood, Dante fights to hold madness at bay. He must think.

The top escape port is open, but that way lies suicide; the Krauts

*will have every gun trained on it, waiting for the rats to run. They'll
have to go out the emergency hatch. Buddy is moaning, bleeding, his
pants slick with urine. Dante eases him down, and goes for the small
emergency door. It won't budge; he kicks at it savagely, injuring his
foot before managing to crack it open.*

*Buddy lies on the floor of the tank, crumpled in on himself like a
big doll, eyes open, blood draining from his smashed mouth. Dante
grasps him and as gently as possible drags him forward. He slithers
through the hatch himself, then reaches back, grabs Buddy's collar,
and hauls him onward. A thought flits through Dante's mind:*

'Boy, is Buddy gonna be sore tomorrow.'

*They're out of the tank and on the opposite side from the German
machine gunners. Panting, mad with pain, Dante crawls, dragging
Buddy behind him toward a line of poplars and thicket a few yards
away. Somewhere nearby he can hear a familiar sound. It's a diesel.
A big diesel. A tank! But whose? Behind him, his own tank burns
furiously.*

Laney stood there, arms folded, eyes interrogating him, demanding
a verbatim version of a hell she cannot imagine and that Dante cannot
bring himself to render. He wanted to scream at her to accept his
perjury and paste it into her scrapbook along with other images of
Buddy.

On the drive to Alabama, he had searched hard for a lie to tell this
woman. A lie for the children of soldiers. Now, standing before her,
half-naked, his blemished skin and confusion a brute testament to
war, he saw her look at the tattoo and the scars. He saw her hand
come gently toward him and coolly trace, with a single finger, a five-
inch rivulet of wound running above his right nipple. Her touch was

not sexual. It was familial. It was in some way conjugal, an effort to reach out to Buddy through his last friend, to regain for an instant contact with the lost man she'd loved beyond loving.

The tenderness of it—the simple womanly tenderness—broke him. Frailty began its evil creep down his spine. His legs trembled. Resolve melted. Anger and love, Maria and Bruno, Buddy and Milo, his grandfather, the Krauts, the blood and stench of the burning tank, a lifetime of fear and woe in an afternoon—it all overwhelmed the cofferdams he'd built to keep himself sane.

Shuddering, hot tears gushing from his eyes, he tottered like blind, fated Oedipus forced to face abominable truths. He reached for the door jamb but found her arm instead. She took the shaving kit from him, supporting him momentarily before he sank slowly to his knees, his hand traversing stiffly down her arm, to her waist, thigh, calf, floor. He was too heavy for her to hold. He was too heavy to hold himself. Burdened to breaking with a malady that doctors give different names in different wars, he cratered onto the bedroom rug, crying silently, quivering like that Centurion of Caesar's, ague-ridden in furthest Gaul.

Without hesitation, she lay down behind him, cupping his form into hers, her arm around him, sleeping spoons as she had so often with Buddy. She would stay until this horror passed, leaching into him her warmth and forgiveness and sympathy, loving him for loving Buddy.

Lying in the corner, his head erect, Sir Plus had watched it all. Now he rose and eased forward, prudent, concerned, his yellow eyes wide to catch and use what light there was. He snuffled at Dante's bare foot, processing abstruse canine data, assessing the torment. Then, matching the woman gesture for gesture, the great gray dog curled himself into a ball and lay down next to Dante, his back against the weeping man whose back was against the woman.

"Oh, God," Dante whispered. "Oh, God."

And then he went to sleep.

Chapter 3

Early the next morning, Laney came out on the front porch, carrying a coffee pot and two cups. Dante was changing a flat on the jeep, his duffel already cinched and loaded. In the night, when she'd heard him snoring softly, she'd gotten up, slipped a pillow beneath his head, draped a blanket over him and the dog and tiptoed out. Now, she sensed the chagrin he might feel, and she had no idea how to play it. Maybe he'd want to talk. Maybe he'd pretend it never happened.

"Coffee?" she asked.

"Absolutely. Black. Ta. That's what the Limeys say for thanks, 'Ta.'"

"Nice."

"Yeah, so, ta for last night," he said, taking the cup.

"No need. I think you showed a lot of courage in just . . ."

He tossed the lug wrench into the trailer. She could see he'd dealt with last night's episode and had put on a face to meet her today.

"You know," he said, "Buddy and me were with Patton . . . but, hell, you know all that. Anyway, Patton was a son of a bitch, but he was our son of a bitch, and he used to have a saying that got around among us tankers. Whenever people talked about courage and all that, Patton would say—he had a kind of high-pitched voice. He'd say, 'Courage is nothing but fear holding on a minute longer.' We liked that, Buddy and me . . . fear holding on a minute longer."

She nodded. He looked away and up at a big red-tailed hawk circling on the morning thermals.

"See that guy?" he said.

"Yeah, he's hunting."

She sat on the edge of the porch, her legs dangling in the soft light.

Down in the dove field, Milo's men had already begun gathering hay bales for the barn. Milo himself sat atop a big buckskin-colored horse, overseeing them.

They drank the coffee, listening to the farm wake up, mourning doves lamenting their slain brethren, bobwhite quail calling for their mates to covey-up lest the hawk pounce, the hay laborers' laughter drifting to them from the field.

"Man, this is just like Buddy described it. A little bit of heaven out in the middle of nowhere."

"We like it."

"You'll stay around here, huh?"

"Oh, yes, it's all I know. And Mama Lou wants us to."

"So does Milo."

Laney caught the tone in his voice.

"Milo's not why I'm staying."

Dante fingered a dark mole beneath his ear.

"You know, Dante, Buddy wrote about you a lot in his letters."

"That so?"

"And you know what he said?"

"Haven't got a clue."

"He said you were like brothers, closer than brothers."

"Yeah, we . . ."

"And he said you had more talent in your little finger than he had in . . ."

Dante gestured it away before she could finish, focusing on the hawk circling high overhead. He could believe Buddy might have said that, but he did not believe it, terrified as he was by his own limitations. No matter what bluster he brought to bear, no matter what compliments his work might elicit, he lived always with an acidic sense of failure. The chasm between the work he'd done and the work he wanted one day to do seemed only to widen.

"Buddy was an awful liar," he said.

"Not when he talked to me, he wasn't."

He finished his coffee and glanced at her. She wore no makeup and appeared as fresh and unsullied as this fine, clean morning.

"You know," he said, "Buddy was right. You're a pretty woman. Real pretty."

She started to speak, but he put up his hand.

"And you're hurtin' now like you've never hurt in your life."

Her gaze shifted from the ground to his eyes.

"And you'll be hurtin' for a long time. Forever, probably. But one day, further on down the road, some other guy is gonna come along, and I hope for little Rafe's sake, for your sake, that you, you know, that you let yourself love somebody again. When the time comes. Maybe not Henderson, but somebody."

She nodded. "Thanks," she said, "Maybe I will, but right now . . ."

"Yeah . . . it's way too soon," he said, fearing he'd gone too far. "I'm just stepping on my tongue here, so I'd better get on the road. Gotta register at the college and all that. . . ." He wasn't coming on to this woman; he wasn't seeking to take advantage. He just thought she was too good to waste.

"Not without breakfast. Come on, I'll scramble you some eggs."

"Powdered or real?"

She laughed. "Real, Dante. This is a farm. They're fresh out of a chicken an hour ago."

"Well, hell, Lieutenant, sign me up!"

Later, after hugs all around, Dante took his leave of Laney and Rafe and Mama Lou, the women saying again how much they appreciated his troubling to visit. Rafe grinned, gurgled, and stretched out his

62

hand to Dante. The man stroked the child's silken head, then turned away. He felt that, all things considered, it'd gone about as well as it could've. Except for his . . . breakdown, or whatever the hell it was there on the floor last night.

About that, he didn't feel so good.

Later, he asked, "So, how far is it to Tuscaloooosa, then?" He pronounced the town in a mock Southern accent.

"Don't you be making fun of us," Mama Lou laughed. "It's about fifteen miles. Highway runs smack through the middle of it."

"Good planning," he said.

Sir Plus was already in his jeep seat, ready for action, when he began barking. It was Milo cantering toward them at a hundred yards. Dante kissed Laney lightly on the cheek—for Milo's sake—and cranked up the jeep.

"Don't be a stranger, Dante," Laney said.

He smiled, saluted them and eased off down the gravel drive toward the highway, meeting Milo and the horse near the edge of the mown field, where he stopped.

"So, Yank, on your way to being a college boy, eh?" Milo said, reining in, his sunglasses once again hiding his eyes.

Dante put his hand on Sir Plus to keep him quiet.

"Yep, fresh meat, that's me." Dante fired up his Zippo and lit a Camel.   "

Take good care of those ladies, Milo."

"You don't need to worry about that, fella."

Dante looked at where Milo's eyes should have been, then away, at the hawk, still hunting.

"Maybe not, but I'll be back to check on 'em from time to time. I'm funny that way. See ya'."

He shifted into first and spun a little gravel on his way toward Highway 11.

* * *

The road to Tuscaloosa wasn't crowded this morning, apart from a few tourists, some overloaded farm trucks and a couple of wagons being pulled by mules—the first Dante had seen. The wagons were all driven by black men who kept two wheels—often car tires—on the shoulder and two on the roadbed. Sir Plus saw them, but he didn't care for the mules at all—there'd been so few back in Germany at the nobleman's estate—and Dante had to cuff him a time or two to shut him up.

Otherwise, with the canvas top rolled back and the sun full on its occupants, the little jeep purred along on autopilot, allowing Dante to reflect on whether he'd accomplished the mission on which Buddy had sent him . . .

With the big diesel sound rumbling the ground around them, Dante drags Buddy from the tank toward the poplar thicket and momentary safety in the high grass. At that instant, two heavy American tanks heave into view and, when attacked, begin blowing the shit out of the wrecked chateau in which the Germans have set up their machine gun nest. Dante and Buddy have a ringside seat at the slaughter, only Buddy doesn't know it. He lies quietly, his bloody head in Dante's lap.

The damn Germans don't seem to know when they're whipped. Despite the Americans' withering fire, two of them rush out the back of the collapsing building and toward Dante and Buddy—whom they do not see. The Germans carry an anti-tank bazooka-like weapon called a Panzerfaust and are trying to gain a better angle for a flanking shot on the American tank treads. Watching them, Dante can only admire as a soldier the courage he fears as a man.

As the Germans approach his position, he cradles Buddy's head with one hand and with the other slips out his .45 automatic from a shoulder holster.

Incredibly, the Germans appear to be running right at him, but at the last moment Dante sees they plan to use his own smoking tank as a shield from behind which to fire. He eases Buddy's head to the ground, gets to his knees, chambers a round in the pistol and waits. The two Germans reach the crippled tank, load their weapon and peer around the back toward the clanking Americans, each maneuvering to finish off what's left of the chateau.

The loader-Kraut taps the shooter on his helmet to tell him he's ready, but as the shooter leans out to trigger a round, Dante, who can't be more than thirty feet behind them, stands and shouts:

"Kameraden!"

The men hesitate, distracted. Dante raises the pistol in both hands, aimed directly at their backs.

He shouts again the word for comrade or friend.

The two Germans turn and look right at him. He sees their eyes when they see him, and he sees that they see what's about to happen. Then he makes it happen. Two quick shots. A third. The shooter-German crumples. The loader spins in place like an abandoned marionette. A fourth shot and it's over.

Dante feels nothing human.

Holstering the pistol, he kneels to check on Buddy. Blood is everywhere: on him; on his friend; on the grass. Buddy's face is a lacerated mess. He smiles crookedly, his lips smashed. Then he does what soldiers do. He asks Dante to go and tell his Mama and Laney *that he was thinking of them . . .*

"But," he lisps, "lie to 'em about the details."

Dante overtook a wagon full of loose cotton being driven to the gin by a black man and his wife, their two children riding up high on the fleecy pile. A pair of mules strained at the load, heads bobbing in unison as they stepped off the miles. Dante waved. They waved. Sir Plus barked. Minutes later, as he crested the next hill, Dante noticed Sir Plus intently looking straight up, searching the sky like a wary air raid warden. Then he heard something, a dull, growing drone. All of a sudden, just as a shadow flicked across the jeep, he was engulfed in a thunderous, ear-splitting roar. He felt the shock wave rasp over his body as he yanked the jeep to a halt.

He knew it was a plane—he'd been strafed by some of Hitler's finest—but in Alabama? At first he thought it might be about to crash, but glancing up, he saw a sleek, silver P-51 Mustang fighter climbing out of its dive and blasting up into the wild blue yonder. Then the plane banked sharply left and—one wing pointed straight at the ground—began a long sweeping turn for what promised to be a second run at him.

"No way, pal," Dante shouted, reaching for the German Luger beneath the dash. Holding the pistol upright, he got Sir Plus out of the jeep and knelt alongside, trying to keep an eye on the circling plane. Tall pines on either side of the road partially blocked his view, but he could hear it now, its engine screaming. Back down the road, he glimpsed the cotton wagon stopped, the black family sitting there calmly as though this were a perfectly ordinary Monday morning event in Alabama.

What kind of place was this?

Sir Plus moaned softly. Dante squatted in the road, whirling from point to point on the compass, unable to get a lock on the Mustang's location.

"Friggin' zoomie, come back here and I'll . . ."

Two seconds before it roared overhead again, he saw it coming right at him. He jerked up the pistol and got off four shots at the fleeting, beautiful bird. It was futile, of course, the plane had come and gone before the last round fired, but it made him feel better. He could smell the lingering gunpowder from his pistol as the Mustang waggled its wings, did a triple roll and headed toward the western horizon. If, at that moment, Dante could have gotten his hands on the guy flying that plane, the guy would have died.

He turned to look for Sir Plus whom he found beneath the jeep, quivering. He calmed the dog while he calmed himself, slowly reloading the pistol and watching the cotton wagon clip-clopping closer. The driver, a dark middle-aged fellow in overalls and red shirt, tipped his straw hat.

"Y'all ain't broke down, is you?"

"Huh? Naw . . . I'm okay. You see that damn fool?"

"Yessir, I seen him. Thought for a second he was gonna take your head off."

The black lady smothered a chuckle, and Dante realized he must look peculiar, standing there loading a pistol, his face red where it wasn't bleached white from the Mustang assault.

"Got any idea where that moron keeps his plane?"

"No sir, but there's a air field up ahead three-four miles on the right. Could be he parks it there."

"Thanks, if he does I'll find him."

From the moment they'd stopped, the two adults and their children had scrutinized Dante's fatigues, the jeep and—above all—Sir Plus.

One of the children sitting atop the cotton, a boy about eight, called down to him.

"What kinda dog is that, Mister? He's pretty."

"German," said Dante, "a Weimaraner, it's called."

Everybody looked at Sir Plus. Something about the big foreign dog, the pistol firing and reloading, the Army man/Army jeep and the strafing incident came together in the children's minds with perfect logic.

The other kid, a girl about twelve, said, "Mama, I thought the war was over. Now they done brought it home to Alabama."

"Hush, child," her mother said. "This man ain't fighting no war."

Dante laughed. "I will be if I catch that son . . . that airdale in the Mustang . . . See ya'."

The driver spoke sharply to his mules, and the wagon began to move on by, but the children, as though their heads rested on swivels, never let Sir Plus out of their sight, and after a few seconds the boy could be heard excitedly.

"Daddy, I want me a big ol' gray dog just like that."

"Be quiet, boy, that dog ain't studyin' you."

Dante got underway, waving as he passed the wagon, and ten minutes later, he saw the Mustang crossing the highway at about 500 feet, wheels down, on its final approach. A thousand meters off to the right, he could see a few hangars and a wind sock, the plane's destination. He slewed the jeep and trailer onto a gravel road past a sign reading:

TUSCALOOSA AIR FIELD

Dust plumed up behind the speeding jeep as it ran nearly parallel with the descending plane. Dante saw the Mustang touch down, bounce once lightly, then settle back for its runout. He also saw that only one of the four corrugated metal hangars had its doors slid open. He pulled the jeep up in front of it and waited as the big handsome tail-dragger swung around at the end of the dirt runway and began taxiing back toward him.

Sir Plus whined softly.

"It's okay," Dante said, tickling him beneath the muzzle. "This jerk is ours."

Red and blue markings highlighted the mirrored silver skin of the Mustang's tail and wings. Its nose insignia was a splashy poker hand—a royal flush. Taxiing nearer, engine deafening, the plane made a final turn toward the hangar and the jeep. Dante got out and stood with his fists on his hips, legs spread, the pistol stuck in his belt. Sir Plus stood up in the seat, his paws on the windshield top.

The plane slowed but kept coming.

"Okay, asshole," said Dante, "Stop the plane. Get out. Climb down. Let's get this over with."

But it was still coming. Dante could see the big prop whirling, knowing it would slice him into fine bologna if he weren't careful. Apparently, they were going to play a little game of chicken. He could see the pilot in his sunglasses and leather flying helmet looking down at him past the long engine cowl. And still it came closer, the prop wash flattening the grass, kicking up a massive dust cloud behind it.

The plane was not fifty feet away and still moving toward him when Dante experienced a profound insight:

This crazy bastard is gonna kill me.

Apparently, Sir Plus gained the dog-equivalent perception at the same instant. Just before the Mustang became a rolling guillotine, the ex-Sergeant fled one way and the Weimaraner bolted another. At that moment, the pilot cut his big twelve-cylinder Merlin engine, which back-fired once, and slowed to a stop.

An apoplectic Dante stopped running and whipped out his pistol, screaming.

"Come down here you zoomie son-of-a-bitch! I want a piece of your ass!"

On the Mustang, the canopy slid back. The pilot, swathed in soft flying helmet and white scarf, stood up, unbuttoned the helmet, pulled it off with both hands—and loosed a mass of blond curls that cascaded onto her shoulders.

"Take a number and get in line, buster," she said.

Sir Plus barked.

Dante, open-mouthed, stood near the Mustang's wing tip, holding the pistol.

"I . . . I don't get it," he said.

"Clearly."

"A dame?"

"Very good."

She clambered out of the cockpit onto the wing and hopped to the ground. Walking toward him, she pulled off a fleece-lined flying glove and stuck out her hand.

"Evelyn Curtis, sorry if I scared you."

Dante had to transfer the pistol before shaking hands.

"Somebody could get hurt, you waving that thing around," she said. "What's your name?"

In her mid-twenties, absurdly attractive, she stood maybe five-seven or eight, her athletic build accentuated by the cinched-in, waist-length leather jacket, trim flying pants and boots. Aware of—and enjoying—her impact, she smiled and cocked her head. Dante noticed a faint scar running from her left cheek to her chin. When she saw him notice, she averted her head slightly as her lips parted to reveal perfect white teeth.

An apparition, Dante thought.

"Dante Larocca, Brooklyn."

"Brooklyn's your last name?"

"Larocca. I'm Dante Larocca. Where'd you learn to fly like that?"

"I was a Ferry Command pilot during the war."

"You flew combat?"

"No," she said with disgust, "Women weren't allowed."

"Well, hell no, I mean, you wouldn't want a girl in combat, 'cause . . ."

Evelyn exploded, mimicking his accent.

"No, I mean, hell, you wouldn't want a goil in combat! What if da' Joimans didn't provide shampoo and hair curlers in da' P.O.W. camp?" She glanced at the jeep. "Were you in the service?"

"Yeah. Sergeant. Army. With Patton."

"Peachy." She was furious. "I was a WASP, Sergeant, and thirty-eight of us goils were killed ferrying planes to embarkation points for the Army. And the Navy. So cut me some goddamn slack!"

"I . . . hey . . ."

Her fury stopped him cold. She turned and strode toward a slick, 1941 maroon Ford convertible which he hadn't seen until now, parked inside the hangar. En route, she spotted Sir Plus, posed upright and imperial in the jeep. She paused, went over to him, spoke, and extended the back of her hand, palm inward. Sir Plus took a tentative sniff, then gazed into her face as though he were scanning a poem.

"Nice Weimy," she said. "Yours?"

"Yeah, uh, yeah, I got him . . ."

"Had to be Germany. How'd you bring him out of the country? They're strict as hell about that."

She laid her flying glove on the hood of the jeep and stroked Sir Plus behind the ears. Dante walked up to the woman and dog, now intimates. His equilibrium was taking its own sweet time to recover.

"Nobody else . . . How'd you know what it was?" he said.

"I was in Germany with my dad before the war. Tried to buy a pair of these, but apparently my pedigree wasn't good enough."

Dante grinned and mocked his own accent.

"Duhh, yeah, well, I guess ya' gotta be from, like, Brooklyn, ya' know what I'm saying?"

She relaxed a bit, even smiled, looking him over in the stone coldest appraisal he'd ever received.

"So, I'm betting you didn't actually purchase this big guy, did you?" she said.

"Not . . . technically." She looked a question at him. "He, uh, came to my attention after a little ruckus with a couple of Kraut Panzers. He was only half grown, and his, uh, owner—former owner—had kind of, uh, gone to pieces, you might say, so . . ."

"You killed the guy for his dog?"

"No. I killed the guy for trying to kill me. The dog was sort of a side benefit."

She looked at him again, her green eyes assessing his.

"Right. Well, he's a fine animal."

She turned and hurried toward the Ford.

"See ya'," he called after her.

She waved over her shoulder, without turning. At the hangar, she paused a moment to speak to a young mechanic who'd ambled over from working on a two-seat, open-cockpit biplane parked nearby. Then she jumped into the Ford and peeled out.

Dante picked up the glove lying on the hood. He smelled something familiar and raised it to his nose.

"Lilac," he said softly. "Jesus . . . Maria . . ."

Turning, he watched a loamy contrail boil up behind the fast-disappearing convertible as he fought to prevent lovely, terrible Maria from invading his head. How was it possible to want so badly something you hated so deeply?

"Keep busy," he said to himself. "Keep moving."

Climbing into the jeep, he noticed the mechanic walk toward the biplane and glance back at him. Dante drove over.

"Howyadoin'," Dante said.

"'Lo." The coveralled mechanic was a small, wiry guy, about 25, sandy-haired and suspicious, sporting a half-hearted ginger mustache. He held a big crescent wrench in one hand.

"Nice plane."

"Yeah, it's a Boeing/Stearman Kaydet. Best little bird in the fleet."

"Yours?"

"Nope. Belongs to the lady you was just talking to—Miss Curtis."

Dante and Sir Plus surveyed the neat open-cockpit plane, its paint scheme a brilliant interplay of green and gold.

"Woman's got two airplanes?"

"This one's for work. The Mustang's for fun."

"What kinda work?"

"Crop dusting—or 'aerial application' as some call it." The mechanic nudged the plane with the wrench, and Dante noticed a line of small pipes and spigot heads attached to the trailing edge of the lower wing.

"She's good," the mechanic said, "got the balls of a brass monkey."

Dante nodded.

"I hear you."

"'Course, when it comes to paying the bill, it don't hurt none being her old man's daughter."

"Big shot, eh?"

"Real big."

"Figures."

Dante gazed at the plane; the mechanic looked at Sir Plus.

"Nice dog."

"Thanks. He's a handful."

"Looks kinda like a German short-haired been dipped in gray paint. Will he hunt?"

Sir Plus turned away in disgust.

"Never tried." Dante slipped the jeep into first. "Well, take care," he said, and started to roll, but the mechanic had something else on his mind.

"Say," he said, "you ain't from around here, are you?"

Dante smiled. "No. From up north a ways. See you."

Chapter 4

With Evelyn Curtis still on his mind, Dante again hit Highway 11 heading west for Tuscaloosa, searching out a good place to pitch his tent. He'd hoped to find a remote corner of the campus or a farmer's field, but he'd also hoped for water and electricity. He had bought the tent in the first place for financial reasons and because the papers were full of stories about how ex-servicemen in record numbers were flooding into college on the G.I. Bill, overloading university housing all over the country. Some smaller schools had doubled in size overnight, and administrators were scrambling to provide student rooms of any kind. At some schools, disputes about living space had even led to fist fights. He didn't need that.

Topping a rise, Dante saw on the left a tree-lined drive leading to a field on which were anchored several small house trailers. A big, home-made sign at the entrance read:

SHORTY'S
TRAILER PARK, CRICKET FARM
AND
BEAGLE RANCH

Dante slowed, liked what he saw, and pulled in. What he saw was an inviting proto-gypsy campsite comprising a dozen live-in trailers—none too fancy—along with the pick ups and dusty cars that had pulled them in. Dante spied wash hanging on lines strung between trees, plus electric cables running from a jake-leg power pole to the various trailers. All this was nicely spaced among tall pines and hickories and lay next to a creek that a tall man with a running start just might jump across. At a narrow place somebody had used field stones to dam up the creek, forming both a waterfall and pretty little swimming hole, the creek gurgling over the falls before running off downstream. Near the campsites sat a white farmhouse with a front porch on which Dante glimpsed a man. From behind the house, he could hear dogs baying.

He stopped, got out, tied Sir Plus to the jeep, and walked toward the man, who spoke.

"Hep ya'?"

"Yeah, howyadoin', I'm looking for a place to set up camp."

The oddly pale man looked to be fifty-plus, with thin graying hair, a round face and beady eyes that peered at Dante through rimless glasses. He sat in a wooden chair, teetered back on two legs against the wall. Dante saw him look at the jeep.

"Got to provide your own trailer," he said.

"Yeah, well, I'm going with a tent, see, 'cause I couldn't afford a trailer, but . . ."

"You a vet?"

"Yeah, Army."

"On the G.I. Bill?"

Dante grinned. "And not much else."

Above the sound of dogs and waterfall, he could hear a pair of blue jays giving each other hell high up in the pines. The man's eyes narrowed. He seemed neither hostile nor friendly.

"Europe or the Pacific?" he asked.

"Europe. Tanks."

The man scratched his elbow and looked off.

"My boy was at Pearl."

The voice was soft, almost a whisper, and Dante sensed a need to tread softly.

"Navy?" he asked.

"Yep. Gunner's Mate First Class . . ."

"Good man, we had . . ."

"On the Arizona."

Now Dante knew what he was being told. The U.S.S. Arizona held the melancholy distinction of having sustained one of the greatest losses of personnel of any American vessel on the Day of Infamy. A great hulking battleship moored to the pier, she was—like the rest of Pearl Harbor—wholly unprepared for the Japanese attack that sank her where she lay, taking the lives of hundreds of shipmates, many of whose bodies were still trapped inside.

"I'm . . . I'm real sorry to hear that," Dante said.

"He was a career man."

"Right."

"Some career . . ." The man stood up. He was short. Muscular, but quite attenuated, maybe five-six. He stretched and yawned, sounding a weary little note.

"Well, so you want a place to pitch a tent, huh?"

"If I can afford it."

The man squinted at him.

"Can you handle five dollars a month?"

"Yeah, but just barely. Thanks, Shorty . . . You are Shorty, aren't you?"

The little man's squint deepened. "Take a guess."

"Well . . . yeah, now you mention it."

"Come on."

He led Dante toward the creek, pointing out a level spot between two hickory trees where a tent could be set up. The place was actually a little plateau down from which the ground sloped ten-twelve yards to the creek, well-shaded and maybe thirty feet from the nearest trailer.

"This'll work fine," said Dante. "I see you got power here, too. What about a latrine?"

"Oh, yeah, power, water, crapper, everything the modern housewife needs to . . ."

At that moment, a spectacular canine-based racket arose nearby. Dante's tying up of Sir Plus had been perfunctory, and while neither man had noticed, the big dog had chewed loose the knot, left the jeep behind and gone exploring. Whatever he was looking for, he'd found. Intermixed with a raucous multi-throated baying, Dante recognized Sir Plus's thunder. Both men ran for the sound. As Shorty disappeared around the corner in front of him, Dante marveled that any guy with legs that short could run that fast.

When he himself made the corner he was greeted by the sight of Sir Plus at war with two dozen enraged beagles. Fortunately, the beagles were all incarcerated inside a long fenced run, while the Weimaraner—safely outside the wire—flew back and forth from one end of the run to the other, hotly pursued by the apoplectic pack. The order of battle proved rather odd, though, because Sir Plus was faster than some of the beagles, so that, while nimbler members of the throng could keep up with him on his mad double-reverse dashes, others could not.

The result was like a psychotic auto race where the leaders overtake slower competitors. Except here, every time Sir Plus and the speedy dozen reversed course at the end of the fenced-in run, the slower dogs were still heading in that direction, so that at every turn, fast and slow beagles plowed into each other with extraordinary violence, sending one another spinning ass-over-teacup and inflicting concussions all around as they battled for the right of way.

A couple of the thinner-skulled dogs—it was impossible to tell whether of fast or slow design—had already given up the chase and were stumbling blindly around the run looking for the number of the truck that had whacked them.

Dante was sure Sir Plus had planned the whole thing.

"Get aholt of your goddamn dog," Shorty shouted, "afore all my friggin' beagles kill theirselves . . . Hey, Bess! Here, Sam! You, Bob, hush up now! Goddamnit to hell, Willy, stop your hollerin'. . ."

And so on for several minutes.

Showing a lamentable lack of discipline, the beagles ignored Shorty completely, their wails, if anything, growing wilder as, for several minutes, Sir Plus danced beyond Dante's grasp. Finally, Shorty entered the run and, in true Biblical fashion, began laying about him left and right with a stout leather lead. This direct application of force proved sufficient to gain his charges' attention. The beagle barking subsided into a low chorus of irritated mutterings mixed with yelps from those whom Shorty did manage to anoint with the lead.

Dante took Sir Plus—looking pleased with himself—back around the house and double-tied him to the jeep.

* * *

By five o'clock that afternoon, Dante had given Shorty a down-payment and, with some help, had set up his 12' x 12' camouflage tent, complete with a central ridge pole, and a drop-flap canvas rain porch over the entrance. Later he would build a wooden floor for it to get everything up off the ground. Meanwhile, he'd met several other fellows—all vets—who lived in the nearby trailers. One, red-headed medic Freddy Wilson, had a wife with him. The others—Karl and Ben, two fierce, rock-hard, 100-proof ex-Marines looking like they'd just returned from severing Jap heads on Iwo Jima, three Army grunts and a couple of former Air Corps pilots—were solo.

The guy in the closest trailer, David Cohen, particularly interested Dante. Tall and well-built, he had dark curly hair and a quick, sardonic wit that sometimes eluded the Marines. He was missing a hand, but with his good arm he was plenty strong, and along with the Marines it was he who'd helped Dante set up the big tent.

All the vets were crazy about Sir Plus, making Dante repeat his story about the dog's history, how he'd smuggled him, sedated with a medic's help, aboard the troop ship home. Sir Plus appeared to regard all the attention as nothing more than he deserved, and Dante recalled what he'd seen so often during the war, that lonely, frightened men will befriend a stray dog or cat or rabbit and shower it with an adoration they'd never be capable of summoning for another human.

Dante had also installed his Army cot, foot locker, drafting table, typewriter, coffee pot, hot plate, and two each of Army-issue cups, plates, knives, forks and spoons. Shorty had loaned him a couple of chairs and a small, neat bureau with attached mirror that had been stored in the barn. All he needed now was a second-hand fridge of some kind.

"Let me pay you for these," Dante said to Shorty.

"No . . . No, this stuff belonged to my boy, Vernon, and that wouldn't be right. When you're through with it, we'll pass it along to the next vet, and that way Vernon'll be helping y'all out . . . making a contribution-like."

Dante knew when to acquiesce.

With the help of Cohen and Shorty, he rigged up lights in the tent, taking power from the ad hoc pole, which itself was stealing electricity from the main line running alongside the road.

"Power company ain't hurting for money," Shorty said, "They'll never miss it."

The last things Dante brought in from the jeep were a portfolio of his architectural sketches, a photography book of Frank Lloyd Wright designs, and several small, wooden scale-model buildings which he set on the bureau.

Just before dark, he flipped on the lights in the tent, looked around and pronounced himself satisfied. He'd come a long way, leaving behind everything he'd known—the city, the war, the old neighborhood, the memories of a marriage—and penetrated deep into a new and alien land. Maybe Maria and Bruno wouldn't follow him here. Maybe.

Get busy.

He plugged in his hot plate and retrieved water from the barn in which Shorty had set up a central shower-latrine facility where formerly Vernon had hosed down thoroughbreds boarded there by the neighbors and wealthier university students.

Dante's first meal would be instant coffee. Waiting for the water to boil, he laid the German pistol on the table and picked up a deck of playing cards given him as a phony bonus by the Toadstool surplus agent back in Brooklyn. Shuffling the cards, Dante smiled at the thought of that chubby little guy standing on the loading dock, his hair plastered to his forehead by the rain, locked in a ram rod stiff salute he'd learned from watching war movies. What a pony-loaf those movies were, Dante thought, a parcel of criminal lies spread among vainglorious youth, hungry for a hero's wreath only to wind up in a sucker's grave. They never got it right, Hollywood.

"Knock knock . . . you gotta get a door, Larocca, or a damn Chinese bell or something."

It was Cohen. Beneath his bad arm he pressed a fifth of bourbon to his side and was carrying in his one hand a mixing bowl.

"Hey, Lefty, come in, man, I was just making my first cuppa joe. Take one?"

"Sure. Here." Cohen thrust out the bowl.

"Whatcha got?"

"Tent-warming gift. One-handed potato salad."

"Hey, my favorite kind. Thanks, man."

"And a bottle of Kentucky's finest," Cohen said, placing the bourbon on the drafting table.

"Now you're talking. I thought this place was dry."

"Not if you know the right people." He winked and whispered: "Shorty."

"I knew God brought me here for a reason."

Dante could tell Cohen had been in the service—he wore a khaki shirt with frayed holes in the collar where he'd pinned the rank insignia. Dante also assumed the amputation derived from combat, but that was none of his business. Cohen moved with an athlete's grace, made more striking by the sometimes awkward gestures forced on him by the missing hand. His left arm ended mid-way between elbow and wrist, the stub encased in a sort of black woolen sock. Pulling one of the chairs back, he spun it on the axis of one leg before noticing the pistol.

"That a Luger?"

"Yeah," Dante said, "took it off a German."

"Sweet piece," Cohen said, picking up the gun and assessing its heft. "Good balance. Nine millimeter, isn't it?"

"Yep, parabellum cartridge. Dead accurate."

"Nice. Gonna sleep with it under your pillow?"

"That's my plan. Got a problem with that?" The two men's eyes flicked past each other. Cohen smiled and replaced the pistol.

"No, no problem. Always good to be prepared. . . . So, did I hear you say you're going to study architecture?"

"Yeah, they don't have a full architectural school at Alabama, but they set up this deal where they cross-breed art with engineering, and they've got a couple of hot-shots teaching building design, strength of materials, that kind of thing."

"Sounds interesting."

"Yeah, and I can do a year or two here, maybe win a fellowship, then transfer to . . . shit, I don't know, to wherever they'll have me."

"Right. . . . What are those?"

Cohen pointed to the little scale-models Dante had lovingly stored out of harm's way on the bureau.

The question embarrassed him.

"Oh, that's just some working models, you know. A vacation home, a church, art gallery, like that."

"They're yours?"

"Yeah."

"This one's nice. How's it work?"

Cohen picked up the vacation home prototype, turning it in his big hand. Dante had fashioned the model out of cast-off cedar, walnut and maple pieces, blending the hues and grains of the three woods to form intricate patterns in the walls, plus a radically shaped, high-arched roof-line.

"Well, if you sited it facing east, see," Dante said, his voice intensifying, "the sun wouldn't wake you up every day in the master bedroom back here, but it would throw great morning light into the kitchen, over here. And on real steamy days, you'd recycle the heat from the attic to help warm up water in the tank. Then, see that little porch there on the other side? That's where you'd have a beer at . . . you know, sundown, or whatever . . . in the shade or, with somebody, your wife . . . or a babe. . . ."

He shut Maria down by checking the temperature of the water on the hot plate.

Dante's hope to design practical structures that harmonized with their inhabitants' lives always conflicted with his reluctance to brag, which itself clashed with his need to dominate, which fell afoul of his artistic insecurities, which were contradicted, in turn, by his vaulting ambition to do good work—and have it recognized. Conversationally, the result could be a mess—except when the excitement of a project took over and he got on a roll. Then he could really talk. Especially when he sensed interest in his interlocutor.

Cohen seemed to qualify.

"That's damned clever," he said.

The water began to boil.

"Hot java, coming up." Dante mixed the water with powdered coffee, apologizing for the lack of sugar.

"Forget the sugar, hand me the bourbon."

Cohen poured a generous dollop into both cups.

* * *

Over the next couple of hours, the two men danced a delicate getting-to-know-you pas de deux. Like strangers on a life raft exchanging selected private information, they drilled into each other's lives, layer by thin layer. A little of Brooklyn and Dante's combat experiences emerged, a wound here, a scar there, a bit of Buddy and Laney. But nothing about Maria. Cohen spoke of the Navy and his life as a

Lieutenant aboard a destroyer out in the far Pacific fighting the Japs.

"So," Dante said, "Cohen's gotta be Jewish, but you sound more like Uncle Remus than Groucho. You ain't from New York."

Cohen laughed. "No, Mobile. Good many Jews down there, you know, port city and all."

"That give you any trouble . . . being a Jew with this crowd?"

"Not really. Unless you count things like country club exclusions and not being a big part of Mardi Gras or . . ."

"I thought Mardi Gras was New Orleans."

"It is. But it started in Mobile; we exported it to them in the last century."

"No kidding?"

"Yeah, I'm, uh, talking about all that—'The Wartime Adventures of a Deep South Jew'—in my novel."

"You writing a novel?"

"Hmm, like every other shell-shocked ex-serviceman who thinks he's got a story to tell."

"Hell, might as well be you as anybody."

"Agreed, and there's this guy, Hudson Strode, teaches writing at the University. He's pretty damned good. Read some of my stuff and admitted me into his seminar."

Dante observed Cohen through muted light thrown off by the bulb he'd shielded with a tee shirt. The handsome Southerner seemed a little more impaired now than he had at first, more shredded on the inside. As the whiskey flowed, his right eye had developed a tic, and Dante caught him staring from time to time at his stump. Then, at the pistol. After potato salad and the first cup of coffee, they'd proceeded to plain bourbon and water—taken from the creek behind Dante's tent.

"Booze'll kill any bacteria," Cohen had said.

*Thank god for night. Kamikazes don't attack at night. It's April,
1945. Lieutenant David Cohen, Executive Officer of the USS Little
(DD-803) slumps on the port wing of the bridge in the pitch-black of
darken-ship conditions—no white lights allowed; only soft red bulbs
glow in interior passageways and gun mounts. Cohen is operating on
eight hours sleep—over the past three days—his brain baked, skin salt-
grimy, eyes red-rimmed. The Little is on picket duty south of Okinawa,
serving as both a radar beacon for U.S. planes en route to and from
bombing Japan, and as a rescue vessel for downed pilots. They've
fished six out of the water during the past week—four dead, two alive,
but one of them stark raving mad from exposure and fear of sharks.*

*As X-O serving under an incompetent skipper named Walcot, Cohen's
concerns are legion, paramount among them: crew-fatigue and the
near-panic induced by Jap kamikazes—flying bombs controlled by the
ultimate analog computer, a human brain. The men of the Little cannot
fathom the motivation of these suicidal attackers. The frightened
sailors talk incessantly about the Jap pilots, unable to bridge a cultural
chasm separating their own ideology of live-to-fight-another-day from
the Japanese concept of bushido: honor above life.*

*Why, the baffled American sailors wonder, why would you
deliberately crash your plane into an enemy ship? Not torpedo it, not
bomb or strafe it, but smash yourself into it at the certain cost of your
own life? Makes no sense, they think. It's crazy, they think. Some of
them say it ain't fair. It's un-Christian.*

*Cohen sneers but agrees; still, what is is what is, and his job remains
to fight the ship, not easy to do with the exhausted crew standing
port and starboard watches at battle stations: four on, four off, 24-7.
Everybody's on their last nerve. Vicious fist-fights over nothing break*

out between friends.

The Little has been attacked three times in recent days by multi-plane flights of suiciders, shooting down four of the screaming terrors, while absorbing one massive explosion of a near-miss on the port side, a blast that killed two gunners manning open-tub 40-millimeter anti-aircraft guns.

Cohen had liked those gunners.

His own hatred for the Japs frightens him.

His right eye has begun to twitch.

Outside, guarding the entrance, Sir Plus lay on a piece of canvas Dante had placed there for him—the lunatic beagles but a happy memory.

About seven o'clock, Shorty came by to deliver a plate of his wife's fried chicken.

"Now, boys," Shorty said, "this right here is the freshest fried chicken you'll ever sink a tooth in. At noon today my big old Rhode Island Red rooster was chasing that there hen around the back yard trying to get him some, and tonight, well, she's dinner."

"So, she was gonna get screwed either way," said Dante.

"You got it," said Shorty. "And far as I can tell, that's the way the world works." He appeared to have sampled some of his own private stash as he whistled his way back home, listing slightly to port.

"Good guy," said Dante.

When he glanced up, David Cohen was looking at him.

"What?"

"Aren't you going to ask me about my hand?"

Dante had stopped drinking once he saw how much Cohen liked the stuff. Now he realized his new friend had a buzz on.

"I figured you'd talk about it when you were . . ."

"Kamikazes." The word knifed across the tent, usurping response. Dante waited.

"Goddamn Jap bastards."

Cohen's voice had gained an unhealthy edge. Dante decided he needed another drink. He gestured a question toward the fifth, but Cohen was back aboard his destroyer waiting for heralds of the Divine Wind to plunge out of the clouds and send him and his shipmates to the bottom of the China Sea.

"Five of 'em hit us last May. We shot down three." Dante listened, quiet. "I was X-O of the U.S.S. Little. Ever hear of us?"

Dante shook his head and emptied the fifth into his cup.

"Doesn't matter. Just chalk up another tin can sacrificed to the Emperor." He finished his drink, looked at the bottle, and turned away. "A hundred men, half the crew, didn't make it. Two of us were nominated for the Medal of Honor, me and a chief machinist's mate named Ralph Graham—bravest guy I ever met." Cohen's pupils dilated in the soft light, his knees vibrating with suppressed tension.

"What about your skipper?"

"Dead. Decapitated. I'd assumed command, but even after we were afire, taking on water, and I'd passed the word to abandon ship, Graham kept going back down into the engine room pulling guys out . . . five or six of 'em. Setting up a first-aid station on the fantail. Incredible stuff. . . just incredible."

"Sounds rough."

"And then there were the sharks."

Outside, the last of the evening crickets chirped and fell silent. Sir Plus stuck his head in the tent, asking with a look where he was supposed to sleep. Dante pointed to a mat placed next to the cot. The gray dog walked over, sniffed the mat, turned around three times and lay down.

Cohen's eyes said that Cohen's mind was far away.

"Crappy thing was," he said, "up the line, Graham's Medal of Honor nomination was 'reduced' to the Navy Cross by . . . by some sorry-ass staff puke back at CincPac that never heard a shot fired in anger. Totally fubar."

"What about yours?"

For a long moment, nothing moved on Cohen but his knees, then he reached into a shirt-front pocket and slowly withdrew a pale blue, starred ribbon attached to a gold medal. Dante knew what it was. He'd attended a couple of Medal of Honor ceremonies in France—but never for a living recipient. Cohen seemed to want him to take the medal, to hold it. He did. It felt heavy with loss and suffering—not only Cohen's but that of every terrified sailor aboard the Little who'd gone down with her in that exploding furnace of gunpowder, metal, and oil.

"Very impressive, Cohen," Dante said softly. "You must have done one hell of a job out there." He extended the blue ribbon toward David, who stuck out his stump, apparently for Dante to drape the medal across. Dante complied.

"The secret is," Cohen said, leaning forward, whispering, "the dirty little secret is that in matters of medals it helps to leave some part of you behind. Visually more compelling, don't you know."

Larocca didn't go in for competitive heroism. He'd done his best in Europe; the Army had decorated him with its second highest award for bravery; he accepted that. But Medal of Honor winners were damned thin on the ground, and the waters parted when one walked into a room, bearing, as he did, an aura of extravagant courage and horror, of things seen and things done beyond the pale. Men made way for them because their very presence raised the warrior's eternal conundrum: 'I don't know what he did, but whatever he did, if I had been where he was when he did it, could I have done it?'

Most of those posing the question secretly knew the answer, which sealed the high esteem in which MOH winners were held. But such homage didn't come cheap, and Dante could see that Cohen was struggling with big demons. The two scarred young veterans looked at each other, both feeling centuries old. Stunned. Spiritually covert. Lame.

"You know, Brooklyn," Cohen said softly, "this war has damaged us—me, anyway. And I don't mean the hand . . ."

"Yeah . . ."

"I mean . . . I mean damaged us, you know, upstairs, in ways we may never understand or be able to talk about."

"I know."

"For the rest of our friggin' lives."

"Right . . ."

"Because to understand it, you know, you have to . . . to voluntarily revisit it—not just at night—and nobody, I mean, nobody wants to do that . . ."

"I know, pal. Do I fuckin' ever."

Sitting there in an Army tent pitched in an Alabama farmer's field, Dante felt a potent link to this man he'd never met before today, a brotherhood of suffering not unlike what he'd known with Buddy. War had scorched all three of them. Luck had saved two of them. Chance had led those two to this modest place.

Dante started to speak. Stopped. Began again, his voice hushed: "Cohen, do you . . . do you have . . . dreams?"

On his mat, Sir Plus stirred. Music from a nearby trailer drifted in on the night breeze.

Cohen sneered, his face warping into dark menace.

"What. Do. You. Think?"

Dante nodded. "Me too."

"I'm trying to figure out," Cohen said, "whether it's better to lie there awake, you know, remembering all that crap, second by second, death by death, or fall asleep and relive it. In full color. Mostly red."

"Yeah, nights are the worst."

"It's like your brain has declared war on . . . on your soul."

"Roger that."

Outside, an owl hooted his intention to hunt tonight.

"Funny thing, though," Cohen said softly. "I can't cry."

Dante looked up.

"I mean, I never cried, you know. First, because of my men with me in the life raft, right? Then, later, in the hospital, not even alone. Funny . . ."

Although Dante couldn't see exactly where this conversation was headed, no option looked good.

"Nothing wrong with a couple of tears, guy. By the way, you mentioned 'fubar' a minute ago. I haven't heard that since . . ."

"Yeah, great all-purpose description of life: 'Fucked Up Beyond All Recognition.'"

Dante chuckled. "About sums it up."

Cohen stared a moment, then, with a deft little movement, he pocketed the Medal of Honor, picked up the empty fifth, and stood, his manner changing to cover an abrupt emotional redeployment.

"Up and at 'em early in the A.M., ground-pounder. The U.S. Navy will lead you poor Army buggers to the enemy at zero eight hundred hours. . . and remember, like Dugout Doug MacArthur: 'I shall return.'" He saluted individually Dante and Sir Plus.

"Damned handsome beast you've got there, Sergeant. Don't let anything happen to him."

"Count on it, sir."

Cohen executed a wobbly about-face, and left the tent.

Larocca prepared for bed.

Night has fallen. Dante's in Paris with Maria. So are the Germans. Searchlights strobe the black sky. Otherwise, the city is war-darkened. Somebody's bombers roar overhead. Dante leads his wife in a mad dash through serpentine Latin Quarter streets, closely pursued by a German patrol. Ducking and running, they cross Boulevard Saint Michel near the Musee de Cluny, desperate for the sanctuary of Notre Dame. A rifle slug flits overhead, making a zissing noise like tearing silk. Maria cries out. He can sense the warmth of her hand, gripping his fiercely, trusting him to save them, believing he will know what to do, where to turn. He feels his duty to her as a massive burden, but one he shoulders without hesitation. It is, after all, Maria.

They sprint. He shouts that he loves her. He shouts that they will be all right, but of this he can't be certain. He's lost, now, but cannot admit it. He must lead. He must find a way out of this labyrinth. In the distance, he can see the twin truncated spires of Notre Dame.

Shots ring out. People fire at them from windows high overhead. The old city is full of collaborators. As they flee through the night, Maria prays aloud—a rosary of despair. Dante is strong and fit but is lost in the warren of alleys between Boulevard Saint Germain and the Quai de Montebello that runs along the Seine. Where is the cathedral now? Where? Which turn to take? Which unmarked alley? Paris is a mazey whore, an ancient Jezebel who has shamefully sold herself to the Germans with hardly a shot fired. Maria has come to warn him of something, but he can't hear her over the noise of sirens and gunfire. What is she saying? Something about love?

They take cover in a little vest-pocket park as the German patrol rushes by only inches away. Bullets ricochet around them, kicking up flakes of dirt and cobblestone. Maria can't take any more; she begins to sob. He comforts her, saying they'll be okay if they can just get onto the Ile de la Cite. She whimpers in terror. They're trapped together behind an elaborate fountain when it begins to rain; he can feel the wet on his face, and a strange heat . . .

Dante awakened on his cot to find something big looming over him, breathing in his face. For an instant he didn't know where he was and lashed out, striking Sir Plus on the nose. The dog yelped and shied away. Ears flat, stubby tail down, he backed across the tent, looking wounded. Dante came to his senses, saw what he'd done, rose and moved gently toward the dog, repeating his name and making apologetic love-sounds.

The man could smell a faint musky odor hovering in the air, a primitive smell of fear emanating from Sir Plus. The dog lowered its head at Dante's approach, not sure what to expect. The man put out his hand, palm inward, breathing the dog's name, coaxing, imploring. Sir Plus looked at him. Dante kneeled and whispered.

"Come here, boy . . . it's okay."

Finally, Sir Plus indicated by his posture that he would allow himself to be touched—and perhaps reconciled. Dante nustled him beneath his jaw, working his hand up to the ears and neck. Sir Plus leaned into him, connecting, forgiving. Kneeling there with both hands on the dog, Dante could see through the tent-flap to the yellow-rose eastern horizon.

Thank God, he thought. Thank God for daylight.

Crouched in a reddening dawn, Dante heard from outside a tapping sound he didn't recognize. The dog, too, stiffened and turned its head toward the tent flap. Dante walked outside, trailed closely by Sir Plus. Nearby, the waterfall gurgled. Behind it, from the surface of the swimming hole, a mist levitated into the cool air. A bobwhite quail called up near the barn, and in a tiny window of David Cohen's trailer a light shone.

It was from this old trailer that the tapping sound came. Dante walked closer, stood on tiptoe and looked inside. At a small desk sat Cohen hunched over a black Underwood, tap-tap-tapping out his novel with the long index finger of his one hand. He was amazingly fast.

After a couple of beats, he stopped, took a drag on his cigarette, blew smoke rings at the ceiling, and stared off. Then, something happened. His shoulders slumped, his head drooped and Dante heard a soft sob escape Cohen's mouth. For three or four seconds his whole torso vibrated in dreadful syncopation, then, with a sharp intake of breath the young ex-naval officer caught himself, ground out the fag, wiped his nose on his sleeve, and resumed his one-finger whacking.

My God, Dante thought, what a way to make a living.

Chapter 5

True to his word, at eight o'clock the next morning David Cohen—driving a dusty black Packard—led a rogues' convoy comprising Dante's jeep, a pickup truck, and two clapped-out 1930s Ford coupes out of Shorty's driveway toward Tuscaloosa. The pickup carried Karl and Ben, the two crew-cut, tattooed, psycho Marines.

Dante had seen these guys at dawn in their green Marine Corps skivvies grunting in tortured unison as they did marathon sets of push ups, their faces red, their neck muscles rippling. Like all Marines Dante had run into, there was something odd about them, a curiously sinister and deracinated quality that mixed hostility and guile with fury, focus, and simplicity. It was as if they were all perpetually looking for a good way to die. Or to make the other guy die. But Dante figured if he could enlist their aid in whatever schemes he cooked up, half his battle was won. The Marine motto of Semper Fidelis was no idle boast: the enemy of their friend was their enemy. Further, they really liked Sir Plus, calling him the "Kraut Hound" and slipping him bits of food.

The other convoy vehicles contained more of Shorty's edgy vets headed for their first encounter with higher education. Dante was loath to admit his nervousness. So he didn't. Earlier that morning, standing outside the tent drinking coffee, Reddy Freddie, the red-haired ex-medic with a wife and a yen to become a doctor, had announced his own case of nerves and asked Dante if he too were worried about going to college.

"Naw, man," said Dante, "piece of cake. Hell, guys like us busted Hitler and Hirohito's chops. Us vets are gonna turn this friggin' college on its head, pal. Kick. Its. Sorry. Ass."

Cohen smiled. "Nothing like a little confidence."

"Damn straight, Lefty."

"And so elegantly expressed," said Cohen. "Okay, since I've been there before, I'll lead. Let's mount up, gentlemen. You too, Brooklyn."

"Up yours, Swabbie," said Dante, grinning.

Now, rolling west toward Tuscaloosa with Sir Plus beside him, Dante didn't feel so confident. What he felt was an overpowering sense of American caste envy. Ambitious and talented but thoroughly out of place, he was driving a surplus jeep, wearing mismatched parts of a uniform, his heavy accent and manner so unlike that of the locals, his educational skills rusty and long untested.

Judas Priest. He imagined himself a foreign intruder, an interloper meddling with a world into which he had been neither born nor invited, but to which he'd gained access by the academically irrelevant route of military service. The question flew through his head: What the hell am I doing here?

Nothing if not pragmatic, he consoled himself with two thoughts: first, that if he could survive the war he could survive this. Second, in the Army he'd met a lot of real dumb fuckers with college degrees— most of them officers. If they could do it, so could he.

Drive on.

At the outskirts of Tuscaloosa, when the veterans' convoy hit heavy university traffic, Cohen pointed and shouted out the window:

"There! Every man for himself."

Dante knew the name of the building he was supposed to head for: Foster Auditorium. He signaled the Marines to follow, and when he saw those words incised in limestone over the door of a red-brick hulk, he slowed. Behind him, Karl and Ben tailgated him to a stop. Just ahead, a freshly washed gray Chevrolet was trying to parallel park.

Dante watched in disgust as the driver cut it too early and hit the curb, then pulled out and tried again, this time cutting it too late and hitting the car behind him. Dante swore.

"This creep's probably got a couple of PhDs."

When the driver's third attempt failed—and before he could begin a fourth—Dante swung the jeep neatly into the targeted parking space, cut his engine, and got out. The other driver came tumbling from the Chevy full of bluster and blow.

"Young man . . . young man, that is my parking space. You have taken my parking space. . . ."

The bespectacled driver looked to be in his mid-forties. He wore a starched white shirt, bow tie and—despite the heat—all the tweed he could layer onto his chubby body. Dante paused in tying Sir Plus to the jeep. As the little round man marched toward him, Sir Plus stiffened.

"Easy, boy," Dante said to the dog who had begun erupting in soft pre-barks. The man stopped, assessing the uncouth pair before him, his eyes big with a mix of anger and caution.

"Got a problem, Mack?" Dante said.

"Yes, indeed I do. You've stolen my place. You know perfectly well that I was attempting to park . . ."

"You got the 'attempting' part right."

"I would certainly have succeeded on my next try."

"Maybe, but meanwhile, you were holding up traffic."

Dante gathered up a mailman's leather shoulder bag he'd snagged in the Brooklyn surplus store. "Like they say," he said, "three strikes, you're out. And I was on deck."

"Now see here. You're a veteran, aren't you? I can tell you're one of those new fellows, so full of himself."

"And I'll bet you're a teacher."

"Professor, young man, professor."

"No shit. Professor, huh?"

"Don't you curse me. . . . Don't you stand there and curse me and pretend . . . pretend to . . ." The professor emitted little sprays of indignant spittle.

"Naw, pal, I didn't curse you. If I'd cursed you, you'd know it."

Angry car horns were blaring now, complaining about the traffic snarl caused by the professor's car. Then, just as that gentleman took an irate step toward Dante, two large, lantern-jawed men with short haircuts and shorter fuses stepped between them, grabbed the professor by both arms, lifted him off the ground, frog-marched him backward to his car—his feet making little walking steps in mid-air—and deposited him next to the driver's door.

"Get-in-your-car, asshole," snarled Karl, the slightly taller Marine.

"And-beat-it," snarled Ben, "before we rip out your guts and feed 'em to you!"

The professor instantly grasped the not-so subtext. In a flash he was in the car and gone.

"Thanks, fellas. Owe you one," said Dante.

"No problem, Brooklyn," said Karl. "Now, Ben, let's make us a parking place."

"Me and you," said Ben.

The two of them walked over to a neat little Plymouth coupe parked in front of the jeep. With Karl at the front and Ben at the back, they bent down and grabbed a bumper apiece.

"Ready when you are," said Ben.

"One . . . two . . . three . . . heave!" said Karl. The Plymouth popped up off the ground like it was mounted on coil springs. A minute later it sat athwart the sidewalk— blocking pedestrians—and a minute after that the Marines' pickup occupied its former parking space.

"Well done, men. Excellent work," said Dante.

"Semper Fi," said Karl.

"Where's the schoolhouse at?" said Ben.

"Follow me," said Dante.

* * *

The mass of students fighting their way into Foster Auditorium was epic in size, determination and variety. Seasoned fraternity boys—wise to roadblocks set up by the university to make them register in sequence—slipped through with the connivance of their frat-brother guards. Sorority girls winked and flirted their way past their own boyfriends, unwittingly placed at the door by the Dean of Students to stem the tide.

Terrified, beanie-wearing male freshmen—their heads shaved—open-mouthed and goggle-eyed, smack off the farm, were seeing perhaps for the first time in their lives more than 50 people crowded together in one place. Older, uniformed Army, Navy, Marine, Coast Guard, and Merchant Marine vets scoped out the terrain, then elbowed aside some bright-eyed Sigma Chi whose indignation was exceeded only by the veterans' disdain.

"Hey, what the heck . . ."

"Outta my way, candy ass."

Dante surveyed the seething mess at the doors, then turned to his Marines.

"Men, this calls for a flanking movement."

"Roger that," said Karl.

"Brooklyn, you want me to kill a couple of 'em, create a distraction, let us slip through?" Ben asked, earnestly.

"Thanks, Ben, but no. Come with me," said Dante. As he led them around the corner, he wondered if Ben, for all his charming loyalty, might not represent a certain . . . what . . . liability, unless carefully supervised. Earlier, at Shorty's, Karl had told Dante that in the Pacific war against the Japs Ben had established quite a record.

"Record for what?" Dante had asked.

Karl had stared off, then said, "Thoroughness. Ben is exceptionally thorough when dealing with the enemy."

"Well, I hope you can keep him on a leash."

"Oh, yeah. Until we need him."

Now, it was enough that Karl and Ben were nominally on his side.

"There!"

Dante had spotted a side door guarded by only one neatly turned out young man wearing a diamond-encrusted Phi Delta Theta pin on the left chest of his letter-sweater. When approached by the three vets, the young man blanched but did his best.

"Uh, hi, fellas. Sorry, but you can't, uh, go in this way," he said. "This way is the, uh, wrong way. This way is the way out, and the way out is not . . . is not the way in, so you can't . . ."

Before Dante could say that they were with university security and had come to police the building, Ben had slid right up into the frat boy's face.

"Karl," warned Dante.

"Ben," warned Karl.

"Move, maggot," explained Ben.

The Phi Delt's pupils enlarged. In his worst rum-and-coke-soaked-nightmare he had never seen a face that terrible pressed so close to his.

"Yes, sir," he croaked and stepped aside.

"Thank you," said Dante, moving past him.

"Wise decision," said Karl, pushing Ben ahead of him.

"Unngghhh," said Ben.

Once inside the building, the vets followed the line of exiting students backward and up three flights of stairs to its source in the big gym where the Crimson Tide played basketball. Here, the hubbub of a thousand voices created a rolling susurrus that rang and echoed off the high metal roof like a cattle auction in an insane asylum.

Co-eds screamed warmest greetings to girlfriends they detested. Young men back-slapped pals whose fiancees they'd plundered over the summer. Interminable lines wound everywhere, and everywhere there were signs instructing the lost. Dante saw the deal: the vets were being channeled through the system separately from the non-vets—and according to their former branch of service.

He grabbed each Marine by the shoulder. It was like fondling two sides of beef. "Okay, boys, here it is: the Army's over there. The Marines over here. We'll meet back at the cars in an hour—or whenever. If I'm not there, shove off without me."

"Roger, got it," said Karl.

"And, Ben," said Dante, "all these people? They're not, technically, the enemy—yet."

"Take no prisoners," said Ben, as Karl grasped him gently by the elbow and led him away.

Watching Ben cleave his way through the mob, Dante thought of Quasimodo heading for the belfry.

* * *

Larocca joined the Army line and saw he was about 500th in a thick triple queue aimed at a row of tables where overwhelmed university staff sat processing mounds of paperwork. All around him vets in their mid-to-late twenties, some still in uniform—or parts of uniform—were craning their necks toward the tables trying to get a fix on the hold-up —and raising a chorus of picturesque complaints.

"Who volunteered me for this chicken shit detail?"

"Is the Pentagon running this fuckin' show?"

"I swear to God, if I have to stand in one more stinking line . . ."

"Shit, this is worse than mustering out."

"I never mustered out. I just walked off the base and kept going."

"Call the Marines!"

"Yeah, and then call the Coast Guard."

"The Coast Guard?!"

"Hey, didja see that chick with the slide rule?"

"Slide rule? Hell, man, that was a pecker checker."

"No shit? Well, she'd better tape a couple of 'em together if . . ."

After five minutes Dante hadn't moved an inch. This wasn't cutting it. He reached into his postman's bag, removed a manila folder, waved it about and started forcing his way through the knot of ill-tempered men, shouting as he went.

"Lady with a baby! Hot stuff! Watch it, buddy! Lady with a baby, here! Look out! Watch your feet, fly-boy. Priority message, here! Stand aside, Captain . . ."

Within 10 seconds he had reached the head of the queue and left a furious pack of vets in his wake. He was about to step in front of a corporal who was first in line when he saw the guy had been terribly burned in the war, his face an ugly purple-red pulp, his hands white-wrapped claws. Dante stepped back respectfully.

"After you, pal," Dante said.

The vet nodded and Dante saw that the only thing alive in the man's face were his darting eyes. To keep from staring, Dante glanced at the next line over where a pompous-but-handsome Air Corps Major was loudly singing his own praises. To hear him tell it, he'd pretty much won the battle for the Pacific alone—which seemed doubtful, since he was wearing only a couple of unimportant campaign ribbons and nothing for heroism. Dante stepped in front of him just as the woman handling the paper work looked up.

"Next," she said.

"That'd be me," Dante said. And then froze.

Sitting there in all her defiant, blonde gorgeousness was Evelyn Curtis, the Mustang pilot who'd blown him off the highway, then nearly decapitated him with her plane's prop. Her deep-set green eyes locked on his in a moment of recognition. He winked. She smiled ever so faintly.

"Registration papers, please," she said.

"Hold it, Sergeant!" It was the Major, staring down his patrician nose at Dante's unbuttoned field tunic and dungarees.

Flustered at confronting Evelyn, Dante tried, with limited success, to shift into New York-overdrive.

"Sorry, Major, but I, uh, I was detailed to help Admiral Larocca, the, uh, big war hero. He, uh, won the battle of—Oh, God—of Mobile Bay."

"Mobile Bay?"

"Or maybe it was Manila Bay. Anyway, he wants these papers signed ASAP." He turned to Evelyn, his eyes pleading. "Here ya' go, ma'am. Can you expedite these for the Admiral?"

Fumbling, he spilled the registration forms in a pile onto the table.

"Christ. Sorry. Must be combat fatigue . . ."

"Sergeant . . ." The Major didn't give up easily. "Sergeant, the Battle of Mobile Bay was fought during the Civil War. The Battle of Manila Bay was fought during the Spanish-American War. Who the hell is this so-called Admiral Larocca?"

"He, uh . . ."

Then Evelyn stepped in to save Dante's ass.

"The Sergeant is mistaken, Major. It was actually the Battle of Matsui Bay, last June. Off the coast of Okinawa. A small but crucial surface-and-air engagement that opened up the way to Japan's Home Islands."

She coolly opened the manila folder and scanned its contents.

"Matsui Bay?" The Major frowned. "Never heard of it."

"The admiral is studying architecture?" Evelyn said.

"Ahh, these dagos," Dante said. "They all think they're Leonardo da Vinci or something. Whatta ya' gonna do?"

As Evelyn checked and marked the papers, the Major fumed. He turned to a Captain standing behind him in line.

"You ever hear of the Battle of Matsui Bay?"

"Sounds Jap. I was in Europe," the Captain said.

Dante grinned at the Major.

"Nice uniform, Sir!" he said.

"Thank . . ."

"But you forgot your ribbons."

"Okay, Sergeant," Evelyn interrupted. "Tell your Admiral Larocca he should proceed through the green door, down the steps, third room on the left . . . and please, convey my congratulations to the Admiral on his sterling war record. The Battle of Matsui Bay was a brilliant tactical victory."

Dante smiled. "Thanks, ma'am. Sorry, Sir."

He spun and was gone. At least, his body was. His mind remained lodged in the gym with Evelyn Curtis. Later, while going through the motions of buying school supplies, he mused about her looks. She was stunning, but it was more than that. He had to admit that her flying the Mustang had impressed the hell out of him. But it was also the way she carried herself, her self-assurance that suggested a woman who didn't take crap off anybody, but who managed in the process to remain astonishingly lovely and open and. . .

He grinned when he thought of how smoothly she'd gone along with his Admiral Larocca baloney against the Major. What a dame, he thought.

* * *

Two hours later, lathered in sweat and carrying forty pounds of books, drawing supplies, and a roll of artist's canvas, Dante staggered out of the student swarm and up to the jeep. He saw that the Marines' truck was gone and hoped that Karl and Ben were back at Shorty's and not in jail for eviscerating some stuffed shirt.

He made a mental note to inquire further into Ben's proclivities for violence.

In the jeep, Sir Plus greeted him with barking and a sustained, full-body wriggle. Dante flung his load into the back, untied the dog and gave him a two-handed head rub.

"Hey, fella, you thought I wasn't coming back, didn't you? Didn't you? I bet you're dying of thirst in this friggin' heat." Sir Plus grinned and licked.

Followed by the dog, Dante grabbed the watering helmet, spotted a hydrant next to Foster Auditorium, walked over and began filling the ersatz water bowl while Sir Plus, barking and biting at the cascading stream, danced around and through Dante's legs like a mad gray dervish. An awkward move, a mis-timed lunge, and soon dog and man were rolling around together in the grass like circus clowns.

"A boy and his pooch. Who needs Norman Rockwell?"

Lying on his back, with Sir Plus straddling him and pretending to gnaw at his forearm, Dante looked up to see Evelyn standing there in black slacks, smiling.

"Oh, hiiya, beautiful. Wanna buy a dog?"

"I might. What's the price?"

"Ouff . . ." Dante pushed Sir Plus aside and got to his feet. The dog went for the water full time, burying his muzzle in it up to the eyes as Dante brushed himself off.

"Naw . . . couldn't sell this mutt. He's my pal. . . . Say, thanks for the help awhile ago. Hadn't been for you, I'd still be in line yapping at that Major."

"What a jerk."

Dante looked around in the grass for his pocket comb.

"May be, but I figure he asked you out."

"He did. How'd you know?"

"Ahh, he was pretty. You're pretty. Likes attract."

She smiled.

He turned and told Sir Plus to get in the jeep. The dog hesitated, lowering his head. Dante snapped his fingers. Sir Plus stared: He'd been in that goddamn jeep for three hours and, by God, he wanted to play.

Dante's body language changed. His voice lowered.

"Sir Plus: Mount up!"

The dog stood a moment, working a primal calculus, then walked to the jeep and with no apparent physical preparation —like an out-sized cat—leaped straight up and into the seat.

"Thank you." Dante gave him a treat.

"Nice. So, back to the Major. He was pretty, but I declined his offer."

"Yeah? Well, that's good. That's good. Make him work for it. Speaking of: you work here?"

"No, I live in town, so I volunteered to help with registration. The G.I. Bill guys are driving the university nuts and . . ."

Dante's face colored. "Yeah, you lower the bar. Let in the riffraff. First thing you know they want to eat in the same restaurants, use the same toilets . . ."

Stung, Evelyn backtracked.

"I didn't mean that, and you know it. It's just that . . . that with all the veterans back, there are so many more students, thousands, and the university's not prepared to handle them . . . and, uh, the housing problems. . . ."

Dante felt his caste sensitivities leak out into plain view. "Hey, it's the American Way. Crack open a door, guy's gonna walk through it, no matter how dirty his hands are . . . Say, you know Sidney Greene?"

Evelyn was glad for the reprieve. "Everybody knows Sidney Greene. Not everybody likes Sidney Greene. . . ."

"Like-shmike. He's the best."

"So they say."

"And I'm gonna work with him. . . ."

"And win a Dalton Fellowship to study in Rome."

Dante blinked.

"I, uh, well, yeah, but . . ."

"You think you're the first hot dog with talent to show up here dreaming of Dalton fame?"

"Well, uh, no. There's lots of guys, but, I mean, I'm not bad and

Greene is tops, and . . ."

"And the meanest old crank in the design department."

"That so? Well, I'm pretty good with cranks. Where's he hang out?"

"Woods Hall." She pointed. "That way. Three hundred meters. Red brick. Looks like a fortress. See ya."

As Dante reached into the jeep, she turned and started away, the tight slacks emphasizing every athletic move of her legs and butt. Dante couldn't resist. He wolf-whistled. She glanced back to object but saw him holding something out toward her.

"Flying glove," he said. "You left it with Sir Plus at the airport."

She blushed and started back, her hand outstretched. He tossed it to her.

"Thanks . . . they were a present."

"So, is this like the old story where the lady drops the hanky and the guy picks it up?" he asked.

"No, more like the lady just forgot. But, if you want a reward, I'll take you up for a spin one day in my crop duster."

"Not me. Never been in a plane."

"Hey . . . piece of cake."

"Yeah, upside down cake." He gestured to show a plane inverted.

"I got it."

They looked at each other.

"Sorry if I insulted you at the airport," he said.

"Happens all the time . . . besides, I deserved it. Good luck with Sidney Greene. You'll need it." She smiled and turned away.

* * *

Leaving a well-watered Sir Plus to guard the jeep, Dante grabbed his postman's bag and a black portfolio and headed for Woods Hall, a long, three-story brick building that looked as though it belonged at a military academy. Its crenelated roof line culminated in raised battlements at each end complete with slits for archers and limestone-capped gaps for pouring hot oil onto a howling mob of infidels below. At each story, deep porches ran the length of the facade. On the ground floor an elegant, symmetrical arcade offered protection from sun and rain. Dante liked the solidity and balance of the building. It was a place where a man could do good work.

As he approached the double doors centered in the arcade, he passed a free-standing, rough-cut granite block seven feet tall, five feet wide, and four feet thick into which had been inset a brass tablet. He paused and read:

1861 - 1865

THE UNIVERSITY OF ALABAMA GAVE TO THE CONFEDERACY - 7 GENERAL OFFICERS, 25 COLONELS, 14 LIEUTENANT COLONELS, 21 MAJORS, 125 CAPTAINS, 273 STAFF AND OTHER COMMISSIONED OFFICERS, 66 NON-COMMISSIONED OFFICERS, AND 294 PRIVATE SOLDIERS. RECOGNIZING OBEDIENCE TO STATE, THEY LOYALLY AND UNCOMPLAININGLY MET THE CALL OF DUTY, IN NUMBERLESS INSTANCES SEALING THEIR DEVOTION BY THEIR LIFE BLOOD.

AND ON APRIL 3, 1865, THE CADET CORPS, COMPOSED WHOLLY OF BOYS, WENT BRAVELY FORTH TO REPEL A VETERAN FEDERAL INVADING FOE, OF MANY TIMES THEIR NUMBER, IN A VAIN EFFORT TO SAVE THEIR ALMA MATER, ITS BUILDINGS, LIBRARY, AND LABORATORIES FROM DESTRUCTION BY FIRE, WHICH IT MET AT THE HANDS OF

THE ENEMY ON THE DAY FOLLOWING.
TO COMMEMORATE THIS HEROIC RECORD THIS
MEMORIAL STONE IS ERECTED BY THE ALABAMA DIVISION,
UNITED DAUGHTERS OF THE CONFEDERACY.
MAY 13, 1914.

Dante reread the part about loyal and uncomplaining death. Terms like "obedience to state" and "went bravely forth" sickened him. He shook his head and started for Woods Hall. In France, Buddy Fooshee used to tell him that the American Civil War wasn't over in the South, "not by a long shot," he'd say, "not by a long, damn shot, my friend." Now, Dante knew it, first hand.

He found a wall directory and searched out Sidney Greene's office number—301. Starting up the stairs, his heart raced and his stomach clenched. Despite Evelyn's warning about Greene, Dante thought he could finesse the old coot. He'd just lay a little New York savvy on him, show him his work. . . . Still, pausing before room 301, he crossed himself and whispered.

"Yo', God. Remember me? Dante from Brooklyn. Lookin' for a little help, here, Sir." He shifted the portfolio to his left hand, knocked on the door, heard a muffled response and went in.

Room 301 proved to be a dazzling studio, filled with light from a row of north-facing windows. Along one wall ran six shelves 40 feet long, crowded with sketches, paintings, and scale models of numerous buildings, all influenced by the Bauhaus School: abstract, rational, unadorned, flat-roofed, and off-white.

At a drafting table in the center of the room stood a trim, aristocratic man of sixty or so with a thin mustache and a full head of gray hair. Looking like an aging photographer's model, he wore a French-cuffed blue shirt, a blood-red ascot and a chilly expression. In one hand he held a silver mechanical pencil with which he'd been examining a set of blueprints on the angled table before him. Not pleased at this intrusion, he stared over rimless glasses at Dante.

"Yesss?"

"Uh, hiiya, Dr. Greene. Dante Larocca, down from Brooklyn. I'm. . . was a pal of one of your students, Buddy Fooshee. . . ."

At the sound of Buddy's name, Greene's eyes narrowed, his chin tipped up.

"You knew Buddy?"

"Like a brother. So, Doc . . ."

"I'm not a doctor. I'm an architect."

"Right. That's why I'm here. And I'm good, too."

"I'll judge that."

Dante hesitated, then plunged on.

"Well, judge away, chief. 'Scuse me . . ."

Larocca advanced, placed the portfolio on the drafting table and opened it. Inside were carefully organized layers of his best work—building elevations, floor plans, architectural renderings.

Larocca drew a breath and grabbed a paper. "Okay, right . . . cliff-side mountain house, cantilevered and earthquake-proof. Heat-absorbing tiles and insulation in the attic. Hidden garage. Minimum water requirements. Perfect for California or Mexico."

"Derivative Frank Wright."

"Well, Frank Lloyd Wright's my hero . . ."

"Pity." Greene stepped back, his arms folded.

Dante shuffled papers and carried on.

". . . And this is an open-form church. Pre-stressed concrete, double-glazed glass, A-frame pitched roof-line. Sun or snow, doesn't matter.

Could be built in Vermont or Florida . . ." He seized another sheet. "Now, this right here, this is a suspension bridge. Uses 15 per cent less steel but has the torsional strength to stand up to a friggin' hurricane. Build this baby in, say, the Tennessee mountains—hundred and fifty knots of wind, nothing to worry about. Hey, eat your breakfast off the roadbed. And this . . ."

"That's quite enough. I . . ."

"No, wait, wait, Doc, this is my pride and joy."

He removed from his leather postman's pouch a shoe box which he placed on the table. Opening it, he held up one of his wooden scale models—a radical structure about the size of a coconut—all acute angles, windows, and overhangs.

"Get this, Doc. Expandable slum housing! See . . . they hook together like an erector set. You need more, you build more—in pods, like. Private and cheap." Dante's enthusiasm grew. "And in the center of, say, 10 or 15 of these babies you stick a grassy play area for the kids. And . . ."

"Yes, mustn't forget the children."

Larocca ignored the sarcasm.

"I mean, poor people they hate crap housing, Doc. But they got no choice. So, they live there but they tear it up or let it run down." He leaned in toward Greene. "I say build 'em something they can buy—own—give 'em a stake, you know, then they'll fix it up, and take pride, and . . ."

"Silence!"

The two men locked eyes, Dante sensing he'd blown it, but not knowing how else to talk about his work except in full missionary mode. He tried to read the older man.

"So, whatta ya' think?" he asked. "Sir."

"Impractical. The poor have no money."

"Yeah, but, hey, low-interest government loans, ya' know? Kind of a G.I. Bill for civilians. Like with the WPA or CCC for home-buying or . . ."

"The New Deal is dead, Mr . . ."

"Larocca."

"And so, thank God, is Roosevelt." Dante blinked. "In addition, your friend Buddy Fooshee did better work."

Caught off-guard, Dante felt at first adrift, then enraged. His voice came out in a strangled rush.

"Yeah, you're right, Doc. Buddy was good. Buddy was goddamn good. Buddy may have even been a fuckin' genius for all I know . . ." Dante was losing it. "But let me point out to you one inconvenient fact: Buddy Fooshee is also dead. Stone, cold dead. Take it from me. I was there!"

He bent forward, gripping the edge of the drafting table, the only thing standing between him and Greene. The professor seemed to sense he'd slipped the knife in a bit too deep.

"All right, son, calm down."

Larocca's eyes had narrowed to pinpricks of loathing and sadness. "See," he said, "like it or not—fair or not—that's the way it worked out: Buddy got killed and I got out. And I'm hungry. And I'm going to Rome on a Dalton Fellowship, and that's it. That's the deal!"

Green offered a tight little smile.

"Not unless I say so."

* * *

Later that afternoon, leading Sir Plus on a slow trek through the campus, a subdued Dante sifted through his hostile encounter with Greene. He hadn't meant for that to happen. He'd meant simply to show his work and let it speak for him. Be humble. Well, maybe not humble, but respectful, at least. But then, he'd come unglued about Buddy. Greene had punched his ticket and he'd just gone to pieces. He was horrified at how close to the surface the war remained for him. Last night he'd glimpsed David Cohen's demons. He'd dreamed of Maria in Paris. Then, this afternoon, his own war-gremlins had been on full display before Sidney Greene.

Now, with the dog, he tried to relax in the shade of huge oaks and magnolias dotting the university grounds. The earlier student-bedlam of registration had subsided into a random mishmash of fraternity boys playing football on the quad, terrified freshmen wandering from pillar to post, and scowling veterans hurrying home to a spam sandwich and a piece of whiskey. Larocca passed two shaven-headed first-year boys clutching books and bemoaning their fate.

"Professor Seldon says we have to read a book a week!"

"Yeah? Well, my math teacher is loco, and the damn veterans made all the rest of us sit in the back of the room. Said they'd kick our asses if we moved up."

"I hate those bastards."

"They all look, I mean, crazy to me."

The kids moved on and Dante smiled, wondering if this was the work of his Marines, Karl and Ben, then he plopped down on a wooden bench to assess the damage to his budding career. His confrontation with Greene ate at him. The cool hauteur of the man had thrown him, emphasizing as it did the enormous gap between those to the manner born and the immigrant rabble of which Dante felt himself a charter member.

As he berated himself, two grizzled vets, wearing mismatched parts of uniforms, walked by.

"Yeah, I was in the 386th," one said. "We pretty much whipped the Japs' ass singlehanded."

"I thought you were a cook."

"Combat cook, man."

"Lofton, you are so full of shit."

The vets walked away, arguing.

Sir Plus parked himself hard against Larocca's foot and leg, demanding a pet. The man stroked the big silken head, causing the dog to point his muzzle skyward in mute ecstasy. From the quad, sounds of the collegians' intramural football game floated to Dante on the warm fall air. Children, he thought, as he watched them, just kids. He'd seen lots of guys like them blown to flinders by German bazookas, shredded by an artillery round, shot between the eyes by snipers. He'd watched them grow up in a morning—from boy to man to corpse in three hours. Then, it was home in a box. Not even home. A patch of French dirt, more likely, in Normandy or Brittany.

Suddenly, Dante Larocca felt very tired.

A beautiful co-ed walked by and smiled at him, perfuming the air with her presence.

"Hi," she said.

"Hi ya' doin'."

"Say, do you know where Woods Hall is?"

"Yeah," he said, "big barracks-looking place about two hundred meters back that way."

"Thanks . . . You must be a vet." She obviously wanted to talk.

He hesitated, then spoke softly. "Naw, just an old guy got a late start."

She seemed disappointed. "Oh, well, thanks then."

She moved off and in her place—down that ribbon of perfume—Maria arrived, nibbling at the edges of his mind. He fought her off, but she was tough, persistent. It was the perfume. That and the girl's perfect skin.

June 6, 1942

On bord ship in the Atlantic

My dearest Maria,

Hi honey. I'm fine as can be expected, given that this big old boat is roling in a storm like me and Bruno on a weekend bender. Anyway, I didn't get sick yet, but a lot of guys are in prety rough shape, pukking their guts out. Enough of that though.

I love you. And I miss you like crazy and when I get back their to Brooklyn I'm gonna take you into that little bedroom and strip you down real slow and then I'm gonna do all those things you like untill you beg me to stop. I'll be so deep in you theyll have to send a search party to find me. Ha ha. And me whispering over and over: MariaMariaMaria.

Hooo! Anyway, we're heading for Europe tomorrow. Maybe I'll get to Italy and see grandpas village. If the Krauts don't get me first (thats a joke).

Gotta go. Just remember that I cant weight untill we . . . you know. Lots of kisses.

Dante

p.s. By now you figured out that spelling ain't my long suite.

xxxx

Dante rose from the bench, gathered up Sir Plus's lead and started away.

"They oughta outlaw the wearing of perfume," he told Sir Plus, "Outside the bedroom, anyway."

Chapter 6

Evelyn Curtis had always known exactly what she wanted. At the age of eleven—blond-haired and hard-wired for competition—she gave up dolls and took up baseball, insisting that she be allowed to play on her beloved older brother, Robert's, team. He demurred. She threw a fit and her labor-lawyer mother brokered a settlement: she was allowed to play the role of bat-girl—not bat-boy, her mother insisted. Robert took heat from his friends for this intrusion, but—loyal to a fault—he defended his sister, pointing out that she had a better arm than the current right fielder and could outrun the catcher. After the team's fourth straight defeat, she replaced the right fielder, hit .298 for the season, made a couple of circus catches in the outfield, and threw two runners out at the plate.

She was also a budding horsewoman and a crack shot with the neat little .22 rifle she had begun pestering her father for when she was nine.

"When you write your age in two numbers," he'd said, searching for a rationale, "I'll get you a gun."

The day she turned 10, she walked into his study brandishing a Sears Roebuck catalog.

"Daddy, I would like this Marlin lever action .22, please. It holds 12 rounds," she'd said. "And I'll need you or Robert to teach me about it, too. But that won't take long because I've already been reading the gun magazines. Except some of the big words I don't understand. But I think this is the best gun for me."

Harry Curtis had nodded.

That was Evelyn. God protect the man she marries, he often thought.

Harry was a big man with a lot of hair, an athlete's body, and an assassin's focus. Accustomed to the deference of the hired help—along with much of Tuscaloosa's gentry—Harry's views on good and evil were forceful, if unsubtle: FDR was a Communist sympathizer; Hiroshima and Nagasaki had been long overdue; and labor unions were the devil's spawn.

As for his problems controlling Evelyn, he figured it was all his wife's, Atlanta's, fault. Who ever heard of a woman labor lawyer in 1940s Alabama? Chicago, maybe. Or that god-forsaken New York, but Alabama? Atlanta Curtis, in Harry's private opinion, was rearing a dangerous child, encouraging the girl in every tomboy foolishness, from riding bikes to climbing trees, from shooting marbles—she usually won—to shooting snakes. He actually had to insist that Atlanta go to Birmingham occasionally and buy his daughter a dress.

The first airplane Evelyn ever touched was the first one she flew in. One Saturday in 1932, a couple of handsome barnstormers had come through Tuscaloosa and were taking terrified local farmers and bolder university boys up for five bucks a pop. Evelyn was twelve. She read about the itinerant pilots in the paper, visited her piggy bank, then inveigled the newly licensed Robert to drive her to the airfield with its single dirt strip. Once there, she slipped away from him, passed a fiver to one of the pilots, climbed into the front seat of an open-cockpit biplane, was strapped down, and took off.

She was hooked. Her father was outraged. Her mother, amused.

"Atlanta, this madness has got to stop," he'd said.

"Oh, Harry," Atlanta had said, "you know Evelyn is not like other girls. She never has been, and—"

"It's a damned disgrace!"

". . . and she never will be. She's just . . . Evelyn."

By 1940, Harry Curtis had become a rich man. By 1945, he was very rich. Harry had a knack. Everybody said so. Besides playing tackle for the Crimson Tide, he had earned an engineering degree from the University but had never really practiced—engineering. What he had practiced was damned clever deal-making, mostly in the coal, wood, and land business. His successes flowed from his ability to talk redneck to the rednecks and bankerese to the suits. That and mineral rights.

Harry understood mineral rights before most others did—especially the state's Depression-wracked, bankrupt farmers and land-owners. Everybody else wanted their timber. Harry wanted their coal. So, whenever land in Alabama changed hands there was a good chance that Harry Curtis' name nestled somewhere deep in the paperwork. When a rapacious Yankee corporation bought the timber, Harry bought the rights to what lay beneath the timber, and the land-owner got paid from two sources. Everybody went home happy.

But timber, in its own way, was also good to Harry. To assist in laying gothic waste to the great swaths of virgin longleaf pine blanketing much of Mississippi, Georgia and southern Alabama, Harry had, in 1920, built three bodacious saw mills, one in Georgia, one in south Mississippi, and one on the banks of the Black Warrior River running through Tuscaloosa. By operating the sawmills—instead of cutting down the trees—he didn't have to maintain a fleet of trucks and drivers and donkey engines and drunken, brawling wood cutters. He also didn't wind up owning a lot of useless, cut-over land. Someone else felled the timber and hauled it to Harry, who bought it for a song. Then his mills cut it into beautiful heart-pine boards which he sold back to the Yankees up north for four times what it cost him. With the standing trees out of the way, he parceled out the coal from the sub-surface mineral rights to other Yankees running the pig-iron smelters in Birmingham. Then he hired somebody to count his money.

But it was the war that had spread the icing on Harry's cake, money-wise. Turned out that almost everything the army and navy moved by rail or ship had to be crated up—in stout wooden boxes and pallets. With the primeval, long-leaf pine forests all but gone by 1942, Harry Curtis changed blades at his saw mills and put out the call for hardwood—more hardwood, boys!—and the tree-cutting industry responded with a vengeance. C-rations, jerry cans of potable water, bombs, artillery shells, toilet paper, spare parts, chewing gum, beer, uniforms, caskets, you name it, if it moved overseas during the war it had to be packed and protected in rough-sawn crates of oak and hickory. The south overflowed with oak and hickory, and Harry had the mills to cut it. In the end, four words had made Harry a multi-millionaire: COST-PLUS GOVERNMENT CONTRACT.

Signing such a contract during the war amounted to a license to steal: "I don't care what it costs. Just get it to me yesterday!"

Harry did. For Harry had a knack. Everybody said so.

But even Harry's knack had its limits. Atlanta and Evelyn simply would not do as they were told. Harry was not an especially introspective man, but when, huddled in a duck blind in a freezing dawn rain, these women crossed his mind, he wondered if in some misbegotten way he loved them because of their hardheadedness. He couldn't figure out any other reason why he put up with them.

And then there was the terrible business about his son Robert's death. That was something Harry Curtis would never forget and could never forgive.

* * *

The day Evelyn buzzed—then nearly decapitated—Dante Gabriel

Larocca with her P-51 Mustang, she drove away from the airfield smiling. Partly, it was the torrid adrenaline rush left over from blasting that sweet silver bird across the landscape at tree-top level. Partly, it was the pleasure of driving home on a clear day with the top down in her convertible. Partly, it was petting that magnificent Weimaraner. And partly it was Dante Larocca's eyes.

Blue. Deep-set in an imperfect face. Honest. Sexy. And that hey-baby-I-know-just-what-you-need crooked grin. The guy had it and knew it. No question. But what an attitude, and what an accent. Sounded like he'd stepped out of a Dead End Kids movie. Then, the next day, she'd run into him at the university and laughed at his outfoxing that hotshot Army major during registration. This was getting to be a habit.

A couple of weeks later and dressed in whites, she was crushing tennis balls on the court at her parents'. . . estate. There was no other word for it. Atlanta Curtis had thought the whole place a bit much— seven acres, two full city blocks half-a-mile from the court house, featuring swimming pool, tennis courts, five-car garage, a brace of squawking peacocks, servants, goldfish ponds, 1,000 camellia bushes, and all the rest of it. But this was what Harry had wanted. This was what he'd bought up 15 adjoining properties to get. And this is, by God, what he got.

Evelyn's tennis opponent was her serious beau, Tim Fletcher—a tall, dashing Princeton graduate and almost as good a tennis player as Evelyn. Almost. Actually, her forehand was running him around the court like a spastic lab on a long leash.

"Take her out, Tim!" Harry Curtis bawled commands as he and Atlanta sat in the shade of an awning, sipping iced tea. "Ace her, boy!" But Tim could only manage a sky-high lob that Evelyn pulverized, sending it into the furthest three square inches of the deuce court.

"Good shot, dear," called out Atlanta.

"Nice one," said Tim between gasps.

"Damnit, man, you can't play her like she was a woman. She'll kill you," said Harry.

Arthur Wilson, a black man wearing a white coat, approached the Curtises holding a silver tray on which sat a telephone. He stooped, placed the tray on the table, and plugged the phone into a water-proof receptacle.

"Telephone for Miss Evelyn," he said.

"Thank you, Arthur. Evelyn, telephone, hon."

Harry stood up. "Here, Tim, I'll play you. Give me the ball—Senior man serves first. And change courts with me. I can't stand looking into that sun." Evelyn and Tim exchanged a chaste kiss and a whisper as she headed for the phone.

"Careful. He'll hustle you," she said.

"Don't I know," Tim said.

Evelyn took the phone. "Hello . . . hey, Betty, girl, how the hell are you?" Paying out the long telephone cord as she talked, Evelyn eased away from her mother. On the court, her father shouted "out" at shots by Tim that were clearly on the line. Atlanta shook her head and picked up Time magazine to read about the latest reports of unspeakable discoveries at Nazi concentration camps, and of the conflicts between Soviet and American troops in Berlin.

This will end badly, she thought.

When she hung up and wandered back to her mother's chair, Evelyn was beaming.

"That was Betty Braxton. Flew with me in the WASPS. Helluva pilot. She once did a wheels-up crash landing in a brand-new P-38 on a frozen lake. Couldn't get the gear down. She's gonna be coming through here soon and . . ."

She was stopped by a look from her mother.

"What?"

"Evelyn, have you decided yet?"

The younger woman glanced down, then away. "Not . . . not law school." She saw Atlanta blink twice, her lips compressed. Of all people, she hated disappointing her mother most, but maybe now was the time to hash it out. "Mama, I'm just too simple-minded. I mean, how do you defend someone you know is guilty?"

"You don't ask."

"See, that's just it. To me, things are so black and white. I'd ask the bastard: `Did you do it?' And he'd say yes and I'd have to run him over with my car or at least recuse myself."

"I'd hoped . . . You once seemed so interested in the law. In joining my practice and . . ."

"I know, I know." This was killing Evelyn. "And with you president of the county bar . . ."

"Well, so many of the men are still in uniform. . . ."

"Baloney! You're good and you love it. And that's what I want. I want to really, really love something and then do it full out. . . ."

"Full out . . ." Atlanta Curtis lit a cigarette, dribbling smoke to the wind. "It's the flying thing, isn't it?" Her eyes bore in, but with no animosity. She loved this eccentric daughter too much for that.

On the court, tennis balls thwocked and soared.

"Afraid so," said Evelyn. "Mother, don't be disappointed in me."

"I'm not, dear."

"I mean, you knew it. Didn't you? Ever since I was a kid . . ."

Atlanta tilted her chin up an inch, took a deep breath and let it out. "I suppose I did. But parents always make secret plans for their children and . . ."

"Yeah. . . ."

". . . then sometimes they just have to let them go."

"The plans or the children?"

Atlanta smiled. "Both."

"Out!" Harry Curtis roared.

"Mr. Curtis, really . . ." Tim's voice betrayed his exasperation.

"Your father still cheats," Atlanta said.

"Game. Set. Match," Harry crowed. "Don't fret, Tim, you're just a little rusty from the war. Hoo, boy, I need some gin." Harry walked over to the women, tossing his racket onto the grass. "Atlanta, ask Arthur to bring us some gin down here. And ice. You women ate up all the ice."

* * *

Dinner that night, served by Arthur, was not a happy affair.

"Crop dusting?" Harry's voice was clotted by steak and ire.

"For right now. I've got other plans for later," Evelyn said, avoiding her father's eyes. Talking to him was a blood sport, one she found more than a little tiring.

Tim's eyes narrowed as he spoke. "I thought it was law school for you. Before the war . . ."

"Blame it on Mama—I'm just following her motto: 'Decide what you want. Then decide what you're willing to do to get it.' This is step one."

"Four years at Vassar straight down the toilet," Harry said, spearing another piece of meat.

"Oh, I don't know, Harry," said Atlanta, "she learned some art history, some French—and to think for herself."

Harry looked up and grunted. "Dirty pictures. How to talk to a frog. And gross insubordination. If there's three things a woman didn't need, that's them." He returned to his plate.

"Arthur," asked Atlanta, "is there any more of that wine left?"

After dinner, Evelyn and Tim strolled about the grounds holding hands and picking flowers. A natural athlete, Tim stood six feet two or more, was rail-thin and hawk-faced, with restless gray eyes that seemed to see more than was in front of them. His sandy hair was beginning to go. He'd be mostly bald by 40, but his infrequent smile lit up the night and made people feel blessed to bask in its warmth. Evelyn had always liked his seriousness and his concern for duty, but since he'd come home from the war he seemed fidgety, unfocused, even cross at times.

"Why won't you ever talk about what you did in Washington during the war?" she asked, plucking a red zinnia.

"It wasn't very . . . heroic."

"Just because you weren't in uniform? Daddy says it was terrifically important. Super top secret and all that. Were you a spy?"

"Actually, I ran a high-class brothel at the Pentagon."

"Ahh. And did you sample the wares?"

"Nope. Off-limits to civilians, you see." He gave a bitter little chuckle. "No. I was . . . I helped create a . . . monster."

They had fetched up at the family's swimming pool. Tim sat on the diving board, spreading the flowers they'd cut into a fan shape next to him. Evelyn walked to the pool house and flipped on the circulator and underwater lights that shed an aquamarine glow on the night air. She turned and looked at Tim, so forbidding, so dignified, so sad.

"Can you talk about it?" she asked, moving to him.

He pursed his lips. "Not supposed to."

"Okay."

Nearby, tree frogs competed with cicadas in their nightly howl-rituals. The water in the pool began to ripple, stirred by a distant pump.

Tim scratched his cheek. "You ever hear of an Army general name of Leslie Groves?"

"Nope." She took his hand. It was soft. Warm.

"Well, he was the military liaison officer for something called the Manhattan Project. Even that name is top secret."

"You were in New York, then?"

"No, I was mostly in Washington and . . . New Mexico."

"New Mexico? What the hell were you doing out there?"

"You wouldn't believe it if I told you."

She saw that her questions troubled him. "Let's talk about it later," she said. "So, why're you so glum tonight? Was playing tennis with Daddy that bad?"

"Your old man never changes." He tossed a flower into the water, watching it spin slowly and float away. "Unlike life. No, I was just thinking how nothing's like it was before the war, how everything's changed. Forever."

"You preferred the Depression? Bread lines? Government make-work?"

"I preferred it when people knew their place. Take these veterans on the G.I. Bill. They've descended on the campus like a swarm of locusts. Loud. Vulgar. Coarse. It just bothers me, that's all."

Snob talk got under Evelyn's skin. She thought of that sergeant, Dante Larocca, pure double-dipped Brooklyn working class, a little bawdy, maybe, but determined to become an architect, to make something of himself. Parents didn't speak much English, for all she knew. At the same time, she sensed that Tim's malaise was not about the invasion of the vets, that its roots ran much deeper.

"So, we're talking about breeding, here?" she asked.

"I guess, if you want to call it that."

"Breeding." She counted on her fingers. "Very important to bird dogs, race horses, lab rats . . . and Virginians."

"Evelyn . . ."

"But not to me. Come on. Let's go to Kilroy's." She grabbed his hand and hauled him off the diving board. "They've got a hot band there tonight."

"I'm not sure I'm in the mood," he said.

Tim Fletcher sits next to Dr. Robert Oppenheimer. It's Thursday, April 12, 1945. Along with Richard Feynman, Enrico Fermi, Otto Frisch, and a gaggle of the world's other leading theoretical physicists, they are crammed into a small lecture hall at a converted boys summer camp in Los Alamos, New Mexico, listening to Edward Teller present on the first experimental determination of the critical mass of pure Uranium 235. Teller, a Hungarian refugee, speaks with a heavy, almost comic accent, but nothing he says is funny. Like the other men in the room, he is engaged in a frenzied rush to build the world's first atomic bomb.

What if the Germans get there first? The Japs?

Tim's stomach is a wreck. He can taste acid at the back of his throat. As a civilian liaison officer between General Leslie Groves in Washington— the man ultimately responsible for the Manhattan Project—and Oppenheimer, the man supervising the bomb-makers, Tim lives his life dancing on the edge of a razor. He must please both masters. He must lie to neither. He must understand everything about the physics of the bomb and everything politically relevant to the bomb in Washington.

It is an impossible task, and it is slowly taking Tim Fletcher down.

Is he the only one in the room who wonders whether he and all these men are going straight to hell for what they are doing in this remote mountain outpost?

As Teller, muttering, scribbles formulae and schematics on the blackboard, Oppenheimer's dark-haired wife, Kitty, knocks on the door and enters.

Teller glances around with a growl. Everyone turns to her. She looks stricken, her face drained of color. She clears her throat.

"Roosevelt is dead," she says.

No one moves. Then, everyone looks at Oppenheimer.

After three beats, he says, "Truman . . ." Then, "Sunday. We'll have a memorial service on Sunday. Tell the wives."

And she is gone.

Oppenheimer turns to Tim.

"Get Groves on the phone."

He gestures to Teller.

"Please continue, Edward."

Chapter 7

Dante Larocca was in like Flynn. The day after he met Sidney Greene, he'd gone by and done a little mea culpa dance for the professor. Greene then agreed to review the ex-GIs portfolio of drawings and consider his application to the hybrid art/architecture/engineering program at the University. A few days later—when Dante called him from the pay phone on Shorty's front porch—Greene had grudgingly said, yes, okay, Larocca was accepted into the program. Dante thanked him, wisely omitting any mention of the Dalton Fellowship.

Earlier, as he was leaving the campus following his first confrontation with the tetchy prof, his attention had been diverted to a construction site where workmen were throwing up ticky-tack temporary housing for married vets and their families.

In the States, after four years of war, everything was rationed except surplus military gear and broken hearts. As Dante cast his practiced eye over the half-finished wooden building, he spotted several items of keen interest: piles of precious lumber, kegs of nails, yards of rope—and an armed guard. The University was taking no chances.

Whistling an Ellington tune, Dante palmed a few bills from his wallet and ambled over to the burly, crew-cut guard who looked like—and was—a former sailor. Baroque nautical tattoos wound their way up both his arms from wrist to elbow: naked mermaids, fouled anchors, gallant ships, war eagles, the lot.

Dante gestured to the tattoos. "Nice work."

"Yeah, thanks. I'm real proud of 'em."

"Where'd you get 'em done at?"

"Well, let's see, this big mermaid I got in Frisco. Watch her ass move when I flex. See? Then the twin eagles, they was done in Formosa. This here ship I picked up in Hong Kong . . . Or Manila? Shit, I forget. All them gook places looked the same to me. You Navy?"

"Nah, ground-pounder. Tanks, actually, with Patton."

"Hooo, mean motherfucker, that guy, from what I hear."

"Yeah. Good one to have inside the tent pissing out 'stead of outside pissing in."

"I hear you."

Dante looked around, then held up his open palm toward the guard whose eyes flew to the money like a ferret's.

Dante said, "Say, iffa guy was to come back here tonight around ten o'clock, reckon he could pick up a few boards, couple of nails, without getting shot in the back?"

The sailor's jaw muscles clinched. He leaned forward, his voice a low growl.

"Trooper, far as I'm concerned, if we're gonna win this here war—Army, Navy, Marines—we all gotta pull together. One for one. All for all." Dante blinked at that. "It just so happens, at ten o'clock sharp I'll be taking a long, happy piss at the other end of the building."

"Good man." Dante shook hands with the sailor, slipping him the money without missing a beat.

That night, precisely at ten, Dante's jeep and empty trailer eased up to the construction site. At ten-fifteen—heavily laden—it eased away. No shots were fired.

The next morning, with the help of Cohen, the mad Marines—Karl and Ben—plus a brawny, cigar-chomping ex-chief petty officer named Davis, Dante set about building a raised wooden floor for his 12 x 12 tent. During the war, Chief Davis had been a Navy Sea-bee—

Construction Battalion—and had assembled everything from floating piers to latrines to landing strips for the Marines in their island-hopping campaign across the Pacific. The Sea-bees' motto was "Can do!" and the experience had been "interesting . . . messy and often fatal, but very interesting," Davis said.

What it had amounted to was wading their construction gear ashore onto a coral beach at, say, Iwo Jima or Tarawa as soon as most of the Japs were dead. Then with draglines and bulldozers, hammers, saws, and brute force, they'd set about rendering a remote, blazing hot, snake-and-vermin-infested volcanic atoll livable for U.S. troops. It was not duty for the faint-of-heart. The surviving Jap snipers—they would not surrender—hid in the jungle at the edge of the Sea-bee camps and took pot shots at the bulldozer drivers scraping out of hard coral a level place for the planes.

It was bedlam.

And then there was the day that Davis, running an armored dragline of his own, had taken fire from an abandoned Jap dugout. He could see the little bastards in there, two of them, and he simply turned the dragline in that direction, ignored their staccato bursts, and drove the big earth-grader up and over their position, burying them alive.

Whatever works. Can do!

To the profoundly irreverent Davis, a construction site amounted to a little piece of heaven, and at Shorty's he took command of the other vets with a vengeance.

"All right, you bunch of lame-ass pussies," he roared around his cigar. "Get your hands off your cocks and get 'em on your socks! Let's go. Dante needs a tent floor. Sir Plus needs a house. Move it!"

Davis had come to college bearing a complete set of tools, figuring to put himself through school on a combination of the G.I. Bill and carpentry work. Sizing up the materials Dante had acquired through his nocturnal requisition, he assigned tasks, cut boards, and planed edges. He measured, hammered, cajoled, threatened, swore, sweated, and occasionally praised. But he took a special, gentle interest in one-armed David Cohen, asking the Navy vet to steady a board while he sawed it to microscopic perfection.

Having labored for three years with Marines in the Pacific, Davis found Karl and Ben ideal workmates. It helped that he was fluent in the piquantly nuanced lingua franca of the Corps.

"Ben, you worthless piece of shit," he'd say, "can't you even drive a fuckin' nail straight with them big meat-hooks of yours? Pull that fuckin' thing up and do it again. I oughta put a fuckin' bullet right between your beady little eyes."

Ben loved it. "OK, Chief, you got it."

While Sir Plus reclined in the shade, Dante watched the workers, amazed. "Man, you friggin' Sea-bees are good."

Davis roared back, "Can do, baby. Can do!"

"Roger that."

"Say, Dago-boy, you providin' the beer for this here project, or what?" Davis winked and gestured toward Shorty watching them from the front porch.

Dante strolled over to his landlord.

"Shorty, as unreasonable as it sounds, the men are demanding beer. I know Alabama is dry, but I thought you might have, you know, connections, or . . ."

Shorty stopped him with a raised hand. "How much you need?"

"Oh, couple of cases."

"Shit, you'll need more'n that. Them two crazy Marines'll drink that for breakfast. Wait here."

Shorty hollered into the house to tell his wife he'd be back in a minute, got in his pick-up and hit the highway. Twenty minutes later he was back with five cases of beer and 50 lbs. of cracked ice in a thick, brown-paper sack.

"Go get that old red cooler out in the barn," he said to Dante. "This is on me."

By six o'clock that night Dante's tent sat anchored atop a solid wooden floor raised on pilings six inches off the ground.

"You want the air to circulate underneath," Davis said. "Much cooler."

"I know that, Chief," Dante said.

Next to the tent—also up off the ground—sat a big handsome dog house, complete with gables, roof-line ventilation, a cantilevered sun porch, and a double floor for insulation. Dante had sketched it off on graph paper while sitting next to Sir Plus at the shaded drafting table while Davis & Co. worked on the tent floor. When he finished the sketch, the other vets crowded around, drinking beer and marveling at Larocca's skill.

"How the hell'd you do that so quick?" Cohen asked, holding the sketch up to the light.

"Hey, when you got it, flaunt it, Cohen," Dante laughed. "Nah, I apprenticed in a Brooklyn drafting shop before the war. My boss kept taking in these big-ass jobs he didn't know how to do, you know, then he'd bring 'em to me." He mimicked his boss's girlish voice: "'Hey, Larocca, got a live one here for you. I could do it myself, but I ain't got the time. Client needs it by Thursday. Stay late if you have to.'" Dante smiled. "You learn fast when the client needs it by Thursday."

* * *

With the housing needs of Dante and Sir Plus sorted out, the vets sprawled in the grass, swilled beer, told lies, and watched the sun set. They had invited Shorty and his—equally attenuated—white-haired wife, Cleola, over to join them, and now the two Alabama natives sat on folding chairs amid the vets, laughing and enjoying by proxy the camaraderie their dead son would have so much loved.

"You know," Mrs. Shorty said, speaking of her husband, "Herman here is a vet too."

"Hush, Cleola, these boys don't care about old-timey history," Shorty said, touching her hand.

But they did.

"Hey, Shorty," Chief Davis said, grinning, "you make it to Pickett's Charge, or what? Shoulda told that glory-hog that Gettysburg hill was too high."

"No sir, and I didn't chase old Teddy Roosevelt's fat butt up San Juan Hill, neither. But I did fight with the Marines in France in WW One. Belleau Wood. Chateau Thierry. . . ."

This news, delivered in the quiet matter-of-fact of someone who has known battle at its worst, sobered the younger men. Shorty busied himself with a bent nail, thinking he'd said too much, and for a moment in the waning light, the only sounds were tree frog trills mixed with bubbling from the waterfall near Dante's tent. Then David Cohen stood up and lifted a beer in his one hand.

"To Shorty," he said. "Thank you."

The other men jumped to their feet, with Karl and Ben executing salutes so rigidly perfect their teeth rattled.

"Semper Fi," they said in unison.

"Semper Fi," said Shorty quietly.

"By God—excuse me, ma'am," said Dante, "but this calls for a celebration."

Agreement to this motion was universal and vociferous.

"You know," said Cohen, "there's a vets' club in town called Kilroy's. They sell beer—no hard stuff—but they have great bands on Saturday night. And, man, dames galore show up there."

"First round's on me and Sir Plus," said Dante.

"All right!"

"Come on to Kilroy's with us, Shorty," said Chief Davis.

Mrs. Shorty smiled. "You do that, Herman, you ain't been out with the boys since . . . for a long time, now."

"Naw, I'm too old to keep up with these guys. . . ."

Karl and Ben may have had tiny little brains, but what little there was appeared to work in perfect synchronicity. Before anyone saw how it happened, they'd slipped up behind Shorty, grabbed both handles of his folding chair, and lifted him off the ground.

"Hey, what the hell . . ."

"You're coming with us, trooper," said Karl.

"Right," said Ben. "Marines don't leave no Marines behind."

Everyone agreed they had to take showers before they left the reservation; otherwise, damage on the dames front was likely to be severe. While the others gathered in the horse barn beneath the two shower heads Shorty had rigged up, Dante used the new pay phone to call Laney Fooshee.

"Hey, Laney, it's Dante Larocca. How you doin', girl?"

"Dante! So good to hear your voice."

Yes, she knew about Kilroy's, and yes, the widows of vets were welcome there, and no, she wasn't really busy tonight—except that

Milo Henderson was coming by later to check on Mama Lou—and yes, she thought it sounded like fun, and no, Mama Lou didn't mind watching Baby Rafe, and yes, she'd meet them there in an hour.

Larocca hung up and stood by the phone a moment, listening to the laughter and hi-jinks coming from the men in the barn. The beer was doing its work.

He liked Laney. She was . . . she smelled good, Dante thought, and she was Southern and soft, and . . . she smelled good. She'd been a good wife to Buddy who had talked of her often in Europe, but always in a shy, respectful way so as not to compromise a husband's secret knowledge. 'Sweet' was the word Buddy had repeatedly used. 'True lovin' and sweet as pie,' he'd say.

Somewhere in England
September 20, 1942

Darling Maria,

Well I cant say much for English cooking. They eat tomatoes and mushrooms for breakfast! and drink about a galon of tea a day. They've sufered a whole lot from the kraut bombing. Beautiful buildings all over London are just guted and burned but they act like it don't bother them. They just go on about their busness always being real polite and talking like lords and ladies.

It don't look like they know what to do with the u.s. army. Well, the girls do, but the men don't. (Don't worry, I'm being good). We're training up a storm here and will be shiping out before too long but I don't know where or when.

I've got that picture of you paystid into my helmet. Seems like you get prettier every day. Lots of guys got married like you and me just before they shiped out and now some of them are regreting it and some others just cry like babbies when they think about there wife back home.

Just so you know, I don't regret it one dam bit and when this thing is over, look out louie, cause I'm coming home to my Maria and inflict some major damage below the belt. Well, got to go. Don't forget me. And write.

Your loving Dante

* * *

Kilroy's was a quonset hut. It looked like God had turned a million-gallon oil drum on its side, then buried it half way in the ground. With a door punched through one end and its barrel-round roof, it was a near-perfect structure from the point of view of efficiency. As the caravan of three vehicles containing six young vets—Reddy Freddy and his wife had joined them—and Shorty roared up to the gravel parking lot, they heard hot jazz flooding out the opened door, next to which stood a hand-lettered sign:

ALL VETS WELCOME

CHECK WEAPONS & GRENADES AT THE DOOR

"Hell, Ben and Karl are weapons," Dante shouted as they piled out of the cars.

"Death . . . death," grunted Ben. But Karl said not to worry. This was just Ben's way of preparing for a fresh social interaction.

The vets' club was owned by brothers Neal and Henry Levy, a couple of ex-Coast Guardsmen who had lived all their lives around boats in Mobile but who, as Jews, had been advised to avoid the Navy. Friends of Cohen—same synagogue back home—their entrepreneurial spirit had sensed an opportunity among the returning vets, and they had recently wangled a federal concession to sell spirits on a limited basis. Essentially, it amounted to a federal liquor license to operate in a dry state. Now they were doing a brisk business slaking the thirst of the returning warriors—and the girls who admired them.

When Neal Levy saw David Cohen come in, he motioned him and his friends to a good table that was just emptying near the bar.

"David, how the hell are you?"

Levy was a tall, uncommonly handsome man with black hair, a thin face, and a smile that made women weep. Cohen introduced his pals while Dante headed for the bar where a black man was popping the tops off bottles with both hands. Dante ordered seven beers, looking closely at the man who seemed somehow familiar. When the fellow placed before Larocca a tray containing the beer, he smiled.

"You ever get up with that airplane tried to run you off the road?"

That's who he was, the guy driving the cotton wagon with his wife and kids.

"Hey, fella, how you doin'?" Dante said and stuck out his hand. The black man hesitated, and a couple of white guys at the bar shot Dante a look. The black man covered the moment with aplomb. "My hands are right icy just now," he said, picking up a bar towel and going through the motions.

Dante let it go. "You work here, then?"

"Yessir, me and my wife both. There she is in the back cutting up sandwiches."

Dante looked and there she was, smiling and waving a huge carving knife at Dante. He waved back.

"So, what's your name?" Dante asked.

"Sammy," the man said, "Sammy Cleveland. And my wife's named Katy."

"Dante Larocca, down from Brooklyn. I was with Patton in Europe." Larocca said.

Cleveland smiled. "I was with the Quartermaster Corps in England, and later in France."

"Oh, man, you guys saved our asses. Fuel. Ammo. Parts. Don't tell me you drove with the Red Ball Express."

Cleveland's smile broadened. "The whole time it was up and runnin' in '44. From St. Lo all the way to Paris. Hadn't been for us. . . ."

"Hell, hadn't been for you guys, our tanks would still be sittin' on the Rhine waiting for gas. You fellas were the greatest."

"Well, they wouldn't let us fight, you know, the colored. So we did what we had to do to help out."

He and Dante exchanged a look and a nod. Again, Dante stuck out his hand, and this time Sammy Cleveland grasped it.

"Real nice to meet you, Sammy." He left a generous tip, turned and gave the two white guys a New York glare.

"Cleveland fought with me in France. You boys got a problem with that?"

They flinched. "Naw, man, no problem. Everything's copacetic."

"Fine," he said, "Terrific. Hey, Sammy, give these boys a beer. Put it on my tab." He grabbed the tray. To the white guys, he said, "Tip him good, he's a close personal friend of mine," and headed for his table.

"Jerks," he muttered.

* * *

Kilroy's was packed and rocking. Sweating vets and their wives and girls jitterbugged on a sawdusted wooden dance floor to the music of a five-piece black combo that was blowing the lights out. Fronted by a woman who could sound like anybody from Lady Day to Sarah Vaughn, the band included a slicked-back cornet player as good as anybody Dante had ever heard in New York or Paris. The guy hit notes high enough to split his lip, then crescendoed down-scale to the lower depths, making his horn moan like something alive was inside trying to get out. Then he handed the melody off to a tenor man standing next to him whose chops were just as good—and was out to prove it.

"Man, these guys are laying down good juice," Dante shouted to Neal Levy over the roar. "Where'd they come from?"

"Mobile, New Orleans, all over. They just got a record deal with Decca in New York. Headed up there next week."

The band had the joint hopping, and Dante could feel a kind of crazed elation in the air. The war was over. The good guys had won. Despite the carnage, most fellas had made it home, and now Uncle Sugar was shelling out the beans to send guys to college. And as an added bonus, the girls absolutely loved the vets. As long as you could keep the war and your past at bay, life was good. Then, suddenly, Maria appeared out of nowhere and tried to carve her way inside his head. Dante locked down and shut her out.

At that moment he saw Laney Fooshee enter Kilroy's, pause, and look around uncertainly. Dante put his fingers in his mouth and blasted out a high, piercing whistle that turned heads—including Laney's. He waved and motioned her over. She looked good. Her hair was pinned up, and she wore white shoes with low heels, a touch of rouge and lipstick. Her pale green cotton dress clung to her body's curves and moved as she did. When she came up, smiling, Dante gave her a hug and a peck on the cheek and turned to his friends.

"Okay, listen up, you bums, this here is what's known in the civilian world as a lady, so no funny business, you got it?"

They applauded. He turned to Karl and Ben.

"Now, for you Marines, who have no experience with the species, a lady is like your sister . . . well, not your sister, Ben, but . . ."

Ben growled. Laney laughed and shook Ben's hand.

"Hi, Ben. Pleased to meet you."

While Karl fetched Laney a beer, David Cohen stood and offered her his chair. She glanced at his stump capped with its clean white half-sock.

"Damn!" he said, "Forgot my hand again."

She started, then saw he was smiling.

"Hello, I'm David Cohen. Sorry about that."

She smiled, relieved. "Hi, Laney Fooshee."

"Glad you could join us. Any friend of Brooklyn's is somebody with a police record. What's your crime?"

She hesitated, "Optimism," she said.

That caught Cohen off-guard. He nodded.

"Fine," he said. "Always room for one of those at the table."

In his jeep on the way into town, Dante had filled David in on who Laney was and why he'd invited her.

"Her husband was my best pal in the Army. I was with him when he bought it. Damn shame. Guy coulda been great. Great."

"Yeah, it always seemed the best ones got killed while the shitheads got lucky."

"Roger that."

Now, Dante was acting as a sort of impresario of the evening. Within half an hour he had lured three cute girls over to the vets' table, drunk two more beers, gotten Laney talking to Cohen, and pissed off a gang of ex-fighter pilots at the next table. Things were going well. Sitting beside Shorty and chatting with one of the girls, he heard Ben—three beers ahead of everybody else—confide his quaint, but comprehensive weltanshauung to Shorty.

"Marine," the big man said, "way I figure it is this: if you can't eat it, drink it, steal it, sell it, grope it, fight it, or fuck it, then I say piss on it!"

"My sentiments, exactly," said Shorty. "Oughta be engraved in stone some place."

"It is," Dante said, "in Ben's head."

Ben paused, trying to fathom whether he'd been insulted or flattered.

"Now wait a minute, Brooklyn. . . ." he said.

But Dante's attention lay elsewhere. On the dance floor, Evelyn Curtis—wearing a creamy blouse, dark blue skirt, and a white gardenia in her hair—and a thin tallish guy were slow dancing to the band's sexy version of "Blue Moon." The girl singer had the room in the palm of her hand:

> Blue Moon
>
> You saw me standing alone
>
> Without a dream in my heart
>
> Without a love of my own. . . .

Larocca shut up and stared. Karl followed his look.

"Now that," Karl said, "is what I would call high tone, table-grade pussy."

"Watch your mouth."

"Hey, the man's in love. Go for it, Fred Astaire."

"You think I won't?" Larocca swigged his beer for courage. Evelyn's partner turned her so that she faced Dante's table. She saw him and winked.

"Green light, pal," said Karl.

"What're you, a friggin' traffic cop?"

"No guts, no glory, soldier," Karl dug him in the ribs. "Five bucks says she's engaged to that pencil-dick she's dancing with."

Dante finished his beer and burped. "Only one way to find out, Jarhead," he said, excused himself to the girl, sailed out onto the dance floor, and tapped the thin guy on the shoulder.

"'Scuse me, Mack. I'm here to put the lady out of her misery."

Tim Fletcher turned and gave Larocca a look usually reserved for roadkill.

"I beg your pardon."

"It's okay," said Evelyn, "I know him. Dante, this is Tim. Tim, Dante."

"Hiya doin'? Bar's over there," Dante said to Tim, slipping his hand around Evelyn's waist.

"I'll be back," Tim said to her and walked off.

"No hurry," Dante said, pulling Evelyn closer. "Your friend don't look too happy," he said.

"Well, a little jealousy is good for the soul."

"Damned little goes a long way, I find," Dante said, lowering Evelyn into a smooth dip.

"My, my, the boy's a pro."

"Hey, neighborhood champ, three years running."

But she was good, too. As they learned each other's moves, Evelyn's body worked into synch with his, and their natural athleticism did the rest. Through his shirt, she could feel the cords in his shoulders and arms flex as he led her in time with the music. At the vets' table, Laney Fooshee watched the dance floor a moment too long.

"They look good together," Cohen said.

"Uh, yes, they . . . do," Laney said.

On the floor, Evelyn laughed, "Hell, I think you are a pro, Mr.

Larocca."

"I jitterbug better than this," he said.

The singer was winding up her soulful rendition:

> Blue Moon . . .
>
> Now I'm no longer alone
>
> Without a dream in my heart
>
> Without a love of my own. . . .

At the vets' table, Reddy Freddie, the former Army medic, turned to Karl.

"Beauty and the beast. Who's the chick?"

"Don't know," said Karl, "but it's gonna require some high-grade sexmanship to get horizontal with that honey tonight. Wonder if her boyfriend is armed."

At the bar, Tim drank a beer and glowered.

On the dance floor, Evelyn said to Dante, "That invitation for a free flight is still open."

"No way, my combat insurance expired last month."

The singer finished. The crowd whistled and clapped. Tim Fletcher drained his beer and took a single step toward the dancers before the band broke into a screaming version of "Take the A Train."

Dante grinned at Evelyn. "Let's see what you got, babe," he said.

"You're on," she said.

As the band roared into the great Billy Strayhorn tune, Dante and Evelyn danced like dervishes on dope, spinning, leaping, twisting, coming together chest to chest only to fly apart, still holding each other at arm's length while their feet flew and the sweat formed. Dante was damned good. Evelyn was better.

When he spun her, the dark blue skirt flowered out, revealing strong legs up to her thighs. The GIs whistled their appreciation while their dates shouted and clapped in admiration mixed with envy. The other dancers gave way until an open space formed around the two kinetic principals in the middle of the floor. The faster they danced the faster the band played, repeating the chorus and wailing impromptu solos even the musicians had never heard, the cornet player vying with the tenor man for supremacy in saluting the choreography of desire spinning out before them.

It was some show. Communal. Primal. Joyful. A cultural anthropologist would have seen it for what it soon became, a shared ritual of sexual beckoning that broke old codes of public pleasure, a hedonistic ceremony shot through with the participants' joy of simply being young and alive, at having fought and won a long, bitter war, at discovering within themselves and their nation a toughness and tenacity they hadn't known they possessed—and at having survived to experience this little moment of pure, erotic revelry.

Tim Fletcher, however, was not amused. Watching from the bar, his dark side surfaced. Apart from a garden variety jealousy at seeing his girl turned into an object of lust by an unschooled thug from Brooklyn, Tim was a man who took life seriously. He understood, as no one else in the room did, that two months ago—in the incineration of a pair of Japanese cities and the deaths of tens of thousands—their world had changed. It had changed forever and for the worse, and he'd been a small but integral part of that atomic tsunami. He felt bewilderment. Sadness. Guilt.

* * *

When the band finally brought the A-Train into the station and parked it, Dante and Evelyn were gasping, laughing, and covered in sweat. The crowd roared its approval as Evelyn spontaneously pulled the gardenia from her hair and tossed it into the crowd. It was caught by a one-legged vet in a wheelchair. The crowd cheered him as he kissed the flower and raised it in tribute to the beautiful laughing girl caught for an instant in the floodlights. She blew him a return kiss and led Dante toward Tim.

"Now we'll see what pencil-dick is made of," said Karl, watching the trio at the bar. "Three to one Larocca gets himself some nocturnal exercise tonight."

"Lucky dog," said Reddy Freddie, turning to see if his pregnant wife needed another beer.

David Cohen and Laney resumed their conversation. He could see she'd been distracted by the dance display, but he wasn't sure why.

"Dante told me about your husband," he said. "I'm real sorry. It must be tough. . . ."

"Oh, thanks. Yes, it's been a little hard, but his mama is real nice to me and the baby, and we do fine."

His eyebrows shot up. "You've got a baby?"

"Yes, a boy, 20 months. A real handful, but . . . but a lot of fun, too, you know." She could see him react, and in his look she recognized what every young war-widowed mother in Europe, Russia, Japan and the States feared: they were damaged goods. With healthy single women outnumbering men—in some cases 3:1—a widow with a baby was a tough sell, their stock marked down at well below par.

"I think that's terrific," said David. "Maybe I can meet . . . have a look at him one day, or . . ."

Laney smiled. "Sure, if you like. Dante can bring you out to the house."

At the bar, Larocca-the-barbarian was behaving more civilly than

Tim-the-aristocrat. He thanked the sulking boyfriend for letting him borrow his girl and apologized for hogging the limelight.

"But, you know Evelyn, she's a bad influence." Then he told Tim an animated version of the story of her buzzing and assaulting him in the Mustang. Tim seemed to find that amusing.

"Whatever you do," he said to Dante, "don't go up in that old crop-duster with her."

"Now hold on," she said.

"No way, pal. My feet stay on mother earth."

Tim smiled at the thought of Dante and Sir Plus splitting in opposite directions with the airplane prop almost on top of them.

"Damn dog figured out what was going on before I did," said Larocca. "Say, why don't you guys join me and my buddies over there. But watch the Marines—Karl and Ben. They're the hulky ones with daggers coming out their eyes."

"I don't think we . . ." Tim said.

"We'd love to," Evelyn said. "Lead on." She took Tim's arm and kissed him on the cheek. Dante registered it.

He shepherded them to his table and attempted introductions, but the band was up and running again on "Chattanooga Choo Choo," and the noise level rose to drown him out.

"Ahh, screw it. Everybody just talk to the one next to you," he shouted, picked up Laney's beer, finished it, and kissed her on the cheek.

"You smell fantastic," he said.

"How many beers've you had?" Laney asked, smiling.

"First one tonight," he said, and squeezed her shoulder. He was on a roll. "How you doin', Cohen? Everything hunky-dory? Hey, Karl, Ben, ain't it about time you muscle-heads bought us a round?"

"You got it," said Karl.

"Unngghh," said Ben.

* * *

Dante Larocca's thorough, bloody pounding of Bruno Kretchmer back in the Brooklyn alley—with Maria watching—was not entirely out of character. While growing up on the streets, and in the Army, Dante had started a number of fights. And finished many that others had started. That night at Kilroy's, as the stars aligned themselves for trouble, Larocca was ripe to cause it.

At some unspoken level, he experienced the evening as the culmination of a mad, weeks-long odyssey. The confrontation with Maria, arriving in Alabama, lying to Mama Lou about Buddy, acceptance into Professor Greene's program and starting school, getting his tent floor built, partying with his buddies, seeing that Laney had a good time, dancing with Evelyn—and, of course, the beer—all combined to bring out the primate in him.

As he moved around the table, laughing and backslapping, grabbing an empty chair here, someone else's beer there, flirting and chatting up whoever would listen, his voice rose as his tolerance for insult fell.

The trouble began with the gang of ex-fighter pilots at the next table who were reliving old air battles with Zeros, Messerschmitts and Heinkels. Victory having many mothers, they gesticulated with both hands to demonstrate their kills—as pilots have since the first Englishman flying a Sopwith Camel took a potshot at a German Fokker with a pistol in 1915.

Now, the Kilroy pilots' boasts of shooting down enemy planes and strafing columns of "Krauts" and "Nips" grew louder. Dante had nothing against hosing the enemy, but these guys struck him as arrogant pricks. Plus—it had to be admitted—there was a Marx-hued hint of class-warfare at work between ground soldiers and pilots—the lowly grunt vs. the glory boys. As the band played on and the pilots replayed more kills, it became harder for Dante to hear what Laney and Cohen were saying. Finally, he turned to the table of hotshots.

"Hey! hey!" They paused to look at him. One guy held both arms aloft, demonstrating how his fighter squadron had screamed down out of the sun on an unsuspecting flight of German Stukas.

"Yeah? What?"

"You friggin' fly boys, if somebody cut your hands off you couldn't talk."

A handsome guy spoke up. "What's your problem, buddy— apart from the obvious?" His pals laughed.

"My problem," Dante said, "is that you bums are so stinkin' loud me and my friends can't talk."

"Let it go, Dante," said Laney.

"No, it's rude," he said.

"Rude?" The pilots laughed. "What outfit were you with, pal, the Bob Hope Brigade?"

By this time, Karl's and Ben's delicate antennae had picked up an arresting new timbre in the voices rising behind them. As they pivoted in their chairs to face the pilots, Ben's neck swelled and reddened. Karl put a hand on his shoulder.

"Not yet, Ben," he whispered. "I'll tell you when."

"Army," Dante shouted. "Tanks. I was with Patton!"

"Riiiight! Now, every mess cook in France rode with Patton. What'd you do, pal, water his pet bulldog?"

Evelyn spoke up. "Forget it, Dante, they're drunk."

"We're drunk?" one of the pilots guffawed. "This greaseball's been a one-man wrecking crew all night." Then he noticed Evelyn's fine breasts. "Hey, babe, why don't you move up to officer's country and join us? Got a chair right here for you."

Dante stood, reached over the table and liberated the chair, dropping it in front of him and sitting in it backwards, his arms folded across the top.

"That's my buddy's seat you got there," a pilot said.

"Tell him to find another one," Dante said and resumed talking to Cohen and Laney. Evelyn chuckled, reminded of spiteful little boys on the playground.

The pilots looked at each other. This wouldn't do.

The band slid into a dreamy version of "Stardust," and Tim asked Evelyn to dance. She declined, intrigued by how the unfolding drama would turn out.

"Hey, dogface," the handsome pilot called out in a cultivated Southern drawl, "how 'bout settlin' a bet for us?"

Dante looked skeptical, but nodded.

"Yeah, see, judging from your accent, we were wonderin' if you could read and write. I said you probably could, 'cause you had to read the recipes in the mess tent. But my buddies here figure you just winged it and let some other PFC take the lead. So, which is it— literate or not?"

Ben rose to his full 6'2" height, snarling.

"Hey, are you flat-peters insulting my pal?" Without a crib sheet, Ben was never sure. Karl grabbed Ben's belt and forced him back down into his chair.

"Not yet, Ben," he said.

At this juncture, Dante changed tactics, becoming the voice of reason. "Yeah, I can write my name and, you know, handle 'Dick and

Jane'—except for the big words. But, say, you're all Air Corps, right?"

"So?"

"So, any you fubars checked out on a P-51 Mustang?"

"Dante," Evelyn warned him softly.

"Come on," Dante said to the pilots, "who's the hottest Mustang pilot in the group?"

A blond guy with a crew cut and freckles spoke up.

"Kevin, here, has four kills, the Air Medal and the DFC and . . ."

The handsome pilot stopped him.

"Why do you ask?" he said.

Evelyn suspected what was coming and didn't like it.

"Why?" Dante said. "'Cause two hundred bucks says I got a woman can out fly your sorry ass from here to breakfast!"

"Dante, don't . . ." said Evelyn.

"Evelyn, is he talking . . ." said Tim.

"A woman!" said the pilot. "Are you shittin' me?"

"Put up or shut up, flyboys!" said Dante, standing and tossing the chair aside.

Kevin rose and wagged a finger in Dante's face. "Pal, let me put you wise: There is no woman, no dame on the planet that can out fly this boy. None! Zero! Take-it-to-the-bank."

Dante turned to Evelyn. "Hear that?"

Evelyn flushed and sprang up. "Put your money where your mouth is, punk," she said. The pilots stared.

"You?"

"Her," Dante said.

"Never happen," said Kevin.

"Try me," said Evelyn.

"Babe, I'd love to try you," grinned Kevin, "but it's tough to do it in a

Mustang cockpit." His friends roared.

Dante turned to his mates. "Did you gentlemen hear that? These putzes just insulted Evelyn."

"Now, Ben," said Karl, releasing his hold on Ben's belt.

"Arrggghhhh!" said Ben.

* * *

Exactly how the pilots' table—and their beers—became airborne that night was never clear to those present. What most did recall, however, was that Ben moved first—and with alarming speed for a big man. He was followed into the fray by Karl, Dante, Cohen, Chief Davis, Shorty, and Reddy Freddie, bringing with them—as General Patton advocated in frontal assaults—overwhelming force.

The fact that no one was killed or seriously wounded had more to do with (1) luck and (2) quick thinking by the Levy brothers, Neal and Henry. They had both been monitoring the developing dispute for some minutes. The instant it flared into open combat Neal signaled his three bouncers to move in, and Henry doused the house lights. In the cacophonous semi-darkness that ensued nobody could get a clear shot at anybody, although Evelyn did manage to wham down a beverage tray on top of Kevin's head with noteworthy force, while the ever-resourceful Ben lifted a drunken pilot above his head, spun him around twice, then threw him six feet into a pack of his friends.

Dante also got in a couple of nice body shots on one particularly offensive pretty boy before the bouncer—former frogman with a shaved head and much facial scarring—pulled Larocca off and laid him out cold with a quick rap from a pair of brass knuckles. David Cohen, fresh from smashing a chair across the back of a guy who was throttling

Reddy Freddie, saw Dante go down. He shouted at Shorty for help and, together with Laney, they dragged him toward an emergency exit.

The musicians, meanwhile, grabbed their instruments and sought shelter beneath the bandstand. This was nothing new to them—the key thing being to protect your lip, your fingers, and your horn. The rest of the patrons were of two minds: some wedged themselves into far corners to handicap the melee, while others flooded from the exits like scalded rats.

Huffing and puffing in the parking lot—and with only three hands between them—Cohen and Shorty poured an unconscious Larocca into the back of the jeep. Laney tried to help, but it was really a two-man job. As they worked, they heard the sirens of approaching police cars. Cohen turned to Laney.

"Thanks, he's okay," he gasped. "But get out of here before the cops come."

Laney's eyes were wide with excitement.

"David, are you all right?" she asked Cohen.

"Never better. Now scoot. But I do wanna see that kid some time."

"Yes, of course," she shouted, heading for her car. "You and Dante will have to come for supper. 'Bye."

David watched until she was safely away.

"Hey, Cohen," said Shorty, still breathing hard, "you mind if we get the hell out of here? I've got a reputation to think about."

Cohen grinned. "So you do, Shorty. So you do. Let's roll."

With Cohen using his stump and good hand to manhandle the jeep, they blasted a fresh exit from the lot, taking out a fence and several garbage cans and leaving behind a roiling cloud of dust to greet the local gendarmerie as they slid to a flamboyant stop in the gravel—sirens dying.

Chapter 8

Princeton had been good to Tim Fletcher. When he matriculated there in 1934 to study physics, he followed a well-trod trail of Southern boys heading for that particular branch of Ivy League, Inc. Tall, handsome, polite, and precocious, Tim soon became a favorite of his professors. To round things out, he played varsity tennis for the Tigers as well as small forward on the basketball team, leading the squad in assists his junior year. His application for a Rhodes Scholarship was a shoo-in, bearing with it such lavish recommendations from his science instructors that the Rhodes committee wondered if they'd been written by his mother.

After 18 enterprising months at Oxford he emerged with an M.S. in physics and three scholarly publications on sub-atomic particles. The following September—1941—he entered the University of Chicago's doctoral program. Three months later, history made a U-turn—America was at war—and within 90 days he was recruited for what would later become the Manhattan Project—the most costly and sensitive secret venture ever undertaken by the United States government.

His job would be to learn how to blow up the world.

On the day Dante Larocca and Maria Costagno married—February 4, 1942—Tim Fletcher was interviewed in Berkeley, California, by Dr. J. Robert Oppenheimer, the brilliant young physicist enlisted to run the world's first atom bomb factory. The charismatic Oppenheimer, who was said by a Harvard classmate to have "intellectually looted" that university as an undergraduate, combined a catholic—and intimidating—knowledge of languages, physics, art, Eastern religions, left-wing politics and much else.

When asked why he took on the dark task of attempting to build the bomb, he had replied that he found the project "technically sweet." Sweet, perhaps, but also enervating, terrifying, and addictive. Before the task ended in colossal fireballs—first at Alamagordo, N.M., then at Hiroshima and Nagasaki—Oppenheimer would tangle endlessly with General Leslie Groves. Groves had overseen the building of the Pentagon in 1940, and it was to him the Army assigned the task of riding herd on the most legendary concentration of scientific intellect ever assembled in one unlikely place—Los Alamos, New Mexico.

In early 1942, Oppenheimer had liked Tim Fletcher, and Groves had hired him. The following week, with America still in shock—and a good part of its Pacific fleet rusting in the mud of Pearl Harbor—Fletcher returned to Tuscaloosa to say goodbye to Evelyn and his mother and to pay respects at the grave of his beloved father, Phil, a journeyman plumber, amateur inventor and unrecognized genius who had bequeathed to his only son a love of mathematics, crossword puzzles, and abstract logic.

Tim had recently returned home once again, to bury his mother, teach physics at the university, and—he hoped—marry Evelyn Curtis. Although not a combat veteran, he nevertheless suffered from a combination of flashbacks and grotesque nightmares, all tied to his four years spent as a midwife to murder in the Manhattan Project. He didn't speak of it, even to Evelyn, but he had been traveling to Birmingham weekly to visit a government-paid psychiatrist about his feelings of remorse and, occasionally, despair. Tim Fletcher was a private man— private, introspective and troubled.

The night of the brawl at Kilroy's, he and Evelyn had escaped together out a broken window, dashed for her Ford convertible, and roared out of the parking lot just as the police plunged into the bar.

Evelyn had been furious at Dante for starting the fight, enraged at Kevin—the ex-fighter pilot—for his condescension, and exhilarated at having gotten in her own licks during the fracas.

Tim's response was similar, but simpler: he was just disgusted with Larocca and his band of gorillas for inciting the ruckus in the first place. But there was also an overlay of something else—a lingering jealousy at Evelyn's sheer joy on the dance floor. Tim had a pretty good sense of his own strengths and weaknesses, and he did not list jungle dancing among the former.

Larocca's animal magnetism, on the other hand, was perfectly plain, his appeal to women transparent. Thus, on a given Friday afternoon, Tim found himself in Birmingham speaking of Dante to the psychiatrist, Doctor Lawrence Feldman, a balding gnome of a man with his own nervous facial tic and a wandering eye. Normally, the subject would be Los Alamos, Oppenheimer, General Groves, and Hiroshima, but Feldman seemed to want to lead him down a different track.

"It sounds as though you may harbor certain, um, hostilities toward this Larocca character," said Feldman, whose client-base had quintupled since Pearl Harbor. He had seen dozens of war-related cases and thought Tim Fletcher's to be arresting.

Tim hesitated. "No, I don't think so," he said. "I mean . . . It's just that he, that Larocca embodies, that he represents all these vast, uh, changes taking place in . . . in American society and I don't . . . ."

Feldman nodded. "'Bottom rail's on top, now, boss.'"

"Beg your pardon. . . ."

"That's what the ex-slave said when he saw his former master after the Civil War." The diminutive Doctor's wall-eye migrated to starboard in conversation—especially when he thought he'd said something clever.

"What's slavery got to do with it?" snapped Tim. These weekly trips to Birmingham wore on him, but Washington had insisted.

"Just a figure of speech," said Feldman, leaning forward over his notepad. "The important thing, Tim, is to realize that in your mind your secret work on the atomic bomb and the rise of this Larocca—and his type—are linked."

"In what way, pray tell?"

"Well, you helped build the bomb, the instrument that ended the very war that liberated all the Laroccas in America to rise up— courtesy of the G.I. Bill—and challenge key issues of collective caste consciousness, especially in higher education, in, um, university life, which of course in this country is the gateway to social acceptance, status enhancement, ego-gratification, and the accumulation of capital."

Tim grew red-faced.

"Yeah, right, and next you'll say that Hiroshima was nothing but a huge atomic orgasm, complete with phallic mushroom cloud, that it was something I helped engender—that I now feel unduly responsible for—that spawned a million lower-class vets . . ."

"Several million . . ."

"Okay, damnit, many millions of vets who now—freed from their bondage by the war—have risen like Frankenstein. . . ."

"Frankenstein's monster."

"Monster, right . . . from their slums and squalor and come to take my job, chop off my head, and steal my woman!" He could not conceal his contempt for such piffle.

"I didn't mention your woman. You did."

Tim fiddled with his cigarette lighter and glanced out the window. In the distance, he could hear the veiled thunder of the steel mills,

Birmingham's source of bad air and big bucks.

Had he said that? Had he just clumped the bomb with Larocca and Larocca with Evelyn—and himself?

He hated these pregnant silences that paid Feldman's bills.

"All right," the doctor said, "I think that's probably enough for today."

"Wait a minute. . . ."

Feldman stretched across his desk and punched a button.

"Mrs. Drake, Mr. Fletcher will be leaving by the side door. Is Father Shanahan here, yet?"

"Yes, Doctor, I'll send him in on the hour."

"You didn't give me the full fifty-five," said Tim, trying to smile. "I'll have to report you to the shrinker police."

Feldman leaned back in his black leather chair, tapped a pencil on the desk, and looked at Tim. His voice gentled, taking on a soft note he'd perfected through thousands of hours spent with tormented patients.

"Son, you've been through a great deal. More than most combat veterans. After all, you believe you've contributed to building a weapon that may one day destroy the world."

Tim's lips compressed into a hard line.

"I did."

"Yes, you did. Brilliantly."

"And it will. Destroy."

"Maybe it will. Maybe it won't. Only our children will know. Meanwhile . . ."

"Then it'll be too late. Doctor . . ."

"Tim . . ."

"Doctor Feldman, you do realize that the Soviets will have this weapon within, I'd say, five years minimum, and then . . ."

158

"Oh, I doubt that. I mean, the Soviets are our allies, and, anyway, they're barely out of the Stone Age. . . ."

"The Soviets, Doctor, just whipped Adolph Hitler's ass all the way from Stalingrad to Berlin. And the Soviets will not be our allies forever." Tim leaned forward, clubbing Feldman's desk with his fist. "The Soviets will keep Poland and Hungary and Romania and Czechoslovakia, and then they will need this weapon to protect what they've got. And the Soviets will get this weapon. They will either develop it or steal it, because they cannot afford not to. And then, and then," Tim strained to keep his voice in check. "And then there. will. be. hell. to. pay, Dr. Feldman, unshirted hell. Oppenheimer knows it. Einstein knows it. The Soviets know it. They must have this weapon!" Tim fell back in his chair, white-faced, a-tremble.

Feldman sat, stunned, the silence echoing between them.

"Perhaps you're right, son. You're certainly in a better position to know than I am."

"Yes, that's true."

"Meanwhile, life, uh, life for the rest of us goes on, and we must grapple with it daily." Feldman sounded like a cliche-ridden hack. "And . . . and you and I have much to talk about. Don't expect your . . . your feelings to disappear overnight."

Tim stood and pocketed the cigarette lighter. "Dr. Feldman, I expect these feelings to be around—forever."

"Forever's a long time, Tim."

"Well, forever is about the length of my average night."

The psychiatrist stood.

"I'll see you next week, he said. "Drive carefully going home."

"Yes, all right." Tim nodded and started for the door.

"And Tim?" The younger man paused, his hand on the knob. "Do you own a gun? A pistol . . . a rifle?"

The question oscillated in the air.

"No. Why?"

"No reason. That's good. I just thought you might be a hunter, you know, or . . . or, well, a gun guy."

The date is 16 July, 1945. Time: 5:25 A.M. Place: TRINITY, the code name Dr. Oppenheimer has assigned to the New Mexico desert site—a high alkaline plain near Alamogordo—chosen for the initial test of the atomic bomb. Tim Fletcher stands between Oppenheimer and General Groves in a hardened command bunker five miles south of Ground Zero. The place is filthy with nervous physicists slathering on sun-tan lotion as protection against the imminent blast.

At Ground Zero, bathed in multiple searchlights, a fiendishly complex five-foot metal sphere weighing perhaps 10,000 pounds hangs suspended from a steel tower 100 feet above the desert floor. Comprising high explosives, electric wires, detonators, and exquisitely machined parts made of gold, nickel, beryllium, uranium, polonium, and plutonium, it is The Thing itself.

In the command bunker, Tim notes for the hundredth time the physical differences between the corpulent, un-military Groves and the ascetic Oppenheimer, his weight now less than 120 lbs. Fletcher dons ordinary welders' goggles and conjures a short, desperate prayer, asking God to forgive them all. Oppenheimer's people have estimated the bomb yield will be maybe one kiloton—a thousand tons of TNT—but no one really knows. Indeed, no one can be sure the bomb—the "gadget"—will even work. Maybe three years of unimaginable expense and labor will end in cosmic farce.

Suddenly, a green Very rocket whooshes into the reddening dawn sky and a siren begins its violent wail. Five minutes. Tim steals a glance at Oppenheimer whose face is a mask, skin drawn tight over the skull, lips working. Oppenheimer mutters something. Tim leans closer to catch it and hears, "Lord, these affairs are hard on the heart." Tim closes his eyes. He feels complicit in a great evil.

At 5:28 A.M., a second Very rocket fizzles but doesn't fire. Bad omen. At 5:29, the one-minute rocket fires properly, casting a flickering blue pall on the faces of the assembled men. Tim's pulse outruns his brain. He grips a wooden stanchion and wonders if, as one scientist has speculated, the bomb will ignite the atmosphere and incinerate the state of New Mexico—or crack the earth's crust.

At ten seconds a gong sounds in the control bunker. Without realizing it, Tim flexes his knees. At 5:29:45, on the suspended steel sphere a firing circuit closes and 32 detonators simultaneously erupt, igniting the outer lens shells of the explosive—Composition B—collapsing the nickel-plated plutonium core into an infinite nothing.

Then, out of that nothing, roars light and heat and destruction and radiation on an order of magnitude not witnessed since the birth of time.

The explosion's flare blanches the face of the moon, temporarily blinding those caught looking. The shattering tumult from the blast itself exceeds human experience. Birds are oxidized in mid-flight. Desert animals eviscerated.

As the giant fireball races into the heavens, the scientists are left to contemplate their handiwork in appalled silence until Groves turns and shakes Oppenheimer's hand.

One of the physicists says to his boss, "Well, Oppy, now, we're all sons-of-bitches."

Tim Fletcher nods.

The bomb's yield is later calculated to be, not one, but 18.6 kilotons. And later still, Oppenheimer, quoting from the Bhagavad-Gita, tells Tim Fletcher that immediately following the explosion a line from that epic poem sprang to mind:

"Now I am become Death, the destroyer of worlds."

Chapter 9

Professor Sidney Greene and his faculty colleagues were working Dante Larocca's butt off. In addition to taking courses in English composition, history of Greek architecture, descriptive geometry, structural theory, strength of materials, and methods of construction, Dante was up to his eyeballs in Greene's advanced design class. He'd been assigned to the latter on the basis of his drawings and models—and because his three-year apprenticeship at the Brooklyn design firm had given him an edge over the usual first-year students.

At the same time, the competition in "Design II" was brutal. The standards were high, the students were talented, and it seemed to Dante that every guy in the class was angling for a Dalton Fellowship.

Which was pretty much true.

The reason for this was partly Greene's reputation. A distinguished architect and public lecturer, he had built a dozen significant buildings—and a crush of lesser structures—across the country. He was also regularly consulted when a half-finished building—or set of plans—had problems. He didn't come cheap, but he had a genius for spotting flaws and suggesting remedies, and despite his imperious demeanor he had developed wide-ranging influence within his profession as a solver of design problems.

"Wide-ranging," however, did not include Frank Lloyd Wright. Greene detested Wright—who returned the favor in the way only a true, untrammeled egomaniac can, by saying of Greene that "neither his work nor his character rises to a level of significance to merit my riposte." Reports of their spiraling mutual contempt and periodic venomous exchanges had enlivened many a professional meeting and dinner party before the war.

Why Greene remained at Alabama was something of a mystery, although it was assumed the reason could be found in the several thousand acres of rolling farm and timber land bordering the Black Warrior River and inherited by his alcoholic wife, Charlotte. A poor-but-talented bootstrapper from a hard-scrabble farm near Huntsville, Greene had gone off to MIT on scholarship as "Sidneydwayne"—spoken as one word—Greene, returning five years later as simply "Sidney"—the New Man.

The reborn Greene loved a show. With imperial squiredom as his goal, in 1922 he had married the hard-drinking party girl, Charlotte Biggers. By chance, Charlotte was the heiress to a bank full of money and half a county of Alabama countryside. And by cosmic coincidence, Sidney himself was deeply attracted to fishing and hunting: deer, turkey, ducks, quail—on horseback—and doves. It was a match made in accounting heaven. Combining two pleasures, Greene entertained clients and far-flung colleagues on this magnificent spread—which he'd named "Halcyon"—employing a staff of six blacks to train horses and bird dogs, plant and cut hay, prepare meals, serve booze, and generally bow and scrape, all to maintain an exaggerated sense of Antebellum splendor.

Besides supplying the joys of hunting, "Halcyon" enhanced Greene's mystique as generous host and regional godfather of the Dalton Fellowship. Twice a year he assembled the Dalton Selection Committee Jurors there at his palatial, multi-bedroomed camp house set atop ten-foot pilings on the banks of the Black Warrior River. The five jurors spent a day interviewing terrified applicants, inspecting their workout of a designated design problem, and debating their merits, before finally announcing the winners at a sumptuous cocktail party attended by a worshipful claque of social and academic mavens from town and gown.

His fellow jurors—picked by Greene—received handsome honoraria to participate, served three-year staggered terms, and hailed from the best schools of architecture in the East: Yale; MIT; Harvard; Cornell; Columbia; Toronto; Georgia Tech; Virginia—and wherever else Greene wished his reputation burnished. Over the years, he'd pretty much covered all the bases, incurring debts of gratitude from a galaxy of fellow practitioners.

All this self-regarding hoohaw flowed from Greene's own sense of his rightful place in the design firmament. Years ago—in the early 1920s—starting out as a young architect, he'd looked around for ways to set himself apart within his profession.

When he heard about Samuel Dalton, a Birmingham industrialist who had made millions during World War I—and who had lost an architect son to the conflict—he researched his quarry, got an appointment, then made a drop-dead brilliant presentation to the old man. His pitch, in sum: to honor and pay tribute to his fallen son, Dalton should endow an obscenely generous fellowship at the University, by means of which the expenses of young men would be underwritten for a year's study in such European bastions of design as Paris' Ecole des Beaux Arts, the American Academy in Rome, and—until it was closed in 1933 by the Nazis—the Bauhaus.

With tears trickling down his jowl runnels, Old Man Dalton had swallowed the pitch hook, line, and sinker, wrote a generous check on the spot and continued to pile money into the Dalton Foundation coffers every year after that. Over time, he came to see himself as a mini-Ford, Rockefeller, or Carnegie, giving back to the nation—the South, really—a portion of that which he had by rapacity and cunning ripped from an indolent social order more interested in mint juleps than minding the store.

Guided by Greene, the Dalton flourished. A prestigious award, it sent its recipients abroad for a year. It paid all expenses, plus a handsome stipend. It placed its winners in the best ateliers in Europe. And, later, Dalton Fellows could name their price in the marketplace. It had also done much for Green's reputation as king-maker, even as it evolved into a pint-sized Rhodes Scholarship of Architecture.

Taken together, the professor and the prize were enough to lure to the University a cadre of students who would normally have dismissed Alabama as they boarded trains for study at tonier universities. Larocca's design class included guys with monikers like Gunderson, Rodriquez, Markowitz, Sternlicht, Goldstein, Wu, and Scharffolovsky, fine names all, but not ones normally found heading up the Birmingham Social Register.

As for Dante's fellow veterans living on loans, dreams, and the G.I. Bill, many came to 'Bama for the same reasons—Sidney Greene and the Dalton. These guys were here to (1) work hard and (2) raise hell. The nearly universal feeling among them was:

"Out of my way, pal. The war stole my life. I want it back."

Growing up on scattered farms or mean city streets, these fellows had never imagined themselves as college material. When they went off to war in '42 they tacitly assumed that it was to scut work they would be returning: a factory floor; a sweatshop; staring up the east end of a west-bound mule. But now that college doors had been flung wide, many of them had stepped forward—although with chips on their shoulders the size of Noah's Ark.

Of course, many of the younger, non-vets were damn good too; but, representing a different class, they lacked the feral need to dominate that characterized many of their veteran competitors. As younger sons of privilege who, by accident of birth, had missed out on the war, they came to Tuscaloosa, often as third- and fourth-generation legacies at the University. And they were accustomed to deference being paid them—by students and faculty alike.

Unfortunately for the sake of social harmony, the vets were not inclined to defer to anybody, whether candy-assed undergraduates or some hoity-toity professor who didn't know his stuff. Woe betide the woolly-minded Ph.D. with no clue as to how to corral 25-30 ex-Marines, pilots, sailors and dogfaces who had spent the last three or four years staring down the gun barrels of Hitler and Hirohito's finest—and who had the scars to prove it. And whose former military instructors might have begun a typical day's lesson with this gentle admonition:

"All right, you panty-waisted, whore-mongering sons-of-bitches, sit down, shut up and pay attention or I'll have your clap-ridden asses out there in full combat pack on that parade ground the whole fuckin' night long! And I mean NOW! Marconi! Look at you, you maggot! You oughta be arrested for impersonatin' a Marine! Drop down and give me 20!"

Effective, but not the collegiate way, really.

* * *

Amid this complex social stew, what ruled Larocca's life was his Dalton proposal—languishing undeveloped and ill-wrought. Most of his waking moments were spent struggling to mold inchoate ideas for post-war, low-income housing into something he could submit to Greene, together with decent answers to critical questions:

— How do you make the housing affordable, livable, and durable?

— How do you maximize its thermal efficiencies to reduce long-term expenses, while controlling maintenance costs?

— What tricks do you employ to hide overhead utilities while still assuring access to buried cables and pipes?

— How do you minimize vehicular traffic and at the same time encourage free pedestrian movement within a complex or bloc of buildings? And what about landscaping? Ball fields? Swimming pools? Playgrounds? Shops? Restaurants?

— What provisions were needed to accommodate the inevitable explosion of families, now that the vets were coming home by the tens of thousands?

— And what construction materials to use: Brick? Wood? Block? Steel? Glass? Aluminum? Composites?

To Larocca, the challenges seemed endless, and nobody in his design class—including Sidney Greene—showed the least interest in his project. The other students did what students do when working at the behest, and in the thrall, of a distinguished professor—they aped his pet theories.

Thus, at night, Dante sat alone at the drawing table in his tent, sketching design ideas, revising, erasing, cursing, tearing up the result, tossing it into the corner, then rolling out another three-foot section of wrapping paper and starting over. Sometimes, the Marines—Karl and Ben—or David Cohen would blunder in, bearing hooch and demanding that he drink with them, and sometimes he did, particularly with Cohen, whom he admired and liked.

"Hell, Larocca," David had said one night, placing a half-filled bottle on the table and kicking back after taking on a load of bourbon, "you work on that damn housing project thing 'bout as hard as I work on my Great, Endless, All-American Fuckin' Novel. I mean, you're in here every night 'til God knows how late."

"Yeah, that thought's occurred to me."

Cohen looked at him.

"Why, do you think, why do we do it?"

Dante took a breath, puffed out his cheeks, let the air whistle through his lips.

"I'm no philosopher, Cohen. That's your—"

"Aww, come on, you must have a notion."

Dante picked up a pencil and began a quick sketch of Cohen's handsome head in three-quarter profile, the eyes at half-mast, a smile playing across his features.

"'Cause we're late," he said as he drew.

"Late?"

"The war. Old Man Time. And . . ."

"Roger that . . ."

"And 'cause we probably think we got something to, you know, contribute, to give back, maybe . . ."

"Yeah, but . . ."

". . . and, 'cause . . ." Dante worked quickly on the sketch, then leaned back to consider the result. "'cause we've seen dark things up close, you know, in the war . . . and we're scared."

Cohen's jovial mood had swiveled into something else.

"Yeah, I hear you." He played with his glass. "I guess I write about those dark things too, you know, to stay alive. To keep gettin' up in the morning."

Dante nodded, "Right, but what kills me about you writers is that you break your ass to get every sentence, every paragraph just so, like a perfect little pearl, or something . . ."

"Yeah, so?"

"So what if, like, nobody ever reads it?"

Cohen smiled. "Then we jump off a bridge or something."

Dante spun the finished sketch around and pushed it toward David.

"That's good, man. Can I keep it?"

Dante leaned forward. "Sure, here, I'll sign it. For prosterity's sake."

"Posterity."

"Whatever."

Cohen stood. "Well, I'm gonna hit the hay. Tomorrow's another day. Unfortunately." He started out.

"Cohen . . ."

"Hmmm?"

"About this Dalton thing . . ."

"Yeah?"

"It's, well, the rules say you have to write up a . . . a thingamajig, to go along with . . ."

"Like a narrative?"

"Yeah, a narrative. And, well, that ain't my strength, you know? And I was wonderin' if maybe you could help . . ."

"I'd be honored."

They exchanged smiles.

"Thanks, man. G'night."

Chapter 10

The cotton crop was late this year. And the boll-weevils were voracious. These nasty little quarter-inch bastards had crossed the Rio Grande in the 1870s and made it into Alabama by 1892, decimating cotton fields and forcing the state's farmers both to diversify their crops and fight for their lives. By the mid-1930s, crop dusting—or aerial application—had become a widespread practice, and the airplane of choice for this dangerous work was the Boeing/Stearman, Model 75 Kaydet, the same gaudily painted two-seat biplane that Dante had been introduced to by Evelyn Curtis' mechanic, Ralph Hobson, the day she had nearly killed him at the Tuscaloosa air field with her Mustang.

The Kaydet had been developed as the primary trainer for both the Army Air Corps and the Navy. Slow, robust and stable, the fabric-covered two-seater was a predictable and forgiving aircraft that even ham-handed young pilot trainees had a hard time crashing. Careless crop dusters, on the other hand, had no trouble killing themselves by smashing into water towers or barns, being decapitated by power lines—or by snagging an extended wheel on a fence post and slamming into the ground nose-first at 90 mph.

In crop dusting before the war, Evelyn Curtis was as good as it got, and all the local farmers knew it. Absolutely fearless, when she returned from service with the WASPS and took up working again, she was the first one they called when the weevils began laying eggs in the cotton bolls. Her slogan

CURTIS CROP-DUSTERS

WE CAN SPRAY ANYTHING YOU CAN GROW

bespoke her willingness to tackle even the most dangerous and awkwardly positioned fields—those surrounded by tall trees or criss-crossed by nearly invisible electric cables.

Her parents hated the whole business but each responded differently. Atlanta Curtis simply asked that she not be told on the days Evelyn was screaming along six inches above the white-topped cotton fields. Her father, on the other hand, had hollered and pouted, ranted and sworn. He knew, of course, it would do no good; thus, he had taken out an enormous insurance policy on her life, identifying as beneficiary the trust fund named in honor of his dead son, Robert. The fund's mission was to provide scholarships to Auburn University's School of Forestry—the place where Robert had been enrolled when he was killed.

The morning at breakfast that Harry Curtis told Evelyn what he'd done, her face froze.

"But, Daddy, you're betting I'll be killed."

"Well, I love you, Evelyn, but, frankly, it's a smart bet."

"And the policy pays into . . . into Robert's trust fund?"

Her father's eyes hardened. "Can you think of a better place for it to go?"

Evelyn leaned on the breakfast table, unconsciously covering her facial scar with a hand.

"No," she said softly. "No, I think that's . . . fine."

Now, flying open-cockpit at 1500 feet over an Alabama landscape flooded by an early-morning autumn sun, she thought about that conversation, shook her head sadly, adjusted her goggles, tightened her safety harness, and nosed the little gold-and-green Stearman into a gentle, spiraling dive toward a massive cotton field beneath her left wing.

The 300-acre field—farmed on shares for a widow-woman named

Louise Fooshee by Milo Henderson—posed particular hazards to any pilot. Bound on the north side by a gravel road and power lines, the ground sloped in a sharp contour down toward a creek bottom, then up the opposite, companion hill that was crested with a fence, plus stands of oak and pine. In addition to two sets of electric wires and tall tulip poplars growing up in the bottom land, the steep angle of the two slopes required the crop-duster to fly her airplane with one wing tip lowered so as to retard chemical drift of the insecticide—especially in windy conditions.

Thus, flying east at an altitude of five feet, you dipped your right wing. Flying west, you dipped your left. That is, until you attacked the second hill and did exactly the opposite. Evelyn did not like this field. Indeed, she so disliked it that the first time Milo Henderson invited her out to take a look at it she stood with her flagman-mechanic on the gravel road and balked. It didn't help that when Milo put his arm around her shoulder in a kind of clumsy bear hug she didn't like him either.

"Now, what's the problem, little lady?" he'd said. "People told me you'd spray any field a man could get cotton to grow in."

"Generally, that's true."

"Well, right there's the field, and that ain't cotton candy you're looking at."

Evelyn's flagman, Ralph Hobson, spoke up. "The problem, Mr. Henderson, is the contour."

"Right," said Evelyn.

"See," he went on, "if I'm standing at one end of this big ol' field waving my flag, when Miss Evelyn drops down to spraying height, she won't even be able to see it 'til she pulls up right on top of me, near-about."

"Well, Billy Lancaster sprayed it last year without any trouble," said Milo.

"Maybe you ought to call Billy Lancaster, then," said Ralph.

"Lancaster's dead," said Evelyn. "Flew his Piper smack into the Jensens' silo."

"True enough," said Milo, "but he sprayed this field and lived to tell it."

Evelyn hated to be goaded by the likes of Henderson.

"I'll tell you what, Milo," she said. "I'll do the damn field. . . ."

"Good . . . Good . . ."

"On a day with no wind, and for my regular fee. . . ."

"Fine by me. . . ."

". . . plus 50 percent."

"Damn, you bargain hard."

"Yeah. But I'm the best. Deal?"

Milo scratched at a mosquito bite.

"Deal," he said.

"Let's go, Ralph," she said. "We'll put props in the crops at sun-up tomorrow."

Milo watched her ass move as she strode away. Shaking his head, he grunted, "Myohmyohmy. . . . like a couple of cats fightin' in a gunny sack."

* * *

One reason Evelyn finally took the spraying job was because of Buddy Fooshee. Or, the memory of him, anyway. She knew that the big field—and most of the surrounding land—belonged to Buddy's family and that Milo Henderson had contracted with Mrs. Fooshee

174

to farm the land. She had known Buddy well in high school, and for a couple of years back then had harbored a secret crush on him before she went off to Vassar, and he went off to work on the farm, and before Buddy had answered the call and joined the Army, and she had answered the call and begun ferrying planes for Uncle Sam—before all that.

And before Tim Fletcher had entered her life with his charm and intensity and Rhodes Scholarship and mysterious war work. And before Buddy Fooshee had met Dante Larocca in boot camp. And before he and Dante had wound up in the same outfit and shipped over to Europe together aboard the old troop carrier, General Ulysses S. Grant—a name that Buddy Fooshee had said, laughing, he was sure glad his granddaddy wasn't around to hear him associated with.

And before he and Larocca had pulled strings with the Major and arranged to get into the same fighting tank together—the lead fighting tank—Dante always said. And before the chateau and the Germans and the Panzerfaust rounds came crashing into the turret of that tank, wreaking bloody, mindless havoc. And before Buddy Fooshee returned to God on a perfect, cloudless afternoon in eastern France. And in so doing changed Larocca's life forever.

Before all that, Evelyn had told her best girlfriend that Buddy was the gentlest, dreamiest boy she'd ever known, and that he was so full of talent and repressed ambition, and that he had the most beautiful, long fingers, and that—with his shirt off in the sun—when he began to sketch her in charcoal out by the river he always smiled, and his eyes absolutely gleamed. Gleamed, she'd said. His eyes gleamed.

And how many boys can you say that about?

These things she'd said, and more. But she'd been only 17, and he 18, and he had a girlfriend too, Laney Michaels, and then one day at the river he'd told Evelyn that even if he didn't have this girlfriend he could never really, truly be her boyfriend because she was . . . her family was too much richer than his was—despite all that Fooshee land—but you can't eat land, can you, he'd said, laughing.

That conversation had just about broken Evelyn Curtis' heart, even though she knew she probably wouldn't be allowed to marry a boy like Buddy Fooshee. And the not-allowing itself would lead to fights with her father, with whom she already had plenty of problems.

In the end, though, Evelyn sensed that perhaps Buddy's gentle rejection of her rested on something else. She didn't know for sure, but she thought it might have been because she was a little too . . . too much for him. Too strong, pigheaded . . . something. You could never be sure with Buddy Fooshee, because while he'd never lie to a girl, neither would he come totally clean about his feelings for her. Always holding something back, he harbored a secret response to life that kept him apart from it.

This separation between Buddy and the world around him had troubled Evelyn. She'd tried to penetrate it by frontal assault; that is, by accusing him gently of hiding or of being afraid. He'd smiled and demurred.

"Being careful ain't the same as being afraid, Evelyn," he'd said.

"What is it, then?" she'd asked. "How come I can't ever feel like I truly know the real you?"

He'd turned those pale, radiant eyes on her, the smile slipping from his face like a faint shadow, his fingers making a small gesture.

"Because . . . because I'm isolated," he'd said. "Alone."

"We're all alone, Buddy, except for God."

"God's not involved," he'd said. "It's a matter of degree, Evelyn. In Latin, I'm an isolato. Disconnected. An observer. That's why I paint. I don't know how else to explain it."

Then he'd looked away. And that was the moment Evelyn knew he was beyond her.

* * *

Flying at 100 mph in the dead calm of sun-rise, she drifted the Kaydet down toward the big mean field—500'-400'-300'-200'—the biplane's radial engine beautifully on song. Glancing at the western horizon, she saw wisps of mare's tail clouds and knew it'd be raining by late afternoon. That was all right, though. Long as the DDT had 2-3 hours to set on the crops the weevils were finito.

Down to 100' now, she could smell fall in the air as—at the far end of a thousand-foot cotton furrow—she spotted Ralph Hobson waving his white flag to orient her for her first pass. Bits and pieces of Buddy-memories flashed through her mind as she tightened her flying gloves, checked gauges, tested the bug-spray jets, then eased the nose of her bright-colored plane down a bit more, watching for the power lines. Then it was time to concentrate, and Buddy Fooshee vanished.

Where were those damn lines? There, shimmering in the early sun! Pull up hard! Count to three, over you go, then forward the stick to bring her down and level out, wheels almost brushing the cotton tops—and canted over five degrees to account for the slope.

Damn, this was tricky!

Now, grab the spray controller with her left hand, pull it hard backward. Feel the sprayer shooshing out the juice, sensing that Ralph was already running to his left to avoid being drenched with DDT—and to preposition himself for her next run.

Hold her now . . . on course and true until the last possible second, then . . . haul back on the stick with one gloved hand and shut off the juice with the other, then both hands back on the stick to make sure you clear the tops of those pines . . .

Goddamn, that was close!

Now, hard rudder kick and slam the stick right, count four beats as the engine screamed—its laminated wooden prop clawing for altitude—then sharp opposite rudder and shove the stick all the way left to complete the Williamson turn—an old Navy trick that would bring her back on the reverse course and almost exactly parallel with her first pass. And there was Ralph again waving that flag to catch her attention. Good old undaunted Ralph and his flag. She reminded herself to boost his salary before next spraying season. Didn't want to lose him.

Now, just skimming—grazing, in fact—the pine tops, the sprayer on, she thrust the stick forward, glanced over and saw the bug juice billowing out in an iridescent, drifting cloud. Take her down, down, careful . . . level out now, this second run headed back into the rising sun, her goggles a little fogged, distances harder to judge as she made herself hold her position, left wing down, roaring across the cotton, coming up on a fence, sooner than she'd thought, very close!

Pull back hard now, sprayer off.

Then the Stearman's engine coughed once, just once—maybe water in the fuel—but it was enough to damp the lift from the ailerons and drop her six inches nearer the fence. She felt a bump—she'd hit something—but she was still going up, up . . . 40 degrees north of horizontal, her head forced back against the padded rest.

She leveled out at 500', drew a breath, and checked gauges and controls, trying to see if anything was broken. Temp, fuel, oil, manifold pressure all okay, but the airplane was flying heavy and trying to yaw to port. She leaned out the cockpit and saw wrapped around her left wheel a length of barbed wire 10-15' long.

She'd hit the fence.

Whipping around like an angry, living thing, the wire flailed crazily in the propwash. As she watched, a gust of wind snicked it up against the fuselage where it ripped a six inch gash in the green fabric. Evelyn's lips compressed. She could feel heartbeats in her temple.

"Okay . . . just be calm," she said aloud.

She cut her throttle to reduce airspeed, then made a wide sweeping turn to bring the airplane back over Ralph Hobson so he could take a look from underneath. As she approached him, flying at 100', she could see him madly flapping his arms, then slicing his hand across his throat in their signal to cease operations immediately. She waved acknowledgment and headed for home. This was going to be the longest twenty minutes of her life. What if the wire had wrapped around and jammed the wheel? What would happen if it snagged the prop as she landed? A vision of the Kaydet cartwheeling down the dirt runway in a boiling cascade of fire and smoke flashed through her mind.

Maintaining a low speed—just above stall—the plane labored, losing bits of its skin to the wire snake trapped against the wheel. Keeping one eye on the evil filament below her, she watched as it continued to tear pieces out of the fuselage.

And now the engine had begun to miss. More fuel problems, likely, trash or water in the line. Whatever it was, the Stearman's engine didn't like what it was getting from the fuel pump. When it coughed and missed a couple of beats she'd lose altitude; then it would rev crazily as pent-up fuel surged into the cylinders. Straining to look aft, she saw she was trailing a thin rope of vapor. Water, no question. Maybe a busted head gasket.

The airplane skittered through the sky like an unbroken colt, sometimes dropping a couple of hundred feet when the engine cut out, then lowering a wing and slithering nearly sideways with prop-torque when the fuel line momentarily cleared and the engine RPMs zoomed up. She fought the torque problem with stick and rudder, but the Stearman steadily lost altitude.

Flying the shortest route from Milo Henderson's cotton field to Tuscaloosa's air field would take her directly over the university, then the county courthouse—and then, a few miles outside of town, over Shorty's Cricket Farm and Beagle Ranch. Now down to 300', she could see people on the streets looking up and pointing at her as she cleared the tallest building in town, a nine-story bank that had never seemed so enormous—or threatening—before. To lighten the plane, she considered dumping her load of DDT, but where? In the Black Warrior River it would kill fish by the ton. Over people . . . well, that wasn't an option. She had to land it loaded.

Her concentration was absolute now, her hands wet in the fleece-lined gloves, sweat streaming down inside her goggles. She ripped the goggles off, losing them overboard in the slipstream. She thought this must be what combat pilots had experienced in the war, returning to an airfield or the pitching deck of a carrier after being shot up by flak or enemy planes. Her body was rigid with adrenaline, her focus infinitely narrow: get-the-plane-on-the-ground.

* * *

At the Beagle Ranch, the vets were enjoying a calm Saturday morning. Earlier, the telephone on Shorty's porch had rung. Cleola came to Dante's tent to say he had a call. It was Laney Fooshee wondering what he and David Cohen were doing for Thanksgiving, and if they weren't engaged would they like to come for dinner around six.

"We'll have dove, quail, turkey and chicken," she said, "and all the fixin's."

"Sounds great. What's a 'fixin'?"

She laughed. "You'll have to come out and see for yourself."

"Hey, we'd love to. Cohen was planning to eat bourbon and ice cream. Can we bring something?"

"Oh . . . do you cook?"

"Best ravioli in Alabama," he said.

"Well, whatever that is, bring it. And tell David he's welcome, too."

"Will do. And thanks, kiddo."

When Dante mentioned the invitation he could tell Cohen was delighted, and he himself was surprised at the twinge of jealousy he felt at that delight. On one hand, his proprietary sense of her suffering and beauty made him reluctant to share Laney. On the other, he knew that Cohen liked her—he'd spoken of her often since the night at Kilroy's—and, finally, Dante didn't trust himself around her. Her. . . he didn't know what to call it, her seeming innocence, or naturalness was so soothing, so accommodating, so unlike the hard-edged New York girls he'd grown up with. Plus, they shared the sacred warrant of Buddy in ways that Dante hadn't been able to fathom but that he experienced as a strong attraction.

To divert himself, he got busy.

"Hey, Cohen, Sir Plus needs a bath. You game?"

Cohen was game and thirty minutes later he and Dante finished giving Sir Plus a three-handed scrub. The great gray dripping dog was now tearing around them in a mad, barking circle at roughly the same speed that Evelyn was flying—60 mph. Nearby, Karl and Ben rocketed a baseball back and forth at a much higher velocity. The brutal smack of the ball into their mitts testified to the pain each was experiencing, but neither would admit.

"Marines," Dante whispered to Cohen. "One more crazy bunch of fuckers."

Smack!

"Yeah, we called 'em 'Bullet Catchers' in the Pacific. Gotta love 'em, though," said Cohen. "Highest threshold of pain in the known universe."

Smack!

"Threshold of . . . what the hell's that mean?"

Smack!

"Means they can stand more of it than you or me. I read about it. I'm putting it in my novel—a Marine with a hard-on for death, you know."

Smack!

"Hey, hard-ons I understand, but . . ."

Suddenly, Sir Plus stopped running and looked straight up in massive concentration. Dante noticed.

"See that?" he said, "Weirdest thing about that damned dog is how he sees stuff and fixes on it—like a rangefinder on a tank gun."

Smack!

"For example?"

"Like birds and squirrels. I mean, I've seen him freeze and stare up at a buzzard gliding around for, like, a friggin' hour, and . . . ."

Smack!

Suddenly the men heard what the dog heard.

It sounded like the town drunk had gotten his hands on a complex piece of machinery and was ripping it to shreds. The noise was that of an engine, but an engine in extremis, rising and falling, cutting out, sputtering, surging, back-firing. The veterans—and the dog—all watched. What they saw was scary: a pretty little green and gold Stearman bi-plane streaming out clouds of white vapor and seeming simultaneously to be losing its skin and trying to fly upside down.

Dante recognized it instantly.

"Come on!" he shouted at Cohen. "Karl! Ben! Grab Sir Plus. . . ."

He ran to the jeep, cranked it, roared backward in a swirl of dust, and motioned for Cohen to get in.

Dante pointed at the dog: "Sir Plus! Stay!"

David jumped in, Dante popped the clutch and they were gone.

Sir Plus stood his ground, whining. The heavily tattooed Ben hurried to him, muttering his name.

"Easy, Sir Plus, he'll be back . . . easy, boy. . . ." The big Marine gently slipped his hands up the Weimaraner's flanks, persuading him to stick around. Still, Sir Plus never for one second took his eyes off the dissipating dust cloud raised by Larocca's jeep.

On the highway, Cohen shouted over the road noise. "Where the hell are we . . . Who's that in the plane?"

"Evelyn."

"Evelyn? That gorgeous dame at the dance? At Kilroy's?"

"Right."

"Oh, brother! She's in a world of trouble."

"Yeah."

Dante had the jeep red-lined in top gear.

Cohen leaned over and hollered. "Well, let's try and not kill ourselves on the way, okay?"

"Yeah."

They could see the plane descending crab-wise toward the air field, its engine complaining bitterly. In the Stearman, Evelyn knew she was almost home. She relaxed fractionally, breathing deeply, and complimenting herself on handling a tough situation well, even offering a little "Attagirl!" to her plane.

Then, as she settled in on her final approach to the single landing strip, she saw a silver Cessna monoplane taking off directly at her, its spinning wheels just leaving the ground. With the sun at her back, she knew the other guy would never see her in the brilliant haze.

Shit!

There was nothing for it but to break off and go around. She did, just managing to lift the plane's nose enough to clear the wind sock fluttering atop her hangar. The Cessna roared past not 60' away, the pilot shaking his fist at her all the while.

Dante slid the jeep to a stop near the hangars. They'd seen Evelyn's near-collision with the Cessna, and he wanted to figure out her plan so he could pick up the pieces when she crashed. They watched her laboring to circle the field.

"She's going around," shouted Cohen.

"Roger that!"

Dante jammed the jeep into first and dug out for the western side of the airfield where Evelyn had made her turn and was struggling to reach the extreme end of the runway.

Now, the jeep and the plane were headed directly at each other. Dante steered off into the grass to give her maximum room, and as she approached, power-slid the jeep around and roared back east, parallel to her glide path. Suddenly, he spotted the barbed wire dangling from the left wheel, and a mad thought occurred to him.

"I'm going closer. Grab the wire!" he screamed at Cohen.

"Are you nuts? I'm not. . . ."

"Grab it!"

Then they saw Evelyn shake her head and wave them away.

"Ease off, Brooklyn. Ease off. . ." Cohen said.

Screaming along parallel to the descending plane, Dante maneuvered the jeep to the strip's margin. Without warning, her engine backfired and quit, bouncing the plane down hard onto its landing gear, and crumpling the left strut where the barbed wire had locked up that wheel.

What saved Evelyn's life was the laminated wooden prop. It disintegrated on impact with the ground, flinging dirt, engine coolant, motor oil, DDT, and razor-like shards of wood everywhere—including into Cohen's right cheek.

When she felt the engine shut down, Evelyn cut the ignition, huddled down in the cockpit and held on. Its wheel strut gone—and minus its prop—the Kaydet plowed down the dirt strip canted over to port, its fuselage and left wing-tip spewing up clouds of dust, grass, blue smoke and dead crickets. Finally dying, it spun lazily around 180 degrees, coming to a stop facing back toward the west, its exhaust manifolds red hot and crackling.

In the jeep, Dante and Cohen stopped 20' away.

Evelyn raised her head, looked around, and saw them.

"What the hell," she asked, "did you expect me to do, land on the jeep?"

"He wanted me to grab the wire," Cohen said.

"Grab the wire," she said.

"Yeah, well," Dante said, "I saw Buster Keaton do it in a movie once."

"Buster Keaton."

"Yeah. Worked poifect. You all right?"

Evelyn nodded and smiled.

"Poifect," she said. "And thanks."

Dante looked at Cohen.

"Your cheek is bleeding."

"Yeah, that tends to happen when I get stabbed by flying propeller shards."

"Uh, fellas," said Evelyn, "hate to interrupt, but could somebody give me a hand here?"

Chapter 11

Despite the carnage suffered by the Stearman, it remained salvageable, and Evelyn—though bruised and shaken—was not seriously hurt. Larocca and Cohen retrieved a steel cable from her hangar, hooked the jeep to the biplane, and dragged it off the runway, just as the silver Cessna made a three-point landing in its wake. When the Cessna taxied by, its pilot and passenger stared in disbelief at the wreck, and about that time Ralph Hobson's pickup roared into view.

"What happened?" he asked, running up to the threesome as they disengaged the jeep.

"Bad fuel, I expect," she said. "Felt like water or trash in the line. Ralph, do you know Dante and David. . . ."

"Hiya. . . . Boy, I've got to work out a better fuel filter," Hobson said, dejected. "I'm real sorry, Miss Evelyn. I just feel awful."

· "Don't worry about it, fella. Take a look at her and let's get back in the air when we can. There's a spare prop in the hanger."

"Yes, ma'am, okay."

"Anyway, dusting season's about over, and Milo Henderson can find himself another pilot for that damn cotton field."

Dante perked up. "Milo? You were working Henderson's property?"

"Well, actually, it belongs to a widow lady named Fooshee. He contracts . . ." She stopped when she saw his face. "What is it?"

Dante shook his head, speaking softly. "Small world. I . . . was with her son . . . Buddy, in the war."

She heard it in his voice and knew not to ask more right now, though she was dying to probe. She wanted to know how Buddy had died, how he'd lived, how he'd befriended this crazy Yankee. She looked at

Dante. Dante looked away. She turned to Cohen.

"David, that cut on your cheek needs cleaning. It could have DDT in it, not to mention oil, fuel, dirt. . . ."

"Cricket crap."

"That too."

"Maybe it'll save me having to shave," he said, glancing down at the trail of blood on his shirt front.

Dante assumed command. "Look, I'll take Cohen back to Shorty's. Evelyn, you follow us. You can do the nursing. Blood scares me."

She hesitated. "Shorty Puckett's Beagle Ranch?"

"And Cricket Farm," said Cohen.

"Yes, all right," she said, "I'll meet you in a few minutes. David, when you get there, irrigate your cheek—with cold water, not beer."

"Beer. Now there's a thought," said Dante, grinning. "Hey, it's almost ten o'clock. Karl and Ben will be miles ahead of us."

In the jeep, on the way to Shorty's, Cohen looked at Larocca, the blood on his cheek congealed now to a dirty reddish black streak.

"She's got your number, pal."

"No dame's got my number, Cohen. . . ."

"Riiiight."

"Except maybe my wife. The bitch."

This was news.

"I didn't know you were married."

"Neither did she. It was a long war."

"She back in New York?"

"Yep, back home and pregnant."

They exchanged a look.

"Not my work, pal," said Dante.

"Women."

Lost in France

Dearest Maria,

How are you baby? Got your last letter, and it was great. I only read it about 500 times. The guys in the outfit were realy ribing me about it. Speaking of which, I've palled up with this old Alabama boy I told you about before, Buddy Fooshee.

He's a real character and about the fightinest son of a bitch you ever met. In the tank we all learn each others jobs and Buddy is the best, and he loves that 50 caliber like it was a woman. It's funny too because when he's not in combat hes calm and quite and is always drawing or sketching. But when the Krauts come out to play he turns into a gangster or somthing. Funny guy. Johhny Reb, we call him. I like him alot.

Anyway, the Captain just ran over and told us to mount up, so gotta go. Be sweet and keep your knees together. Just kiding. I know you are. I miss you so much at night somtimes that, well, you know what I'm saying.

Write more often. Please.

all my love

dante

* * *

Sitting in the grass by the swimming hole at Shorty's Beagle Ranch and Cricket Farm, Evelyn was treated like an honored guest. Ben and Karl, Reddy Freddy and his wife, Chief Davis, and Shorty sat nearby, all remembering her from Kilroy's. They were riveted by Dante and Cohen's hair-raising rendition of her one-wheel crash landing.

189

". . . and then," said Dante, "the damn thing spun around 180 degrees, slinging oil and propeller parts all over the place . . . look at Cohen's face. . . and this dame, she just waits in the cockpit for the dust to settle, then leans out and hollers at us for trying to save her."

"Tell 'em about Buster Keaton," she said.

"Buster Keaton?" said Chief Davis.

Embarrassed, Dante gestured the question away.

"No, come on, hero, tell 'em."

"Well," he said, "once in a movie I saw Keaton climb up on a low-flying plane from a car, and I thought we could. . . ."

"He thought I could. . . ." said Cohen.

The vets laughed at Dante, who blushed but joined the mirth. He pointed at Evelyn as if to say, 'I'll get you for that.'

"Anyway, he's embellishing the whole thing," she said.

Wanting the spotlight moved off her, she turned to Shorty.

"Mr. Puckett, I was so sorry to hear about Vernon at Pearl Harbor."

"Yeah, thanks, Evelyn. It's been pretty tough—especially on his mama."

"I'm sure. . . ."

"You know," said Shorty, "Vernon's still down there in the Arizona. . . . His body is, anyway."

No one looked at anyone.

"I 'spect they'll get him out before long, and we can give him a proper burial," said Shorty.

Shorty's wife, Cleola, joined the group carrying a tray of iced tea and cookies. The men jumped up to help her, glad for the distraction.

Cohen was trying to make the connection.

"You knew these folks' son, then?" he said to Evelyn.

"Sure," she said, "I boarded a couple of saddle horses out here in high school—remember, Mrs. Puckett? And it was Vernon, really, who taught me to ride."

"Oh, yes, dear, I remember your mama bringing you out here when you was just a little bit of a thing."

"And Vernon was magic with horses, wasn't he?"

Cleola's eyes shone with the memory.

"Lord, yes, child," she said. "That boy could talk to 'em like they was people. Always carried little sugar cubes in his shirt pocket, you know, and the horses would just follow him around like a pack of old hound dogs."

The vets chuckled and nodded.

"Boarding them horses," said Shorty, "and giving riding lessons was how he made his spending money back then. He was always writin' us from the Navy saying how he was gonna come back and get into it again, wadn't he, Hon?"

"Yes, that's what he'd say," said Cleola.

"But I think he was hooked on ol' Uncle Sam," said Shorty. "He sure loved them boats."

"Ships, Herman. Vernon always said to call 'em ships."

"Ships, then."

"What about it, Cohen?" said Dante, "You're the expert. Ships or boats?"

Cohen smiled. "Subs are 'boats.' Ships are 'ships.' And it's mighty easy to fall in love with one."

"Guess that's why they call them 'she,'" said Evelyn.

And so, sitting out here on the grass, next to the waterfall, the vets sampled an old woman's iced tea and cookies while chewing the rag about Vernon Puckett and horses and ships and war and college and their shared, vanished past. Out here in the quiet of a rural Alabama

191

fall, where mockingbirds sang from tree tops, and hawks sailed by overhead, out here two generations talked and remembered. Parents who had lost a beloved son to a Sunday morning of butchery in a far-away island paradise spoke to these grown children who had joined up to fight back—and who had somehow survived the four years of slaughter and terror that followed. All these folks connected to one another across barriers of age and class and education and experience, joining hands over the consecrated memory of the dead and wounded.

Out here, no one looked askance at David Cohen's missing hand and dark moods, or at Dante Larocca's shrapnel-torn body and clamorous nightmares, or at the former Army medic, Reddy Freddy's endlessly repeated memory of powdering sulfa drugs into the sucking chest wounds of dying soldiers, or at Karl and Ben's mental and physical scars that would haunt them until their last day on earth. Out here, Evelyn Curtis was accepted as one of the guys, a helluva pilot, a game dame—a volunteer.

Out here, the old and the young, the lame, the halt, and the fit sat and laughed together. Young men—and a woman—who had signed on the dotted line and had taken their chances; these parlayed with an older couple who had watched their son march off to follow the flag. He had followed it to the bottom of Pearl Harbor, and now his parents—with no corporeal remains to bury in that flag—moved through life awash in memory and grief.

Sitting across the group from Evelyn—and with Sir Plus's head in his lap—Dante copped a glimpse at her. Although she usually looked a person directly in the eye when she spoke, she also had a way of turning her head and glancing down in a sort of shy gesture that Dante found devastating. These odd combinations in her—polarities of beauty and strength, self-assurance and modesty, fire and ice—kept him off-balance. He could never tell in advance how she would respond to a particular comment or anecdote.

Then she locked those strange radar eyes on him.

"So, Dante, how's God's gift to modern architecture doing? You and Sir Sidney Greene best friends now?"

Dante extended his palm. "Got Old Greeney right there. Guy loves me," he lied. "I even passed a test last week."

"Well, there's a first time for everything," she said.

"Hey, show a little respect."

David Cohen watched the two of them interact.

"Evelyn," he said, pointing, "have you seen inside Dante's sanctum sanctorum? His artist's atelier—better known as a U.S. Army tent?"

She looked around.

"That's where you're living?" she asked.

"Summer home," he said.

"And when it gets cold?"

"Cold? Cohen! You lying dog! You said it never got cold in Alabama."

"Only in December, January, February, and March," Cohen said.

"Ah, well," Dante said. "Maybe I'll go underground. Dirt makes great insulation, you know."

"Well, Alabama's mostly dirt," she said. "Does it work?"

"Oh, definitely. Got a better thermal coefficient than wood, for sure. Fact, I once designed a rammed earth house that I calculated would make it through a New York winter with only a little oil burner for heat."

"I don't believe it," she said.

"Show her, Brooklyn," Karl said.

Dante Grouchoed his eyebrows at her and spoke out of the corner of his mouth. "Say, babe, wanna come up and see my etchings?"

"Of a dirt house?"

"Sure, come on. I've already bored these bums to death with it."

He stood, put out his hand, and when she grasped it, pulled her up in one quick movement.

The little impromptu party was breaking up now, with many thanks to the Pucketts for tea and cookies. The Marines went back to their beer and baseball as Cleola told Evelyn she was welcome to come for dinner one night soon, and that she had some pictures of Vernon she'd like to show her, and Evelyn said she would and that she herself had pictures of Vernon giving her riding lessons and that she would bring them, and Cleola said she'd like that.

The two women hugged. The men looked off.

* * *

With Dante leaning against the ridge pole and Sir Plus watching her, unblinking, Evelyn marveled at how clean and comfortable the inside of an Army tent could be—especially one set on a raised wooden floor. Since moving in, Dante had rigged up several shaded lights and bought a small fridge for $10. A tall stool and his drawing easel dominated one corner. Shorty had also loaned him a chest of drawers, small table and a couple of scuffed chairs that had belonged to Vernon. Dante's cot, crisp and clean, would have passed a white gloves inspection, and Sir Plus's padded bed lay at its foot. A phonograph, radio, and textbooks occupied a clever wooden rack he'd built himself, and along the walls of the tent he'd pinned several of his architectural renderings.

"That's the rammed earth house," he said, pointing to the drawing of an odd semi-buried structure. "Walls packed with dirt two feet thick. Warm as toast."

"Hmmm, got a telephone out here?"

"On Shorty's front porch. Nickel a shot."

"Running water?"

"Head's in the shed, and room service is dead slow."

"In the barn?"

"Yep, showers, sink, johns, all that. Shorty converted it from where the rich. . . where your horses used to board."

"Convenient."

They stood side by side, she looking around, struck by how efficiently he'd wedged so much stuff into such a small space.

"Impressive. You'll make somebody a good wife," she said and saw a cloud flit across his face. "Just kidding. Jesus. It's really quite comfortable."

"Okay for a wop vet, eh? Want a drink? Me and the bootleggers are real tight."

"I'll ignore the first part of that, but yes to the drink. Thanks." She looked around. "Only potential problem I see is security, somebody sneaking in and taking something."

"Yeah, my books and stuff, but I've got this." He took a step, reached under his pillow and withdrew the German Luger pistol, holding it with the barrel pointed up.

"Impressive. But, hey, nobody in Alabama ever stole a book—unless it had dirty pictures in it."

"Roger that."

While he busied himself with the bottle and glasses, she ran out to raise the top on her convertible and to phone her mother in case someone had seen her fly over town at tree-top height with a faltering engine. When she returned he had laid out both his glasses, both spoons, a bottle of scotch, and some peanut butter fudge that David Cohen had whipped up the night before.

"Brunch," he said. "Dig in. Or, jeez, I guess you don't 'dig in' to brunch, do you."

"Boy, have you got a chip. And, say, don't you owe me an apology, anyway?"

Dante squinched his eyes. "For . . ."

"For Kilroy's."

"Ahh, Kilroy's. Did I step on your foot when we were dancing?"

"No, Larocca, I'm talking about the fight. The scuffle. Battle. Fracas. With the zoomies. Don't you recall? Or did the brass knuckles erase your memory?"

"Is that what I got hit with? No wonder. . . . Nahhh, I remember. Okay, I apologize. You satisfied? But I was right, you know. You could outfly any of those airdale scrubs."

"Maybe. Maybe not. But I prefer to speak for myself."

"Fair enough. You ain't shy."

He poured two fingers of scotch for each of them and slid the plate of fudge toward her.

"Thanks," she said. "I was hungry and didn't know it."

He watched her long fingers take a sweet and raise it to her mouth. Their eyes met. Her hand stopped.

"What?"

"Nothing. It ain't poison."

"Yes, but what are you looking at?"

He smiled. "The fudge."

She laughed, and they talked. For two hours they talked. Mostly, though, she held the floor—still jazzed from her crash.

She asked him about Buddy Fooshee—without telling him why she cared. He evaded the question and said it was a long story that had ended badly—for Buddy.

Instead, he questioned her about her past, and if he'd known her better, he'd have known that her loquacity this afternoon was unusual, that she seldom went on about herself, that it was his attention, his gentle inquiry into her past that eased the restraints and freed her to talk. In short, he listened, something she found very few men did.

She told him about flying for the Women's Air Force Service Pilots during the war, about how she volunteered in '42 and became one of the 28 so-called "Originals," women with at least 500 hours in the air (she'd had 1100) who ferried planes from factories in the Northeast and West to Army Air Forces training bases all over the country.

At his urging, she recounted tales of jockeying the hottest airplanes the Army had: the P-38 Lightning ("a demanding, but lovely bus"), P-39 Bell Airacobras ("hated those damn things"), P-40s ("okay, but couldn't hold a candle to the P-47 Thunderbolt, a big handful of killing machine"), and, above all, the glorious, responsive P-51 Mustang ("just about the finest airplane anybody ever put in the air").

"You know," he said, "when you talk about flying, you do what the zoomies do, hands all over the place." He gestured with both arms.

She laughed. "Yeah, pilots are bad to do that."

Sitting on his cot and listening to her, Dante heard thunder overhead, followed by the first patter of rain on the tent. He put out a hand and stroked Sir Plus's head to calm him.

"How'd the men pilots, you know, how'd they take it when your plane pulled up and a woman popped out?"

She laughed. "About like you did at the airport."

"Yeah, but did you try to kill 'em all?"

"Truth is, a lot of the men resented us," she said, "and at first it really bothered me. But in the end we ignored them: just picked up our orders, smiled politely and flew the wings off those beauties."

"By yourself?"

"By yourself. With other pilots. Whatever they wanted. Cross country, through rain and snow and sandstorms, over mountains, right down on the deck, a lot of times with no friggin' radio, following highways and twisty rivers from city to city. Je-sus, but I loved it!"

She leaned forward, her body complicit with her voice in making him understand her past, heedless of the many distances between them, anxious that, as a fellow veteran, he witness what she'd done and how she felt about it, the pride, the daily proximity of death, the defying of insulting female stereotypes, the existential rush dispensed to those few who dare.

"The women proved we could do it, Dante, and after a while we said, well, if the men resent us, then screw 'em, you know? Hell, we were helping the war effort, releasing male pilots to fly combat, taking chances, living right on the edge. Boy, we were drunk on it. . . ." She drifted off.

He stared at her, then down.

"Yeah, you guys did good," he said softly. "Damn good."

She glanced up at the tent roof as the rain ballooned into a drumbeat. Then she looked at him.

"You know," she said, "it was the proudest feeling I ever had, flying those planes for the Army. We didn't try to be hotshots, like the men; we didn't booze up before a flight. With us, it was always 'eight hours from bottle to throttle.' And some of us died. . . ." Despite her best efforts, her voice cracked. "I. . . Dante, I don't expect to ever feel that. . . needed, that . . . absolutely vital again as long as I live. I'm only 25, but for me it's kind of already over, in a way. . . sheee."

The shaded bulb illuminated her lovely face, etching it with light and shadow, accentuating a melancholy, revealing the scar on her cheek.

"Sorry," she said.

"No. . . hey, it's okay." He reached and touched her hand. Her fingers opened, then closed gently on his, threading them together. Their other hands came forward and joined the grip, like teammates praying together before a big match, holding on for a moment, capturing a fleeting spirit. Then she withdrew her hands, leaned back and rearranged the hair that had fallen over her eyes.

"Sorry," she said, again. "Not like me."

"Maybe it should be."

He wanted her to go on, to know how proud he was of her, how much he admired what she and the other women had done.

"How'd you get hold of the Mustang you assaulted me with?"

She laughed, pulled a handkerchief out of her flying pants and wiped her eyes.

"She was what we called a 'war-weary.' A plane that had been shot up over Germany. Flown by these incredible Negro pilots trained down in Tuskegee. Fantastic squadron. Never lost a bomber they were escorting over Europe. Anyway, my Mustang had been surveyed—written off—by the Army, but I heard about it and took a train up to Long Island to check it out."

"You musta liked what you saw."

"Ohh, fell in love with her the minute I walked into the hangar," she smiled, "despite the flak damage, the bullet holes in the wings and the flat tires."

With the war winding down, she'd bought it at auction from Uncle Sam for $3,500 and had it trucked to a refurbishing yard in Virginia, where, for another $5,500 or so she wound up with a perfectly good example of the hottest fighter plane in the American arsenal—minus its 50 cal. machine guns.

"I guess your old man shelled out big bucks for all that," he said.

She leaned back and selected a piece of fudge. "No, Daddy and I don't see eye to eye on flying. I saved some from crop dusting, and my mother loaned me some. . . and I have a sort of small trust fund. . . ."

"Yeah, nothing like a little trust fund to get you over the humps, I hear."

But he said it with a smile while pouring her more scotch.

"Nice paint job on the Mustang, anyway," he looked at her. "You ever, uh, crash?"

"Not counting today, once. . . ." Then, her face darkened. "Well, twice really, but only once with the Army. I was trying to ferry a clapped-out P-38 Lightning from Santa Monica down to Louisiana, but the hydraulics went kaput right on take off."

"And . . ."

Her eyes lit up. "Well, I couldn't get the damned gear down. Tried everything. Santa Monica tower told me to come around low and slow and let 'em look at the undercarriage." Her hands were at work again. "So, I racked it around and nearly creamed the tower. Rowwwrrrr! After they ducked, they reported I was pouring out oil."

"You couldn't bail out?"

"Yeah, sure, I had a 'chute, but the P-38 is a bitch to bail out of because it has those twin vertical stabilizers, and a lot of pilots got, you know, decapitated when they tried it during the war."

"So?"

"So, I retracted the other wheels, flew out over the ocean, and dumped fuel while they cleared a runway. Then I came back and did a kind of wheels-up controlled crash. Totally greased the landing. Very exciting, actually."

Dante drew his finger across her chin and cheek. "So, is that where you got that? If you don't mind my asking."

She looked off.

"I do mind, actually."

"Sorry, forget it."

"That'd be nice."

He could see he'd overstepped.

"So, was that Santa Monica. . . problem the worst thing that happened to you?"

"No, the worst thing was accompanying the body of one of my best friends on the train all the way across the country for burial."

With the rain pounding outside, he watched, letting her decide whether to go on.

"Nancy Fleming," she said, talking to the air. "Best pilot I ever flew with. Absolutely fearless. Which is what killed her. The week after my lucky trick in Santa Monica, she tried the same thing up in Seattle with a brand new Thunderbolt that had come out of the factory with its electrics fouled up. She knew. . . we had laughed about my P-38 story, and I think. . . I know she was determined to pull off the same caper."

"Not your fault, though."

"No, but listen to this." She leaned closer. "When Nancy reported the problem—smoke in the cockpit, gauges all kaflooey—the tower told her to bail out, and she refused, told 'em, 'If Curtis can do it, I can. Hold the fort, boys!'" She paused. "That's what she said to the tower: 'Hold the fort, I'm coming in.'"

"Didn't work?"

"She caught a power cable. Went in nose first at 120 mph. Airplane burned."

Dante grimaced.

She shook her head. "Nancy Fleming. One fine pilot."

He could think of nothing to say. Then Buddy Fooshee's fiery, bloody death raced through his mind with a vicious snap.

"More booze?" he said.

She checked her wristwatch.

"Cripes, look at the time. I've bored you blind. And you've hardly told me anything about your war. Patton. Tanks. France. Damn! I want to hear all of it, but . . ."

"Another day."

"Yeah."

They looked at each other, both knowing that in their friendship some Rubicon had been crossed, though neither understood what lay on the other side.

"You're some dame," he said. "A real handful."

"My life's story," she said. "It has its liabilities."

They stood and shook hands, a gesture of equals, a confirmation of the intimacy their long conversation had bred. In her grip he felt the strength and self-confidence that both impressed and unnerved him.

"So," he said, "what's next for you, then? Gettin' married, havin' kids, settlin' down to, you know, domestic bliss and diapers?"

She laughed and looked out the tent flap at the rain.

"Nope. Well, not yet. No, I'm gonna become the first woman to fly commercially for a major airline."

He arched his eyebrows.

"Hundred bucks says I do it."

"You're on."

Another handshake.

She smiled. "Don't bother to walk me to my car. It's a little mooshy out there. See ya', Dante . . . and remember, you owe me the full story of 'How Brooklyn Won the War.'"

"Sure. . . . Maybe."

She picked up her flying kit, reached down and tickled Sir Plus behind his ears, made a kissing sound at him, and left. A minute later, the little maroon convertible cranked up, and she was gone.

Dante stood in the tent watching her tail lights disappearing through the rain.

"Sir Plus," he said, "we're in a world of trouble, pal."

* * *

Maria Larocca's letter arrived at Dante's tent on that cold, dreary Christmas Eve. Her handwriting was clear and precise, her spelling better than his. Turned out she'd had a miscarriage around Thanksgiving. She'd thrown Bruno Kretschmer out on his ass. She begged her husband's forgiveness:

". . . I still love you, Dante, and I always have, even when I was being bad while you were overseas. You have every right to want me dead, because there's no excuses, I know. I'm not trying to offer any, but during the war I was missing you so much and it looked like it was going to go on forever, and you might not come back, and I was so afraid and so lonely.

Bruno's a creep. You were sure right about him. But a long time after you shipped out he started coming by, and he paid attention to me, and helped Mama when Poppa died, and took me for ice cream and stuff, and I don't know what to say except

I'm so sorry, and I apologize, and if you could stand to have me back, maybe we could work something out. I've always loved you, and I still love you, and I miss you like crazy.

Much love from your wife,
Maria

P.S. I got your address from Vinny Moroni. Don't be mad at him. He told me you was really messed up about Bruno and all. Like I said, I'm so sorry about all that.

With Sir Plus curled in a tight ball next to him and with temps in the mid-30s, Dante sat on his cot wrapped in four layers of foul-weather gear, handling his wife's letter with leather flying gloves. Overhead in the tent, two strings of colored Christmas lights festooned from corner to corner, meeting at the ridge pole. Near him a little coal-fired stove radiated what heat it could manage, but Dante could still see his breath vaporing into the cold.

From the dinky wooden radio he'd bought for five bucks, the announcer said, "And here, folks, is that great crooner, Bing Crosby, singing the new holiday song that everyone is so crazy about." And then Crosby's mellow tenor filled the tent:

"I'm dreamin' of a white Christmas. . . ."

Dante set the letter on the cot next to him, stared at the flames dancing in the judas-hole of the stove, and scratched at the whiskers he hadn't shaved in days. Maria's deft combination of apology, evasion, and remorse ripped him like a blunt Ka-bar knife, opening half-healed wounds, reminding him of both her beauty and her treachery. For the past four months he had struggled to shut down his memory functions and live in the moment: burying himself in schoolwork and his half-baked architectural project for the Dalton fellowship, indulging in the occasional bout of industrial-strength hell-raising with his pals at the veterans' club, and day-dreaming about Evelyn Curtis and Laney Fooshee.

The war and Maria—the two things he'd fought hardest to suppress —he'd more or less avoided, at least while he was awake and working. The dark hours were a different story. More than once over the past weeks David Cohen had crept into Dante's tent after midnight and gently called to him from a few feet away, telling him to wake up, that he was having a nightmare.

Cohen's first attempt at such rescue work had been a near-disaster. He'd reached down and touched his friend to shake him awake, and Dante had roared up off his cot with a demon's fury, knocking Cohen to the floor and splintering a mirror.

Now, in the wet-cold of an Alabama December, Dante stared at the fire and doubted if he were going to make it. He just couldn't see past the obstacles. Professor Greene hated his Dalton Fellowship proposal. Plus, his vet buddy, Reddy Freddy, the ex-medic who'd wanted to become a doctor, had already beaten up his pregnant wife, pulled a knife on a classmate, flunked out of school, and driven away, hauling his few worldly possessions and rusty trailer to God only knew where.

The crazed Marines, Karl and Ben, were hanging in there—although their majoring in Phys Ed, and fistfights, and fucking had lowered the academic bar somewhat. Chief Davis was surviving in civil engineering, but he studied ten hours a day to make barely passing grades. For some vets, transitioning into civilian life was proving to be tougher than winning the war.

As for David Cohen, Dante worried about his handsome friend. The guy's moods seemed to whip through enormous arcs depending on variables Dante couldn't assess. One day the aspiring writer would pop into the tent juggling a pint of bourbon, two glasses, and a sheaf of typescript, cackling over some genius scene he'd just completed and insisting on reading it aloud to Dante. The next day he couldn't be roused from black slumber, and more than once Dante had jimmied the door in Cohen's trailer to check on him, only to find him lying in bed awake, surrounded by overflowing ash trays and pages of ripped-up novel.

Was the book going well or going to hell? Who knew? Were the searing pains from his phantom hand driving him mad? A good possibility. Or, was it the regular night-visits by his former shipmates, those screaming, terrified sailors from his fated destroyer—the kamikazied U.S.S. Little?

"General Quarters! General Quarters! All Hands Man Your Battle Stations! The Smoking Lamp is Out Throughout the Ship! Bogies Inbound! I say again, Bogies Inbound!"

Kamikazes. A dawn raid by the Divine Wind.

Aboard the Little, exhausted sailors fly to their assigned positions at 5" guns, radar scopes, ship's boilers, and radio transmitters. Leaping through hatches, men slip and fall and are trampled by those running behind them. Below-decks, emergency diesels are lit off and ammo is run up to the gun mounts. Topside, the air-search radar silently interrogates the sky. On deck, with frantic intensity, lookouts scan every inch of horizon, seeking deadly blips streaking toward them out of a brilliant sunrise.

Fear is as common as sweat.

On the bridge, Captain Walcot's blood-shot eyes vibrate as he jams on his helmet and shouts orders bringing the ship up to flank speed.

Although a 1924 Annapolis graduate, Walcot is hopeless as a destroyer skipper: a punctilious, overweight martinet whom the men hate and the officers contemn. Drunk and loud in port, in battle cowardly and slow, Walcot presents a liability that Lt. Cohen must negate.

Standing behind Walcot, Cohen steadies the men on watch, acknowledging with a quiet "Very well," or "Make it so," each battle station report as it flows in from around the ship. He has already discovered about himself that he is good in a crisis, that when battle-borne trauma flares, his brain shifts into a secondary mode that allows him to see a path through the mayhem and to make decisions without panic. This revelation secretly pleases him. He had never thought of himself as a warrior, but war makes its own acolytes.

The incoming kamikazes are plainly visible now, five of them, swarming high above the Little like horse-flies at a fish fry, their engines shrieking, the tropical sun glinting off their canopies, the blood-red rising sun meatballs visible on their wings and fuselage.

Far below, and despite attaining a speed of 25 knots, the ship seems like a pigeon at a convention of raptors. Frightened young officers shout orders to gunners, and the 40-millimeters open up at too-great a range, their tracer rounds arcing into the morning sky, but always leading or trailing the attacking planes.

Captain Walcot has released the main batteries to fire at will on the incoming Zeros. As a Nip pilot rolls over to begin his dive on the ship, one of Little's 5" rounds, triggered by a proximity fuse, explodes in his face at 1000 feet, disintegrating the airplane in a roiling ball of fuel, metal and human tissue. Cheers and vile racial curses pound through the ship, and Cohen experiences a brief epiphany: the hatred! the hatred! What have we come to?

Now the Jap airplanes are everywhere, jitterbugging across the sky in a rhapsody of menace, toying with the Little's crew, side-slipping down to the water, skimming the waves, always on the attack. But the ship's gunners are damned good. Stripped and breathless in their boiling, impossibly loud mounts, they splash another Zero and damage a third. On the bridge, Captain Walcot seems frozen at his station, face red, eyes wide, mouth agape. The ship is effectively being fought by her Executive Officer. And crew.

Running out to the starboard wing of the bridge, Cohen spots an enemy Zero streaking in from astern, not 20 feet above the water. He also sees a fat gray bomb with a red-painted nose snugged up to the fuselage right beneath the pilot. He grabs a telephone and shouts warnings to the fire control officer, though something tells him that this is it, this one will get them. A moment later, with a dazzling roar, it does.

The kamikaze has struck Little squarely on the aft 5" gun mount, blowing it overboard and killing all six men inside, before flushing flaming debris down into the powder magazine and ammo handling rooms, incinerating another 10 there. It has also demolished the ship's steering gear, jamming the rudder over hard to port. Finally, it has sliced open the destroyer's hull like a fine steak knife. Now, taking on water and listing to starboard, the ship can only steam to the left in a haphazard, smoking spiral. Cohen feels Little shudder as though she has been struck by the hand of God. .

DIVINE WIND, indeed.

In his brutal mood swings, David Cohen sometimes visited lower depths to which even Dante's terrible tank experiences did not reduce him. Perhaps Dante's will was stronger, his imagination less rich, his superego differently developed. Or, maybe Dante's regular oiling and dry-firing of his 9-millimeter German Luger pistol was a warning signal to himself from his own private hell, an omen saying that he must exercise maximal vigilance to keep at bay the memory of Maria's betrayal, of Buddy's death, of the shocking firepower of Hitler's Wehrmacht, and of weeks spent in an Army hospital.

Meanwhile, in addition to his problems with Sidney Greene, Dante's own academic record—despite what he'd said to Evelyn—was, frankly, not great. His highest grade was a 'B-' in English comp. Also, Laney Fooshee and Cohen—on his good days—were hitting it off pretty well without any help from him. Evelyn Curtis was probably Christmas-partying about now with her boyfriend, Tim Fletcher, and other fellow caste members. As for the remaining vets living out at Shorty's, most had shoved off for the holidays.

And now, Maria.

He reached down and stroked Sir Plus behind the ears. The dog raised his head, saffron eyes searching the man's face. He sniffed Dante's hand, then, shifting his body a bit, eased his head down on the ex-GIs booted foot, nose to the stove.

On the radio, Crosby continued romancing the season.

Outside, it began to sleet.

PART II

January - June, 1946

Chapter 12

Despite a couple of logs burning low in the fireplace, Tim Fletcher's living room was freezing on a blustery Saturday afternoon. Earlier, he and Evelyn had dragged a mattress in from the bedroom, heaped it with blankets, poured themselves glasses of bourbon, stripped off their clothes, and made a nest. Evelyn knew something was amiss inside Tim's head but feared barging in to ask. Professionally, he was doing okay, teaching over-crowded physics courses at the university where he had modified his view of at least some of the veterans thronging the classrooms.

"The good ones are brilliant," he'd said. "Rough-edged and socially inept, but damned smart. And ambitious. I mean, they'll swarm over any problem you throw at them. Absolute bulldogs."

He seemed to enjoy his interactions with the better students who played it no-nonsense, guys who had gone to war when asked, then had turned on a dime and leaped into college, hungry to get their degree and get on with it. His own Oxford-Rhodes graduate work with sub-atomic particle physics—together with rumors of something mysterious and taboo he'd done in the war—made him a bit of a local star, his status cemented by a well-chosen wardrobe and the whiff of a toffish accent he'd picked up in England.

When he left the university each day, however, and dropped his professor's mantle, things changed. Over the past couple of months Evelyn could sense his emotional palette darkening and a preoccupation with his war-time bomb-making polluting their relationship. Especially in bed.

Lying now behind and against her, with a little sour-mash coursing through his veins, he stared past her shoulder into the fire, gently stroking her thigh with his fingertips beneath the blanket. Then his hand stopped and he spoke softly.

"At Los Alamos, they called it 'The Gadget.'"

"What?"

"And later, 'Little Boy.'"

"Tim . . ."

"And 'Fat Man.'"

"Who? What are you. . . ?"

"Oppenheimer, Teller, General Groves. All of 'em."

"I don't know what you're talking about."

"The bomb."

Evelyn sat up, the blanket drifting off her shoulders to reveal firm nipples and a tangle of blonde curls framing her oval face. He reached up and drew the back of his hand across the cool skin of her breast.

"You unhinge me," he whispered.

"Tim . . . thanks, if that's a compliment. Tim, you've got to get help."

He closed his eyes. "I'm getting help. It doesn't help."

"What do you mean?"

"The trips to Birmingham. I'm seeing a head-shrinker. Paid for by your tax dollars. Courtesy of Uncle Sam."

She stopped to consider this news.

"What's he. . ? I mean, is he helping?"

"Oh, sure, he's got it figured cold. Says it's all Larocca's fault." He lifted his bourbon in mock salute.

"Larocca? That's nuts."

"Says I feel immense guilt about the bomb, and that's compounded by a corresponding fear that Larocca will bag my girl." The edge in Tim's voice hardened. "Says that between all those incinerated Jap women and children—the Hiroshima-Nagasaki Effect—between them and the newly freed and rampant, oversexed Laroccas of this world I'm trapped and depressed and, get this, potentially suicidal." He gave the last word a dramatic snort, then returned to his bourbon.

"Did he actually say suicidal?"

"Didn't have to."

She stared, silent.

Tim Fletcher was in love but couldn't act on it. From the waist down, he was dead as a mackerel. It felt to him as though some switch in his cerebral cortex had been opened, disrupting a neural link between his brain and his crotch. For weeks, despite, or because of, his best efforts, he hadn't been able to perform with Evelyn. The situation ate at him day and night.

It was not as if Evelyn wasn't willing—or patient. She was a grown-up. She knew men's bodies weren't always sexually on call. She'd been pursued by would-be lovers since she was fifteen, and in her own time, on her own terms, she'd taken one here, one there: a Yalie football star who could actually talk to women; a furloughed bomber pilot who played a mean jazz piano and had a terrific sense of humor—but who'd later crashed his crippled B-17 into an Italian Alp during the fighting after Anzio.

And, for that matter, carnal collapse was not unknown to her, either. Over the years, she'd had prospective lovers wilt in her hand when called upon to live up to their own romantic bombast, the men's voices subsequently full of alibi, humiliation. Still, despite her discreet background in the romantic arts, she remained fuzzy on the precise intersection of male plumbing and erotic performance.

For Tim, the hours spent with Evelyn alternated between torture and nirvana. He loved how they talked endlessly like the old friends they were, and he appreciated that she never pushed him, sexually, that she seemed content to let time heal what wounds it could. But that was cold comfort to a young man toting a big psychic load.

"Do you think you're suicidal?" she asked, watching him for any readable sign. Outside, a chill wind whipped around the house, driving wisps of smoke into the room from the smoldering fire. Tim wrapped himself in one of the blankets, hobbled on his knees to the fireplace, grabbed a poker and stirred the embers into a blaze. He tossed on another log, sending sparks shooting up the chimney, then sat back, pulled the blanket around him and considered his handiwork.

"I don't know, Evelyn," he said to the fire. "I don't . . . I mean, how does one gauge a suicide vector? I'm a scientist. I measure things. I make hypotheses, test them, develop a thesis, experiment, reach conclusions. Suicide is, you know, it's not an empirical question. . . ."

"Its results are pretty empirical. Definitive, I'd say."

"Yeah. But all that Freudian mumbo-jumbo . . ."

"Introspection has never been your long suit, Professor."

"I am what I am."

"You and Popeye."

"Mmmm, hand me the spinach. I need it," he said, and lay back to contemplate the ceiling.

Truth be told, Tim's sudden, dour reference to Dante Larocca had stunned Evelyn. If the ambient light in the room had been stronger, if Tim had not been so entangled with his own demons, he would have seen in her face a dead giveaway expression of embarrassment and guilt: Evelyn Curtis couldn't get Dante Larocca out of her head.

* * *

Spring semester had started badly for Dante. Although he knew by heart the guidelines for a Dalton Architecture Prize submission, he had chosen to ignore a couple. For one thing, the rules limited any proposed structure to:

   a. single-family dwelling
   b. office building
   c. religious edifice
   d. cultural or sports complex

That was it. Four categories. Slum housing was not among them, but slum housing—or restricted income development—was what interested Dante. Housing the poor presented an architectural challenge he had mulled over for years. He had seen first hand the effect of tenement life on his own family. Although the hard-working, piano-tuning Laroccas had at some point moved from the Lower East Side of Manhattan over and up to better digs in Brooklyn, the memory of those childhood years south of Delancy Street never left him. He could recall with perfect verisimilitude the yells and smells of the poor from twenty nations jammed together in dark, chicken-coop apartments and rancid stairwells.

He remembered the violence, lack of privacy, and assaults on the senses. And he remembered his grandfather, Angelo—driven nearly mad by the hellish cacophony in the tenement—killing a man. The neighborhood bully, an Irishman named Flaherty, had done what bullies do, he baited the smallest man in the crowd, Angelo Larocca, calling him a "dago bastard" and "guinea faggot" because he painted pictures.

Late one afternoon, pushed past his limits, the elder Larocca felled the Irishman, striking him in the temple with a sculpting hammer. Small and compact, but imbued with the deep strength of one who has worked for years with his hands, Larocca brought to the blow a decade of resentment and a lifetime of precision. In an alley, in the presence of two other men, Angelo had whipped out the ironwood hammer from his tool belt and, with one perfectly aimed wallop, relieved the neighborhood of a major nuisance. The other two men stood behind him in the alley, silent, curious, newly respectful. When the bully crumpled to the pavement, and it became apparent he wasn't getting up, one of them motioned for Angelo to leave. Angelo did. But not before lighting a cigarette, dropping the dying match onto the bully's face, stepping over the body and walking away, his tool belt jangling at his waist.

Dante had not heard this story from his grandfather but from one of the men who was present at the murder, Stefano Moroni, the father of Dante's best friend, Vinny.

"Like a sack a' turnips, da' bully went down, Dante," Stefano had said. "Pow! Flop! Sack a' turnips lyin' in da' alley."

Dante had listened, wide-eyed. He was 14 and revered his grandfather above all other men.

"Your grandfather is a very brave man, very strong, Dante," Stefano had said. "Dis is sometimes what must be done with da' bullo!"

Dante often thought of this conversation—and of his grandfather— when things were going badly for him. It wasn't so much a matter of his prospectively murdering anyone—Sidney Greene, for example— but of his instinct to lash out when the going got tough. Remembering the murder of Flaherty as a species of pro-active self-defense had gotten him through much of the war as well as his three months in various critical care Army hospitals in Europe. In those institutions he could safely have been described as not a model patient, unless one asked the nurses. Or at least that nurse.

218

2 March, 1945

Dear Mrs. Larocca,

My name is Elizabeth Rhodes, and I am an operating room Army nurse here at the 346th Special Surgical Unit near Fountainbleau, France. I expect the Army has already contacted you, but to be sure I am writing to let you know that your husband, Sgt. Dante G. Larocca, is alive and, although badly wounded, is doing as well as can be expected.

Along with a small medical staff, I attend Dante (and the other patients) every day. He is not able to write you as his arms and hands have been injured in a tank accident. Or, maybe not an accident, but a combat incident in which every man in his tank but him was killed. Your Dante has been put up for a top award for bravery, even though he won't talk about it.

I am just writing, at his request, to let you know he is fine. That's what he has instructed me to say. But as a wife myself (my husband is an Airborne Ranger) I am taking the liberty of telling you that Dante's injuries are quite serious, and that he would have died on the battlefield if two medics had not found him by chance soon after he was wounded.

I know that you know without my saying it that he is a brave, good man, and I just want to mention that he may need some special attention—love and patience and understanding—when he gets back stateside. I'm sure you will see to it that he receives such attention.

We all believe the war will be over soon, as the Jerries are on the run. But, still, they're bringing in badly wounded GIs every day, and we nurses are kept mighty busy, sometimes with tears in our eyes.

Sincerely,

Lt. Elizabeth T. Rhodes

P.S. Dante's best friend, a boy named Fooshee, was also killed in the tank incident. You will find that Sgt. Larocca is having some difficulty adjusting to that death, but I believe in the end, because he is so strong, he will pull through just fine. He speaks of you often and with great affection.

* * *

Larocca steered his jeep into the faculty-only parking lot and began a fruitless search for space. After three trips around the perimeter, he said to hell with it, squeezed his vehicle in between two cars so that neither occupant would be able to open his own door, climbed out the back of the jeep, reached through the window of another car, liberated the faculty parking permit hanging from the rear view mirror, placed it on his jeep, and walked away, carrying his mailman's bag.

A few minutes later, climbing the steps to the student union, he saw a guy he recognized standing with a pack of other men, enjoying a coke and a smoke, relaxing in a weak winter sun.

"Whoa, Kelvin the Plane Jockey," he said. "Long time, no see."

"Kevin, meatball, not Kelvin." It was the handsome pilot and his friends from the bar fight at Kilroy's quonset hut.

"Whatever you say."

"Well, if it ain't Loud-Mouth himself," said one of the other pilots. "You still hanging around here? I figured they'd have kicked you out on your butt by now."

"Yeah, they tried, but I bribed your mother with this." Dante grabbed his crotch.

"You. . . !" The pilot surged toward him.

"Ease off, Porter. The guy's a trouble-maker," said Kevin.

"Yeah, that's me, with a capital T," said Dante. "Listen, Kelvin, you still got time to sweat it on that head-to-head fly-off bet I mentioned. You know, where the dame kicks your ass for you in the Mustang? And I make a pile of moola? She's been busy crop-dusting and. . ."

"Yeah, yeah. And flying around the world, solo, too, I expect. Some broad. You're full of it, boyo. You know that?"

"Tell you what, hotdog. Let's double the bet. Make it four hundred on the dame's nose."

"Works for me, wise-ass. Easiest money old Kevin ever made. Right, boys?"

They shook hands on it, Dante grinning.

"By the way," Kevin said, "who's furnishing the Mustang?"

"It's hers," Dante said, winked, and strolled away.

"Hers?"

As he headed to Woods Hall and a date with Sidney Greene, Dante couldn't have said why he was moved to beard the pretty-boy pilot in such a way as to seriously endanger his own financial well being. Four hundred bucks. Christ! He didn't have fifty, but the guy's cock-sureness got up Larocca's nose. Ah, well, just something else to worry about down the road. Meanwhile, he had his hands full with Professor Greene who had directed Dante to meet him in his office at three o'clock today. It was already ten-past.

At three-twenty, Dante climbed the stairs and knocked on Greene's studio door.

"Enter."

The voice rang with the impatient authority of a man unaccustomed to being kept waiting. Dante went in, expecting the worst. He knew what this meeting was about: his Dalton application. Throughout the fall semester—far into many nights—he had worked on it, struggling to move forward from rough sketches through a fuller rendering, to the preliminary plans, specs, and elevations that were required to meet the first stage application deadline.

As though that weren't tough enough, the Dalton rules required that the applicant submit, in addition to the design work, a written narrative describing his project in detail and laying out a theoretical argument in its defense. This requirement had given Dante fits. Although he possessed a superb spatial imagination and could visualize complex structures in three dimensions with no difficulty, his relationship to the mother tongue—especially in written form—had been soiled by years spent tough-guying his way through a Brooklyn youth and a world war. In Larocca-speak, orthographic niceties and the punctilio of rhetorical protocol gave way before the majesty of brute force and animal zest.

To solve this problem, Dante had enlisted David Cohen's literary sensibilities in aid of his proposal. The deal had cost Larocca nearly a case of bourbon, but Cohen had come through in spades, helping to transform Larocca's raw linguistic formulations into something approaching a legitimate, semi-professional prose style.

But it was not the prose that troubled Sidney Greene.

When Larocca came into Greene's studio, he saw the older man standing at the long bank of windows, cigarette in hand, surveying through rimless glasses the campus beehive spread below him.

"Sorry I'm late, Sir; couldn't find a parking space."

"Yes, no doubt." Greene exuded ice. "With the veterans having returned, everything at the university is changed. Including the traffic patterns and the general level of civility."

Larocca bristled but squelched an impulse to engage.

"You wanted to see me, Sir?"

"Yes, I did, and you can imagine what it concerns."

"I'm guessing the Dalton."

"Quite."

To Dante, the room seemed hot.

"So, uh, what'd you think of it? Affordable housing for the teeming masses and all that."

"The teeming masses don't interest me very much, I'm afraid, Larocca."

Dante went for a lame joke. "Well, sir, maybe that's because you outrank them."

"Hmmm." Sidney Greene offered a thin smile, turned and consulted a set of architectural plans that Dante recognized as his own.

"Larocca, you have talent. Considerable talent. I'd be a liar and a fool to deny it."

"And we know you ain't either one, right?"

"Indeed. However, you are also as refractory and willful as a damned mule. For example, it is widely known among your fellow design students that the Dalton guidelines are narrowly prescriptive regarding the type of structures eligible for an award, and your plans for a low-cost . . ."

"And low maintenance."

". . . housing project. Yes, and low maintenance. Thoroughly admirable, I'm sure. But hear me, son: these plans, whatever their potential merit, simply fall outside the purview of the Dalton rules. To include your project in the competition, I would have to hear a very persuasive argument on its behalf, and, while your written narrative is well done—congratulations on that, by the way. I didn't think you had that quality of work in you. . . ."

"Thanks, sir. Worked like a demon on that baby." Dante made a mental note to reward David Cohen with more hooch.

"Yes, I'm sure. Still, the project itself, while perhaps marginally worthwhile—from a sociological point of view—is just not . . . not pure enough. Not unadorned and simple enough. There's no theory at work here. It's not sufficiently revolutionary, Larocca."

"Yes, sir, not Bauhaus enough. I see. But the need for this kind of housing complex . . ."

"It will never win you favor among the giants of the profession, those men and women of genius, and yes, some perhaps influenced by the brilliance of Bauhaus principles. Mies, Gropius and so on. Still, like it or not, it is they whom you must impress, whose favor you must curry, in order to rise up . . ."

A knock on the door interrupted Greene's peroration.

"Yes, what is it?" He hated being disturbed in mid-rant.

"I'm here for my Dalton meeting, sir, a little early, I guess." It was Ole Gunderson, a short, stout, bespectacled undergraduate classmate of Dante's, and the apple of Greene's professional eye. Gunderson combined a genuine design talent with an epic capacity for sycophancy. His flattery of his superiors was legendary, but Greene ate it up, particularly that part of Gunderson's hagiography that positioned Sidney Greene higher in the pantheon of architectural avatars than that old fraud, Frank Lloyd Wright, whom Greene detested.

"Come in, Gunderson. Come in. Lovely to see you. Larocca and I were just discussing that very thing."

Ole Gunderson hailed from Minnesota. His beady blue eyes, set in a bland, perfectly round face, reminded Dante of something one might see scurrying around in a Bronx Zoo cage. Perhaps in the gibbon section.

"Oh, sorry, sir. Didn't know you had company. Hello, Larocca." Gunderson's voice was lackluster with the contempt and apprehension he experienced in the presence of his older, veteran colleague—and rival.

"'Lo, Gunderson." Dante pointed to the rolled up set of plans Gunderson carried. "Still peddling that Minneapolis sports arena for the Dalton?"

"As a matter of fact, yes. I think you'll find that, although deeply influenced by Professor Greene's seminal work in large-structure design, my own vision can be seen asserting itself in . . ."

Dante snorted, grabbed the plans and unfurled them onto a slanted drawing table.

"You know, Gunderson, I've watched this piece of crap develop since your first presentation to the class back in October. To me, it's nothing but phony, derivative Bauhaus. And it's dull as a widow-woman's laundry."

Gunderson's eyes flitted to Greene, but the Professor seemed content to let the two of them fight it out.

"Try and understand, Larocca," the younger man said, "the structure makes use of a vernacular urban grammar to, as it were, coerce patrons into meaningful cultural intercourse. . . ."

"That the same as the other kind?"

Gunderson hesitated, not sure whether to fight back or dismiss this heathen.

"Look, pal," Dante grabbed a pencil and advanced on the plans like Napoleon at Borodino. "You got a ninety-foot-high, flat-roofed ice rink here. Right?"

"Exactly."

"For Minneapolis?"

"Correct."

"Correct. So, what happens in February with a ten thousand-ton static load of snow sitting up there and a full gale blowing?"

"I've calculated sufficient redundancy . . ."

"Bull shit! It'll collapse here," Dante savagely penciled the plans, "and here and here."

"What are you doing to my . . ."

"I wouldn't send my mother-in-law to a hockey game in that pit. My wife, maybe, but. . ."

"Lousy vets . . . Really, sir, I must pro . . ." He wheeled on Dante. "And you, what's your project, then, Larocca, a penitentiary?"

"Matter of fact, I'm doing high-density, low-cost housing with both public and private green space and modular units that can be added as the population expands . . ."

"Oh, yes, of course. Charming. But has Professor Greene approved that?" Gunderson smirked.

"We ain't got that far, yet, have we, Prof?"

"You ain't?" Ole smirked. "Goodness, better get busy; the deadline is in two weeks. Right, sir?"

Larocca was past caring now. It was the undergraduate's smirk that did it.

"And I'll tell you something else, Gunderson, you chubby little prick: in case you didn't notice, the world is seriously fucked up just at the moment. In Europe, they got twenty-thirty million dead, and another five million Displaced Persons wandering the roads without a pot to piss in."

"Serves them right for starting a war."

"Work with this concept, my man: The women and children didn't start the friggin' war!"

"Well, their men did."

"Yeah, and we killed most of them! And I helped. So. . . by the way, where did you spend the last four years?"

Gunderson shifted his shoulders.

"Uh, high school, and. . . here."

"Ohhh, very dangerous, high school. Look, kid, right now we got eight-ten million vets coming home with their wallets in one hand and their peckers in the other. Am I right?"

"And so elegantly phrased."

"Right. So, this here is gonna be the horniest homecoming since the last Crusade. Now, these fellas—mostly worker types, right? These guys, what do they want?"

"Tell us, do."

"I'm about to, since you missed the war. Okay, if they're like the joes in my outfit, they want, one, a wife, two, a house, and three, an education. The G.I. Bill is liberating guys like me, pal. So, stand by for a ram."

"And your point is?"

"Marriage causes children, fat boy, in case you ain't got that far in your studies, yet. So, for the next twenty years, as GIs like me age and move through the system, there's goin' to be a housing explosion like this country never saw. Also . . ."

"Pure speculation."

". . . also, the Depression may be over, but we got beaucoup folks sleeping in the rain out there. From Birmingham to LA to Chicago to New York, we got cities packed with people—your colored, your immigrants—living in . . . in squalor. Now, there's a five-dollar word I don't use much. But it applies in this case. Somebody, somebody's got to provide housing for these people. And that's what my Dalton project is all about, my friend. Rural or urban, don't matter. My design is adaptive to both."

Gunderson glanced at Greene and tried a parry.

"Well, Larocca," he said, "the Bible tells us the poor we'll have with us always," and grinned.

Larocca pitched forward, placing his face within inches of his adversary's nubby little nose.

"The-poor-ain't-laughin'-boy!"

Gunderson backed away half a step.

"So, you'll design for these people, I suppose," he said, "niggers and wetbacks."

"Fuckin' A, pal."

"All right, gentlemen. That's enough." Sidney Greene fluttered his hand dismissively. "Larocca, you may go. I'll contact you later with regard to your Dalton submission. Gunderson, I want to talk to you about the landscaping of your building."

Chapter 13

At blustery dusk, David Cohen's black Packard Super-Eight wound its way up the half-mile, inclined gravel drive to Laney Fooshee's farm house. This was the same road Dante Larocca and Sir Plus had negotiated six months before, en route to complete the heartbreaking mission requested by their dying friend, Buddy. Now, though, the fields lay quiet, with the hay bales removed and stored in Milo Henderson's—and Mama Lou Fooshee's—barns.

The Packard forded a shallow, cement-bottomed creek, and slowed to a stop several hundred yards from the house. On either side of Cohen, undulating pastures stretched out to distant tree lines, and he could see a pair of white-tailed deer—buck and doe—cropping the grass, the buck's big-antlered head suddenly high and cautious, catching the wind, ready to herd his lover into the protective trees at any threat. Laney had once told David that her family owned about 2500 acres, but, semi-city-boy that he was, he really didn't grasp what that amounted to in actual land. To him, an acre was a quaint, rural abstraction, on a par with league, hectare, or Ukranian verst.

Still, from where he sat, idling, he was captivated by the subdued beauty of the dormant landscape. As he did with many inanimate objects, Cohen assigned to it a functioning cognition and was struck by the idea that the land seemed to want to cycle-on according to its own primordial logic. He mused that if men just went away and left it alone, this bucolic lithograph of tans and grays would return to the elemental, fluxing balance it had enjoyed for millenia. Before European settlers set out to improve it.

Cohen shifted the big Packard into first, eased the clutch, glanced down, and considered for the umpteenth time the stub of his left arm, ending in its blunt black sock. By now, he was grown proficient at compensating for the diurnal insults of its absence, successfully opening jars and cars, typing the novel, dressing, shaving. But his rage at the maiming never fully left him. And the memory of that day never faded, for deep in his midnight memory the Japanese kamikazes never stopped attacking his ship, and his men never stopped dying, and he never stopped regretting.

The USS Little (DD-803) is in extremis. The order to Abandon Ship has been passed more than once. But now, fire disables the 1MC loud speaker, and no crew member hears anything but explosions and screams and the sound of doom pounding in his ears.

Struck by three flying bombs, Little is down by the stern, awash in sea water and sailors' blood. The aft 5" gun mount, carrying its five-man crew, has long gone to the bottom of the China Sea. Below decks, the powder magazine has exploded in a cataclysm of smoke and flame, rending the ship and killing dozens more.

Little has assumed a permanent starboard list as she steams in a broad left-hand circle, black smoke billowing from her stacks and hatches.

In the competing nightmares of her engine and fire rooms, Little's oil-drenched machinists and boiler-tenders struggle to save their ship by plugging holes and redirecting superheated steam that thunders through the lines at 850 deg. F. When they fail, an invisible fillet of air, escaping through fatal ruptures in a steam pipe, slices off the arm of a red-headed sailor cleaner than an executioner's blade. The boy stands there a moment transfixed by the sight of his own limb lying on the metal deck, dark blood arcing from his wound.

A chief machinist mate named Ralph Graham, a burly blond with close-set eyes and the body of a prize fighter, rips off his own shirt, grabs the broken, fainting sailor, and ties an impromptu tourniquet around the kid's stump. Then, he props him up against a bulkhead, crouches and allows the boy to slump gently onto his back. Then he staggers through fumy mayhem to the nearest ladder and begins a desperate climb toward the main deck, carrying his burden topside. Before they can escape to daylight, all lamps in the main engineering spaces flicker and go out.

Little is dying.

On the ship's bridge, chaos reigns. Captain Walcot has been struck in the head by a wicked fragment of kamikaze engine, the force of the blow strewing his brains all over—and into the mouth of—David Cohen. Cohen chokes and spits, not able to identify the strange, warm flavor. Then he sees Walcot's body, more or less headless, lying at his feet, and knows.

Next to it shines a single pale green eye ball. As he stares at it, the eye's expressive color begins to fade and grow viscid, but in that first two or three seconds, it lodges its image in his brain for good.

Cohen is now in charge of the ship. He calls for Reynolds, the bosun's mate of the watch, but Reynolds has been blown overboard. He shouts for Froggy Mathews, the junior officer of the deck, but Mathews is crouched in a corner of the bridge, cradling his stomach, from which a rope of moist intestine has escaped. Mathews whimpers, trying to stuff his own body parts back into their cavity.

Stepping over Walcott's fugitive eye, Cohen rushes out to the port wing of the bridge and tries to assess the damage to his ship. Canted over to starboard, smoke and flames streaming from a hundred fissures, she is slowly losing headway. In a few minutes, she'll be dead in the water, a hulk.

Miraculously, the number 2 forward 5" gun mount is still firing at a crippled Japanese plane overhead.

The plane is hit. Shouts go up from the mount. Then Cohen hears fervid shrieks of a different note from there, fear piercing the voice of John Stonewall Struthers, the gun captain.

"Put it down, Jarvis! Drop the fuckin' projectile. . . . Jarvis, it's hot, leave it!"

This is followed by a terrific, muffled explosion from within the sealed mount. The ship bucks slightly. Smoke begins leaking from the escape hatches at the rear of the mount.

David Cohen hears nothing more from there.

Back aft, Ralph Graham has grabbed a flashlight and a stretcher and is descending again into the fiery abyss that is the forward engine room.

Waiting for Cohen in the Fooshee farmhouse, Laney shared a coke with Mama Lou. Around them, the living room walls were clotted with Buddy's oil paintings, water colors, pastels, and charcoals, freshly matted and framed. Many of the pieces had been brought to them from out of a war and across an ocean by Dante Larocca. It had taken the women months to choose the right mountings, and now the room resembled a crowded museum devoted to the work of a single artist. Lately, though, Laney had begun to feel the paintings' presence as vaguely oppressive and unremitting, and when Milo Henderson had wondered aloud if maybe they couldn't do with a few less, she'd secretly agreed, although she didn't admit it to him.

"I'm so sorry Dante doesn't come visit us more often," Mama Lou said.

"I am too, Mama Lou."

"I mean, of course, I'm glad David comes as much as he does—such wonderful manners he has—but I miss that crazy Yankee, sometimes."

"Yes, ma'am."

"You know, the funny accent and all."

"Yessum."

"Don't you, hun?"

Laney cocked an eye at her mother-in-law.

"It's not to be, Mama Lou. Dante's married."

Mama Lou stared back at the younger woman and listened to the wind whip around the house.

"Married, huh? Hmmm . . ." She didn't seem convinced, although it did explain some anomalies in her daughter-in-law's recent behavior.

"Well, I'll say one thing," said Mama Lou, sipping her coke, "if he is married, and she ain't livin' with him, then that is one fine man that's going straight to waste."

"Yessum, I agree." Laney stood and peeked through the front curtains on the lookout for Cohen's car.

"So, when is David coming by, darlin'?"

"Should be any minute. Asked me to keep Rafe up 'till he got here. He does love that child."

The older woman surveyed her beautiful, doe-eyed daughter-in-law. An image of the vanished Buddy flashed across her vision, but there was another fatality that drew these women together. In 1938, Buddy's father had died in a stupid accident: hunting alone, he had climbed a fence with a loaded pistol in his pocket; the gun discharged into his groin, and Will Fooshee had lain there in the woods for hours—stoic, helpless—the life ebbing from him, his old squirrel dog, Sam, sprawled nearby in bitter mockery of an idealized American tableau. It had taken two days to find the body, and only then by trackers following the sound of Sam's mournful baying.

Forty-two years and four months old when he went, Will Fooshee's departure had driven Mama Lou to her knees. It was Buddy who'd saved her, really, rescuing her from a black sojourn in the lower depths of grief. Buddy, with his sweet bravado and promises that things would be okay, despite all evidence to the contrary. For the next three years, she and Buddy—and six colored men—ran the big farm and had it going good, profitable, but only because her son worked ten-hour days between his classes at the university and managing the fields.

Then, in the spring of '41 Buddy had up and married Laney Michaels, snap, just like that. Mama Lou hadn't objected—Laney was a lovely girl—but a mother knows, and what this mother knew—or suspected— was that her son had been crazy in love with Evelyn Curtis, the beautiful, rambunctious daughter of that millionaire fool and loud-mouth, Harry.

Later, when the horror of Pearl Harbor had wafted in on a cool December Sunday's radio broadcast, Laney was a beloved member of the family. The next week, Buddy had signed up with Uncle Sam, then asked Milo Henderson to take over his farm duties—temporarily, and for a share of the profits. A year after that, Laney was pregnant and Buddy had shipped overseas. Two years after that, he was dead. And five months after that, a badly damaged Dante Larocca had showed up on the doorstep, bearing condolences and the proffered residue of a young painter's genius.

"David's Jewish, isn't he?" asked Mama Lou.

Laney turned. "Yes, he is. Why?"

"No reason. I never met a Jew before. Nice people."

"The Nazis didn't think so. The Nazis thought they were vermin, from the look of it. What's that place, Auschwitz?"

"Mmmmm."

The gleam of a car's headlights flared across the front window, swung left, and stopped.

Mama Lou's first Jew had arrived.

* * *

Akers and Zeiler.

It had the cheesy sound of a B-Grade Vaudeville act, but there was nothing soft-shoe about the glint-eyed twosome standing on Tim Fletcher's front porch when he opened the door.

"Can I help you?" Tim said to the men.

"Yes, we think you can," said the runt, Zeiler. "And we hope you will."

They might as well have had "HELLO. WE'RE FROM THE F.B.I." stamped on their foreheads in 30-point type. Akers, the bulky one with the third chin, was clean-shaven to a fault, his hair—beneath a bad fedora—buzzed short, his shoes well polished, his suit tight and cheap, his weapon bulging in its shoulder holster beneath the jacket. He appeared to be senior man in this rollicking duo. His sidekick, Zeiler, drooped in a gabardine suit a size too big, wore a pencil-thin mustache and reeked of the sort of hair oil college boys bought by the quart.

Where do they get these guys? flashed through Tim's mind.

"May we come in, Mr. Fletcher?" Akers said.

"I take it you're from the Bureau," Tim said. "May I see some identification?"

As they fumbled with their badges, he could tell they didn't like being so quickly made, but through his war-time work with the Manhattan Project, Fletcher had enjoyed a more robust exposure to Edgar Hoover's pavement pounders than he'd liked.

As soon as he'd joined Oppenheimer's team, agents from Washington

235

had descended on Tuscaloosa, Princeton, and Oxford asking security-linked questions of anyone who might have an opinion on his suitability to be permitted access to, ahem, sensitive material. Was he honest? Did he go to church? Was he a homosexual? Had he ever been a member of the Communist Party? What sort of people did he associate with? Was he a gossip? Did he display good mental hygiene—whatever that meant. Fletcher had received several letters from innocent friends in England warning him of an ongoing deep-background check.

Later, he'd discovered that those letters had been intercepted and steamed open by someone before delivery. This, in turn, required him to get word back to his informants via intermediaries urging them to keep quiet. It didn't matter that Tim Fletcher was a choir boy's choir boy: If he'd ever stolen so much as a pack of BBs, the F.B.I. was gonna nail him.

Now, Tim led his visitors into the living room where a packed suitcase rested, draped with his overcoat.

"Going somewhere?" said the runt.

"New Orleans. What's this about, please? I'm late."

"May we sit down?" Akers said.

Tim gestured to a couple of chairs, then sat on the couch.

"Mr. Fletcher, this is not about you. So no need to get in a huff."

"I'm not in a huff. I'm in a hurry. I've a train to catch in less than an hour, and . . ."

"We won't detain you long, sir."

Akers leaned forward on the edge of his chair.

"I believe you have a student in your advanced physics class at the university by the name of Victor Rangle."

Akers had a way of narrowing his eyes to mere slits when he talked, his eyeballs all but disappearing behind fat lids.

"So?" Already, Tim didn't like where this was going. Rangle was brilliant, easily the best student in his physics seminar, and Tim was about to recommend the young man for a fellowship working directly with him in his fission lab.

"We have reason to believe that 'Rangle' is not this individual's real name."

Akers' eyes had grown mean and beady. Tim glanced from man to man.

"So, what is his name, then?"

"Ronchipov. Vladimir Ronchipov. Born in Minsk, Belarus, 1921, to a Canadian mother and Russian father. Joined the Youth League of the Communist Party in 1937 or -8. Studied astrophysics and high-energy accelerators at Moscow University during the war. Speaks impeccable English." Akers pronounced it impessable. "Graduated first in his class in 1941. Recruited straight out of university to join the Soviets' failed deuterium oxide crash program trying to develop a Soviet nuclear weapon. Made significant contributions to said program.

"Married physicist Olga Semynova in 1942. She was later abducted, raped—and killed—by retreating Wehrmacht troops. Has one child, Irina, now living with his mother in Moscow. This past September— shortly after Hiroshima and Nagasaki—he slipped into the U.S. from Canada on a forged—nearly perfect—American passport. Following orientation sessions and a brief stay in Chicago, where he fraternized with known Communist sympathizers, suspect Ronchipov came straight here," Akers manufactured a pregnant pause, "to study with you."

Tim's mind reeled. Rangle? Ronchipov? "How good is this information?" He played for time.

"How good does it sound?" Zeiler the Ferret chimed in with a leer.

"It's good," said Akers. "From the beginning we've been on to him as a rising star in the Soviet effort to build a bomb."

"Yes, but . . ."

"His university roommate in Moscow was one of ours," said Zeiler. "We know how many times a day that boy craps."

"Crapped," said Fletcher, absentmindedly.

"Craps!" said Zeiler. "Today. This morning."

Tim stared at the fetid little agent.

Akers intervened. "His landlady's supposed husband here in town is one of ours, too. Noisy plumbing."

Tim Fletcher took a deep breath and settled back on the couch to try and absorb all this.

"You want a cigarette?" asked Zeiler, pleased that he and his partner had clearly just knocked this hotshot professor for a big loop.

Ziggy Zeiler had spent the previous two days paging through Fletcher's impressive F.B.I. dossier, in part to prepare for this meeting, and in part because Zeiler knew that serious security questions hovered in the air around Fletcher's former boss, Dr. J. Robert Oppenheimer. Some in the Bureau—at the highest levels—thought the brainy Jew was way too politically soft to be left in charge of something as critical to world peace as the A-bomb.

"No . . . thanks, I don't," Fletcher struggled to regain equilibrium. "Why do you think he came to Ala. . .? You're saying he purposely came here to study in my lab? I don't. . ."

"Don't be modest, Mr. Fletcher," Zeiler said. "You're hot stuff."

The stolid Akers waved his partner silent.

"Tim," he said, "you're very highly respected within the, uh, atomic, the nuclear fraternity." Fletcher noted the softened use of his first name. "Although you don't make a big thing of it, your role in the Manhattan Project is well known within. . . within security circles. I've read Oppenheimer's letter to President Truman recommending you for a special, uh, service award. And large financial settlement."

Fletcher felt violated, defenseless: these bastards knew everything.

"If the, um, funds should come through," Akers continued, "if the President approves the settlement, then it would make it easier for you to marry Miss Curtis, and, you know, live better. Nice car, house, vacations and such. I mean, college profs don't make, well. . ." Akers smiled, his gold eye-tooth showing.

Tim's breathing had grown shallow. Evelyn. Well, of course, if they knew about Oppy's letter to Truman . . .

"Who said I was to marry . . ."

"Still, with all her jack, it might not make that much difference, huh?" The leering ferret was back in the game. "Her old man being rich as fuckin' Croesus, and all."

Tim ignored Zeiler.

"What do you want me to . . . I was going to recommend Rangle . . . Ronchipov, for a top university fellowship to work with me. I presume . . . I mean, surely you don't want me to go ahead. . ."

"That's exactly what we want you to do." Akers was back on the leading edge of his seat.

"But, my chairman . . ."

"We know. You've discussed the recommendation with Gilmartin, your chairman. He's discussed it with Beidler, the Dean. Both of 'em are for it. Neither one knows shit about Ronchipov."

Tim's head swiveled from agent to agent.

"Fletcher." It was Zeiler. "In this game we have a few simple rules. One of 'em is: screw the bad guys until you kill 'em. In other words, embrace your enemy. Keep 'em close. Squeeze 'em, you know? So they don't suspect anything, don't know what you know.

"Ronchipov figures he's top dog in your class, right? He knows none of these American kids can touch him. I mean, what the hell, he made 99 on his mid-term, and only two other guys—" he turned to Akers— "who was it, Everett and Hale? They made, what, 58 and 70? If you give the fellowship to anybody else, Ronchipovski might suspect he's been made. Bingo. Game over. Back to Moscow."

The depth of their penetration into his life left Tim Fletcher weak, barely able to summon the remnant of a value system to guide him. Should he throw these guys out and call . . . call who? Campus police? Should he drop to his knees and thank them? His native patriotism— and horror over the atomic bomb's hellish effects in Japan—argued for doing exactly as they asked. On the other hand, his moral repugnance at the stories emerging from the smoldering ruins of German death camps at Bergen-Belsen, Birkenau, and Treblinka urged him to think independently.

Befehl ist Befehl. An order ist an order, and ve vere just following orders!

"So," he said, standing. "I've still got a train to catch. What do you want me to do?"

Akers and Zeiler stood, too.

"Work with us," Akers said. "Go ahead and recommend Ronchipov for the fellowship. Get him on board. Keep him close. His job in your lab can't start until the fellowship kicks in, and that's not until, what, the first of June."

"By then," Zeiler was grinning. "By then, we'll have him and his Commie friends by the short hairs. And we'll start twisting."

He actually said Commie, Tim thought.

"Important thing, here," said Akers, "your security clearance is in the stratosphere. You don't want to jeopardize it. And you don't want this Russian to find out what he's here to find out about nuclear fission, or whatever the hell you guys call it. So, keep it general until 1 June. Treat his class as, you know, a long review session for the sake of the GIs who're still catching up after the war, or something."

"Right. I see." Tim glanced at his watch.

"Okay, we're outta here," said Zeiler, grasping the front door knob. "But I do have to commend you for the job you and your Los Alamos pals done on those Jap bastards in Hiroshima and Nagasaki. I mean, you fried their little yellow asses good. How many was it, like, two hundred thousand or something?"

"Something like that," Tim said, softly.

"Served the stinkin' nips right. My brother was a POW of theirs in the Philippines. His buddies didn't find nothing but his head. Well done, Fletcher."

He winked, opened the door, and moved out into the sunlight. Akers made a face to Tim, as if to say, 'Hey, whatta ya gonna do with guys like Zeiler?'

And then the two G-Men walked to their green, government-issue sedan, cranked up, and drove off.

Tim Fletcher felt dizzy.

It's the evening of July 25, 1945. Fletcher is a restive guest on board the heavy cruiser, USS Indianapolis (CA 35), steaming en route from San Francisco to Tinian Island in the Northern Marianas, far Pacific.

ETA, 0800 tomorrow morning, the 26th. The ship is flying through the soft tropical night, making 29 knots, thin ribbons of smoke pouring from her twin stacks. No one on board knows that in five days—having delivered its two guests and top secret cargo to the military base on Tinian—this ship will be sunk by the Japanese submarine I-58 with the loss of approximately 880 lives in what will come to be regarded as the worst U.S. Naval maritime disaster on record.

In one of the hangars of the ship, guarded around the clock by U.S. Marines—and the joint responsibility of Fletcher and Army Major Joseph Bolden—are two objects: a lead "bucket" weighing some 200 lbs. and containing the uranium core that will be used in the first atomic bomb to be exploded in wartime. It has been welded to the deck.

Alongside the bucket, secured by stout lines, is a large wooden crate some five feet high and wide and 15 feet long. It contains additional critical components of the bomb—code named "Little Boy."

Working alongside the scientists at Los Alamos, Fletcher has seen this bomb designed, labored over, and finally perfected—a project that has consumed over three years and two billion dollars. He has watched one like it ignite the dawn sky at Alamogordo, New Mexico, vaporizing ground zero at a temperature of 5400 degrees F. and changing the face of warfare forever.

Now, he has been entrusted to help courier the weapon to Tinian where its final assembly will be completed, and where it will be strapped into the belly of a glistening, silver B-29 Superfortress, flown to an unsuspecting— yet to be determined—Japanese city, dropped, and detonated, with the express intention of killing as many human beings as possible, all in an effort to end the most appalling war in the planet's history.

Alone, Fletcher climbs up three decks and enters the hangar where four well-armed Marines stand guard. These men do not know what the bucket or crate contain, only that whatever it is it's damned important, because their orders are to shoot on sight anyone caught tampering with either. By now, Tim is well known to the guards. In fact, the *sergeant in charge thinks this young civilian spends way too much time nestled up to the secret cargo.*

The Marines do not demand to see Fletcher's papers. Instead, the sergeant nods and offers to pour him a cup of joe from the coffee mess. Fletcher accepts. He asks how things are going and is told that everything's shipshape. He takes the coffee and strolls to a metal folding chair facing the crate and bucket—which are bathed in the soft red glow of electric battle lanterns.

The sergeant watches out of the corner of his eye as Fletcher sits and stares.

As a courier with an inter-galactic security clearance, he is one of only two men aboard this ship who know what fierce evil lurks inside the two containers—and that knowledge is slowly coring him out.

Chapter 14

At almost the same moment Tim Fletcher was admitting Akers and Zeiler to his living room for an unnerving lesson in realpolitik, Dante Larocca, on his way home, drove past the L & N train station and spotted Evelyn Curtis's '41 maroon Ford convertible turning in to the parking lot. On a whim, he wheeled around and pulled up beside her as—dressed for travel in a stylish black pants outfit and red scarf—she wrestled a folding, Valpac pilot's valise out of the trunk.

"Hiiya, babe, thought people like you had servants to do that for you."

Her face broke into a smile. "Larocca, you handsome bum, how are you? Get over here and give me a hand, will you?"

Dante got out and manhandled the valise up onto the platform. "Christ! What you got in here, spare parts? Body parts?"

"Make-up," she said, laughing, "and flight manuals. How are you, anyway? I've really missed seeing you around." She seemed genuinely pleased to run into him.

"Yeah, me too. I'm good, you know, working my butt off for your friend Sidney Greene, but . . ."

"Oh, yes, I wanted to ask about your Dalton project. Any word?"

"Well, next week we hear who made the first cut. I'm not too, uh, optimistic, you know, 'cause my design don't really match the criteria, but I met with Greene and made my case and, hey, you never know, you know? . . ."

She could see how much it meant to him. "You really want this, don't you?" she said.

He looked at the ground, then at the sky.

"More than you know, lady. More than you know."

"I'm pulling for you, Dante."

"Yeah, thanks . . . so, flight manuals?"

"Uh, right, I'm headed for New Orleans to interview with Pan American for a job."

He looked at her, certain he was going to screw up whatever he said next.

"As a pilot, right? Not a stew."

"As a pilot."

"Yeah, I remember our conversation about that. Are they hiring, uh, women?"

"They're hiring pilots."

Standing there next to each other on a late winter's morning, both of them felt a powerful, quasi-magnetic impulse to move closer, to smile, to accommodate and flatter and smell the other, to please, to touch. Evelyn's blonde hair had darkened a bit through the winter, but she looked fit and gorgeous. With her suntan faded, the razor-thin scar leading from the corner of her mouth toward her right ear was more evident, and Dante wondered again about its origin.

Meanwhile, she gave him an appraising once-over. "You're looking good, Brooklyn. What do you do out there at Shorty's Beagle Ranch to stay in shape?"

"Oh, cigarettes, beer, pretzels. . ."

"Got a girl?"

The question threw him.

"Right," he scoffed, "twenty naked midgets under my cot. No, the mad Marines, Karl and Ben, you know, they get everybody up at dawn and make us bathe in enemy blood, take us out on forced marches, calisthenics, push ups, hand-to-hand combat. . ."

She laughed. "And David Cohen? What does he?. . ."

Dante flinched. "Ah, well, Cohen . . . Cohen's having sort of a tough time, just at the moment. And push-ups are not his thing, as you can. . ."

"Yeah, I expect not. . . ."

"But, he's got his novel up to, like, 600 pages or something, and his prof, this Strode guy, says he's gotta cut it down to maybe four-five hundred before he'll send it to New York. It's killing him." Dante chuckled.

"Poor guy."

"Fuckin' writers," he said, "crazy, all of 'em."

"Have you . . . has he let you read any of it?"

Dante heard a train whistle and glanced back down the track.

"Yeah, um, he asked me to look at the first, you know, couple hundred pages or so."

"And?"

Dante focused on her again, absorbing the angular symmetry of her face, forcing himself not to reach out and touch her cheek, or, for that matter, simply hug her.

"It's dark, Evelyn," he said softly. "Real dark. And stone autobiographical, you know? His ship, his war, his wound, his Japs. . ."

"Yes, he seems rather. . . preoccupied, or. . ."

"Lotta hate in that book, I'm thinking. Lotta hate. . . . But, hey, I'm no critic," he smiled. "I can barely read and write."

"You goofball. . . ." She tapped him lightly on the arm and held on a moment, signaling. . . what? Call it an affectionate co-conspiracy of self-deprecation.

"Well, there you are. Sorry I'm late. Hello, Larocca." It was Tim Fletcher who had driven up, disembarked, and approached them without either being aware of his presence.

246

Evelyn blushed to the roots of her hair. "Oh, hi, Tim. Thought you'd stood me up."

The train rolled into the station, steam venting, brakes screeching.

"Had a couple of visitors." Tim had to raise his voice. "I'll tell you about it later. Or, maybe I won't. Anyway, there's the train. Gotta hurry, doesn't stop here long. So, Larocca, you, uh, boarding too?"

Larocca smiled. "No. . . no, I just happened by and seen Evelyn wrestling with her steamer trunk. Have a good trip, the both of you." He turned to Evelyn, said. "Good luck, kiddo," and winked so that Tim missed it.

Minutes later, Dante sat in his jeep at the rail crossing and watched the train pull out in front of him. As her car chugged past, gaining speed, Evelyn gave him a wave, a smile, and a sweet lift of her chin. Through the moving train window, Dante could see Fletcher standing behind her, placing luggage on the overhead rack.

Too bad. Tim missed that wave, too.

* * *

Driving home, Dante settled into an Evelyn-Curtis-besotted reverie. Although on one level she seemed miles out of his league, there was no question she was giving off charged vibrations that got into his head and wreaked serious havoc. When she kidded him, or laughed at his jokes, or touched his arm, the natural shyness he felt around women he liked evaporated, and he knew, somehow, that she was there for him. Right there, to be held or kissed or made love to. It was crazy in a way, because he had no concrete evidence of her feelings for him, nothing that would stand up in the court of love. It was just something he felt but was so unsure of that he derided his own presumption. Although he didn't know the word, Evelyn possessed for him a natural, if sexually charged companionate quality, a pre-verbal chemical beguilement that evades the best efforts of art and science to describe—it must be experienced to be known. He smiled and shook his head.

"Some dame," he muttered, "some red-hot dame."

He pulled into the Beagle Farm and Cricket Ranch, stopped, and ran up on Shorty's porch to check his mail box nailed to the wall. Nothing, as usual. After half-a-dozen false starts, he had never answered Maria's mea culpa Christmas letter begging to be taken back. The truth was, he didn't know what he thought of her anymore. He just felt numb. The emotional woe she'd inflicted on him had superficially healed over, but every time she flitted across his mind—whenever he saw an ex-GI with his wife or girlfriend, for example—the memory of her infidelity exacted its pound of flesh.

As Dante started toward his tent, Sir Plus ran out barking with joy and doing his usual full-body wriggle that included hurling himself between Dante's legs and demanding to be petted instanter. Hearing the racket, David Cohen glanced out his trailer window and waved. Then he did something odd: he pointed at the tent and arched his eyebrows.

Larocca laughed. "Cohen, you're one crazy rabbi, you know that? Go cut another fifty pages out of that Moby Dick novel of yours."

"Very funny, dago-boy," Cohen yelled. "For that, you should be beaten, and driven from the land."

"Never happen. You know, where I come from, Moby Dick is a venereal disease."

"Yeah? Well, one thing's for sure: if it's contagious, you've got it."

Dante chuckled, shot him the bird, raised the tent flap, walked in, and froze. Standing by the ridge pole was Maria Larocca, looking pale, pretty, and a tiny bit petrified.

"Hi, Dante."

He couldn't summon his tongue.

"How you doin'?" she said. "You look great."

"I . . . how did you . . ."

"Rode the train. I had your address. Took a cab. I think it was the only one in town."

"Yeah, New York it ain't." Violently contrary emotions flooded his brain. He reached out and grasped the drawing table to keep from tipping over.

"Maria, I . . . I don't . . . what do you want here? Why'd you come all this way to . . ."

"Didn't you get my letter around Christmas? Where I said, where I asked you to forgive—"

"Yeah, I got it, but—"

"You never answered, Dante. You never wrote nothing back. I said I was sorry. I said—"

"I know what you said. I did read it. A lot. Maybe a hundred times."

"So?"

With them both standing there, the tent felt like a small, packed closet. Then, Sir Plus came in to add to the crowding. He stood staring at the two people appearing for all the world to understand every word out of their mouths.

"Nice dog. I remember him from . . . He's yours?"

"Yeah."

"What's his name?"

"Sir Plus. You know, surplus army stuff. Left-overs. Discards. Like me."

He gestured for her to sit on one of the two chairs while he led the dog outside and tied him off.

Back inside, his heart racing, he offered to make her coffee. She asked if he had tea. He said no. She settled for coffee. While he fumbled with the drip pot and hot plate, she surveyed her surroundings.

"This is nice. I wouldn't have thought a tent could be so . . . you know, cozy."

"Yeah, well, the wood floor helps a lot."

"It's so neat." She smiled. "You weren't always so neat before, you know. Like, with your pants and stuff."

This conversation was draining the life from him.

"Well, the army has a way of shaping a guy up. Besides, this place is so tight, if you're a slob, pretty soon it gets where you can't find your ass with a seven-hand working party."

He handed her the coffee and sat on his tightly made-up cot. His head was clearing a bit now, and he'd begun fashioning scenarios for what was about to happen. Or could happen. Or shouldn't happen.

Then, he struck.

"So, Maria, how's Bruno?"

She looked off.

"That's low, Dante."

"No! You want low? I'll give you low. Low is your steady givin' blow jobs to my draft-dodging, so-called buddy while I was gettin' my ass shot off for two-plus years. Low is gettin' pregnant by that same sleazy, chicken-shit kraut. Low is lying to me in every friggin' letter you ever wrote—which, I might add, were fewer and fewer as time went on, including while I was lying in a hospital for three months."

Maria flushed and struck back.

"Yeah, right, big deal; I got a couple letters from some nurse saying you couldn't write because you was hurt. I'll bet. I'll bet you were all over her like white on rice. I'll bet you were putting it to her right there in the hosp . . ."

She stopped, horrified at having gone off the rails so quickly.

"No . . . no, I'm sorry, Dante, I didn't mean that . . . I don't believe you would . . ."

She glimpsed in his eyes a look she'd seen only once before—that terrible day in the alley with Bruno—a deep pool of pain and anger and incipient homicide. When he spoke his voice was husky with threat.

"Let me tell you something about that nurse. Her name was Liz Rhodes. She was pretty. She was smart. She was damn good. She worked 15-hour days to try and keep as many of us shot-up G.I.s alive as she could. She was married to a captain in the paratroops, but she liked me too. She liked me a lot, and I liked her. We laughed at the same things, Maria. Remember that part?

"Sometimes her and I, we held hands in the dark and talked. We talked about after the war. About what we were gonna do and where we'd go with our . . . her with her guy and me with you.

"Then, while I was recuperating in her unit, her husband got killed in a parachute drop over Germany. The night she heard the word about him she ran to my bed and cried like a child. I never saw nobody cry like that before. Absolutely wailing. Crushed by the pain of it.

"I did what I could—I held her. I kissed away the tears. She crawled up in my bed and I held her all the rest of the night, and for that night . . . for that night, I loved her, and she loved me, and we told each other so. She was beautiful. She was magic to touch. I was confused. Here I was married to you and . . . and caring a lot for another woman. . . ."

"Dante, I take it back. I didn't—"

"No! Let me finish! . . . So, when I got better, when my wounds healed up some, and I was walking, and they stopped the morphine, she came in late one night and asked me to go to bed with her, practically begged me to make love to her, said the war had already half-screwed us both up, so we might as well finish the job. I wanted to do it. Man, I never in my life wanted but one thing more than I wanted her, then. You.

"So, can you believe it, I said no. I said I had to be true to you. Crazy, huh? But she understood. She said fine, okay. She kind of laughed and said, 'Well, your wife's a lucky woman, Larocca, but if you ever change your mind . . .'

"A week later she was killed in a truck accident, ferrying wounded guys back from the front. That was Liz Rhodes."

Outside, the wind rustled the trees and Sir Plus whined, reminding his master it was time for the late-afternoon repast. In the tent, Maria's untouched coffee had gone cold. She looked down into her cup, then placed it on the table.

"I guess . . ." she said, "I guess you're through with me then, huh?"

"I . . . I don't know, Maria. I ain't saying that. But you hurt me. You hurt me good. I'm kinda simple when it comes to women, you know. I take 'em at their word. And I did that for you, and then you . . ."

"I'm so sorry, Dante."

She leaned forward and took his hand in hers, rubbing the back of it with her thumb, caressing the prominent blue veins, feeling his strength.

"It's gonna take a long time, Maria, a long time. That's all I can say right now."

"I understand," she said and gently released his hand.

He offered a faint smile.

"Can you call me a cab, please?" she whispered. "And, Dante, I'm still in the phone book, you know. Under 'Larocca.'"

* * *

The train ride from Tuscaloosa to New Orleans took a little
over five hours, including the possibility of an evening meal in a
remarkably good dining car. Before that, while Evelyn pored over
her flight manuals and Pan American pilot application, Tim stared
out the window of the rocketing train, processing the radical counter-
intelligence summary dumped on him earlier by Akers and Zeiler.

Rangle. Ronchipov. Incredible.

Disciplined as always, Fletcher worked his way back through all
his interactions with the bright, articulate physics phenom. It was
true he was a bit older than the standard-issue students, but then
so were all the ex-servicemen fresh back from the war. It was also
true—when Tim thought about it—that the guy spoke in a clipped,
precise accent inflected with a kind of exotic warble in the vowels.
But Tim had linked that to Rangle's casually mentioning one day that
his grandmother was Welsh, and that he'd spent a number of summers
with her as a child near Swansea, learning the language. Clever
bastard, masking a potential liability with a plausible cover.

As the train clacked through south Alabama and Mississippi, dusk
began to fall, and the western sky reddened. Tim retrieved a couple
of bourbons and bags of peanuts from the club car. Evelyn yawned,
stretched and laid aside the Pan Am material.

"Ready to take 'em by storm, old girl?" he said, handing her the
drink.

"Yeah, I am. I feel good about this. Real good." She smiled. "I figure
in six months I'll be flying a big ol' Clipper from Frisco to Honolulu or
somewhere. And, boy, I can't wait! Here's to the ladies."

She lifted her bourbon to him.

"Yes, well, that's just it. . . . I mean, the gender thing and piloting.

You'd be the first . . ."

"It's time, Mr. Fletcher. Long past. The war's changed everything. Women have proved themselves. They can't use that old 'weaker sex' crap against us any more."

"Yes, but . . ."

"Besides, I've got 2,500 hours of cockpit time in more than a dozen planes. I'm instrument-rated. I can outfly . . ."

"Hey, hey, save it for the Pan Am big wigs. You don't have to convince me."

She blushed. "I know. Sorry. Anyway, what, uh, you said back at the station that you'd had visitors or something this afternoon. Sounded rather mysterious. Tell, tell."

"That's . . . I can't really . . . Look . . ." He pointed with his chin.

At that moment, a badly burned, decorated Marine Corps Major entered the train car and began making his way toward them. He moved in pained lurches, his face and hands swathed in white gauze. Behind him, a black porter carried the Marine's Valpac. Every pair of eyes in the car followed the progress of these two, but not one word was said. The porter placed the Major's valise on the overhead rack. The officer smiled, pivoted his hip toward the black man and said something. The porter hesitated. The Major spoke again, and the porter gingerly reached in and withdrew the Major's wallet from his back pocket. The Major spoke a third time, and the black man extracted a couple of bills before slipping the wallet back into the pocket, nodding his thanks.

Suddenly, someone behind Evelyn and Tim yelled out, "Semper Fi, Marine!" and the whole car broke into sustained applause. The Major smiled, raising one white-matted club of a hand in thanks.

"You know," Tim said to Evelyn, "there's a kind of hierarchy among the vets. I've seen it in my students."

"You mean, by service?"

"No, by suffering. A sort of echelon of pain. The worse hurt, the higher status. Deference, respect, and so on."

"Mmmm. Do you disapprove?"

"Absolutely not. Completely deserved."

She watched as a woman helped the Marine off with his tunic. Someone else handed him a pillow as he wrenched himself into the seat.

"Are you . . . it almost sounds like you're jealous."

"No. It's not that, really. I was just thinking how the war busted up a lot of people badly—but in totally different ways. Inside, outside, you know? Minds and bodies."

She looked at him. "And for some, both," she said. "Like David Cohen. You remember, Dante's friend. Missing a hand? You met him at Kilroy's that night."

The temperature of Fletcher's voice dropped a couple of degrees.

"Oh, yes, Cohen. And Larocca. Funny, him showing up at the station today."

"Pure chance. But Cohen, Dante told me once that Cohen won the Medal of Honor for . . . for something in the Navy, Jap kamikazes sank his ship or something. Sounded awful."

Tim glanced out the window at the sharecroppers' shacks whistling by.

"Medal of Honor. . . Well, not many of those around. Live ones, anyway. Kamikazes, huh? Must have been rough. Almost enough to make you think the . . . Japanese had it coming."

"Almost?"

He turned on her. "The women and children, Evelyn. The women and children didn't deserve it."

She leaned forward in her seat and looked him in the eye.

"Tim, I know you had something—I don't know what, but something—to do with the bomb. So are you ever, can you ever tell me what you did in the war, and why you still see a psychiatrist in Birmingham about whatever it was, and why . . . what effects whatever you did are having on you?"

He grimaced and drained his glass.

"Probably not," he said. "No time soon, anyway."

She held his eye a long moment, then settled back in her seat.

"I'd like another drink, if you don't mind," she said.

* * *

Dinner on the speeding train came early and passed quickly. It was not the shared romantic flirtation Tim had anticipated when he'd volunteered to accompany her to New Orleans for the job interview. "Pass the salt, please," was about as intimate as it got. It seemed to Fletcher that some cardinal essence was ebbing from their relationship. The war, flying, competing with the men, all had changed Evelyn. She was less respectful or, not respectful, but—he didn't know what exactly—less forgiving, more competitive than she had been earlier. And back there at the train station parking lot he'd seen—he couldn't deny it—seen some . . . some sizzle between her and that semi-literate Yankee vet. Although Tim was not by nature a particularly jealous lover, for Larocca and his crude strut he made an exception.

When they alighted from the Checker cab at the Roosevelt Hotel in New Orleans, Tim paid the driver and turned, only to see Evelyn already half-way up the steps, headed for the lobby. By the time he reached the front desk she had told the clerk they would be taking two singles. When she handed him his room key, he looked a question at her.

"In case Daddy calls," she said. "Or . . . I'm really just too nervous about Pan Am to, you know . . ."

"Sure. I'm tired anyway. See you in the morning. What time's your interview?"

"Nine."

"Breakfast at 7:30, then?"

"Sounds good."

She could see the hurt in his eyes before he bent to pick up his suitcase.

"Tim . . . why don't we have breakfast in my room instead of down here?" She put her hand on his shoulder. "You can give me a pep talk, like you always do."

He nodded. "Okay, fine, I'll beat on the door at half past seven."

"Great." She rose on her tiptoes, gave him a hug and a kiss on the cheek. "You're the best," she said.

On different grounds, it was a long night for both of them.

* * *

Pan American conducted its interviews at their regional offices on Canal Street, not far from the Roosevelt. Evelyn decided to walk it, suggesting that Tim amuse himself in the French Quarter while she did the deed.

"Knock 'em dead, Ev," he'd said, standing in the hotel lobby. "Just don't lose your temper if they act like jerks, because . . ."

"I won't. . . ."

". . . because they may try to goad you, just to test your temperament under duress."

She'd laughed. "Ha, duress. . . duress is a wheels-up landing in a crippled P-38 on one engine, no fuel, and dead electrics."

She'd meant it in the spirit of tough-gal bonhomie, but his look told her he'd taken it amiss, as though she were ridiculing his concern.

"I just meant . . ."

"No, I understand, dear," she'd said. "Thanks for the advice. Gotta go. Wish me luck."

"Break a leg," he'd said in a voice of rue.

Now, on a beautiful morning, as she strode down Canal wearing gray slacks and a black jacket, her hair pinned back and an alligator handbag slung over her shoulder, she had the world firmly by the balls.

Her mind was roaring down a dozen tracks at once: visions of the tense train trip yesterday: sleeping alone last night—and preferring it; reviewing potential pilot questions she would be asked in the next hour; remembering to boost Tim's flagging morale—when she had time; recalling the image of a smiling Dante Larocca leaning against his jeep, sporting tight jeans and an attitude; flashing thoughts of her dead brother Robert and that terrible day years ago; thinking of one-armed David Cohen struggling with his novel and his demons; recollecting the beautiful Buddy Fooshee, before the war, secretly painting her nude out in his barn on a perfect summer's afternoon. . . .

Later, in the Pan Am waiting room, Evelyn sat with two well-dressed men about her age. All three showed nerves, some of her confidence having been drained away by the overwhelmingly male presence all around her. She'd seen maybe five female secretaries answering the phone and whacking away at their typewriters while forty or more men ran the show, from young flunkies delivering files, to self-important gray-suits hurrying down corridors engaged in whispered conversations. And, of course, the occasional uniformed Pan Am pilot ambling along with that familiar hot-shot swagger she'd dealt with—and fought off—a thousand times during the war.

"You, uh, in the right room?" It was one of her fellow waitees speaking to Evelyn.

"Yes."

"Mmm, guess they're doing stews, too."

"Guess so."

The door opened. A well-built guy walked out and flashed the OK sign to his buddies.

"Piece of cake," he confided to them. "They're definitely hiring. Blood flow and a pulse seem to be the prime criteria."

"What'd they emphasize?"

"Well, one big thing is your flight log. But I've got, you know, nearly a thousand hours, so I was good there . . ."

"Yeah, still . . ."

"Curtis!" The voice came from the interview room.

Evelyn stood and breathed deeply. The three men appraised her, the new guy moving forward.

"Say, babe, I'm Buford, you busy for lunch?"

"Piss off."

He recoiled. She opened the door and walked through it.

Inside, behind a long table covered with file folders, wearing white shirts and nearly identical dark ties, sat three middle-aged men. There was a pretty one, an ugly one and a bald one. Each looked confused by her advent. Indeed, when Evelyn walked in, the ugly one even stood up for a moment, caught himself, and dropped back into his chair.

"Uhhh . . . mmmm . . . Curtis?" said the pretty one, holding a folder.

"That's correct. May I sit down?"

"Umm, yes, of course."

The men all strained to read the file at the same time.

Evelyn said, "You might have it listed as 'E. Randolph Curtis.'"

"Yes, yes, we do. But he's flight-rated in," he counted down the page. "eleven different aircraft . . ."

"Actually, it's thirteen."

They stared at her like a set of 'no-evil' monkeys.

"Ma'am, these interviews are for pilots," said the ugly one.

"I know."

"Stewardesses are down the hall. Room 101-B."

"I know."

"You're telling us you're applying as a pilot?" said the bald one.

"That's what I'm telling you."

"But we don't have any women pilots."

"Whose fault is that?"

The pretty one leaned back in his chair.

"This is a joke, right?"

"That depends on what happens next."

"Miss Curtis, we're short-handed, and we're hiring a lot of cockpit crews . . ." said the ugly one.

"That's what I heard."

". . . but I can assure you, none of them will be women."

"Why not?"

The men were regaining their equilibrium now, and they were not amused. The bald one seemed to be the head monkey.

"Look, Rosie the Riveter," he said, "there are hundreds of combat veterans out there applying for these jobs . . ."

"Are you hiring pilots to fly combat missions?"

"No, goddamnit, we're hiring them to fly passengers!"

"Then combat experience isn't relevant. Whereas, flying hours, time-in-the-air, will be."

"And how many hours do you have?"

"Twenty-five hundred. It's there in the record. All documented."

The men gaped and clustered over the file again.

The bald one narrowed his eyes, his voice dripping.

"You claim to have logged two thousand five hundred hours in 13 different aircraft?"

"That's affirmative, including bombers and C-47s, which I believe make up a large part of your fleet."

They were impressed, she could see. She had these bums on the run.

"How many hours do you have flying over water?" The bald one asked.

"Water? I don't . . ."

"The ocean, Miss Curtis. Many of Pan Am's long-distance routes fly over water. We expect our pilots and co-pilots to be competent in celestial navigation. Are you?"

"Of course I am. I've flown cross-country twenty-seven times."

"Not the same, ma'am." He was gloating. "But of course you wouldn't know that."

Out in the anteroom, the two waiting pilot-applicants could hear voices raised behind the closed interview door.

"Ten to one she cries," said one.

"Pass," said the other. "She looked tough. Great tits, though."

Inside the interview room, the three men had fallen to squabbling among themselves, almost as though Evelyn weren't present. She was pleased to see that the pretty one was half-taking her side, and although he didn't appear to be senior man, he did seem sharpest. Maybe that would help.

Pretty boy was speaking to the others, "Look, fellas, I'm just saying, she's qualified. Hell, she's overqualified. Her hours are off the chart; she can fly anything with wings; and her letters of recommendation make her sound like the second coming of Lindbergh."

"Possibly forged," said the bald one.

"Excuse me!" said Evelyn.

"Oh, shit, Harry. They're not forged, for Christ sake. I say give her a shot. If she makes it, we get a load of free publicity. How does this sound: NEWS FLASH: PAN AM HIRES FIRST WOMAN PILOT! OPENS THE DOOR TO THE FUTURE OF AVIATION! Blah, blah. Everybody will know about it."

"Yeah, same as when she crashes," said the ugly one.

"Paul," said the bald one to the pretty one, "do you really think anybody in his right mind would knowingly fly as a passenger in a plane that some broad . . . excuse me, ma'am, that a lady was piloting, no matter how qualified she was?"

"I would," said the pretty one.

"I rest my case."

"Besides," said the ugly one, "your wife flies."

"So what?" The pretty one was annoyed.

"Miss Curtis—" It was the ugly one. "While we appreciate your many fine contributions to the war effort, it appears you have applied for a position with us under a false name, and . . ."

"No. That's the right name. You made the wrong assumption."

He steamrolled her, ". . . a name that, if not assumed, was at least calculated to mislead us as to your true identity. . . ."

"Sir, my middle name is Randolph. It's one I sometimes use."

". . . and thus, for that reason, among others, we cannot hire you at this time."

Her throat was choking her.

"What . . . what if I'd applied as an obvious woman?"

"We wouldn't be sitting here, unfortunately," said the pretty one. "Miss Curtis, I want to echo my colleague's compliment concerning your war work. It is most impressive. However, we three have obvious differences. And the main difference is they think your sex disqualifies you, and I think you'd make a helluva fine command pilot on any route Pan Am flies. And not only that, but I promise you I will take up this whole issue with higher authority. Today. This matter is not closed."

The four of them sat silent, each stunned in a different way by the pretty one's little speech. Finally, Evelyn found her voice.

"Thank you, sir. I'm only asking for a chance to compete. And to you other gentlemen, I would just say: think about it. Women make up about fifty percent of the population. In a group that large, there's gotta be a few keepers. Thanks for your time."

She gathered her purse, stepped forward, shook hands with each man in turn, spun on her heel and headed for the door. As she passed through the waiting room, one of the jerk-applicants grinned.

"Heyyyy, hon, get the job?"

"No, asshole," she said, "I got the shaft."

From the interview room, she heard the ugly one's screechy voice: "Robertson? . . . Robertson? You out there?"

"Yo' that's me," said the jerk, jumping up.

When Evelyn emerged from the Pan Am office building, she saw Tim standing on the sidewalk, looking worried. He hurried toward her.

"How'd it go?" he said.

"Not well, but it's not over, either."

"Evelyn, are you sure you—"

"If they don't give me a shot, there're other airlines."

"Maybe you should rethink this whole—"

"Don't talk to me right now, Tim."

It was going to be a long train ride home.

Chapter 15

Although he mispronounced it, David Cohen had recently discovered the female clitoris. More accurately, Dante Larocca had informed him about the magical properties of this recondite appendage, making Cohen one of only half-a-dozen non-medical men in the entire state of post-war Alabama to be so privileged.

Now, in his trailer, in the middle of the night, in the middle of a storm, in the middle of his bed, David Cohen was in the middle of making love to Laney Fooshee like there was no tomorrow. Lying on his back, with her grinding away on top of him, and calling out his name at every jolt, Cohen grasped her ass with his one hand and propelled her hard against him in a gorgeous, rhythmic sexual cotillion that, first, launched her into breathless, shrieking orbit, then left her a wet, whimpering, grateful mess, trembling against him.

"How . . . how . . . oh, God, how did you do that?" she whispered.

"Beginner's, whew . . ." he was in no better shape than she, "beginner's luck, I guess."

Outside, the rain poured down. Tonight was the first time for them. It was the first time for her since her husband's death. It was the first time for him since the kamikazes. It was wonderful.

David Cohen owed Dante, big time.

As for Laney, it wasn't supposed to be this way. Since the day last September that Dante Larocca had rolled into her living room recounting stories of Buddy's life and death, praising his art, bemoaning his loss, finally collapsing in tears on the bedroom floor, she'd been hooked on the rough-edged, vulnerable New Yorker. She vaguely understood that in falling hard for Dante she was attempting to recapture Buddy vicariously, to annex the missing, purest love of her life. Yet, she couldn't govern her emotional response to Larocca's laugh, his body, his gentle touch.

She and Mama Lou had invited him out to the house numerous times, and at first he always came, regaling them with tales of Paris, of London, of a Brooklyn youth. Then, he began finding excuses: too busy; working mighty hard on his Dalton project; trying to keep old Sidney Greene off his back. Still later, after the riot at Kilroy's, when invited he would ask if he could bring Cohen along, saying that Cohen didn't get out much, that Cohen was too moody and needed to be around people, that he was worried about Cohen.

Of course, she was happy to include the handsome, shattered ex-Naval officer from Mobile, in part because his elegant cynicism and articulate critiques of the nasal, hum-drum President Truman (whom he could mimic perfectly), or a partisan, self-dealing Congress and the fumbling military brass kept them all laughing—and in part because his presence gave plausible cover for her infatuation with Larocca. Then, one Saturday in February, when Cohen had been too depressed to accompany his friend to the Fooshees, Dante had gone alone.

And Laney had made the biggest mistake of her life.

After dinner, she'd gotten him to go for a walk, and there she told Dante how she felt about him. She told him she knew it was too soon, really, after Buddy's death. She told him she wouldn't blame him if he wasn't interested in her. She said she knew that a woman with a baby was no great door prize.

"But," she told him, "Right or wrong, I think I've fallen in love with you."

The moment her words flew loose in the air, she felt she'd overstepped, that she'd violated some unfathomable code of male friendship and loyalty. At that moment, she saw herself as a pitiful, begging grass widow, desperate for the love and attention of a man who didn't want her. And she'd said as much to Dante on the spot.

She'd wheeled around to return to the house.

"No," he'd said, and caught her arm. "No, it's not that way. It's not about you. It's me. I'm married."

She'd never even entertained the thought. Married. Well, of course. Why wouldn't he be? How could she have been so stupid? On the walk back to the house, Dante had revealed enough about Maria's infidelity for her to understand and sympathize.

"That woman ought to be shot down dead in her tracks," she'd said.

"I considered it, believe you me."

And then he'd said the thing that sealed it, the thing she would never forget until her dying day. He'd said how much he liked her, how pretty he thought she was, even how much he loved the smell of her hair but, "You know, Laney, I could never . . . I mean, if we got together, it would always be like there was three of us in bed, you, me, and Buddy. I mean, I could never get his face out of my head. I can't even now when I'm lying in my cot out in that crazy tent. If I were with you, in that house there, in his bed, I would just feel like I was. . . cheating on him, in a way. You know?"

"That's okay, Dante, I understand," she'd said.

But she didn't.

Now, with David, things were advancing. But whatever she and Cohen had—and at times it was very good—whatever they had, it was not what, in the deepest recesses of her heart, she desired. It was fine and pleasing and comforting. It was even good enough to settle for. But it was not It.

David got out of bed, pleased with his prone performance. He lit a cigarette, turned on a small electric fan to cool them, and poured two shots of bourbon.

"You enjoy that?" he asked, smiling.

"Seismic," she said. "Isn't that the word for earthquakes?"

"Yeah. Earthquakes. Funny, I was in a couple, you know?"

"Earthquakes? Where?"

"California. San Diego. We were going through predeployment training, and I was living ashore in the BOQ . . ."

"The what?"

"BOQ, Bachelor Officer's Quarters, on the naval base. And one night I was sitting around in my skivvies reading . . . I remember I was reading Don Quixote, and suddenly I felt something odd, and I looked up, and the booze in my drink was shaking like jello, and the overhead hanging lamp started swaying, and I said, 'What the hell is this?' and I ran out in the passageway. . . ."

"In your drawers?"

"Oh, yeah, and the place was just crawling with guys dressed like me—and worse—and nobody had any screaming idea what the hell was going on, and then somebody yelled 'EARTHQUAKE'! and, man, that was it, we hauled ass out of there, I mean there were naval officers coming out the windows, sliding down drain pipes, shit, it was raining naval officers there for a while. Funniest damn thing I ever saw."

They laughed together at his story as he repeated, "'. . .it was raining naval officers,' you coulda bought 'em by the bushel. Cheap."

Lying down beside her, he pulled the sheet over them, his drink balanced on his chest, looking at the ceiling, his one hand gently stroking the inside of her thigh where she was still damp.

"Do you . . . does my hand, the absence of a hand, bother you? I mean . . ."

"No, it doesn't, you mustn't think that . . ."

". . . I mean, I know it must be a little gross or freaky or something, because even I think it's freaky, but . . ."

"David, it doesn't bother me. I think you're handsome, and . . . delightful, and . . ."

"Sexy?" He laughed.

"Yes, sexy," too quickly, "and so smart and such fun to be with. Don't worry about the hand . . . as far as it affects me, anyway."

He turned his face toward her.

"You do know I'm just another fucked up, neurotic Jew, don't you? And a writer to boot. Or at least, a typist, so far, but one day . . ."

"I don't like that word."

"Jew? Writer?"

"Fucked up. I don't say that, and I wish you wouldn't."

"Sorry. You're right . . . But I am."

She set her drink on the floor, turned to him and began gently tracing designs on his bare chest with her index finger.

"Was it bad, the war? I mean, I know, obviously, it was terrible, but . . . but do you still think about it a lot? Or, does it, with time going by, do the memories sort of recede a little, become less harsh?"

Her question was really a disguised expression of hope, for she saw how their relations were developing. Dante had worried aloud often enough about Cohen's mental health that she knew she must try and discover the worst of his condition while she could—while there was still time to climb back from the ledge, if need be.

"Guys like me, Laney, we'll never be totally the same," he said. "I won't lie to you." His voice was low, but strong.

"Men who've experienced such fear, who've seen what combat does to a human body—or to a mind, how it drives some guys stark raving nuts—they can never put that image away. It's there for the duration. Everything else is a footnote."

"Yes, but can't you try to think about something else and . . ."

"Sometimes, there is nothing else . . . No, it's . . . I think it's like a virus, you know, that, once it's in your blood, is there forever."

"Forever?" She closed her eyes in the dark.

"Maybe. Too soon to tell, really, but it's something you carry around inside you, waiting for it to bloom into full view—whenever it wants to. On its own schedule, prompted by its own logic."

He smiled and caressed her cheek with his fingers,

"Fortunately, it's not catching."

"Memory's a funny thing," she whispered.

"No . . . no, it's a cruel, brutal thing, and it can kill you." Then, he chuckled, " 'Course, you can't get to heaven if you don't die."

"Please don't say things like that."

His mind seemed to have drifted away from her, not sleepily, but into a state of lulling reverie in which his voice sounded slightly disembodied, as though he were talking to God—or speaking for God.

"Memory divides us against ourselves, Girly Pearlie, it sets up a war inside our heads. It's sort of like that earthquake I was telling you about, you know? Out in California they're always going on about aftershocks, little temblors that strike periodically, for seconds at a time, sometimes hours after the bigger, initial quake."

"That must be strange."

"Yeah, you'll be walking down the street and suddenly, without warning, you'll feel them in the balls of your feet, small realignments of the cosmos right beneath you. Aftershocks. Unpredictable, scary reminders of the quake itself, and very destabilizing in their randomness.

"I see the war as like a really massive earthquake that lasted for years. And then it ended. And for those of us who were trapped in it, for the rest of our lives there are these memories—the aftershocks— that send tremors through our brains and into our lives, and the lives of those around us . . . And we either deal with it or succumb to it. Aftershocks . . . Dante has them. You ought to hear him scream in the middle of a nightmare."

To make him stop, she kissed his chest, his ear, his mouth.

The USS Little is sinking.

Avoiding body parts scattered along the port-side weather deck, Lieutenant David Cohen forces his way aft through a chaotic jamboree of fire, smoke, and terror. His uniform spotted with bits of his captain's head, he reaches the stern.

On the way, he has grabbed stunned, bleeding sailors and put them to work saving their shipmates. He has organized rescue and fire-suppression parties to try and keep his ship afloat long enough to salvage what's left of the crew. He has slapped some men across the face, hard; others he has bear-hugged and encouraged, all in an effort to bring them to their senses, to jump-start their brains.

Working with the burly Machinist Mate Chief, Ralph Graham, he sets up a first-aid station on the fantail and sees to it that the worse-wounded and burned are cared for as well as possible. Graham, his hair and eyebrows singed black, has now made six trips back down into the flaming engineering spaces, bringing up wounded sailors on each passage.

But carrying a 170 lb. man 20 feet up a vertical ladder is proving— even for a man of Graham's enormous strength—nearly too much. He lies haggard and heaving on the deck. Cohen thinks the man's dying, but Graham manages to rasp out, No, he'll go back down in a second.

Cohen orders Graham to refocus: We've got to cast off the motor whale boat!'

Graham tells him it's smashed.

'Then we've got to release the life rafts into the water! We've got to get the wounded into the rafts! We've got to get away from the ship before she takes us all down!'

The young chief and the even younger officer lock eyes in the midst of this ruinous hell.

Graham nods.

'Aye, aye, sir,' he says, then staggers to his feet, collars a couple of nearby sailors who're kneeling paralyzed with fear, and calmly tells them to start loosening the life rafts, throwing them over the side, and tying them off so they don't drift away.

In a voice made almost tranquil by violence, he tells them that if they don't do it right and on the double he will personally kill them on the spot. This forceful directive has the desired effect; the men go to work, followed by others, helping.

Cohen turns to set the same task underway on the starboard side, when, suddenly a scorching explosion roars up out of the gaping hole left by the missing 5" gun mount. Cohen takes the full force of the cooking-off ammo's blast on his left side. Parts of his uniform are shredded, the surface of his face is blackened and peeled, and he is blown against a bulkhead, injuring his back.

This fresh tragedy has added bodies to the pyre. As Cohen struggles to his feet, he reaches out with his left arm to grab a support, only to recoil in horror at the mangled remains of his hand—fingers missing, wet and shiny tendons, bones and blood vessels exposed as though displayed in the pages of a medical student's anatomy text.

With this wound, he knows he will either die or lapse into shock—or both—if he doesn't get immediate help.

Meanwhile, the Little now lists a good 15 degrees to starboard. Ambulatory men have difficulty walking, while—like a macabre corps de ballet—the dead and wounded slide across the deck to the lower side and into the water—now up to within a foot of the scuppers— before anyone can save them.

A medical corpsman sees his skipper's wound and produces a tourniquet, morphine and sulfa powder from a shoulder bag. Within minutes, he has Cohen stabilized and the bleeding stanched.

His hand wrapped in gauze, Cohen now gives orders to begin loading the life rafts, and—working with Graham and the few undamaged sailors clustered on the fantail—they effect a singular rescue at sea, tenderly lowering the wounded into the rafts, tossing in food and water, assigning stations and duties to the dazed.

By now, the initial confusion over what is happening to them has abated somewhat, and their training kicks in. Men are doing what they should to help each other, to load the rafts, to clear the ship.

Thirty-seven minutes after the first kamikaze struck her, the Little— sleek, lethal greyhound that she was, her back broken—slips beneath the waves with a sigh of escaping steam. The surface of the sea is left calm, oil-soaked, and flecked with life rafts, debris, floating bodies, and a few swimmers struggling in their cumbersome kapok life jackets to keep their heads above the waves.

Cohen in one raft and Graham in another see to it that all rafts are lashed together for safety. It's not even noon, yet the hot Pacific sun has already begun to do its work.

Everyone is thirsty.

In Cohen's raft a Radioman second class, named Stotsenburg, tells his captain that after the Abandon Ship order was passed he managed to key off a Morse code S.O.S. twice. He thinks it went out, but he can't be sure. David commends the petty officer for his actions. Then Stotsenburg groans and points at something in the near-distance.

Cohen looks and sees a shark's fin cutting a leisurely, inquisitive wake through the water, heading on a roundabout course for the lashed-together rafts.

They've been in the water less than 16 minutes.

* * *

Evelyn Curtis sat in her brightly lit bedroom pounding on a typewriter. Seven envelopes—all addressed to different airlines—lay on the table next to her elbow. Try as she might, she couldn't get the Pan-Am rodents out of her head—particularly the Ugly One and the Bald One. Something about the overt pleasure they took in denying her the opportunity to fly commercially—when she knew she was more qualified than half the men they would actually hire— "boiled her gizzard," as her mother, Atlanta, would say. Still, the Pretty One had stood up for her like a champ, and he had said he would take the issue to higher authority. She figured no news was good news.

Evelyn's fingers paused over the keyboard as she wondered for the hundredth time whether this dream of flying with the big boys was reasonable, nuts, or both. Nothing, nothing gave her more pleasure than being in the cockpit, testing herself, man-handling a plane through the sky right at its limits . . . Well, great sex ran a close second, maybe, but she hadn't had much of that lately. This thought, in turn, vivified both Tim Fletcher and Dante Larocca simultaneously—but differently—in her mind's eye. She shook her head and went back to work.

"Evelyn? . . . You in there?" It was her mother.

"Come in, Mom."

"Dear, you have a telegram." Atlanta Curtis entered the room looking 10 years younger than her age, a handsome, patrician woman with the bearing of a soldier of the Old Guard and the temperament of a saint.

Evelyn jumped up and took the telegram.

"Oh, maybe it's from Pan-Am, I hope, I hope, I hope . . ." She tore it open, and her face fell. Then she tacked.

"Well, it's not from them, but it's good news. Betty Braxton and two other girls I flew with in the WASPS are coming through in a few days, and they want to stay here, if it's okay."

"Of course, hon, I love to meet women who can do something besides sew, gossip, and cook. They're more than welcome."

"Swell." She glanced again at the telegram. "And they have a 'business prop' they want to put to me. Wonder what . . ."

"Maybe they want all of you to apply to law school together."

This old running gag between them had never died, and when Evelyn returned, crestfallen, from New Orleans, Atlanta half-hoped the disappointment might lead her headstrong daughter to consider other employment options. That did not, however, appear to be happening.

"Motherrrrr . . ."

"Just a thought. And here's another: your father . . ." her voice caught in her throat, making Evelyn look up sharply.

"What about him?"

"Evelyn, your father isn't well." She drew a breath, stood up a little straighter and continued. "He, uh, he's had some tests in Birmingham, and the doctors don't like what they're finding. It could be stomach acid. It could be stomach cancer."

The daughter looked at the mother, then reached out and took her in her arms. They stood there, embracing, each woman cascading through her own memories of this man who had so dominated their lives in different, sometimes intemperate ways.

Atlanta drew back slightly, her eyes red.

"Darling, I know he can be a difficult old son-of-a-bitch. Indeed, he is often coarse, opinionated, and vulgar and sometimes throws his weight around like a rich gorilla . . ."

"All true . . ."

"But, at the end of the day, I love him. And I love you. And it just kills me that you and he are not able to get past . . . to completely reconcile all these years after . . ."

"I'll try, mother. I really will. But I've tried before—more than once—and he's rebuffed me."

"Yes, darling, but it may be different this time. He's frightened. He thinks, rightly or wrongly, he may be dying. I know this sounds like something out of a dime-store novel, but if you'd consider approaching him, I would appreciate it more than I can say."

Evelyn took her mother's hands in hers.

"I will, Mom, I will consider it very, very carefully."

"Thank you, sweetheart."

An hour later, Evelyn parked her convertible at the university post office, ran inside, and posted her seven airline-bound letters. On the way out, she spoke to a couple of local fellows she'd gone to high school with, guys who'd dropped out of college, joined the Marines and fought their way across the Pacific. One had been badly burned on his face and neck in the fighting on Guadalcanal, but both were back in school on the G.I. Bill and doing okay.

"Hey, Curtis," said the burned one, "you still flying around up there with the zoomies?"

"You know it, Silkwood, gonna get a job with an airline real soon. Then I can ferry you and Mrs. S. out to Hawaii for a vacation when you graduate."

"Hell, I'd fly with you any day. I've seen you crop dust. Say hello to your old lady for me."

"Will do."

They moved on. As Evelyn walked toward her car, fishing keys from her purse, someone grabbed her arm from behind.

"Hello, sugar cakes, long time no see." It was a good-looking man with a crooked grin and 'fighter pilot' imprinted all over his face.

"Do I know you?"

"Kilroy's. Back in the fall. You were with that guinea greaseball that claimed you could out-fly me in a Mustang. Name's Kevin Marshall. But I never caught yours."

She remembered now, without pleasure.

"Evelyn. Evelyn Curtis." Dislike of this bozo competed with the happy memory of her whamming down a tray of drinks on the head of one of his buddies after the lights went out that night.

"Well, hello, Evelyn Curtis. You're lookin' good, babe. Say, I ran into the guinea again awhile back, and he's still runnin' his mouth about you and that Mustang. What's the deal, there? You two sack-mates, or what? 'Cause if you're not, I like to offer my services . . ."

"You insufferable shit-heel! Who're you calling a guinea? That guy's my good friend. As for the Mustang, I could take you apart!"

Marshall recoiled, his expression changing from would-be lover-boy to outraged male insultee, his voice taking on an ugly snarl.

"Well, like I told the wop: bring it on. I could use the dough. What was the bet, anyway, four hundred or so bucks?"

"I don't recall," she said, "but, tell you what: I'll add five thousand of my own money to it. How's that sound?"

Their shouting and body language had attracted a crowd of the curious. The big-money offer threw Marshall on the defensive.

"Hell, woman, I don't have those kind of bucks."

"Okay, then, make it a thousand. Plus the original four hundred. Surely you can handle that?"

He couldn't, but he wasn't going to say so.

"Oh, yeah, easy. Name the day."

"Wait a minute. Who's gonna judge this little flying shindig? And who'll be holding the money? I wouldn't trust your pals as far as I could spit."

A tall man who stood nearby watching the dust-up said, "You two talking about an aerobatic contest of some kind?"

"Yeah, what's it to you, pal?" Evelyn was in no mood for more incoming crap from another wise guy.

"Easy, lady, I'm neutral here. But I flew Corsairs off a carrier in the Pacific, and I've got some fighter pilot buddies here at school. If you two are serious and want unbiased judges, I think I could round up a team for, maybe, fifty bucks or so."

"Consider it done. That okay with you, Marshall?"

Kevin had nowhere to hide.

"Yeah, sure. Great." To the tall guy he said, "What's your name and phone number? We'll get in touch when it's set up."

"Name's Britton, Bill Britton. Number's 994. It's a party line, but you can usually get through, if the women aren't talking about recipes and hair . . ."

A look from Evelyn silenced him.

Chapter 16

Dante Larocca sat on his cot, face wreathed in bliss. In one hand he held a glass containing two inches of bootleg bourbon whiskey on which he'd just gotten started. In the other, a one-page letter from Professor Sidney D. Greene containing this sentence: "I am pleased to inform you that your proposal has been chosen as one of the five finalists for this year's Dalton Fellowship Prize."

Pleasure so obliterated Dante's other senses that he failed to hear Cleola, Shorty Puckett's rotund wife, calling his name.

Finally, she appeared at the tent flap.

"Danny?" as she called him. "Danny, you got a call on the telerphone. It's that pretty lady, Evelyn Curtis, used to board her horses with us and flies them planes, and all."

Dante jumped up, thanked Cleola, knocked back the bourbon, and sprinted for the al fresco phone mounted on the wall of the Pucketts' screen porch.

"I need to talk to you."

It was, sure enough, Evelyn.

"Hey, kiddo, no problem, what's up?"

She explained briefly about running into Kevin Marshall and asked Larocca to meet her at her airport hangar.

"I thought, since it was Saturday, maybe you had some free time."

"I'll be there in twenty," he said, and rang off.

He considered taking a quick shower. Decided against it. Whiffed his pits, reconsidered, grabbed soap and towel, and scrambled toward the barn where Shorty had set up a full-service latrine for the resident vets. Twenty-three minutes later, he and Sir Plus rolled up to Evelyn's double hangar, housing both the mustang and the crop-dusting Stearman biplane—now repaired.

Her hair pulled back in a bun, dressed in a black sweater, rolled green scarf at the neck, and tight khaki flying pants stuffed into short boots, she was waiting. She looked like something off a Vargas calendar.

"Jesus wept," Dante muttered to himself. "But then Jesus never saw this dame."

Sir Plus bounded out of the jeep and over to Evelyn for a quick hug and a coo, got both, set off in a series of mad dashes around the dirt-and-grass strip, then spotted and chased a blue monoplane rolling down the runway before taking off into the afternoon sky. Dante whistled for him, but Sir Plus was running dead out, convinced he could catch the plane.

"Crazy damn dog, that one," said Dante, approaching her and shaking hands. "You okay? Sounded a little strung out on the phone."

"Yeah, not bad. I just needed . . . I wanted to discuss this Mustang flying-the-bet thing."

Truth to tell, some of her furious confidence about going up against a veteran combat pilot in a test of aerobatic skills had waned a tad.

That, plus she simply wanted to see Dante Larocca, period.

"So, how'd it go in New Orleans?" he said.

"Not good. Not bad. One of the Pan-Am guys seemed open to it. Two others didn't. They haven't said no yet, and I've applied to half-a-dozen other airlines."

"One of 'em will bite."

"For sure."

"Well," he smiled. "I know you're disappointed, but it didn't hurt your appearance any."

"Thanks. Come inside the hangar; I've got an old fridge with beer in it. I mean, if you'd like one."

"If? IF? Lady, you forget who you're talking to."

She laughed as they strolled toward the old Kelvinator ice box. He seemed genuinely interested in her situation.

"Tell me about your run-in with Kelvin the Krud."

"It's . . . isn't it 'Kevin?'

He chuckled. "Yeah, but I call him Kelvin just to piss him off."

As the afternoon wore on, and the empties piled up around them, Evelyn and Dante drank and talked and broke down barriers. The thing about him, she realized, was that no matter how outré he seemed at first glance—or first hearing—if you paid attention to what he said and the enthusiasm and conviction with which he said it, he reeled you in to his world, his passions, his values and loves. Then, she noticed that he had stopped talking and was just looking at her around a sly, smirky grin.

"All right, Brooklyn Cat, where's the canary?"

"Chomp-chomp. I ate it. And I made the finals for a Dalton Prize."

She screamed her delight, jumped over and hugged him tight, her breasts pressing against, her arms around him.

"Congratulations, Dante, that's fabulous! I'm so happy for you."

They stood holding each other a second or two longer than was strictly required by custom, then separated.

"Thanks, I was pretty happy, and—by the way—did you know that Frank Lloyd Wright is God?"

"God's a woman."

"Oh, yeah, I forgot. Okay, God's right-hand man, then. Get it: Wright/right?"

"Lame, Larocca."

They laughed; he admitted it.

"But what makes you say that? Why's he different from a hundred other 'greats'?

"Well, a lot of people hate him—including Sidney Greene—and from what I can tell, he's a total loss as a human being—vain, arrogant, hates Jews—but he's also, even at his present age of, what, nearly 80 or something, he's still way ahead of everybody else—at least in my opinion—with his vision."

"Because?"

"Because he builds what he calls 'organic architecture,' which means folding your designs into the landscape so that the structure and the site blend perfectly."

"Yes, I've seen photographs of . . ."

"No, no, photographs lie! You have to go there. You have to stand in front of his buildings, penetrate them, examine the details."

His eyes shone.

"Have you done that?"

They were sitting on an old couch covered with a chenille bedspread and jammed up against one wall of the hangar, a place for Evelyn to take cat naps on between crop-dusting missions. Suddenly, Dante jumped up and began pacing, waving his beer around and proselytizing like a mad-dog revivalist.

"Lady, I've seen 22 of them—up close and personal. Most of the Prairie Style homes. Plus, the Unity Temple in Oak Park, Illinois, 1905. Hey, and on that, get this: a church with no steeple, no pitched roof, just bare poured concrete molded like plastic. Or . . . or, the Robie House in Chicago. Oh, God! Built in 1909 and still looks like the day after tomorrow, and the Boynton House in Rochester, 1907, and the Willits House, 1902, in Highland Park, and the Heurtley House, also 1902, and . . ."

"But how did you get there to . . ."

"Hitch-hiked, rode the rails . . ." he laughed. "Even stole a truck once in Milwaukee to get out to the Bogk House, 1916, where the trains don't go. Nearly wound up in the klink on that one. Stupid cops . . . And, oh, yeah, I got over to Wingspread, 1937, in Wind Point, Wisconsin. Fabulous, big house, and, oh, jeez, I don't know how many others. And you know what? There're a couple dozen, maybe, out in California that I haven't seen, like Hollyhock House and the Storer House—but I will—but no time soon, you know, because, well, travel costs and school . . ."

He was electric, a man on fire. She watched him pace back and forth, his mind leaping from structure to structure.

"Okay, wild boy: Which is your favorite?"

Without a beat: "'Fallingwater.'"

"Falling what?"

"'Fallingwater,' Bear Run, Pennsylvania. 1935. Built for the Kaufmanns. His masterpiece."

"An over-used word, if I ever heard one." She got up, retrieved two beers from their dwindling supply, opened both with a church key, and handed him one.

"Still, masterpiece. No question. A cubist sculpture, really, pretending to be a house."

"So, how close did you get to this one?"

She settled back on the couch, legs outstretched and crossed on the cushions, arm lying across the back.

"How close is inside?"

"They let you in?"

"Hell, I broke in."

"What?"

"God's own truth. Sneaked up on it around midnight, see. Nobody home. Wild country around there, near Pittsburgh. The property is real hilly, with a pretty little river running through it."

"Hence, Bear Run."

"Check. A river, like. So, anyway, there I am hiding in the trees. I got drinking water with me, some food, heavy coat. And there's a full moon distributing light all over the site, like something . . . something in a movie. And the rocks in the river there cause a water cascade right under these massive cantilevered balconies—God knows how he got them to suspend like that. And I can hear and see the water, and about four A.M. a bear, a black bear and her cubs come down and drink from the river, and then they sort of amble off.

"And then, and then"—he thrust his beer up toward the roof— "the sun starts to rise, just a hint of yellow and rose glow in the east. And as I sat there watching—the sun coming up—slowly you see this incredible . . . thing, this series of brilliantly balanced horizontals and angles emerging, and it's turning from black and white to full color, and it looks like it grew straight out of the hillside.

"Wright's got stone walls repeating the stone cliffs, and staggered bays that step back one above the other. And these parapet edges, they're curvilinear, you know, rounded, something he'd never done before, and their pale color and . . . softness just . . ." He took a deep breath, his eyes closed. "It just breaks your heart that something—that a house—could be so beautiful."

He stopped, drained, embarrassed that he'd let his enthusiasms run away.

"And you broke into this place?" she said.

He sat on the couch next to her. "Ehh, jimmied a window and roamed around. The Kaufmanns never knew. I didn't take nothing."

"Amazing story."

"Sorry to be so, you know . . . noisy," he said, "don't often get a chance to talk about that sort of thing."

She watched his every move.

"Don't apologize," she said gently. "To care about anything that much is good. Noble, even."

"Well," he smiled, "don't know about that, but . . ."

Suddenly, from outside they heard a plane landing and a dog barking, then the dog screaming in agony. Both bolted for the wide-mouthed hangar door just in time to see Sir Plus cartwheeling down the runway, ass-over-teacup, while the pilot of the blue monoplane struggled to keep his craft's left wing from digging into the dirt, flipping and killing him.

Sir Plus had been hit by the plane.

Dante is once again at war. Bleeding from a dozen wounds, he struggles to drag Buddy Fooshee through tall grass away from their burning tank and the two German soldiers he's just shot with his .45.

Behind him, he can see several other Wehrmacht soldiers crouched and hidden, maneuvering to blast the one remaining American tank that hasn't been knocked out. Two other Shermans are ablaze, with surviving members of their crews climbing out the top hatch, guys pulling their crew-mates out behind them. But every time an American shows his head, he gets shot at, and often hit. It's turning into a turkey shoot, and the Americans are the turkeys.

Buddy is a moaning, ruined wreck, his mouth shattered, face lacerated, hair matted with dirt, leaves, and snot. He tells Dante over and over to leave him, to save himself. He curses Dante for a fool. He tells him that if the situation were reversed he'd leave Dante on the battlefield and run for his life.

Dante knows his friend is lying; he also knows he's screwed if he can't stop the Krauts.

Then an idea hits him. He pauses and tenderly props Buddy against a tree some 100 meters away from the tank vs. troop skirmish going on behind them. He gives Buddy his canteen and tells him to lie still and feign death if any Germans discover him. Buddy grins, his tooth-stumps wet with blood and saliva.

''Fore long I won't have to pretend, will I, Brooklyn?'

Dante ignores him. He can hear firing and shouts rising back at the tanks. He pats Buddy on the knee and scurries away, almost on all-fours. Within two minutes he's arrived at his burning tank, now fully engulfed in flames. Lying near it are the two dead Germans and their Panzerfaust, the lethal hand-carried bazooka that has dealt such misery to the Americans. Dante knows it's loaded because he saw the Germans at work before he shot them.

With the separate battle raging nearby, he crawls to the bodies and rolls the gunner off his weapon, a crude pipe affair with a big explosive charge attached to one end. The German's blood makes it slippery. Dante wipes it off with his shirt tail.

Heat from the burning tank drenches him in sweat.

He examines the weapon. He's seen these before in training and knows vaguely how they work. He shoulders it, fingers the trigger, cocks his head, and peers through a crude sight. When he thinks he's got it figured, he crawfishes away from the tank and takes cover behind an overturned German staff car.

About 50 meters away, he can see a cluster of enemy soldiers preparing to blast the remaining American tank that struggles to pull back, trying to escape what has turned out to be a vicious trap set by a well-managed, retreating army.

Dante props the heavy Panzerfaust on an axle of the wrecked staff car and takes aim. Then, he notices something strange. Near the cluster of Germans, but maybe 20 meters away, is an animal of some kind.

He looks closer. It's a dog. A large gray dog tied to a post. The dog is terrified, his yowl adding a mammalian keening to the metallic horror that is the sound of battle.

Dante's attention flits from dog to men, men to dog. Then he aims the German weapon at the middle of four soldiers as they fire a .50 caliber machine gun against the Americans. He squeezes off a round.

The Panzerfaust roars and almost leaps from his grasp. A second later, the round explodes right in the midst of the Germans, hurling bodies in all directions.

The dog is stunned into silence.

Then, it's all over. This is the last remaining quartet of Germans in the vicinity, left behind to retard the enemy's advance. And they've succeeded. Dante drops the Panzerfaust, unholsters his .45 and creeps forward to check the Germans.

When he gets to them, it's plain they're dead. Hell, they're in pieces. He spies the butt of a beautiful Luger pistol protruding from a holster attached to one of the officers' bodies. He grabs the Luger, sticks it in his belt, and signals to the American Sherman that it's all over.

Then he moves to the dog who crouches, quivering, a low growl gurgling in its throat. Dante whispers to him, makes a clicking sound with his tongue, then reaches out and strokes his flank. The dog responds.

Each has found what he needs.

Dante unties the dog and runs with him back to check on Buddy. As he approaches, he calls out in a low voice:

'Buddy, Buddy, man, look what I found. You ever seen a dog this

color . . .'

But Buddy Fooshee is dead.

*Dante's knees buckle. He collapses on the spot from blood loss and
delayed shock.*

The great gray dog whines and lies down next to him.

The war, for all three, is over.

* * *

Tim Fletcher sat in a comfortable leather chair placed near the center
of Dr. Lawrence Feldman's Birmingham office. The dapper little
psychiatrist appeared to be working through a significant conundrum
while Tim stared a hole in his face.

"A Russian spy?" Feldman said. "In Tuscaloosa, Alabama?"

"I said it was conjectural. And unlikely. But, if you were in my shoes,
what would you do—assuming, against all odds, that it were true?"

In positing the "Rangle Hypothetical" to Feldman, Fletcher had
omitted any mention of the two Bureau apes who'd sat in his living
room, saying simply, "what if . . . ?"

"Tim, really, I think . . . I understand that your experience with
the weapons—the atomic bombs—has induced great psychological
trauma, and that those experiences continue to haunt your waking
thoughts . . ."

"And dreams."

"Quite. However, I find it exquisitely unlikely that the Soviets have
sent a spy—a secret agent of some kind—to, to your laboratory. I
mean, don't you see that this is almost certainly a delusion on your
part, born out of . . ."

"So, you think I'm crazier now than when we started these chatty

288

little visits eight or nine months ago?"

"We don't use words like 'crazy' in the practice of psychiatry."

"Pity."

"Tim, I suspect it more likely that you have taken a strong dislike to this student—if he exists—possibly because . . ."

"He certainly exists, doctor."

"Very well . . . possibly because something about him vividly reminds you of someone you detest or fear. A kind of transference, for example, to the student from one of the scientists who worked on the bomb at Los Alamos."

"Seems highly unlikely to me."

"Stranger things have happened. Believe me. Now, it's my understanding that several of the top theoretical physicists out there were foreigners—east Europeans, even German-born, perhaps. And your . . . your difficulties in assimilating your experience of the bomb might have led you to suspect this student of something nefarious."

Off of Feldman's theory, Tim ran through the miscellany of nationalities and types Dr. Oppenheimer had convened in the wilds of New Mexico early in the war: a little something for every taste, and no taste too weird. Hungarians, Italians, Englishmen, Danes, red-necks, heathens, Mormons—but this, he had to remind himself, was beside the point. Victor Rangle was a brilliant student of his, and had been for months.

Not only that, but ten days ago two agents from Hoover's F.B.I. had shown up on his doorstep advancing the fully developed and documented Rangle/Ronchipov parable—although not having seen the documentation, Fletcher had to trust what they'd said.

Still, he hadn't made them up. Akers and Zeiler, however ill-dressed and dull-witted, definitely existed. They had knocked on his door, and they had scared the living crap out of him with their whispered tale of nuclear espionage, subterfuge, and intrigue. Now, the question, as he saw it, was what was he going to do with the information? His options were limited: 1. he could keep his yap shut, award the fellowship to Rangle, and wait for the feds to pounce—maybe killing the guy, right there in Fletcher's own lab if the Russian resisted. Or, 2. he could tip Rangle off in hopes that he might disappear before the Bureau jumped him.

As strange as the latter alternative sounded—even to Tim—it had a certain appeal. In the first place, he truly liked the young man and respected his intelligence and charm—as he might an exceptional younger brother who was treading in his older sibling's professional footsteps. Over the past months he had several times invited him, along with two or three others of his brighter students, to his house for sherry—an academic tradition he'd admired at Oxford.

Together, they'd sat around discussing physics and baseball—and the physics of baseball—poetry and art, wine and music (Rangle favored Borodin, Rimski-Korsikov, and Stravinsky). Any subject, in short, except the war, which Tim had made off-limits—for personal reasons, claiming, falsely, the death of two cousins in the Pacific fighting.

In those afternoon gatherings, Rangle had shown himself a man of culture and refinement, master of several languages—Russian not among them, interestingly—an accomplished pianist, raconteur, athlete, and connoisseur of single malt scotches, which, he said, he'd discovered while hiking in Scotland before the war.

Tim's other American students, no matter how capable as budding physicists, were neither socially sophisticated nor well-traveled, and not one of them had ever heard of single-malt scotch. It's true that several had journeyed the world—in the sense of visiting remote, steaming Pacific atolls filled with heavily armed enemy soldiers and murderous booby traps, or, perhaps, had fought or flown across France, Italy, North Africa, or Germany—but that hardly amounted to the same thing.

No, Rangle was a breed apart, and he knew it, the other students knew it, and Tim Fletcher knew it.

A final, more complicated consideration also shaped Tim's thoughts regarding what he should do about Victor Rangle. At Los Alamos, late in the war, as it became clear that Oppenheimer's claque of geniuses was overcoming the last of the theoretical obstacles to building an atomic weapon, some of the participants began to grow queasy about the applied implications of their work. No matter how long they'd labored on the project, often for years, several of the scientists had begun to have second thoughts.

Recognizing a Faustian bargain when they saw one, they knew that in the name of saving the world for democracy they'd been lured by Oppenheimer and General Groves into pursuing the holy grail of particle physics—splitting the atom and fashioning out of the result the most destructive weapon on the face of the planet. The more they thought about it, the less bewitched some of them became by the fruits of their labor.

In fact, during the last frenzied weeks leading up to the dawn explosion at Alamagordo—then Hiroshima on 6 August—a number of prominent scientists associated with the Manhattan Project in New Mexico, or Oak Ridge, or Hanford had written letters or pled their case in person at the highest levels of government. They argued for, at the very least, what was being called a demonstration bomb that might be exploded under controlled circumstances in some manner designed to convince the Japanese military high command that they must accede to the Allies' demand for unconditional surrender.

Privately, Tim Fletcher had adopted their view. Not that he'd acted, but he had come to share those doubters' dread of what the bomb meant in its practical application. In the process, he also absorbed these men's attendant guilt over what their prodigious technical skills had wrought. This guilt had haunted him ever since.

But it was too little, too late. If the bomb worked, the bomb would drop. And some hapless Japanese city, its civilian population notwithstanding, would be converted to energy.

The geo-political corollary to all this was what had led Tim to advance the "Rangle Hypothetical" to Dr. Feldman in the first place. As posed, the question turned on an argument proposed by some bomb-makers that the Americans were duty-bound to share their recently developed nuclear technology with the Soviets—their nominal partners in the long war against tyranny.

Scientists favoring this view believed it was the only way to internationalize atomic energy and thus to avoid a world-wide arms race that would last 100 years and conclude by destroying civilization.

Others considered this contention to be the most woolly-minded, credulous piece of drivel they'd ever heard.

And they said so.

Tim Fletcher was somewhere in the middle.

Meanwhile, the "Rangle Hypothetical" remained unresolved—and Dr. Feldman, unconvinced.

* * *

Life—viewed from the perspective of canis familiaris weimaranis—comprised one long happy parade of pleasure and folly. But dogs didn't domesticate themselves for nothing, and Sir Plus's appraisal of others' potential for pleasuring him bore a striking resemblance to the one voiced by that subtle observer of human desire, the heavily tattooed Marine, Ben, when he told Shorty Puckett that night in Kilroy's that "if you can't eat it, drink it, grope it, fight it or fuck it, then I say piss on it."

Although, strictly speaking, Sir Plus did not comprehend the full range of tumult embedded in each of those active verbs, he did grasp their essential tenor. To Ben's List of Desirable Options (BLODO) he might have added "sniff it, lick it, and bite it," and he would certainly have included "chase it."

When he and Dante pulled up to Evelyn's airplane hangar that afternoon, he'd leaped out and copped a sniff off her, then blasted away to mark a ton of prime local territory. In the midst of washing a tire on Evelyn's convertible, he'd looked up to see a most alluring sight: a blue car-with-wings thing trundling down the grass air strip, roaring to beat hell and with CHASE ME written all over it in a hound idiom universally recognized by the species. He had forthwith complied, reaching a terminal velocity of approximately 31 mph before falling behind in the monoplane's wake as it gained speed and left the ground.

Left the ground!

That was the part that so nonplussed Sir Plus: the flaming thing went airborne on him. He was not amused. With that extraordinary attention span that Dante had commented on the day Evelyn nearly crashed her Stearman into Shorty's field of dreams, Sir Plus had aborted his mad dash, but he had not ceased to follow the plane's every move with his laser vision.

Never having seen the dog, the poor student pilot took off with a particularly nasty ex-Marine flight instructor at his side and now had all he could do to keep from bailing out in response to his teacher's shouted "Do this! Don't do that! Why the hell did you do THAT? Are you trying to kill both of us?"

Down below, panting, Sir Plus stood his ground in the middle of the strip, rotating slowly as he followed the plane with rapt intent. Five hundred feet above him, the kid struggled to keep it straight and level while he circled the field, fending off the Marine's running disparagement of his marginal flying skills.

Thus, while, in the hangar, Dante regaled Evelyn with the many charms of Frank Lloyd Wright's Fallingwater, nearby a drama of imminent collision played itself out between dog and plane.

"All right, private," growled the Marine, gesturing down toward the air field, "let's see if you can manage to put this bird back on the deck without taking out half the civilian population of the county."

"Yessir," said the farm kid, banking the plane through 90 degrees of sky, en route home and unknown danger.

Sir Plus missed nothing.

As the little blue, high-winged monoplane lined itself up with the runway, reduced power, and began its approach, the Weimaraner's antennae quivered on all frequencies. Crouching so that his stomach almost touched the dirt, he eased over into the higher grass near the edge of the preferred touch-down area and waited, positioning himself so that a quick sprint should get him a mouthful of tire with no trouble—but never bothering to solve the key canine paradox: "what will I do with it if I catch it?"

Down drifted the airplane, its wheel struts protruding like the outstretched arms of a blind man in a strange house, its Marine instructor whispering invective, mixed with encouragement, to the young pilot.

"There you go, son, easy now . . . check your airspeed, check it, that's it . . . nose up a little . . . you're too fast, boy, throttle back . . . lookin' nice . . . left, ease it left, now . . . attaboy, sweet, now set her down and let's roll out . . . What the hell is that?"

He was referring to a streaking gray blur ahead that had come lunging out of the grass verge on a near-perfect vector to intercept the plane as it began scrubbing off ground speed. The farm boy pilot saw it as well, had no idea what it was, but knew that hitting it was contraindicated.

In a panic, the kid tromped on his rudder pedal and yanked the yoke—at precisely the moment the Marine did the same thing, but in opposite directions. The net effect was to throw the plane into a skittering crab-walk down the runway—and fouling up Sir Plus's carefully calculated intercept in the bargain, so that when animal and machine collided, the dog had already seen how badly the humans were screwing things up here and had just turned away to prepare for a second try, later.

That's what saved his life.

By avoiding both the prop and the main weight of the wheel, he'd simply been knocked into the howling, cartwheeling, whirligig that Dante and Evelyn saw when they emerged on a dead run from the hangar.

Dante got to him first and found his four-legged pal in a state of quivering semi-consciousness, his eyes open but unseeing, his mouth gaping in a rictus of confused pain.

"How the hell did that happen?" the dog seemed to be asking.

When Evelyn ran up to the crime scene, she took one look—and then she took over. Down on his knees next to Sir Plus, Dante crouched, frozen with horror, both hands hovering over the dog.

"Don't touch him, Dante," she said, "he could bite you without meaning to."

"I know, I know, what do we do . . ." Dante was weeping.

"We'll get him to Dr. Patterson," she said. "He's the best vet in town. Give me your keys."

Blindly, Dante handed her his key ring, then slumped in the dirt next to the dog, whispering to it. Evelyn sprinted for the jeep. In three minutes she was back with the vehicle and the bedspread she'd ripped off the old couch.

Together, they wrapped Sir Plus in it and gently lifted him into the back of the jeep, cradling his head. By now, Sir Plus had begun to regain his senses and recognize Dante, but he wasn't able to stand, or even to move his legs in a coordinated fashion. Drool leaked from his mouth onto the bedspread.

"Follow me to the vet," Evelyn said, "and, Dante," she took his face in her hands, "Listen to me. I think he'll be okay. Maybe some nerve damage and a couple of ribs, but he doesn't look too bad. You listenin' to me?"

He nodded. "Yeah, I'm with you." He gently drew her hands away from his face and kissed her palms.

"Thanks," he whispered. "'Preciate it."

Twenty minutes after he was struck, Sir Plus was resting in the exam room of former defensive tackle, Dr. Joe Patterson, a bluff, large-animal vet and practicing good ol' boy who'd trained and played ball at Auburn. Patterson told Evelyn and Dante he wanted to keep Sir Plus a few days for observation, but it looked to him like the young fella would pull through.

"Not so sure about you, though," he said to an anxious Larocca. "You look like shit."

"Yeah, well, him and me, we been through a lot together, and . . . and

I'd hate to lose him, you know?"

Patterson cocked an eye. "You got this dog in Germany during the war, didn't you? Offa some kraut. Dead, prob'ly."

Dante didn't like the tone this big, gruff jerk was adopting.

"Yeah, matter of fact, I did. You got a problem with that?"

Evelyn started to intercede, until she saw Patterson smile.

"Naw," he said. "I've been readin' about this breed for years but never saw one. Beautiful animal. We'll save him for you, soldier."

Chapter 17

Driving home from the vet, Evelyn played back the last couple of hours and had to admit that Dante Larocca was taking up firm residence in her head—on several fronts. One tip-off lay in her instantaneous, unfeigned delight in the news of his making first cut on the Dalton Prize. She had reveled in his joy over this success, wanting to share it fully by, frankly, giving him a big, wet kiss.

Further, his unbridled enthusiasm for architecture in general, and Fallingwater in particular, captivated her. She'd sat on that old couch in the hangar and watched a man transform himself from a wise-cracking Brooklyn street tough into a passionate, articulate defender of Frank Wright's best work. Right in front of her, Larocca had become a man possessing a developed aesthetic, a sense of mission, and a willingness to take risks in order to embrace the rocky-sited house-sculpture in the wilds of Pennsylvania, to, as he said, engage it.

"Gettin' intimate with it," he'd said, without irony.

She smiled, remembering that she'd asked him whether, when he was inside the Kaufmann estate he'd stolen anything, some little token, as a memento, perhaps.

"Hell no, woman," he'd said, "that'd be like knocking over St. Patrick's Cathedral."

And then there was the Sir Plus incident. When she'd caught up to Dante kneeling in the dirt next to the wounded dog, his hands suspended helplessly above the quivering beast, she'd seen a man in extremis, a man unafraid to show his emotions in their rawest state, a man whose great love had been struck down in front of him and who, for that moment, had been sundered by the loss, inconsolable.

Evelyn well knew that in another few seconds Dante would have come to his senses, would have refrained from doing anything stupid, would have gotten the dog into the jeep and transported him to a vet, but at that critical instant of her arrival on the scene, Dante was emotionally derelict, and she, Evelyn Curtis, had had to take over and direct their joint response.

Strangely, she liked that reversal. It had about it the hint of a partnership, somehow, of a woman stepping up when a man was temporarily hors de combat, of two people who—however disparate—could work together under stress, through good times and bad. Odd, that.

Still musing, Evelyn drove up to her family's massive, columned, red-brick home and saw a travel-dirty station wagon parked in the drive.

"They're here," she shouted, jumped out and ran for the front door.

In the living room, she found her mother having a high-ball with three younger women: Betty Braxton, Mavis Raleigh, and Jill Taylor, all girls she'd flown with in the WASPS—good buddies all. Looking at this younger set, a stranger could have been forgiven for invoking Amelia Earhart four times over.

Trim, athletic, self-assured, hair clipped short, they wore slacks and sported ready grins; they talked with their hands; they laughed aloud; they took chances; they sat on the floor; they swore; they drank; they smoked; they slept with whomever they pleased—or with nobody; and they didn't take shit off of anybody. And there was very little about airplanes they didn't know.

Evelyn loved them.

"Hey, Curtis, you tart, you're lookin' great," said Betty Braxton. "How d'you do it? Haven't gained a pound."

"Ohh, Betty, you lie like a rug. I'm fat as an old sow. But look at you three. You could be gracing the front of Look or Time or something."

"Long as it ain't Ladies Home Journal," said Mavis Raleigh, and they laughed.

"Better it was Aviation Week," said Jill Taylor.

"It will be," said Betty, "one day."

Then they fell to talking.

Oh, how they talked. And often at the same time.

Atlanta Curtis sat there listening and thinking of her youth, recalling among old friends the few women her age who had dared to challenge the barriers erected by law and medical and graduate schools to keep women down. She'd felt a special kinship with those women, a bond similar to what she imagined men experienced in military boot camp, or—more ominously—that enforced solidarity recently felt by piteous prisoners of the Germans and Japanese. She saw that bond at work among her daughter and these young women, and she was proud of them all.

Now, as foretold in the earlier telegram, the newcomers had a business proposition to put to Evelyn. They wanted to form a company to fly packages and mail around the country in surplus C-47/Douglas DC-3s, workhorses of both the military and civilian fleets. Betty was their ringleader, but the other two were fully committed, having already put down money to hire a lawyer to draw up incorporation papers.

"We'll call it United Parcel Delivery, or something," Jill said.

"No, 'parcel' is too little-old-ladyish," said Betty. "Let's call it, I don't know, maybe Federal Package Express, FEPEX for short. We'll fly stuff all over the country, even people, overnight, rain or shine, next-day delivery within 500 miles. Two days for further."

"People? Like who?"

"Well, executives. Civilian brass. You could even add refrigeration and fly sea-food from, say, New Orleans to, I don't know, Omaha or some-damn-where. We'll make a mint."

"Right, the Tuna Fish Express. I don't know." Evelyn was intrigued, but skeptical.

"Well, whatever the hell we call it," said Mavis, "I love it. And you wanna know why? Because most of our package or parcel handlers will be men, and they'll be taking their stinkin' orders from us!"

They laughed.

"Yeah," said Evelyn, "but you gotta hire women for some of that work too, so they can't say, you know, that women can only do stuff while sitting on their butts . . ."

". . . Or lying on their backs," said Atlanta, then blushed. "Oh, my, did I say that? No more drinks for me."

This sally immediately endeared her to the visiting threesome.

For another hour, the young women talked, with these visitors laying out their plans, making their case, trying to convince Evelyn to join in their enterprise. Meanwhile, Atlanta Curtis wandered off to see about dinner—and to keep her husband away from the animated conversation in the living room, knowing that his ham-fistedness would kill the moment, if given a chance.

Finally, Betty pulled the trigger.

"So, Curtis, you on board with this, or what?"

Evelyn pursed her lips and glanced around.

"Okay, first, I believe in the business model you're describing. I think, given the right level of cooperation by various airport authorities, the truckers unions, the mechanics unions, male pilots, the post office, the government, and the weather, it'll work—although it'll take one hell of a lot of coordination . . ."

"I hear a big fat 'but' coming here," said Mavis.

"Girls, there's almost nothing I'd rather do than join up on this, but—yeah, there's the 'but,' but I'm gonna get on with Pan Am or American, or one of the other big airlines."

They were incredulous.

"As a stew?" said Jill. "I can't believe you'd . . ."

"As a pilot," said Evelyn, softly. "As a pilot."

"It won't happen," said Betty. "This is exactly why we're forming our own company. The crummy airlines will never hire us to fly their planes. Don't you think we've thought of that? Don't you think we'd all rather join up with a going concern, a major carrier, than buy old planes at auction and try and hammer out deals with unions and regulators, and break our asses building a new company out of nothing, and with nothing? I mean, we've hardly got $10,000 between us."

The room had darkened with the waning day. Now, it grew silent as well. Evelyn looked at them.

"Well," she said, "I've already interviewed with Pan Am, and they haven't said no. If they do . . ."

"When they do . . ."

". . . I've already mailed applications to seven other carriers." They looked at her. "I'm doing this, girls. I'm gonna be the first one of us to fly commercially. Or die trying."

"That could happen," said Mavis.

They could hear cooking sounds coming from the kitchen.

"No, Evelyn's right." It was Jill. "She's got the hours. She's got the skills. She was about the best pilot in our bunch. I say go for it. If anybody can do it, you can, champ, and if it doesn't work out, well, maybe you can join up with us later. No hard feelings."

After a pause, Mavis said, "Yeah, hell, me too. We just really wanted you along. With your looks and brains, you could have charmed even the surliest bastards into helping us."

Evelyn looked at Betty.

"All right," Betty said, "I know when I'm licked. I won't push it any further. And I wish you all the luck in world. You'll need it."

Evelyn smiled.

"But you know what?" she said, "I do have a little something going on in a few days that might interest you."

And she told them about flying-the-bet against the hot-shot Army Air Corps pilot, Kevin Marshall. They loved it.

"In your Mustang?" said Mavis.

"Right."

"Can we watch?" said Jill.

"Watch, hell, you're my ground crew!"

"Yoooo hooooo," crowed Betty Braxton. "We're gonna kick some serious Air Corps ass on this one! Gonna whip ol' Kevin Marshall like a red-headed step child, yes!"

At that very moment Mr. Harry Curtis walked into the room and halted in his tracks, his mouth agape.

"Daddy," said Evelyn, "I don't believe you've met the three musketeers. Girls, Daddy."

* * *

A couple of days after Sir Plus got blipped while trying to subdue an airplane, the two tattooed Marines, Karl and Ben, sat outside their trailer at Shorty Puckett's place drinking beer. The morning was lovely. Sun bright, temps in the mid-70s. The hordes of red-breasted robins had already passed through, heading north and pooping on every surface in sight. From Cohen's trailer, the two men could hear the steady sound of one-fingered typing.

At the university, it was the week of spring break, and Karl and Ben embraced that concept literally; indeed, they took it as an edict:

THOU SHALT NOT COMMIT SCHOOLWORK DURING SPRING BREAK.

This despite their combined GPA of about a D-. Karl, the more humanoid of the two, had given at least some thought to catching up on the reading in his Today's Health textbook—that is to say, opening it for the first time.

Although academically a snooze, this was the toughest course he'd enrolled in. They actually had quizzes. But he'd also discovered early on that the young prof teaching it had served as a combat medic with the Marines in the Pacific, until being invalided home with a gaping hole in his back and missing an eye, and—old school ties being what they were—Karl had bonded with his Semper Fi brother so tightly that it would take a particularly violent force majeure for him to fail the course.

His buddy Ben was another matter.

Like Cohen and Dante and Tim Fletcher, Ben had brought the whole war home with him. Thus, he took it to bed every night, never sure what perverse mental morsel might creep out from its dank hiding place and infect his dreams with battle mayhem, dying Marines, and acts of his own brutality to rival those of Genghis Khan.

As Karl had told Dante way back last semester, in dealing with the Japs, Ben had been very, very thorough. Dante had known better than to ask for exposition of this assessment, but he'd seen Ben participating in a couple of bar fights at Kilroy's, and the sight had not been pretty. For the other guy.

At the same time, Ben was beastly loyal and would defend to the death any of the fellows living out at Shorty's, even though he sometimes had caustic, conversationally brutal ways of showing it.

"You know," Ben said to Karl, sitting there in the sun, "Cohen's real fucked-up these days."

"Yeah? How's that?"

"You don't notice?"

"Notice what? Most of the vets are fucked up."

"No, no, Cohen's different. He's a Jew, for one thing. Smart guy, sensitive-like, a writer and all. One-armed writer. Weird, huh?"

"Big deal. He's fucked-up because he's a Jew? I don't think so. The hand? . . . maybe."

"I'm right. Put your money on it. Hey, you gotta start noticing these things, Karl. You gotta be a . . . a observer of your fellow men. Didn't the Corps teach you nothing 'bout guys gettin' their heads dicked-with in combat?"

Karl smiled. College was making little dents and dings in Ben's language and sense of the larger world—proving that no substance is perfectly hermetic. Overhearing others' conversations in class and bars, he had a way of expropriating the simplest random elements of more complex concepts and making them his own. And on his own terms.

"I'm gonna get him to come drink with us," Ben said.

"Maybe he don't want to, Ben. Maybe, 'cause he's a Jew he's afraid of sunlight. Like a vampire. Right. Man, you are fuller of shit than a sausage factory. Leave the guy alone, for Chris'sake, can't you hear him typing in there?"

"Ahh, hell! He's always typing. Friggin' book's longer than the Bible by now." He let out a piercing whistle and a shout.

"Hey, Jew-boy! Naval officer! Medal-winner! Get your sorry one-armed ass out here and drink with the big boys!"

Inside his trailer, Cohen heard the whistle and refined summons. He paused in the midst of revising—for the eleventh time—a crucial scene in his novel. Heartily sick of the whole affair, it seemed he could neither quit it nor finish it, and thus, like Mistah Sisyphus, he was doomed to keep grinding his rock up the hill, then chasing it back down, forever.

Hudson Strode, his writing mentor at the university, had much praised his work and promised to help sell it, but insisted on a typescript no longer than 500 pages. Still, Cohen believed his story couldn't be told in less than that much half again. After all, he had 38 major characters and four years of war to recount, plus a century of Alabama racial and social history to weave into the text. And then there was the Jewish stuff. . . .

Wham, wham, wham!

Ben was pounding on the side of the trailer, standing on tiptoes and looking right into Cohen's face.

"Cohen, you neuronic Yid, get out here and drink a beer with us."

"Neurotic, Ben, neurotic."

"Whatever you say, but come out or I'm comin' in, and you don't want that, I promise you."

More to appease Ben than in anticipation of pleasure, David Cohen joined his two friends in broken-down lawn chairs, accepting a beer from the Marine's beefy grip and looking around at spring's happy effect on nature as though, like that vampire, he really had been living in a cave—or a coffin.

"Nice jonquils," he said of a patch of yellow flowers, twittering on their stems in the breeze. Twenty meters away, several brilliant, red-orange quince bushes lit up one corner of the yard as though plugged into an electric circuit. Planted years ago when Vernon Puckett was just a pup, they formed a temporary golden halo.

"So, David, how's the big book coming?" Karl asked, thinking to smooth the interface between Ben's simian bluntness and Cohen's more delicate sensibilities.

"It's what keeps me alive, Karl," said Cohen, surprising all of them with his vehemence.

"Why you write that crap, anyway?" said Ben. "I mean, it's all about the war, right? Hey, I figure it this way: if they was there, they don't want to read about it, and if they wasn't there, they won't understand it. So, I mean, what the hell? Let it go, you know what I'm saying? Write about, I don't know, pussy or something. Now that they'll read . . ."

"Ben . . ." Karl said.

"Well, am I right, or what?"

Cohen smiled. "You're definitely right, Ben. For pussy, they'll line up every time."

"Yeah, and speakin' of which, the other night during that rain storm? Somebody in your trailer was layin' down some serious horizontal boogie. Man, that was one happy woman, wadn't it, Karl? Coulda heard her yelpin' all the way to Birmingham. Had a nice rhythm to it, though, ya' know? Yes, yes, yessssss . . .!"

Cohen blushed.

"Must have been the guy I rented the place to for the evening."

"Yeah, bushwha! Not unless his name was 'David.'" The Marines chuckled over their ribbing.

"No harm done," said Karl. "All in a night's work, eh, Cohen?"

"Roger that," said David.

The three men sat there, soaking up the spring sun, with bees buzzing around them, sipping their beer, and ruminating—at various levels of intellectual rigor—over the meaning and fragility of life and/or the infinite allure of, well, pussy.

Then, David Cohen blinked, sat up, turned to Ben, and spoke in a soft, slow Mobile drawl that grew in power as he went on.

"You want to know why I'm writing about the war, Ben? I'll tell you. Because I can't write about anything else. Because my every waking and sleeping moment is suffused with the memory of what happened to me, to you, to Karl and Dante, to all of us, a whole generation of guys.

"I don't mean the friggin' cooks and bottle-washers and staff pukes and draft-dodgers and cowardly lurkers slinkin' around back behind the lines or the gold-brickin' 4-F-ers stayin' here at home. I mean guys like us and Karl, guys who got caught in the shit up to our throats, guys who will never be the same. Fellows like you, Ben, who killed and mutilated a lot of people—a lot of people—and who, at the same time, were being killed wholesale by Japs and Krauts.

"I'm writing about my ship and my shipmates who were turned into shark-bait by some crazy flying Jap suiciders. I'm writing about savoring the delectable taste of a man's brains blown into my mouth by a direct kamikaze hit, of watching sailors being vaporized by exploding ordnance, of seeing 18-year olds grow up and die between eight bells and twelve. I'm writing about a fear so disabling as to make a strong man shit his pants and cry for mama. And about the crippling experience—that only a sailor can know—of watching his mortally wounded destroyer slip beneath the waves. And . . . and . . ."

His voice took on a darker timbre, "I'm writing about how it feels to . . . take care of business when one of your own men loses it and endangers the others. Trust me, pal, for me, writing about the war is not a volunteer mission."

A moment of silence passed as Ben and Karl exchanged looks.

"Sorry, man," Ben said. "I was out of line."

Cohen sat back in his lawn chair.

"No sweat, Ben," he said, "I knew you'd understand."

David Cohen and Chief Machinist Mate Ralph Graham are having trouble maintaining order on their lashed-together life rafts. The sun is withering the 90-or-so parched sailor-survivors huddled in the rafts or clinging to their sides.

Cohen—his wounded arm throbbing—has set up a rotation scheme so that the men in the water are to be pulled onto the rafts while the same number already aboard them exchange places by slipping back into the water and holding on.

But some men already on the rafts are refusing to comply. To remind them of the pecking order of survival, Graham has smashed one loud-mouthed belligerent in the face, breaking his jaw, but silencing him, at least, and quieting the others.

Telling his men they cannot be sure they will be found and rescued quickly, Cohen has ordered that spare kapok life vests—sometimes stripped from the bodies of the dead—either be laid out in the sun to dry or used for pillows and shade for the burned and wounded—moaning in the bottoms of the rafts.

He has inventoried the amount of potable water available for the survivors—only 21 gallons for 90+ men. Working with a medic and Chief Graham, he calculates that amount will keep the hardiest alive for, at most, five days. The others will die before that.

Gray sharks circle the trussed-up life rafts bobbing on the rolling surface, the sleek dorsal fins cutting clean, sssssing wakes among the terrified men. One sailor screams long and gargling, then disappears beneath the water—his chest clamped in the mouth of a shark.

Another's torso turns topsy-turvy in its life vest before the man can utter a word, his legs severed just below the waist.

Any bad storm will finish off the Little's survivors, and Cohen knows it. He also knows that a big low pressure system is approaching their position from the east.

Two rafts over from Cohen's, an especially recalcitrant gunner's mate named Largent is causing real trouble. Brandishing a wicked knife, he threatens to cut the lines holding his raft to the larger pack, saying he doesn't want to go down with the others when they begin to sink, as they will, he shouts.

Cohen can't tell whether Largent is temporarily insane or just realizing his maximum potential for disorder—he's been a keen troublemaker for months. David shouts for Largent to shut up and obey orders. Largent shouts for Cohen to 'Go fuck yourself, you lousy kike.'

In Cohen's life raft, Radioman Stotsenburg taps Cohen on the leg and discreetly hands him the .45 automatic he is authorized to carry to protect the ship's secret radio codes. As ordered, Stotsenburg has already destroyed the codes by placing them in lead-lined bags and tossing them overboard. He has no further use for the weapon but sees that his captain does.

"It's loaded," he whispers, "with one in the chamber."

Cohen nods and slips the pistol inside his belt at the small of his back.

Meanwhile, the sun bakes them to crisps, their skin reddening, blisters forming. Chief Graham has set up a watch schedule, in part to keep the men busy and in part to search for rescue. He orders that—in one-hour rotation—four men in each raft remain on watch at all times, two scanning the sky for airplanes, two keeping tabs on possible surface ships headed their way. Graham then rigs up a large triangle of white canvas to signal airplanes.

Over in his raft, Largent refuses to obey the order to establish watches, saying that nobody's coming for them, claiming that the stupid radiomen were too chicken-shit to send out an S.O.S.

Stotsenburg screams at Largent, telling him he doesn't know what the hell he's talking about, that the message went out twice, and might have been picked up. Largent's response—beyond vulgar—is deeply personal and filled with venom. Stotsenburg, sinewy, broad-shouldered, and furious, leaps up and starts crawling across to the next raft, on his way to confront Largent.

Things are getting out of hand.

Men are taking sides in this stupid dispute, with Largent-supporters shouting epithets at the others. Chief Graham grabs a loud man and holds his head under water for 50 seconds. Another sailor attacks Graham.

Then, Cohen acts. With his good hand, he grabs the .45, points it at the sky and fires one round. The effect is unrehearsed. Everyone freezes. Everyone except Largent.

Cohen has known for months that Largent was a foul-mouth anti-Semite, that he regularly made cracks about him behind his back. Now, Largent stands up in his raft and dares Cohen to shoot him, calling him every disgusting name a fertile and practiced imagination can muster. Cohen orders Largent to sit down. Largent screams that he will kill Cohen, that Hitler had the right idea about the Jews.

'Kill 'em all! Fuckin' blood-suckers.'

Before Cohen—or anyone else—can speak, Largent begins a frenzied crawl out of his raft and into the next, which is tied adjacent to Cohen's. Largent seems fully mad now, having vented himself into a blind fury.

Woozy with pain, his left arm a bloody mess, Cohen grips the .45 in his right hand, pointing it at Largent's chest. He orders the enlisted man to stop, warning that he will shoot him if he comes any closer than the eight feet now separating them.

Some of the men, sensing the gravity of the situation, try to restrain Largent, a big man with flaming red hair and a temper to match. He slices one man with the knife, hurls him out of the raft, challenges the others, then turns on Cohen and says, 'So, shoot me, motherfucker, if you got the balls.'

When nothing comes, he starts a menacing crawl toward the young officer, vowing to kill him. He's now less than six feet away, balancing in the raft against the ocean swells, his knife glistening in one hand.

Later, Cohen could never piece together exactly what happened next. He recalled only four things: Largent's terrible, red-rimmed eyes; Chief Graham's screaming, 'Shoot him, shoot the son-of-a-bitch!'; the gun leaping violently in his hand; and the look of shock and disbelief on Largent's face as he comprehends what has just happened—and that he is going to die.

And then he does, slumping into a bloody heap on the floor of the raft. Not another man speaks until Chief Graham says:

'Throw the bastard overboard . . . but keep his life vest and knife. And go through his pockets for valuables, like chewing gum.'

The gum will induce saliva and might keep a weak man alive a while longer.

An hour later, one of the look-outs spies a ship on the horizon. An hour after that, they are safely onboard a rescue vessel, where the doctor (a dermatologist)—using the wardroom as an operating theatre—amputates Lieutenant Cohen's hand, clumsily.

Chief Graham finds Stotsenburg in sick bay and commends him for successfully getting his S.O.S. out.

As for Largent, the sharks finish what Cohen began.

Or, what Largent began.

Chapter 18

In some years—though not all—spring comes stealing into Alabama with enough warmth, fecundity and deep, lazy beauty to stir the soul and fibrillate the heart. Pine pollen dusts the cars to a faint yellow. High in tree-tops, elegant gray mockingbirds blast out in full cry, giving to the world—free of charge—one of the richest, most complex bird-song patterns in North America.

Borer bees buzz about looking for new places to drill holes and lay eggs. Squirrels grow rampant in their lust for pecans they've buried over the winter—and forgotten. University students emerge from hiding, the men doffing shirts, drinking beer, playing sports, and showing off, while the stunning co-eds, radiant with the untested élan of youth, rehearse a species of savory, seasonal danse macabre that takes as its unwitting—though contented—victims, men.

The flickering, erotic chiaroscuro of desire playing out between the sexes on the campus of a Southern university at this time of year is a thing to behold. Indeed, it's almost enough to ease the memory, in Alabama, of a century of institutional slavery, ethnic disenfranchisement, fundamentalist religion, and retrograde politics.

Such a year, in any case, was 1946.

Through some beguiling concatenation of just the right amount of rain, sun, wind, and temps, that year one could, within the span of a week, see—all in bloom at the same time—the first of the azaleas and the last of the camellias, the remnants of plump Japanese magnolia blossoms along with dancing yellow jonquils and stout forsythia, lovely, pink flowering almond, the first of the Carolina jasmine, the tail-end of the red quince, and the first white buds of Bradford pears, along with fabulous, densely white cherry blossoms, early wild purple iris, white lavender, the velvety pink red bud, and even an old-fashioned rose, mutabilis, that changes color in the course of the day from reddish to yellowish.

And all this before the first mauve wisteria or white dogwood showed its face.

It was on a day like this, a Saturday in early April, that Evelyn Curtis, Betty Braxton, Mavis Raleigh, and Jill Taylor headed out to the Tuscaloosa Air Field to flight-check Evelyn's P51-D Mustang and prepare for her to fly the bet. Resting in its hangar, the silver bird with the bubble canopy and red and blue markings appeared spectacularly lethal, seeming to snarl just sitting there. It was a perfect fighting machine—widely regarded as the greatest air-to-air fighter of its day. Flown by some of the hottest pilots in the Army Air Forces, it had accompanied thousands of heavy-bomber raids over Germany, flying some 214,000 sorties and accounting for nearly 5,000 Luftwaffe losses.

The design team who developed this marvelous airplane, gave it a British Rolls Royce Merlin engine that produced nearly 1500 h.p. In full battle regalia, the Mustang could reach speeds greater than 400 mph in level flight—over 500 mph in a dive—and was capable of seven-hour missions without refueling. In fact, with wing tanks, the plane could outlast the pilot. It had become the first Allied fighter able to fly all the way from Britain to Berlin—and back. Armed with six .50-calibre machine guns, it could out-fly and out-fight anything the Axis Powers could put in the air—until the startling jet-powered Messerschmidt 262 came along in the last months of fighting.

It was also, as it happened, the most beautiful aircraft of the war.

Every man who flew it, loved it. As did every woman.

This was the airplane in which Kevin Marshall and Evelyn Curtis would now test their mettle.

And, apparently, the competition would be witnessed by a crowd numbering in the hundreds. For weeks, word had been dribbling out on campus that something interesting was afoot in the age-old domain of male-female rivalry. People were hearing that a hot, former AAF pilot was going up against . . . against a woman! That money would change hands. That the plane in question was a rebuilt Mustang. That the woman owned the friggin' plane. That she wasn't a half-bad pilot. That some dago vet from New York, or somewhere, was promoting the rivalrous affair. That he was calling it

FLYING THE BET

That he and his buddies—plus some unnamed source of outside funds— were covering all wagers on offer. That the amount in the betting pool had grown to a figure that, by local standards, was astronomical. That the university graybeards, upon hearing these rumors, were trying to chase the story down and quash the deal. That nobody was telling them crap. That this was too good to be stopped.

With his usual gusto, Dante Larocca had designed—and persuaded the former Sea-bee Chief, Homer Davis, to build—a sort of uber-betting-cage-bred-to-a-lemonade-stand with drawers, a desk-area, a canopy top, and a hand-lettered sign reading:

HELP A VET.
PLACE A BET.

The object of this apparatus was to give Dante a visible spot where he could manage the betting, hand out markers and, working with the tall Corsair pilot, Bill Britton, keep the money safe.

To judge the flying contest, Britton had assembled a team of four former fighter pilots with no prior connection to either party. He had also promised to pay them a fee of fifteen bucks apiece for their services. They would inspect the plane before each flight and would assess both pilots' aerobatic performance through binoculars. Britton himself would make the fifth judge.

The day of the fly-off dawned a perfect rose. By nine o'clock the early-morning cumulus had burned away, and there was nothing up there but blue. The contest was set to begin at one o'clock; by 10:00 A.M. the road out to the field was awash in a steady stream of old cars and new, trucks, motorcycles, and kids on bikes—even some folks walking.

Four of the latter were Sammy Cleveland, his wife, Katy, and their two young children—the black family Dante had met driving the cotton wagon on the day last fall that Evelyn had buzzed him. Since then, Dante had seen Sammy and Katy at Kilroy's many times, and always paused to visit with them. Because Sammy refused to accept tips, Dante had evolved a trick to make the black man take a little something extra for his services. After he'd pay for his beer and pick up the cold bottles in one hand, Dante would stick out his free hand toward Sammy, fist closed.

"Here, pal, hold this a second for me, will ya'?"

Instinctively Cleveland would extend his hand to his crazy Brooklyn friend, and Dante would drop a fifty-cent piece into it, turn and hurry away, laughing. It was just a frivolous game, but it cemented their friendship in a way few things could.

On his drive out to the field, Kevin Marshall rode with a couple of buddies he'd brought along for moral support—although he wouldn't have termed it thus. Pretty confident he could take the girl, he was still cautious. Although he had kept his flying skills well-honed by weekend stints at the Montgomery Air Station, he hadn't flown this particular Mustang, and he was smart enough to know that when you climb into the cockpit of a powerful fighter, anything can happen.

"You can take her, right?" said one of his pals in the car. "I got the rent money riding on it."

"The dame is dog meat," Kevin snapped.

"You okay, Kev?" said the other.

"Never better."

"You know," said the first friend, watching the landscape slip by, "I was thinking: the war has just about ruined our women. Take my girlfriend, Gertrude. You know what she said to me last night?" He mimed a squirrelly woman's voice. "'Bobby . . . Bobby, I think I want to be an engineer.' An engineer, fellas. A dame. I mean, what the fuck is this world comin' to?"

"Ahh, tell her to lie back, relax, and enjoy it. Sheeesh!"

"That's exactly what I told her. She got pissed, if you can believe it."

"Next thing you know, they'll be wantin' to serve in the Army, right alongside the guys."

"Won't happen. Take it to the bank," said Kevin.

"I say, if they want to, let 'em. They coulda took my place on Okinawa, that's for damn sure."

At the air field, flanked by two scowling bodyguards—the tattooed Karl and Ben—and sounding like a hallucinating circus barker, Dante was swamped with business at his betting kiosk. Chief Davis and the two Marines had rigged up a sound system, taking power from Evelyn's hangar and stringing the cord across a couple of pylons to keep it above the crowd. Dante's voice rang out of a cheap loud-speaker suspended from atop the kiosk.

"All right . . . all right . . . all right. Step up, folks, and stay in line . . . no need to push; there's room for everybody to play . . . we're covering all bets here . . . there's still time to . . . Okay, sir, you're taking Miss

Curtis for twenty? Fine, here's your chit . . . You, sir, forty on the other guy? Smart move. You won't regret it . . . Here you go . . . Here you go! HELP A VET, folks, PLACE A BET . . . Whoa! a century note on the dame! Now that's classy, pal, no guts, no glory, right?"

Betty Braxton and Mavis, wearing tight leather fighter jackets, had fought their way to the front of the line.

"Five hundred on Evelyn," Betty called out, waving the bills.

Dante looked up. This was the biggest single bet he'd covered.

"Whoa, Nelly! Five big ones on the dame." He noted their jackets and tough-girl manner.

"Who're you two?"

"Friends of the family," said Mavis. "Cover the bet."

"Yes, ma'am. Your wish is my command."

Betty looked at him.

"You're the bad boy Evelyn told us about, aren't you?"

"Depends on what she said."

"All good."

"That's me."

With the help of Evelyn's employee, Ralph Hobson, the women had rolled out and engine-checked the Mustang earlier that morning. It now sat gleaming in the sun, nose up, tail down, a panther hungry for prey.

Nearby, Evelyn and Marshall stood together, talking to Bill Britton.

"Her flight logs look good," Britton said to Marshall. "Maintenance records are in order. Nice job, Miss Curtis. She looks like a fit bird."

"Yeah, thanks. Everything's kosher, I believe."

The time of reckoning had arrived. Dante cleared a few last-minute bets—including one for five dollars from Sammy Cleveland, on Evelyn.

"Ain't no way I'm betting against that woman!" Sammy said, and laughed.

"My sentiments exactly, Cleveland. Say hello to Katy for me . . . and how about you go get Evelyn and bring her and the other guy over here, will ya'?"

While Cleveland threaded his way through the crowd, Dante conveyed all the money to Bill Britton for safe-keeping, then climbed up on the deck of the betting stand, grabbed the microphone and addressed the crowd.

"Okay, folks, listen up . . . quieten down, now. . ." but the excited hubbub wouldn't subside. Dante looked around, disgusted, then handed the microphone down to Ben.

"Ben, speak to the people."

Ben lifted the mike to his mouth and let out an ear-piercing whistle intimidating enough to stop birds in flight. The crowd—grown to more than three hundred souls, about two-thirds of whom were vets or their wives—covered their ears.

But they shut up.

By now, Cleveland had returned with Evelyn and Marshall.

"Thanks, Ben. You have such a way about you . . . Okay, folks, here's the deal. What we got here is a contest of flying skills between 'Ace' Curtis here in the green shirt . . ." Applause and appreciative whistles rang out, mixed with a few boos.

". . . and Hollywood Handsome Kevin Marshall, the hero of his former Mustang squadron." More applause and whistles.

"Now, the judging will be done by three ex-Navy carrier pilots and two AAF guys, all fighter-jockeys. And none of 'em, Bill Britton here tells me, know either one of the contestants. I'll flip a coin to see who goes first."

Some guy in the crowd hollered: "What happens if it's a tie?"

"Five judges, pal, it won't be a tie. Somebody walks away from here top dog. Now . . ." he pointed at Marshall.

"Boy Wonder, you call it. Loud and clear."

"Right."

Dante flipped the coin.

"Tails!"

"Tails it is! You're up, hot-dog."

The crowd murmured and bunched up a little tighter, straining to glimpse both pilots. One could hear voices among them muttering, "Girl . . . woman pilot . . . ought to be ashamed of herself . . . it ain't fair, he'll mop the floor with her . . ."

Evelyn walked with Marshall toward the Mustang. She held her soft leather flying helmet in her left hand.

"By the way," she said to him, "without her guns and ammo she's a little . . . mmm, frisky during snap rolls and when you go inverted."

"I'll keep that in mind," he said.

"Good luck." She shook his hand. "And meet the ground crew."

Betty, Mavis, and Jill had already chocked the wheels and spun the big four-blade prop a few times to send lubricant through the engine. Now, they shook hands with Marshall, jumped up on the wing and helped him into the cockpit, tightening his safety harness and adjusting the head rest. He checked the gauges, tapping one a couple of times, then double-wrapped a white silk scarf around his neck below his own soft flying helmet.

When he indicated he was all set, the women jumped down and Betty, acting as ground control, stood in front of the plane, pointing up at the cockpit with one arm and rotating the other overhead in a signal for him to engage the starter—that the area was clear. He did so and after a coughing hiccup, the big 12-cylinder Merlin roared into life with a blistering crescendo of noise and blue smoke that caused the crowd to fall back a dozen paces.

Hot Damn! This big son-of-a-bitch meant business!

Mavis and Jill unchocked a wheel apiece, Betty gave him the all-clear thumbs-up, and Kevin Marshall was on his own. He taxied out to the field, fishtailing back and forth to see past the Mustang's long snout that impeded forward vision—one of the few complaints pilots lodged against this tail-dragger. At the end of the runway he wheeled around, ran up the revs, checked his instruments, said a short prayer, and gunned it.

The result set men's hearts alight.

The spinning prop took a couple of seconds to grab a full quota of air, but when it did—and the superchargers kicked in—the Mustang began hurtling down the runway like a thing alive, anxious to free herself from the sullied bonds of earth.

Gaining ground speed, first the tail came up, enabling Kevin to see where he was going, then, gathering herself like some wild beast going in for the kill, she hit rotation. Kevin drew the stick back and simultaneously punched the gear-retract switch, so that the wheels began to collapse into their wells almost before he was fully airborne.

It was a little trademark trick he'd developed when taking off from short air fields scattered around the lush English countryside during the war. A quirk, something to get himself noticed and talked about among the other fighter pilots. It was also a remarkably stupid stunt, as any failure of the engine at this crucial moment meant a wheels-up crash landing on her belly.

Standing near the crowd, Evelyn and her women friends saw this gesture of bravado and shook their heads.

"They never change, those guys," said Betty.

"Yeah," said Jill, "once a dick, always a dick."

The Mustang climbed out in a rolling, silver pirouette of noise that the crowd could feel in their ears and feet. The fighter-pilot judges had their binocs trained on the airplane, moving their heads and arms together like five synchronized chimps. Out on the edge of the crowd, Tim Fletcher stood alone, his head tilted back, watching Marshall begin a series of snap rolls and figure-8s. Then he walked over to Evelyn, spoke, and gave her a hug. She introduced him to the girls as "my friend."

He shook hands with Dante.

"How ya' doin', Fletcher? Long time, no see."

"Been busy, Dante. You're not going to get my girl hurt today, are you?" He smiled thinly, but the question hung in the air.

"Your girl can take care of herself," Dante said.

Kevin Marshall was a good pilot. Not great, but good. He did some barrel rolls, and dives and a wing-over or two, and he completed an impressive, hard, swinging turn right over the field during which he pointed one wing straight down at the crowd, the other at the sky—as he roared over the hangars, full-out.

Then he tried to hang the plane from its prop, but got it a bit cross-eyed, and fell off too soon. After maybe 12 minutes in the air, he made a rather bumpy landing at the far end of the field and rolled out near the hangar, cutting his engine, unharnessing, and climbing out of the cockpit, wringing wet.

"You got a problem with the ventilation in that bird," he said to Evelyn. "Hot as a bastard in there."

"Did you open the supplementary air duct?"

He'd forgotten. He lied.

"Yeah . . . yeah, I did, still hot. But never mind. She's all yours," he said, and walked over to join his friends and drink a beer.

Ten minutes after Bill Britton had completed a quick inspection of the Mustang, Evelyn was in the air. Her take-off had been purposely unremarkable as she'd waited until she was well up before reeling in her wheels. Then, to everyone's mystification, she disappeared.

They saw her. They heard her. Then she was gone. Nothing.

The crowd searched the sky in confusion. Some wise-guy made a crack about her running away from the fight. The judges looked at each other and arched their brows.

What the hell was this about?

Those with good hearing then picked up a faint, distant growl. People spun in place tying to spot her. Suddenly, before anyone knew what'd hit them, there she was, screaming along ahead of her own sound wave, at 400 mph and 80 feet above the runway. Inverted.

Inverted! Upside down!

Ohhh, my Great God A'mighty! But that woman could fly an airplane!

The crowd cowered. Women screamed. Men stood gape-mouthed.

Evelyn rolled the Mustang upright and put it into a yowling climb nearly straight up, executing a series of heart-stopping vertical rolls, pushing the brute of a Merlin to and beyond its design limits.

Up, up, she went, right over the field, the big engine shrieking as though in mortal agony, sounding like it would tear itself apart in protest.

Then, far above the crowd, finally running out of airspeed—angry that it couldn't climb forever—the beautiful beast faltered, and Evelyn hung that sucker on its four-blade prop, nose up, engine still wailing, perfectly perpendicular to the horizon until . . . until—oh, Sweet Jesus!—until the laws of physics prevailing, it hesitated and fell back toward earth, momentarily defeated, slipping into a wild, barely controlled flat spin, from which Evelyn rescued it at the last possible moment, and—still over the field—went inverted again and disappeared beyond a row of tall pines.

The fighter-pilot judges stared at each other in disbelief.

Betty Braxton smiled.

"We're gonna get well on this, girls," she said to her friends.

"Ohhhh, yeah," said Mavis, "I'm only sorry we didn't double our bet."

"I did," said Jill, grinning, "just before Marshall took off." They clapped each other on the back, laughing.

Tim's face was a tight mask.

Dante was grinning like a mule eating briers.

The crowd loved it, twittering and gossiping, talking with their hands, saying, "did you see that?. . . how the hell did she . . . did you know she could do that? . . . I told you she could do it."

All of a sudden, here came the Mustang again, roaring low and upright over the field as fast as before, only a bit higher. Evelyn rowed back on the stick, sending her airplane into a giant loop, and imposing such g-forces on herself that she very nearly blacked out.

Up the silver bird went, higher and higher, the engine bellowing to beat hell, her nose passing right through vertical; now—on her back—sliding down inside the second half of the loop, aimed straight at the crowd, and just when people began running for cover—sure they were about to die—she completed the circle, flattened out, and blasted away in a series of perfectly executed rolls, at tree-top level.

Dante turned to Chief Davis, Karl, Ben, and Sammy Cleveland.

"Any questions, boys?" he said.

"Larocca," said Ben, "don't you never get in a plane with that woman."

"Not a chance, my man. Not a chance."

He looked around.

"Say, where's Cohen? He said he'd be here. Guy coulda made a nice pile of jack betting on the babe."

Nobody had seen Cohen. But everybody had a new problem to worry about.

Police.

Three squad cars containing a total of six cops approached the crowd. On the roof of each car, a single red light whirled. If Evelyn's engine noise hadn't been quite so loud, if the crowd hadn't been quite so into her performance, they might also have heard the lame sounds of sirens dying. Now that she had once again disappeared over the horizon, everyone turned around and realized that John Law had come to visit.

Dante surveyed the situation and got to Bill Britton.

"Quick, give me five hundred, and split the rest between your judges, five ways," he whispered. "Take it home. We'll pay off later. Don't tell the cops shit. I've got your number. I'll call you."

Britton corralled his judges and led them away.

Two policemen piled out of each patrol car: four fat guys, a stork, and a runt. They swaggered around, asking questions, demanding to know who was in charge. People pointed at Dante, his money stuffed into his shorts. The cops called him over.

They didn't care for his accent or his attitude. He didn't care for theirs. They demanded to know what was going on. He told them everyone had just come out to watch a flying exhibition.

They called him a liar. He called them an unprintable name.

They threatened to jail him. He asked on what charge.

"Frightening livestock," the stork said.

"Felonious cattle-spooking?" Dante said.

"We've had multiple complaints."

"From the cows?"

"What are you, some kind of smart guy?"

"I am in this bunch."

Evelyn, meanwhile, figuring she'd done about all she could in the air, was shooting her final approach when she glimpsed, near the hangars, the three red lights winking atop the police cruisers. Something told her to abort. She hit the throttle, pulled up, retracted her gear, flew herself over the crowd, figured out what was going on, and resolved not to go without a fight. Executing a final, nice wing-over above the hangar, she turned and headed east.

To hell with 'em. Let 'em catch her if they could.

* * *

Hours later, Dante and the boys—including Sammy and Katy Cleveland—were celebrating Evelyn's performance—and their financial windfall—with mixed beverages at the Beagle Ranch. Cohen still hadn't showed, but he'd left Dante a note apologizing and saying he was going out to Laney Fooshee's place to write in peace. At Dante's feet lay Sir Plus, back from the vet, with a couple of cracked ribs and some pretty severe nerve damage that had him walking like a land crab, but nothing fatal. Everybody was talking at once about the air show when Cleola Pucket hollered that Dante had another 'telerphone' call. It was Evelyn.

She was in Birmingham.

In jail.

Meanwhile, the police had had no luck pinning the rap on Kevin

Marshall who'd been spirited away by his dismayed—more than dismayed—mates as soon as the law arrived.

"Kev, shit, man, how'm I gonna explain the rent money to Gertrude?" said hen-pecked Bobby on their way back to town.

"To hell with Gertrude, Bobby. How'd I know the woman could fly like that?"

"Well, hell, you gave it your best shot," said Mack. "Probably just a little rusty, is all."

"I wasn't rusty, Mack, that woman is damn good!"

"Yeah, even I could see that."

Now, Evelyn was in need of immediate assistance. When the Birmingham police—alerted by their Tuscaloosa brethren—had arrested her at the airport, then agreed to allow the usual one phone call, she debated contacting (1) the family lawyer, (2) her father, (3) Tim Fletcher, or (4) a displaced Yankee veteran screwball architecture student with little money and no connections—but great eyes. She chose the latter.

"Drive your jeep to the airport," she told Dante on the phone. "Exchange for my car. Key's in it. Come get me."

"Roger; wilco."

"And," she added, "bring me two sandwiches and a beer."

"Got it," he said. "Ninety minutes or so. Hang in there, girl. Hey, you were outstanding this afternoon."

She smiled into the phone.

"I did okay?"

"Okay? You butchered that bastard. I spec' he's home right now, slitting his wrists. I mean, I knew you were good, but today you were . . . you were friggin' great!"

"Thanks, Dante, that means a lot coming . . ."

"Sorry, Miss, time's up," said the cop at her side.

"Gotta go, Dante. Hurry."

Ninety-four minutes after he hung up, Dante parked in front of the Birmingham police station. He'd brought four of the five C-notes, six beers, three sandwiches, and some change. He had no idea how to spring Evelyn, or how big bail would be, but there was only one way to find out. Inside the station house—and on his best behavior—he introduced himself to the desk sergeant, a blond, formerly handsome guy in his late twenties with vicious red burns on his face, neck, and head—burns bad enough that his hair would never grow back to conceal what had happened to him—whatever that was.

The time was 6:30 P.M.

"Howya' doin', sir. I'm Dante Larocca, and I . . . you have my sister in the slammer, here, and I was wonderin' if I could spring her . . . or, uh, meet bail, sir, if you have time to . . ."

"Your name's Larocca, and her name's Curtis?"

"Yeah, well, half-sister. See, my mama and her mama are the same, but, uh, her dad and my old man . . ."

"I got it, I got it. Five hundred bucks."

Dante's face fell. The sergeant saw it.

He studied Larocca.

"You a vet?" the sergeant said, without blinking.

"You know it, Sarge. Rode with Patton. Across France. Berlin. The whole megillah."

The sergeant stared at him, then down at his day book for a long moment. Then, he gestured at his own disfigured face and head.

"I got this fightin' with Patton. This and two ribbons. One said I'd been wounded—as if I didn't know—the other one said I was a hero—which was bullshit."

Dante nodded. The only sounds in the station house were faint curses and shouts floating in from down the cell block, located behind a pair of swinging double doors, painted a putrid green.

"Well, pal," Dante said, softly, "I guess me and you, we're sort of in the same boat." He grabbed his shirt tail with both hands and slowly lifted it to his shoulders, revealing the vivid hodge-podge of multiple scar-rivulets and wound-welts crisscrossing his stomach and chest like a savage road map.

"That Panzerfaust is a bitch, ain't it, Sarge?"

Something—a moat of dust, perhaps—caught in the Sergeant's eye. He wiped it. He wiped the other. He reduced charges to fifty bucks. Dante paid it with one of the hundreds.

"Break this and keep half," he said to the burned, blond man.

When they brought Evelyn out, she looked tired. Dante thanked the sergeant, letting Evelyn know he'd been most helpful in arranging her release. She stepped around the desk and kissed the cop on the cheek.

"Thanks, Sergeant," she said, "You're a peach."

Then she and Dante walked out, arm-in-arm.

Chapter 19

Professor Tim Fletcher stood looking out the third story window of his university office in the Physics building and thinking of Evelyn's wild flying-cum-jail escapade from the previous weekend. Although he could sense her slipping from him in some mysterious way, he refused to accept the evidence of his own observations. At the same time, a reckoning was approaching; he knew that and he would deal with it when it came.

Now, from up here, he could see the back of his black 1938 Plymouth coupe resting in a faculty parking lot. Since the veterans had begun flooding the campus last fall, three issues had come to trump all others in local priority: parking, housing, and classroom space. These chronic shortages had led to bizarre situations in which senior professors pulled academic rank, of sorts, on younger colleagues, ordering them to remove their cars so that the older men might have the spot.

In the near-distance, Tim could hear the shouts of intramural softball leagues gearing up for the season on freshly green playing fields, spring having worked its usual hormonal magic in favor of sports and against schoolwork. The bucolic charms of university life were not, however, what he was here to contemplate on a late Friday afternoon. Instead, he awaited a visitor who posed, potentially, the most dangerous encounter of his life. That said, Tim felt remarkably calm.

A sudden rap on the door caused him to half-turn.

"Come in."

The story swung open, admitting an uncommonly handsome, young, black-haired man, carrying a bag full of books. The man's broad shoulders stretched the limits of a white tee shirt; his khaki pants were still pressed, even at this time of day.

"You wanted to see me, Professor Fletcher?"

Tim listened for any hint of aural anomaly in the voice—as he had been doing for several weeks in class. He heard nothing sinister, although he had begun to pick up a definite something there, some hint of a youth spent far from Alabama—or America.

"Close the door, please, and lock it."

The young man's dark, oddly liquid eyes reacted, although his manner remained casual.

"Sure, sir." He eased the door to and flipped the lock. The noise of the dead-bolt sliding home sounded doom-laden to Fletcher.

"Sit down."

The man sat.

"What is your name?" Tim asked.

The man's eyes narrowed ever so slightly.

"I . . . my . . . Victor Rangle, sir."

"No, it's not. What is your name?"

They watched each other a long moment in what Tim's father used to call a Mexican stand-off, neither man quite sure what the other knew or didn't, would do or wouldn't.

"They know," said Tim. "They know who you are, Vladimir Ronchipov."

Tim thought he caught the merest hint of a slump in those broad shoulders. But he definitely saw Ronchipov swallow, as though the saliva in his mouth burned to find somewhere to go—fast. In his student's eyes Fletcher detected a hint of the caged beast, and a thought flitted across his mind:

"I wonder if he will kill me."

"Your parents are Canadian and Russian. You graduated first in your class from Moscow University," he said. "You worked on the Soviet heavy-water crash project to build a bomb. Your wife was raped and killed by Wehrmacht soldiers. You have a daughter named Irina." Ronchipov inhaled sharply. "You entered this country through Canada. You have friends in Chicago. Vladimir, they know your bathroom habits. They know it all."

Ronchipov looked as cool as the other side of the pillow.

"I see. Well, in that case, perhaps I should offer you this as a memento of our friendship."

He bent, reached into his shoulder bag on the floor, then straightened up. In his hand he held a snub-nosed .38-caliber revolver, pointed at Tim's stomach.

Tim's composed response surprised even himself.

"So, you're going to shoot me? In my own office? With the campus swarming with people? Not, perhaps, the most clear-headed response."

Ronchipov hesitated. Tim's brief litany of his life history had left no room for doubt. He'd been made. The only question was how much damage he could do on his way down. And the pistol would determine that.

"Did you tell them?" he asked.

"They told me, Victor . . . Vladimir. How the hell would I have known your background? I just thought you were a superb physics student and a gentleman. Turns out, I was only half-right."

"Gentleman," Ronchipov sneered. "Typical. Your sycophantic Anglophilia is showing, Professor. God knows how you and the English won the war. Well, actually, we know how you won in the Pacific. The bomb. Thanks, in part, to you."

"I played a minor role. It seemed like a good idea at the time."

"Quite."

"Would you mind putting that pistol in your pocket, or something, it's making me rather nervous."

Ronchipov wavered, then settled for holding it, barrel down, pointed at the floor.

"So, Professor, what now?"

"My thought, exactly. I've considered this quite a lot, Ronchipov, and I've decided what I'm going to do. It's unorthodox. It's illegal. It could quite possibly get me hanged for treason. Do you understand?"

A glimmer of something, recognition perhaps, flickered in the younger man's eyes.

"I . . . I'm not entirely sure, but go on."

"Yes, well, as they say, all decisions in life are at some level political, and so, in its own way is this."

Tim turned again to the window, his back facing Ronchipov. He figured that if he were to be shot, now was as good a time as any, and, too, if it were going to happen, better they got it over quickly.

Nothing happened. He began to speak in a low voice.

"My automobile is parked just there in the lot, a 1938 black Plymouth coupe. License number . . ."

"JA 904."

"Exactly. When I leave here in a few minutes I will go to my car, get in it, and push the starter button without turning the key. It will turn over but, obviously, not crank. I will get out and express anger, perhaps by slamming my hand on the hood . . ."

"Not like you. Just frown and glare and walk away."

Tim hesitated.

"Very well. I will then leave the car and go home. You, meanwhile, will remain here with the door locked and without making a sound. If you have to pee, do it into the trash can, not in my desk drawer."

Ronchipov smiled, despite himself. "It's Friday. Soon, the campus will be clearing for the weekend. Sometime after dark, you will go to my car where I will have left the key beneath the floor . . ."

"No. Take the key. I will hot-wire it. Removes suspicion from you."

"Yes, good."

"Even so, you will have many questions to answer for why I took your car among the many available to me."

"Yes, I don't have an answer for that, yet. I'll just have to brazen it out."

"'Brazen'? I don't know that word."

Tim smiled. "You should, because you are. Look it up when you have a moment."

Each man was now fully engaged in saving one of their lives.

"Now, here's thirty dollars," Tim said. "It's all I have on me." He dropped the money onto his desk. "You must not, under any circumstances, stop at your apartment on the way out of town, no matter how sensitive, how important, things you may have there are to you. Your landlord is F.B.I."

"I understand. I've money hidden in my bag."

Suddenly, a sharp double-knock sounded from the crazed glass of the office door. Inside, neither man moved. Had their voices grown too loud in their rush to puzzle out this escape?

From the hallway Tim heard a colleague.

"Tim, you in there? You stoppin' by Kilroy's on the way home?"

A second voice said, "Guess he's already left. Probably gone to check on his girlfriend. See if she's in jail again."

"Yeah, crazy dame, that one . . ."

"Pretty, though. And a helluva pilot, I hear."

The two men laughed and walked off, their footsteps echoing down the empty hall.

Fletcher took a deep breath and whispered. "Use this additional dough to buy gas, food, and tickets," he said. "Drive north through the night, to Memphis, St. Louis, and so on. But do not go to Chicago, because . . ."

"They traced me through there. I sensed it."

"Yes. Go to . . . what about New York?"

"I have good contacts there."

"All right. I will have to report the car stolen by sometime tomorrow. So switch to a train or bus—or, better, both—by late Saturday afternoon. Get to New York as quickly as you can. And from there . . . from there, I suppose, to Canada. You speak, among other languages, French, I know. You could be safe in Quebec, Montreal, wherever."

Ronchipov smiled.

"Canada is my mother's country. Russia is mine."

The telephone on Tim's desk rang. Both men jumped. It rang eight times in all. Then silence. Their voices continued low, conspiratorial.

"One's country," Tim mused. "Patriotism. Honor. Integrity. The flag. Funny concepts, eh? But I understand. So, you . . . you'll be returning there? To Russia?"

Ronchipov slid the pistol into his pants pocket.

"Better for me that you do not know more than I can afford for you to repeat against me."

"Of course." The slightly arcane structure of that sentence struck Tim.

"What time is it?" said Ronchipov.

"Nearly five. Dusk in an hour. Full dark in two."

"How do I know that if I allow you to leave you won't go straight to the authorities and give me up?"

336

"You don't," Tim said. "On the other hand, I summoned you here. I revealed what I knew, and I have provided you an escape route."

"However imperfect."

"Beggars and choosers, Ronchipov. Your own clever schemes for secrecy having come to naught."

Vladimir nodded and walked to the window, easing to one side to peer out. Tim suddenly felt exhausted. He'd been standing for an hour and felt he hadn't taken a full breath the entire time. He slumped into his desk chair, with Ronchipov behind him.

"Professor, I have to ask, of course: why? Even though I believe I know." At this proximity, Tim could smell Vladimir's after-shave lotion.

"Do you?" said Tim. "Why, then?"

"The bomb. You are wracked with . . . with a bourgeois sense of penitence and culpability about the weapons you helped create in New Mexico and exploded over Japan, the very devices that ended the war and saved, what, 150,000 American lives if you'd had to invade the home islands."

"Yes, well, that is the argument that the proponents made. It's complicated, Vladimir, and I'm suddenly very tired. Perhaps we can discuss it at another time."

"Yes, over sherry at your house, Professor," Vladimir chuckled. "Nice afternoons, those, lovely tradition. Borrowed, once again, from the English, I believe."

"Mmmm, like so much else here. I really have to go now, if you don't mind."

Tim stood and picked up his briefcase. Ronchipov eyed it.

"Want to look inside?"

"I do, actually, if you don't mind." The Russian took the case, rummaged through it, handed it back.

"So," said Tim, "Am I free to go, or are you going to shoot me in the back?"

"Not my mode, I'm afraid. Yes, you can go. Since, in a way, each of us holds the other's life in his hands. The Americans, I understand, take rather a dim view of nuclear treason."

"Indeed."

Tim started for the door and paused, wondering if good manners required one to shake hands under such circumstances, decided against it, and grasped the knob. He pointed with his chin at a hidden corner of the room. Vladimir moved to it, standing quietly, his pistol held once again in his hand.

The two men looked at each other in the gathering dark. Vladimir Ronchipov mouthed the words, "Thank you." Tim nodded, opened the door, walked out, locked it behind him and headed for the parking lot. Twenty minutes later, he was walking home down a sidewalk paralleling a busy thoroughfare, crowded with what, in Tuscaloosa, passed for rush-hour traffic.

Vladimir Ronchipov did, in fact, have to pee into the trash can, a first for him. Then, at a little after nine o'clock that night, he opened the office door, pistol gripped in one pocket, bag over his shoulder and stepped out into the darkened corridor. He had already decided not to take Fletcher's car. No explanation for that coincidence would convince a good interrogator for two minutes. He owed his benefactor that much, at least.

Instead, Vladimir had waited until he saw a '36 Ford sedan wheel into the lot. The middle-aged driver—reeking of 'Professor'—got out, strode away and entered the building. Within four minutes, Ronchipov had the Ford's hood up, and three minutes later he was easing out of the parking lot. Fifteen minutes after that he motored quietly across the city limits, heading north.

He drove all night, stopping only for gas and the occasional hit of Coca Cola and greasy road food, including bar-b-que—another first for him. By seven the next morning he was well into Kentucky, the little Ford still beautifully on-song. At noon, Saturday, he had to take a break, pulling into a road-side rest stop to sleep in the back seat.

Two hours later he was again on the road and an hour after that he parked near the bus stop in downtown Cincinnati, bought a ticket for New York, and fetched up in the great metropolis only three hours after the Tuscaloosa police had completed filling out paper work on the Professor's stolen vehicle.

In Tuscaloosa, Tim Fletcher lay awake most of the night trying to convince himself he'd done the right thing. But Ronchipov's question spun in his head: Why? Why? Why? Was he now a criminal? A seditious felon? One of the bad guys in the newest international scenario of duplicity, espionage, and death? Death. Since the war, the word had lost its power to awe. What was the head count, now? Twenty million? Fifty?

Finally, shortly before dawn, he sat up on the edge of the bed. He had done it, he decided, for the very reasons Vladimir had identified: guilt by association. Guilt and a staggering culpability for which he and his fellow scientists would never live long enough to be exculpated.

He lay back down.

It wasn't good enough. What if the Germans or the Japs had gotten there first? Would they have hesitated one minute to drop the thing on Washington, or San Francisco? He knew the answer.

At least, he thought, at least I didn't reveal the design. At least I didn't give away any secrets.

That afternoon, Fletcher was shocked to find his Plymouth still parked in the Physics lot.

Four days after arriving in New York, presenting as Flying Officer, Captain Cyril Rayburn, and dressed in a perfectly tailored RAF uniform—including an impressive array of battle ribbons—Ronchipov crossed the border into Canada. Walking with a slight limp—while aided by a carved Malacca cane—he spoke a perfect replica of an Oxbridge accent, and traveled on a British diplomatic passport designating him as in the employ of the Foreign Office.

At the crossing he was queried politely by Canadian customs officials regarding his war-time experiences. Captain Rayburn proved to be the soul of generosity and good breeding. He had served with several Canadian flying officers in his squadron, he said, declaring them among the finest pilots he'd ever met or fought with.

"Frightfully brave, those chaps. Jolly good mates. And wonderful sense of humor about Jerry and the war, don't you know. Never got rattled in air-to-air combat. Absolute dragons, those men."

This evaluation pleased the Canadian officials immensely.

Three days after arriving in Quebec, and speaking heavily Gallicized English, Monsieur Pierre LeVec—French businessman specializing in Parisian couture and expensive scents—boarded the trans-continental train for Vancouver, B.C. The ride across Canada proved difficult. Not because anyone suspected him of anything—his French was as good as his English, and his acting skills were hardly challenged by the odd traveling salesman and drunken, demobbed soldiers he encountered in the club car.

No, it was difficult because Vladimir Ronchipov/Pierre LeVec couldn't get a cluster of three or four ideas out of his head. First, and most understandable, was the image of his beautiful, blond daughter,

Irina—a picture of whom he carried in his wallet—waiting for him at his mother's Moscow flat.

Second was the prospective interrogation he knew he would undergo at the none-too-gentle hands of the secret police—the NKVD. He had, after all, been sussed out by the F.B.I. He had cost his government a lot of money to train, transport, and conceal. And he had not discovered what he had been sent to discover. Still, he had managed to outwit the enemy, escape and return home. He could, he decided, handle anything the NKVD would throw at him; then, when appropriately vetted and cleared, he'd probably be reassigned on a mission to England or France.

But the most troubling puzzle he couldn't resolve had to do with Professor Tim Fletcher and the simple question: Why? Americans, he concluded, were strange beasts, a racial, cultural polyglot of moral confusion and willful blindness. They knew nothing of realpolitik; thus, they tended toward a naively romanticized, sentimental world view that was, to Ronchipov's mind, both Manichean and guileless— and that would inevitably lead to their historical obsolescence.

Brave bastards at times, though, he thought. And smart, some of them. Lucky, too.

Twelve days after his confrontation in Fletcher's office, Ronchipov/ LeVec boarded the good ship Stalingrad for the long sea voyage to Vladivostok, to be followed by another ten-day train ride to Moscow.

Travel tired one so.

But at least he was going home.

To Russia.

To Irina.

On the small Pacific island of Tinian, early August, 1945. The bomb—

and Tim Fletcher—arrive safely aboard the USS Indianapolis on July 26th. Four days later, the ship is torpedoed and sunk by a Japanese submarine. Through a series of colossal blunders, the U.S. Navy takes no notice; therefore, as plans for loading, arming and detonating the Hiroshima bomb go forward, over 800 U.S. seamen who served aboard the ship that brought the weapon to its embarkation point are dying in the open ocean of exposure and shark attack. No one knows this but the Indianapolis sailors themselves.

Although the first nuclear bombing mission over Japan has been authorized by President Truman to commence any time after 1 August, the weather has been terrible. A typhoon roils the island, driving banks of dark gray clouds like speeding freight trains across the sky, releasing massive rain squalls onto the B-29 heavy bombers resting on their hardstands, and flooding the impromptu runways.

In the knock-about huts housing the well-guarded "Little Boy" bomb, the scientists and the AAF men who will fly it to its fatal destination, wait and worry. Tim Fletcher, the bomb's courier from the States, waits with them.

Lieutenant Colonel Paul W. Tibbets, 30, the son of a Florida candy wholesaler—and said by some to be the best bomber pilot in the Air Force—has been chosen to command the lead plane on the bombing run. Earlier, he had led the first B-17 bombing mission from England into Europe and had done the same with the first bomber strike in the invasion of North Africa. He is, as one observer later describes him, "a man of medium height and stocky build with dark, wavy hair and a widow's peak, full-faced and square-jawed, a pipe smoker."

He and his air crews have practiced this mission for months. They are as ready as training, determination, and skill can make them.

By 3 August, the weather has begun to clear, and the forecasts look good for the next three days.

August 6 is designated as D-Day.

Hiroshima as the target.

These decisions unleash a complex choreography of destruction that will end 1,900 feet above that Japanese city in what many of the survivors will recall all their lives as the brightest light they ever saw.

Over the next two days, the bomb is winched onto its transport dolly, eased into a 13- by 16-foot loading pit, and finally lifted into the belly of the strike ship—the Enola Gay, named for Tibbet's mother. It's a tight fit, the bomb suspended within the plane from a single shackle. It is said by one crew member to resemble an elongated trash can with fins. Ten and a half feet long, 29 inches in diameter, weighing 9,700 pounds, in color it's a dull black.

Tim Fletcher thinks it is the ugliest, most barbarous thing men have ever conjured out of the brains God gave them. He is present for the key final assembly procedures of the weapon; he attends the midnight briefing on 5/6th August and eats breakfast with the air crew: ham, eggs, and pineapple fritters.

At 0227 hours, with the crew at their stations aboard the Enola Gay, Tibbets orders the engines started. Standing in the control tower, Tim Fletcher hears the pilot request clearance, using his code-name for the day:

"Dimples Eight Two."

At O245, Dimples Eight Two is cleared for take-off. Weighing 65 tons, the B-29 is 15,000 pounds overweight. Five minutes later, using up almost all the two-mile runway, Tibbets has lifted the massive silver bomber into the night sky and disappeared from view.

The men left behind on Tinian must now wait to discover what will come of their labors.

Tim goes back to bed.

He does not sleep.

Hours later, her dark work done over Hiroshima, Enola Gay touches down once again at Tinian. When the big props stop spinning, the scientists and military men who've been waiting, mob the plane and air crew. A thousand questions are fired at them. Tim Fletcher stares into the faces of Tibbets and his men, all young, all a bit bewildered.

Tim wants to see in their eyes the effects of what they've seen, and in those eyes he notes—along with relief and pride, something else. This day, the crew of Enola Gay have touched the face of God and unleashed a quantum transition in the endless epic of battle.

The cancer of war has metastasized.

Tim asks the co-pilot what it was like.

The man says, "You don't want to know."

Tim says, "On the contrary, I do."

The man wheels on him.

"Horrible," he says, "Unspeakable. Fire. Smoke. A mushroom cloud up to 20,000 feet. The shock wave nearly blew us out of the sky . . ." Then he leans forward, speaking in a low snarl.

"You fuckin' civilians have really done it this time, pal."

He shakes his head and walks away.

Chapter 20

On the same day that Victor Rangle/Cyril Rayburn/Pierre LeVec/
Vladimir Ronchipov departed Quebec for Vancouver, B.C., a
woman named Rachel Birnbaum caught the train from New Haven,
Connecticut, to a small university city in Alabama—Tuscaloosa. At
51, and standing 5' 10", Rachel was entering later middle-age with a
characteristically fierce resistance to the inevitable.

Keeping herself trim with a home-grown work-out regimen that
included push-ups, sit-ups, stretching, free weights, and long walks,
she operated on a restricted diet of fruits, whole grains, vegetables and
premium scotch. She refused to dye her hair—now heavily sprinkled
with gray and pulled back into a tight, silvery chignon—wore a size 7
dress, and served as the only woman on the faculty of the Yale School
of Architecture.

She'd been born in 1895 in Charleston, South Carolina, to a family
of privilege, gone north to Smith College in 1913, become engaged
to an impossibly handsome Harvard boy in 1916, seen him march
off to fight a war in France in 1917, received word (from his friends)
of his heroism in battle in 1918, and lost him to the flu pandemic of
1919, three months before they were to be married in a big Charleston
wedding. He was buried in an American military cemetery in France.

She never recovered.

"Some things," she would say, when asked, "are too perfect to be
replicated."

She had studied architecture at Tulane, had designed several
outstanding homes and public buildings in New Orleans, Mobile,
Savannah, and Charleston, and then, in one of those quirks of fate that

transfigure lives, had won a commission to design the second home—a large coastal cottage on Martha's Vineyard—for a Yale faculty member, R. Reid Badger. This so-called cottage—seven bedrooms, six baths, three floors, two kitchens, and maid's quarters—had so pleased Professor Badger that he prevailed upon his good friend—the dean of the architecture school—to consider the novel idea of adding a woman to his faculty.

"She really is a dream to work with," Badger had said of Rachel to the dean. "And we love the house. The day it was finished, it looked as if it'd been there for decades."

The Dean had surveyed a portfolio of Miss Birnbaum's work and agreed to the proposal. She was good. Thus, in the fall of 1931, at the age of 36, Rachel Birnbaum, permanently unmarried, keen-eyed, talented, and opinionated—but Southern enough not to flaunt it— arrived in New Haven, and found a home.

Her students at Yale loved her admixture of Southern charm and Yankee steel, the way she could, with a couple of well-ordered questions and quick sketches, demolish your design, and show you the error of your ways, yet leave you with your manhood intact. Her own buildings had garnered praise in several professional journal articles, and in 1941 she had come to the attention of Sidney Greene at the University of Alabama through a home she built in Birmingham for a local coke-and-iron-ore magnate of infinite resources but limited taste.

"Ah want mah house big, honey," the magnate had said to her, by way of illuminating his aesthetic. "Ah want it so goddamn big that when mah friends walk into that son-of-a-bitch they just about shit, they're so jealous. You understand what ah'm sayin'?"

She did, indeed. Coming from Charleston, she was familiar with a more refined version of this gentleman, and if she could build for them, she could build for him.

The resulting house was a magnificent rococo honeypot set atop Red Mountain in the middle of Birmingham and surveying the whole city— smoking hellhole though it often was when the wind blew wrong. The iron-ore client proclaimed himself mortally satisfied, and even gave her a $3,000 bonus.

"Just 'cause you're so damned good and . . . and attractive. Woman smart as you oughta be married, gal."

Sidney Greene had heard Rachel Birnbaum speak at several professional meetings, and he'd toured the Red Mountain house more than once. He'd then resolved to invite its designer to serve as a member of the Dalton Prize Jury at the first opportunity—which, delayed by the war, turned out to be the current, 1946 award.

On the train down to Alabama, Rachel reviewed the five Dalton applications she'd been sent a couple of weeks before—the local faculty, led by Greene, having winnowed them down from the 23 original contenders. She didn't particularly like Sidney Greene but understood that no one really liked him: people curried favor with him; they tolerated him; they sucked up to him; they stroked his ego; they praised his work; they feared his ire; but nobody could actually be said to like Professor Greene.

Still, she had to admit he'd done a terrific job with the Dalton money, creating for himself not only a professional power fiefdom of note but also producing bang-up good students and sending them off to some of the more glamorous ateliers in Europe to complete their education, acquire a modicum of social polish, and burnish their accents.

Sitting in the speeding train, she spread out the Dalton apps in her sleeper car berth and looked them over: there were two very nicely done knock-off Bauhaus-style homes, one for the beach, one for the mountains; there was a neo-Renaissance court house, well rendered, but looking like it came right out of 17th century Florence. And then there were the two that interested her most: one was an enclosed, multi-purpose sports complex designed for Minneapolis-St. Paul by a guy named Gunderson that had good possibilities. It was called:

A VISION OF AMERICA AT PLAY

The other, the one that really stirred her, was entitled:

AFFORDABLE HOUSING FOR POST-WAR AMERICA
by
Dante Gabriel Larocca

She admired what this young man had done in his design with new materials (pre-stressed concrete & plastics, for example), with thermal efficiencies (increased insulation, recycled heat and double-glazed windows), with linked, extensible unit-construction, and with abundant, humanizing green space and play areas. She particularly liked Larocca's well-grounded argument—advanced in his narrative defense of the design work—that the war had changed everything, not only in the realm of geo-politics but with respect to the way architecture would collide with daily life in America during peace time.

Also interesting to her was the fact that in developing his thesis Larocca had reached for design antecedents outside a rote recitation of the history of domestic architecture. He had done some of that, to be sure, but he'd also invoked, of all things, the G.I. Bill to argue that the combination of delays in family-formation caused by the long war, together with federal intervention at the pocket-book level—

represented by veterans achieving higher education through the G.I. Bill—meant that America's whole attitude toward the importance of home (or cooperative apartment) ownership would rapidly shift from renting to buying. That shift, in turn, would mean a moving up the housing scale for those formerly trapped in sub-standard living quarters in cities and towns. Finally, he was offering a partial solution to those societal shifts.

She liked that.

When she arrived at Tuscaloosa's mock-Victorian, yellow-brick train station, Sidney Green was waiting to greet her, which he did with a big grin and double-hand shake. Their little set-piece scene on the train platform reminded her of the oxymoronoic view of him she'd always held: that he was antiseptically oleaginous. She wasn't sure that was possible, but if it was, he'd achieved it.

"So, my dear Professor Birnbaum, how was your trip?"

"Long," she said, "but it gave me the chance to spend more time with the applications."

"Ahh, yes, and what do you think," he said, taking her elbow and guiding her toward his car.

"Very promising material, Professor Greene, I'm honored to be among this year's judges."

"Ohhh, not a bit of it. Call me Sidney, and we're thrilled, absolutely thrilled to have you join us."

There it was, in that second "thrilled," a sort of over-ripe rhetorical supererogation that—combined with his lying eyes—always, always masked a darker sub-text.

* * *

As Sidney Greene was driving Rachel Birnbaum out to his country house on the Black Warrior River to meet the other Dalton Prize Jury members, Evelyn Curtis was sitting down in her father's study for a difficult conversation.

Harry Curtis wasn't well. The doctors knew it and so did he.

Having just returned from a two-week stint spent inspecting his sawmills and being put through the medical wringer at Ochsner's Clinic in New Orleans, Harry had missed Evelyn's flying misadventures and brief Birmingham jailing, although he'd heard several versions of the saga from friends. In their accounts, Evelyn had emerged as a combination of heroine, daredevil, nut case, and wonder-woman, but Harry wasn't impressed. On the subject of flying, Harry and Evelyn remained deeply divided and had long ago reached an unspoken agreement never to talk of it unless forced to.

On this day, they were forced to.

"I suppose there'll be court costs and a fine to pay," he said, lighting up a 10" Cuban cigar.

"No doubt, yes . . . I thought the doctors had you off those things."

"To hell with the doctors. In the long run, we're all dead, anyway. I'm just gonna go a little sooner than I'd planned. That's all."

He blew out the match, dropped it into an ashtray, took a big drag, exhaled, and sat back in a leather chair big enough to accommodate William Howard Taft.

"So, what can I do for you?" he said. His tone—not calculated to win any Best Parenting awards—made it sound as though he were talking to a bill collector rather than a daughter.

It flustered her.

"Daddy, I just . . . I wanted to ask how you were, and what the doctors in New Orleans said. We haven't seen each other in so long, and I was worried . . ."

"Oh, right, sure. Well, you should be. I've got cancer. And it's gonna kill me in a year. Maybe less. That what you wanted to know?"

The silence hung there between them like rotting meat as she glanced out the window at the ravishing spring sunshine.

"Maybe . . . maybe they're wrong. We could go to New York or Boston or somewhere and get a second opinion, and . . ."

"We're not goin' anywhere. What I just told you is a second opinion. Doctor Daly here in town gave me the same news in the first opinion, last month. Those Jews at Ochsner's just confirmed his diagnosis. They seemed real proud that an old country G.P. 40 years out of med school had gotten it all just right—without benefit of any of their fancy machinery."

It was precisely this combination of anger, bigotry, and bluster that made Harry Curtis a difficult man to talk to. Especially for Evelyn. But it had also made him very, very rich.

"I'm . . . I'm so sorry, Daddy."

"Well, I am too, Evelyn. And so is your mother. We're all sorry. Just as sorry as we can be. The only person who isn't sorry is Robert. My son Robert. And the reason, you'll recall, that he isn't sorry is that he's dead."

Evelyn suddenly felt hot. She wanted to jump up and flee the room, sensing what was coming, hearing in her father's voice the first spilling of a seasoned, long-stored venom now released by his death-sentence diagnosis of cancer.

"And so . . ." he went on, growing red-faced, ". . . and so, Evelyn, now that I'll be dead too before long I have to sit down to the complicated—and infuriating—business of disposing of my assets in some way that will both deprive Uncle Sam of as much of it as possible and at the same time protect you and your mother, when what I ought to be doing—what I desperately want to be doing—is writing out a one-sentence last will and testament bequeathing all my worldly goods to my only son, Robert, together with the directive to take care of his mother and sister in the manner to which my fortune has long made them accustomed. But that won't be happening, will it? It's too late for that, ain't it?"

The pain caused by this bilious explosion crushed her. She shrank into herself. She could hardly catch air as she realized that she had been half-holding her breath around him for nearly twelve years, awaiting this cascade of malice to descend upon her head.

She stood.

"We crashed," she said softly, "because he panicked and grabbed the stick . . ."

"No, NO! It wasn't 'we' crashed. 'You' crashed, Evelyn. You crashed that stupid, little biplane that you should never have taken him up in because you were so sure of yourself, so goddamn smart and . . . smug about yourself!"

Harry Curtis was very nearly out of control. Evelyn stood, walked to the door, paused, and glanced back at her father, seeing in his face a look of enmity born of hurt and loss and heart-break, a look that no daughter should ever see in the face of her father.

"As I've said many times, Father, I'm sorry. It is, without question, the most horrible experience of my life, and I will take the knowledge of it to my grave—along with this." She grazed her finger along the scar running from her mouth toward her ear.

"Right. You got a scar. I lost a son. Get out."

The year is 1934. Evelyn Curtis is sixteen—and already a pilot.

352

Instructed by Joe Pierce, a World War I naval aviator and former barnstormer, she has been brought along slowly and allowed to get the feeling of the old Jenny—a first war trainer—a piece at a time. Pierce has taught more than 200 young men to fly, and he sees in her a natural talent he's seldom encountered in his other students, military or civilian.

She sits the plane like some women sit a horse—with confidence and poise and with a natural feel for stick and rudder that will, Pierce believes, make her a champ. He especially likes that she takes instruction well, that she has memorized the flight manuals, that she hangs around the airport asking better questions—and listening to the answers—than most beginning pilots much older than she.

She soloed weeks ago, and now Pierce watches as she circles the air field at 500 feet, making smooth transitions, shooting a clean approach, and setting the Jenny down with nary a bump. Then he sees a car drive up and Robert Curtis, Evelyn's older brother, get out. They exchange pleasantries as Evelyn taxies toward them.

Robert asks if she's any good. Pierce tells him she's the best pilot of her age and experience he's ever taught. Robert seems impressed.

"Maybe I'll go up with her," Robert says.

"Maybe you should."

When Evelyn approaches nearer, she wheels the Jenny around sideways to them and cuts her engine. Robert runs over and asks her to take him up. She's not sure about that. Daddy wouldn't like it. Robert insists, saying Daddy doesn't have to know. That Joe Pierce says she's good, and Robert wants to see for himself.

"I thought you were afraid of flying," Evelyn says.

"Gotta face what you fear," he grins, climbing onto the lower wing and vaulting into the front seat.

She tells him to buckle up, Pierce spins the prop, and the Jenny, still hot, fires up. Three minutes later, they're airborne, flying toward town. Robert's hair blows in the wind. He looks back and the two siblings exchange big grins. He gives her a double thumbs up.

It is the proudest moment of her life.

Following a spin over the court house, she heads back to the field. The plane feels a little squirrelly on this return leg, and Evelyn realizes the wind has picked up as the temps have risen. She runs through a down-wind check-list in her mind, cinches her shoulder straps a little tighter, and shouts for Robert to behave.

Having overcome his initial trepidation, he has now loosened his harness and is half standing in his seat, pretending to emulate the barnstormers he's seen in the newsreels.

Evelyn orders him to sit down, screaming at him over the roar of the engine. Finally, he does, but unknown to Evelyn— and intrigued by the view from up here—he neglects to refasten his harness. As they circle the field, Evelyn seeks out the wind sock. Sure enough, it's stretched out like a fat lady's stocking: gusts a good 20-30 mph, she figures. Okay, good test of her cross-wind landing skills.

A thought flashes through her head:

I wish he were not aboard.

On her approach, the wind begins to catch her, drifting them left. She fights it, keeping power on and her nose pushing back against the moving air. In the front seat, Robert can feel the buffeting of the little laminated-wood-and-fabric plane and sees them being eased off course. He gets nervous, glances around at his sister, and grows alarmed by the look of pure concentration on her face, behind the goggles.

He calls her name, demanding to know if she knows what she's doing. His pupils dilate as his head swings back and forth, looking ahead, looking at her, ahead again. He calls her name again, loud.

She yells, telling him to shut up and let her fly the damn plane.

Then, just feet above the field, a sharp gust catches them and pushes the plane's tail out of line. Evelyn decides to put it down quick, and cuts her engine. The abrupt loss of power panics Robert.

For reasons known only to him, he both grabs the stick and rams the throttle home. The engine revs scream higher, torquing the little plane sideways; then it floods, misses, sputters, and dies. Robert's rigid hand clutching the stick throws the plane into an abrupt maneuver to starboard, and a second later, they crash.

Robert is thrown out. His neck is broken.

The prop shatters. A razor-sharp sliver of it flies back and slices Evelyn's face open from the corner of her mouth nearly to her ear. Blood pours down her neck and chest.

The last thing she remembers is old Joe Pierce cooing her name as he struggles to extract her body from the crumpled airplane.

Chapter 21

The Dalton Prize student-interviews took place in Professor Sidney Greene's Woods Hall studio, a wonderful space featuring a range of north-facing windows along a forty-foot wall in a restored 19th-century red-brick building—one of the first structures rebuilt after Yankee soldiers burned the University to cinders in April, 1865.

In this exemplary room, Greene arrayed the jury of professional architects around a U-shaped table covered in green felt—rather like a Vegas poker table—the better to hurl questions at the hapless finalist caught in their cross-hairs. Each judge had brought with him a pile of student applications, together with his own scribbled questions—and a rank-order of preferred designs.

On a luminous, early May morning, as Green introduced Rachel Birnbaum to her fellow jury members, she appraised each man on the basis of what she knew about his work and reputation. Along with Greene and herself, there were three others: Ferguson, the rotund, hirsute homunculus from Georgia Tech who—years ago—had done a fine neo-classical-revival private home on the banks of the Mississippi River, then did it again and again and again, getting rich and regionally famous (and more rotund) in the process.

The fourth judge was Braithwait, a gawky, younger, eager-to-please fellow from the University of Virginia, a real comer, it was said. He'd done—among other things—a couple of big commercial buildings on the West Coast and—with his dual degrees in structural engineering and architecture—was considered something of a rising star in designing complex structures that would withstand the effects of high-Richter earthquakes and their aftershocks.

Finally, she was relieved to see an old friend, Donald Noble, a native of blue-collar Yonkers, New York, a prematurely balding farceur and all-purpose anecdotalist who could keep people in stitches at a party and—she hoped—would defuse with his wit any nasty awards-decision contretemps, should they arise in choosing Dalton winners—of which, this year, there would be two. Noble, now at Columbia, had succeeded chiefly in urban design, with a sub-specialty in lavish city landscaping. He knew how to get along with both contractors and the unions. He knew northern, foul-weather construction practices. He was a nice addition to the mix.

Of the five students to come before the jury, three were vets; two were not. They would appear at nine, ten, and eleven A.M., followed by a catered lunch, then the final two applicants would be grilled at two and three o'clock. That evening at six, Sidney Greene would host a sumptuous cocktail party at his river home, "Halcyon," where the two winners would be breathlessly announced before all and sundry—Greene being rather a fan of the Academy Awards practice of public humiliation for all but the winners.

The first student up was a vet from Los Angeles named Threlkeld. In the war, he'd fought with an artillery unit in Europe, and he'd designed a Bauhaus-influenced private home for the California coastal highlands north of San Francisco. Following protocol laid out in the Dalton guidelines, he presented his model and drawings, made his oral pitch, then sat down to await evisceration.

The questioning was—and was meant to be—brutal. The judge from Virginia attacked the earthquake-proofing elements in the home, taking the young Californian deep, deep into the mathematics of the strength of materials, seismic reverberations, sympathetic oscillation, and much else. The younger man did his best but soon realized he was swimming with the Great White Shark here and didn't try to fake it—any more than was strictly required to save face.

And so it went.

The second, non-vet Bauhaus-derivate got beaten about the head and shoulders by three members of the committee who charged him with simply copying his famous mentors' theories without inspiriting his building with a vision of his own.

The Renaissance-inspired courthouse, in turn, seemed to ignite some shallow-graved, class-based ire in Noble who posed a series of scalding questions about its relevance and the suitability of deploying such a retro-design in modern, post-war America. The applicant argued for restoring classicism to a world architecturally adrift. Noble ate him for lunch.

Meanwhile, Greene seemed caught between pleasure at seeing the blood flow (he believed a designer should be able to defend his work) and dismay that his students were taking such a pounding—even though in his written instructions to the jury he'd encouraged them to engage in a "robust critique of each design." Maybe it was their scorched-earth interpretation of "robust" that was making him squirm. By noon, all three candidates had retired from the fray bloodied and bowed—and with a fresh trove of Dalton-Prize horror-stories to add to campus lore already surrounding this competition.

Lunch for the five judges, by comparison, was quite civil, with everyone swapping tales of the post-war surfeit of vets—some very good, indeed—freshly home from the war, of the difficulty everywhere of acquiring decent construction materials, of a rampant black market in such things as cement and reinforcing steel, of innovative building techniques pioneered by the Sea-bees and other military engineers, and of a brave new world of design they hoped might arise from the ashes of Europe and the Far East.

While all this was going on, Dante, scheduled for the fifth slot at three o'clock, was lying on his cot trying to visualize the interrogation room and the questions he might be asked. With the arrival of warm weather, he had rolled up or staked out two sides of his tent so that his place took on the air of a breezy, rustic pavilion.

At 12:45 P.M. Cohen came out of his trailer, called Dante's name, and walked in, carrying a gray sport coat over his bad arm and holding a drink in his hand.

"What're you wearin' to your date with the firing squad, dago-boy?" he asked, plopping down in one of the two chairs.

"Don't know, maybe camouflage fatigues—but fairly clean ones, you know."

"Wise ass. Wouldn't put it past you. Here, try this on." He tossed the tweed coat to Dante, who stood and shook himself into it.

"Nice fit, Brooklyn," Cohen said. "Keep it. You can wear it to your next wedding."

"Not on the horizon, my friend. And I won't keep it, David, but I will wear it. Thanks, man."

Cohen had not looked well lately. When he wasn't out at Laney's writing, he'd been keeping to himself, and when asked, he'd repeat a version of the same line: "I'm in the home stretch on the novel, baby. I'm pedaling downhill now, man, fast as my old legs will carry me. I can see the ending rising up before me like heaven's gate. Either I finish this thing or it finishes me, etc."

He always laughed when he said these things, but his eyes never joined in the joke.

"No kidding, Dante, best of luck, fella. You deserve it, hard as you've worked on your design. I'm pullin' for you."

The unusual candor and warmth of Cohen's voice embarrassed both of them.

Dante nodded and said, "Well, screw it, know what I'm saying? If I lose, there's always next time. Tomorrow. Whatever. But I'm givin' it my best shot. Can't ask more than that."

David Cohen stood.

"Break a leg, pal," he said, leaned over, and stuck out his hand. Dante hesitated, then shook it.

"I gotta go to the shindig later at Greene's place," Dante said. "But, look, tell the gyrenes and Chief Davis that we'll throw a good drunk when I get back: win, lose, or draw. What'dya say?"

An enigmatic smiled played across Cohen's face.

"Sounds good to me. I'll pick up a bottle from Shorty's bootlegger while you're gone."

"Yeah, and none of that rot-gut crap either, Cohen. We're semi-rich now, after Evelyn kicked that Kelvin jerk's ass for him in the Mustang. Man, I wish you'd seen that. She was . . . she was . . ." His voice fluttered into the middle-distance. "just . . . unbelievable."

Cohen laughed.

"You pathetic dick-head, Larocca. You're pussy-whipped to a fare-thee-well, and that's the straight dope. I'll see you back here after the—" he made a face, "—cocktail party."

* * *

F.B.I. agents Akers and Zeiler bordered on the homicidal. Sitting in Tim's university office—with Zeiler occupying the very chair Rangle/Ronchipov had sat in when he pulled the pistol on Tim—they grilled Fletcher like a piece of fresh tuna:

Had he told Ronchipov anything to tip him off?

No.

Had he detected any change in the younger man's behavior beforehand?

No.

Why had they met right here in Tim's office the day the Russian spy disappeared?

To discuss the forthcoming fellowship.

And on and on it went.

Tim was pretty sure of three things: they thought he was lying; they didn't know how to prove it; they wouldn't be able to nail him unless Rangle/Ronchipov were captured—and talked.

Tim wondered vaguely if he would—talk.

"Now, Professor," said the bluff Akers, straining for cordiality, "I'm sure you know this development has highly displeased the Bureau in Washington. . . ."

"Immensely displeased," said Zeiler.

"Yes, immensely, and including the Director, too," said Akers. "In fact, Mr. Hoover himself was on the phone this very morning letting us know just exactly where the bear defecated in the buckwheat, if you catch my drift."

"Buckwheat?"

"This is serious, Professor," said Akers.

"I know that, gentlemen."

"Yeah, about as serious as it gets, pal," said Zeiler. "And the thing we want to know—as we follow the dots—is why would Ronchipov come here to meet with you late one afternoon and then that very night disappear from view, just like, poof, a spirit or something."

"I'm afraid you'll have to catch him and ask him," Tim said, "because I don't know. He seemed perfectly calm when he was here, though excited about the fellowship; interested in his research topic, and so on."

"You know," said Zeiler, changing the subject, "this office smells like piss to me. Do you, uh, do you ever, like, pee in the trash can, Professor?"

"Are you mad?" said Fletcher. "Pee in the trash? Really, Mr. Zeiler."

Tim felt the color rise on his neck. He'd smelled it too the morning he'd returned here after Ronchipov left. He'd washed the can out twice, but the urine must have mixed with something in the trash, and he hadn't been able to eradicate the smell completely.

"It's probably chemicals or acids or something from my lab," Tim said, struggling to remain composed.

Zeiler stood, approached the can, and bent over it.

"Yeah, you mean like uric acid, maybe?" he said.

Tim held the gaze of the suspicious, ferret-like Zeiler.

"Mr. Zeiler, I give you my word: I have never urinated into that trash can."

"You think Ronchipov might have?"

Zeiler grinned. Tim held his gaze steady.

"Not in my presence, Agent Zeiler. Not in my presence."

"Okay, okay," said Akers, "enough with the piss. Sit down, Ziggy. Look, we got a situation here. We've lost our man. We know—or believe—he stole Professor Eddins' car out of the lot there. The car has been located in Cincinnati. A man matching Ronchipov's description bought a bus ticket to New York—and that's where we lost him. He's probably gone to ground in Canada or somewhere. The thing is, Ronchipov is an important asset of the Soviets, and he's disappeared. And you were the last person to talk to him. Now, you can understand,

Professor, that that makes you . . . well, it makes us just a little suspicious."

Fletcher leaned forward in his chair, placing his elbows on the desk and looking sternly from man to man. His deceased father, a closet alcoholic, had once told Tim that if he ever got into a situation where he absolutely had to lie, then he should (a) change the subject or (b) stick as close to the truth as he could. That way he would have fewer fabrications to remember to conceal. And that's exactly what the older Fletcher always did when questioned about his drinking by his missionary-minded, teetotaling, lay-preacher Methodist wife.

"Gentlemen," Tim's voice took on a husky tone, half an octave below his normal phrasing, "believe me when I tell you this: I do understand the seriousness of the situation. Indeed, I would argue that few people in America understand that seriousness better than I do. I have been . . . my soul has been scorched by exposure to three years of the Manhattan Project. I was one of two couriers who accompanied from San Francisco to Tinian Island the bombs we dropped on Hiroshima and Nagasaki. I understand that the Soviets want an equivalent weapon, and I believe they'll have it within five or six years . . ."

"What? Not a chance," Zeiler sneered. "Not unless Ronchipov shows up in somebody else's lab."

Tim looked at him.

"Mr. Zeiler, excuse me for saying so, but you don't know what the hell you're talking about. The technology here isn't all that complicated, once you grasp the theory involved. The Soviets are not stupid. They have captured—and taken to Moscow—roughly half the German scientists who worked on Hitler's nuclear weapons program. We captured the other half—some of whom are in Alabama, by the way. Nuclear technology is fungible, Agent Zeiler. What works for us will work for them." Tim's voice dropped another half-octave. "Listen to me when I tell you this, gentlemen: the Soviets will get the bomb, with or without Ronchipov."

Outside the open window, shouts from a spirited volley-ball game whispered into the room. Inside, the three men sat, exchanging sullen glares. Akers and Zeiler thought the professor was guilty as hell, but of what?

They'd known he was smart, brilliant, even, but they'd calculated he would not warn Ronchipov—and assume the enormous personal risk that act involved. On the other hand, the facts were the facts, and Zeiler thought Fletcher might be a pinko sympathizer, influenced by his buddy Oppenheimer and thus willing to take the chance of paying the ultimate price—on strongly leftist political convictions, alone.

For his part, Akers thought Ronchipov, smart bastard himself, had probably just sniffed their presence and split before-time. Real bad luck, he guessed, though he knew that explanation would not fly in D.C.

Akers stood.

"Well, Professor, you'll be hearing from us again, and probably some people from Washington, too, you know. This isn't over, by a long chalk."

"Yes, I'm sure of that."

"By the way, Fletcher," said Zeiler, grinning, "we hear your girlfriend, Miss Curtis, got her ass in a sling recently over a flying incident out at the field."

"That's true. I believe she's paid a fine of some sort."

"Three hundred and fifty bucks, my man, plus six months probation, and a stern warning from the judge," said Zeiler. "See, Fletcher, we know everything."

"Do you, indeed?" said Tim, unable to resist.

"Indeed we do." Zeiler leaned in toward Tim. "Which reminds me: don't leave sweet Miss Evelyn alone too long with that wop architect from Brooklyn, Larocca? He'll have her panties off so fast it'll leave burn marks on her butt."

"Come on, Ziggy," said Akers, "cut the crap. Professor, we'll be seeing you again. Enjoy your afternoon."

They left.

Tim Fletcher sat back from his desk, staring at nothing.

* * *

In Sidney Greene's high-ceilinged studio, Ole Gunderson, non-vet designer of the multi-purpose sports complex for Minneapolis, was in the middle of defending his Dalton project to a panel of judges who seemed favorably disposed. The building had good shape and proportion; it was cleverly situated on its site; it pointed to the future of competitive athletics in some inventively combinatory ways. And Gunderson himself—sharply dressed in a bow tie and dark, double-breasted suit to hide his paunch—was good on his feet.

"I believe," he was saying, "with both the war and Depression behind us, our post-war economy will, after some transitional problems, likely explode with pent-up demand for all manner of goods and services. Those will include entertainment, of course, and I think that sports will then assume unprecedented importance in American life . . ."

"And that's a good thing?" said Rachel Birnbaum.

"Yes, Professor Birnbaum, I believe it is. As ancient Athens demonstrated through sponsorship of the original Olympics, organized sport—if properly managed—diverts the common people and provides a viable alternative to warfare. Indeed, contemporary conflicts were known to have been suspended during the period that the Olympics were . . ."

"Perhaps Athens should have told Sparta," Rachel said.

"Well, ma'am, the Spartans were a special case."

"Ole," Greene spoke up. "I'd like you to explain the dual-use aspects of your complex."

Rachel could see that Gunderson was Greene's first choice for one of the winning slots, and—given his powers of persuasion—she figured the only issue on the table was the second. Thus, she was waiting to support—in the strongest terms—Larocca.

"Yes, sir," Gunderson beamed, "For hockey, as you can see here, the floor of the auditorium remains frozen by means of a labyrinth of 2 inch piping charged with a powerful refrigerant. However, for basketball . . ."

Out in the passageway, Dante, wearing a pair of pre-war slacks, Cohen's tweed jacket, and his black, army necktie, paced and waited.

* * *

The telephone at the Curtis estate rang. Arthur, the black butler, answered, asked the caller to wait a moment, then spoke on the house intercom to Evelyn. When she picked up, she found an agitated Tim Fletcher. He'd now undergone his second visit from special F.B.I. agents from the Washington office, and, while they hadn't accused him of anything directly, they were also clearly skeptical of the uncanny coincidence of Ronchipov's late afternoon visit, followed by his disappearance.

Tim stuck to his story that Ronchipov had come to discuss the pending physics fellowship and that he seemed in good spirits—

although Tim did allow that Vladimir seemed, perhaps, a little tetchy or preoccupied, when he thought about it. Perhaps that in itself suggested nervousness? Tim didn't know. When asked why he'd left his car in the parking lot that night, Fletcher said he couldn't get it cranked. Flooded, he guessed. By the next morning, it was fine, he said.

Now, the young professor was caught in the trap of (a) being consumed by the subject of Ronchipov, yet (b) unable to talk truthfully to anyone about it, anyone. Still, he wanted to see Evelyn that night. For her part, Evelyn knew that Dante was undergoing the Dalton interrogation at this very moment, and that the six o'clock cocktail party would tell the tale.

She'd called Larocca that morning to wish him luck, and they'd had a funny chat, with him pretending to have completely forgotten that today was the day. He'd promised to call her ASAP with any news after the party.

"Tell you what, Tim," she said into the phone, "let's get together later, after eight, maybe. I've got a bunch of letters to write, and mother and I need to talk about . . . about Daddy and all that."

Tim acquiesced, knowing of Evelyn's terrible run-in with her father, but he also said he and she needed to have a frank discussion about several things. She heard what lay between the lines there but let it pass.

When she hung up, she looked at the clock: 3:32.

* * *

Dante sat in the Dalton hot seat, his head swiveling to face each questioner in turn. So far, it was going fairly well, he thought, although Greene had raked him over the coals on what Dante regarded as pretty small issues of social impact and choice of materials.

As far as Larocca could tell at this point, he enjoyed support from Professors Birnbaum and Noble—the fellow Yankee from Columbia—plus, he thought/hoped, the little fat fellow from Georgia Tech, Ferguson. He needed three votes and had already written Greene off as a strike against; meanwhile, he was trying to assess Braithwait, the gawky genius from UVA—without much luck. It was all a bit like arguing before the Supreme Court, where the rigor of the justices' questioning didn't always reflect their final vote on a case.

Dante was now pitching his design like mad.

". . . and you have playing or sports fields, movie theaters, food stores, retail shops, churches and schools right here close by the living units, within walking distance. The electric tram running through the complex reduces traffic noise, exhaust fumes, and the danger to pedestrians. Plus, underground, ventilated parking gets cars off the street and turns what would have been garage space into workshops or studios or bedrooms.

"On the thermal front, you have much thicker insulation and, new, double-glazing for windows. These two things will give privacy from sound intrusion, plus long-term savings in heating oil. I calculate the added initial costs will be recovered within 6-8 years, depending on weather patterns."

Professor Noble spoke up. "You're proposing a rather high ratio of green area to resident here, aren't you?"

"Yes, sir, I am. In my experience—and I've lived there—the worst aspect of public housing is the hostile external environment. It's created by other people living nearby, and of course, it ain't possible to make it go away completely, but it's essential that we make these places seem more like," he smiled, "home."

Rachel Birnbaum lobbed him a soft-ball question regarding his chief architectural influences.

"Well, Professor Birnbaum, as I see it, Frank Lloyd Wright and his 'organic architecture' are basically at war with Le Corbusier and so-called modernism . . ."

"Yes."

"Corbo, for instance, calls houses 'machines for living in,' while Wright says architecture 'puts man into possession of his earth.'"

"And where do you come down there?" asked Ferguson of Tech.

"Well, sir, if those are my choices, I'll go with Wright."

Braithwait tapped his pencil on the desk.

"Mr. Larocca, Wright was a fine, perhaps even great, architect in his day, but he's very old now . . ."

"Seventy-eight," said Dante.

"Quite, with respect, the man is finished, isn't he, and isn't it time we moved on?"

"Yeah, I mean, you can't let one architect decide what's kosher for the whole world, I agree, but you know what? I cabled his office last week and asked—just for information purposes—how many projects they've got on the boards right now."

He let that fragment of news hang in the air. Rachel smiled at his chutzpah. Finally, Braithwait couldn't wait.

"Well?" he said.

"Twenty-one," Larocca said, "including a New York museum for the Guggenheim that may, just may, be his masterpiece."

Braithwait half-sneered, "It's said to resemble a mollusk."

"Mollusk?" Ferguson said.

Donald Noble spoke up. "Larocca, in your proposal narrative you seem to take a damn dim view of the whole Bauhaus style, along with its subsequent adherents."

"Yes, sir."

"So, I mean, why? When it's considered by many critics to be the most influential movement of the 20th century."

Larocca sat forward on the edge of his chair.

"Some Bauhaus . . . in my opinion, sir, some Bauhaus work is obviously brilliant, inventive, ground-breaking—Gropius, Mies, and so on—but a lot is cold and . . . and anonymous, you know? I'm just saying that mass-produced boxes are not the answer for public housing. For any housing.

"You said 'anonymous' just then," said Rachel.

"Yes, ma'am."

"Why does that matter?"

"Because," Dante said, "where you live tells you who you are. And if you plop down two-three thousand people in identical sets of high-rise, eight-foot-ceilinged, square-roomed apartments they'll eventually get very unhappy. And when a lot of people—living right on top of each other—get unhappy at the same time, there's gonna be hell to pay."

"Social engineering," sneered Greene.

"All public housing is social engineering, Professor Greene—in my opinion, at least."

Rachel Birnbaum admired Dante's combative attitude toward Greene, whom she knew to be fierce in dealing with his students. It was the veteran thing, she thought; you shoot bazookas and flame-throwers at a guy for three or four years and he loses his fear of a mere professor—no matter how much influence he wields in your life. At the same time, Greene's antipathy for Larocca and his project was palpable, and Rachel hoped this street-smart Yankee could keep his temper in check.

"Mr. Larocca," Greene said, sarcasm dripping, "Do you think Corbusier's ideas about worker housing are devoid of any merit as a solution to . . ."

"No, sir, I don't. Corbusier's high-rise apartment blocks have one virtue: they're cheap to build. That's it. Unfortunately for the occupants, they're soul-destroying."

"Oh, really, come now, Larocca . . ."

Greene's face reddened as his voice rose.

* * *

The university's Student Union served as the chief watering hole for Alabama students caught with only an hour between classes—or those for whom playing marathon games of cutthroat bridge constituted the daily bread of life. In one corner, at 4:30 P.M., Dante sat, drinking coffee, his tie adrift, his energy depleted. The Dalton Hour in Greene's studio had been the longest of his life, ranking in intensity with some he'd spent in combat.

Now, exhausted, he toyed with a sketch pad on which he'd assessed his own performance—along with guesses as to how he'd done with each judge. He still figured he had Birnbaum and Noble with him. Greene and Braithwait he'd conceded, based on their hostile questioning. That left Fat Little Ferguson as the swing vote. This guy's inquiries had been fairly mild, and Dante thought he'd listened closely to the colloquy among him and the other four. But it was all a crap-shoot now. Well, no use losing sleep. But, Christ, what else was there to think about? Evelyn, maybe . . .

"So, Larocca, how'd it go?" It was Gunderson, still looking fit for a fashion show, but emitting none of his former antagonism.

"Say, Gunderson. Not bad, I guess, y'know? Greene was on me like stink, but maybe that's just his way. How 'bout you? Knock 'em dead?"

"Hard to say. Professor Birnbaum didn't seem especially friendly, and that Braithwait," Gunderson laughed, "he totally killed me on some structural stuff. I didn't even know what the hell he was talkin' about."

"Yeah, he was some tough." Dante gestured, "so, sit down, take a load off. No need for us to be enemies."

This weary invitation flattered the younger man. The battles between vets and non-vets had raged all year in intramural sports, in the school newspaper, in fist fights at various events. He was happy to join Dante.

"So, Gunderson, I don't even know your first name."

"Ole."

"No kidding, really? Ole? Just like the old country. Well, Ole, you've got a lot of talent. I gave you a ration of shit that day in Greene's studio, but in fact, I admire your work."

This off-hand appraisal set Gunderson's heart a-beating.

"Well, you too, Larocca. Everybody in the class really liked your design. But, you're . . . you're a little hard to get . . . you know, to get to know, sometimes."

Dante smiled. "Yeah, Brooklyn upbringing, I guess. And the war."

Gunderson grew animated.

"That's the thing with all of us who were too young for combat. I mean, I'da given anything if I could have gone and, you know, fought the Fritzes or the Japs. For the rest of my life, I'll never get over . . ."

Dante raised his hand, palm out. He'd heard it all before.

Gunderson stopped.

"Ole, my friend, let me put you wise to something," Dante felt like an ancient, battle-scarred veteran of some lost culture trying to explain it all to the younger, would-be warrior. "The two most over-rated things on the planet are home-cooking and the glory of war. I know you feel like you missed out on something great, some huge, like, life-defining experience. But take it from me, it was the worst thing that ever happened to the guys who were really in the heat. And you should thank your lucky stars that your mama and daddy didn't get together quite early enough to see you killed 18 or 19 years later."

Gunderson looked directly into Larocca's hundred-year-old eyes.

"I still wish I'd been there," he said.

Dante smiled.

"Sure you do. I understand. And, unless I miss my bet, you'll get your chance. I'm thinking the Far East, maybe. Indo-China, Korea, some place like that."

"What about Europe? You don't think we'll wind up going to war with the Russians one day?"

Dante was very tired.

"Could be, Ole, could be. But wherever it is, I know you'll be there. And good luck to you."

* * *

The Dalton cocktail party at "Halcyon," Greene's river house, proved quite an affair. To protect it from the hundred-year flood-line, the house was raised twelve feet above the ground atop creosote pilings. On the rough, knotty-cypress interior walls Greene had hung taxidermied bodies or heads of wolves, an entire polar bear, fangs bared and rared up on its hind legs, a leopard, five kinds of duck, three huge wild turkeys, a dozen stuffed trophy fish, and half an elk. The place seemed a cross between a gentleman hunter's retreat and an abattoir.

Mingling with the Dalton judges were 75-80 members of the local gentry, mixed with faculty types, plus the five Dalton finalists. The guests milled about, examining and commenting on the detailed scale-model architectural prototypes each finalist had built.

Meanwhile, Dante had squared his shoulders, re-knotted his tie and was attempting to make small talk over a beer with a nice-looking middle-aged woman of improbable hair color and uncertain designs on his body.

"You veterans," she breathed, "are about the best thing that's ever happened to the university. So alive . . . so vital, you know?"

"Yes, ma'am, we're pretty vital, all right." He moved away.

Rachel Birnbaum eyed Larocca from across the room. The time elapsed between Dante's interview and now had not been pleasant. The Dalton panel's discussion of the projects had been heated in the extreme, and no one was entirely happy with the outcome.

The heart of her argument had been that Larocca was 20 years ahead of the rest of them on the subject of public housing, that his design could actually make such places something America could be proud of. Greene's response might be summarized by saying 'Great architecture is about great buildings, Rachel, not clever slum management.'

At that moment, Greene himself stepped up to a microphone, asking for the crowd's attention.

"Ladies and gentlemen, thank you all for coming out on this fine evening. The Dalton Prize announcements each spring are a highlight for me, my colleagues, our students, and, of course, for our worthy judges."

He then introduced each of the judges, supplying brief encomiums and summaries of their major achievements.

The student finalists were dying in the crowd. Larocca could see Threlkeld and Gunderson standing side-by-side near the bar.

"And now," said Greene, smiling, "it is my distinct privilege and pleasure to announce the two winners of this year's Samuel Dalton Traveling Fellowship in Architecture. As you'll see from all the models arrayed behind me, our choice this year has been especially difficult. But it was our task, and we rose to it . . . heh, heh. So, the first winner is a brilliant design for living (and playing) in post-war America and was submitted by Mr. Ole Gunderson of Minneapolis. Ole, come forward, please."

Gunderson's smile was cracking his face. To strong applause, he stepped forward, accepted the certificate, and had his photograph taken with Greene.

"And now, for the second of this year's two prizes. The jury panel engaged for quite a long time in a most spirited discussion of this choice, but in a close vote the winner is. . ." he shuffled the papers he was holding, "Lester Threlkeld, for his superb design of a beach home for coastal California. Congratulations, Lester."

Dante, blinked, breathed deeply and, amid the applause, moved toward the door. Rachel Birnbaum blocked his path.

"What are your future plans, Larocca?" she said.

"Plans? I'm gonna get drunk as a lord, ma'am."

"Anything for further out? Like next year?"

"No, Professor. I'd pretty well been counting on being in Rome, you know? But, hey, I'll think of something. Good night."

And he was gone. The time was 6:36 P.M.

Chapter 22

The 25 mile jeep drive back into town and then out to Shorty Puckett's Beagle Farm took forever, but Dante—for some reason—didn't mind. The clean, rushing air and late spring evening provided solace, and a kind of tranquility had settled on him. He was experiencing something very like a cluster of emotions he'd known before, in Europe—post-combat fatigue. He'd fought as hard as he'd known how. He'd defended his ideas well—a couple of the jury members had congratulated him at the party. He strongly felt he had a good design, but this time he hadn't quite gotten it done.

Apropos Professor Birnbaum's question, he wasn't sure what he was going to do now: stay on at Alabama working with Greene? Try to transfer to another school? But where? Give it up and return to Brooklyn? That had no appeal.

He dreaded having to break the news to Evelyn, Cohen, the Marines and Chief Davis. They'd believed in him and, he could see in the days leading up to the final assault, they were sure he'd win. The task now was to rein in Karl and Ben so that they didn't rush out in full battle dress, barricade the doors to Greene's river house, and set it ablaze with Greene—and everyone else—inside. But, what the hell, he'd tell 'em a few war stories, they'd get drunk, the next morning their heads would all feel the size of watermelons.

And that would be that.

Turning into Shorty's place, Dante saw with dread that Davis, Karl, and Ben had rigged up celebratory colored Christmas lights, linking trailer to trailer to tree to tent. The lights were lit, but no one was in sight. On his tent-flap a note told him that the jarheads and Davis had gone to pick up some beer and bar-b-que and would be back instanter. Cohen's trailer was dark.

He walked into his tent, got a warm, crippled-up greeting from Sir Plus, and knew immediately that something was wrong, that someone had been in the tent rummaging around, looking for something. He noticed the pillow on his cot. It lay slightly askew, not the way he'd left it that—and every—morning. He walked over, lifted the pillow and saw that the German Luger pistol was gone. He stood there silent, calculating. It didn't make sense. All the guys at Shorty's knew he slept with it there, and none of them would steal it. Had they had visitors?

He went outside, looked around, walked to Cohen's trailer, and knocked. Nothing. He knocked again. Nada. He moved to the window, stood on tiptoes and looked inside.

In the half-light thrown by the strings of colored lights, Dante saw a slumped-over shape at the table. His pulse, already elevated, nearly doubled. He leapt to the trailer door, grabbed the handle, and nearly wrenched the whole door off its hinges.

He stepped up and inside and froze.

* * *

The intercom in Evelyn Curtis' bedroom buzzed.

"Miss Evelyn, you have a call. It's Mr. Larocca."

"Thanks, Arthur." Evelyn rushed to her phone.

"Dante, tell me, tell me everything."

She barely recognized the strangled voice on the line.

"Cohen's dead. I need you."

"Dante? What? Dante, what are you say . . ."

"Get out here!" He hung up.

David Cohen was quite dead. A red towel wrapped around his head to minimize splatter, Cohen had shot himself with Dante's German Luger. In front of him on his writing desk lay a neat pile of manuscript, maybe 500 pages thick. Next to it were propped three sealed envelopes with names typed on each—Larocca's, Laney's, and Cohen's parents'.

* * *

As it turned out, the thoughtfully swathed towel wasn't red, after all. It was white, stained a deep rose by Cohen's blood. After Dante called Evelyn, he called the police, but before they arrived—and just as Karl, Ben, and Davis were driving up—he reentered the trailer, picked up the envelopes addressed to him and Laney, and stuffed them into the inside pocket of the jacket Cohen had loaned him. Then, he stepped outside to greet the three ex-servicemen who were lustily singing "The Marine Corps Hymn" as they advanced on Dante's position:

"From the halls of Montezuma

To the shores of Tripoli,

We will fight our country's ba-attles

On the land and on the sea. . .

. . . Hey, Dago-Boy! How'd it go? When d'ya leave for Rome, you lucky stiff . . .?"

They shut up when they saw his face.

"Cohen's dead. Suicide."

The three men halted, arms filled with food and beer. Dante's eyes told them all they needed to know. Instantly, they were sober. Soldiers again. Back at war.

"He used my gun."

"The Luger?" said Karl.

Dante nodded.

"I just found him. Cops on the way."

"Did he leave a note, or, like, a reason?" Davis asked.

Dante hesitated fractionally.

"There's a note addressed to his parents. I didn't open it. And there's his manuscript next to him on the table. He's written on it: "Finished, May 31, 1946. David P. Cohen.""

"That's today," said Ben.

"Right. Here's Evelyn."

The maroon Ford convertible skidded sideways into Shorty's gravel drive and slid to a stop near them. Evelyn jumped out and ran to Dante, her arms extended, pleading for an explanation, desperate to comfort and soothe him. Then, they hugged each other like few people ever have, crying, murmuring, hurdling in a second's time a thousand emotional obstacles and hesitancies that bar us from each other, making the two of them all-but-lovers right there on the spot. In that moment, the remaining barriers between them fell. She whispered that she loved him. He whispered that he loved her.

She said over and over, "I'm so sorry, Dante; I'm so sorry."

"I know . . . I know . . ."

The other men moved off to one side, awaiting the police.

* * *

None of the Tuscaloosa people ever read the letter addressed to Cohen's parents. The elder Cohens were notified of the death, and when they arrived the next day, the sealed envelope was handed to them. They never discussed it with anyone outside the family. Along with a four-sentence note, it contained their son's Medal of Honor.

The note to Larocca was brief.

"Dante—Sorry to use the Luger, but it's such a great piece, I hope
you won't mind. I know you won the Dalton Prize today and will
spend next year in Rome or somewhere. You deserve it. I never saw
a guy work harder on anything in my life. By the way, I finished my
novel. I would appreciate your getting it to Hudson Strode, my writing
teacher. He seems to like it. Take care, pal. You're the best.
                    David
p.s. Marry Evelyn.

In the envelope, Cohen had included a couple of things: five one-
hundred dollar bills, money he'd won earlier by having Karl place a bet
on Evelyn's flying skills; and the quick sketch Dante had done of him
months before while they discussed their strange need to write books
and design buildings.

After the police and coroner had done their work, taken the body,
sealed up the trailer, and left, Dante and Evelyn sat in his tent together,
drinking. He lit a candle, saying any brighter light would be more than
he could stand. Their earlier passionate embrace and joint confessions
of love had left each feeling a little unmoored. At every opportunity,
they touched hands, stroked cheeks, held each other. But nothing more.

"Look," he said, sitting on the cot, "There's something you need to
know about me . . ."

She smiled. "You got secrets. I got secrets. All God's chillun got
secrets."

He couldn't tell if she was joking or serious.

"Go ahead," she said. "You tell me yours; I'll tell you mine."

He paused a long moment.

"Yeah, okay, here it is: before the war, early in '42 when things looked so bad, in the space of one week I joined the Army, big patriot, rah-rah, and, got, uh . . ."

"Married?"

This woman killed him.

"Yeah."

"Well, that does sort of change things, doesn't it?"

"The thing is, while I was overseas, she . . . uh, she got involved with a guy, a friend of mine, and, uh, got pregnant."

She saw the pain in his eyes.

"I'm sorry, Dante."

"One of my buddies wrote me. So, when I got home . . ."

"You kicked the guy's ass."

"I kicked the guy's ass. Big time. Then I came down here. Fact, that day you buzzed me in the Mustang I still had his blood on my pants."

She recalled him standing at the air field, hands on hips, scowl on face, his beautiful Weimaraner upright in the jeep.

"So, now she wants you to support the kid?"

"The kid . . . she miscarried."

"And the guy left her?"

"She threw him out."

"And she wants you back."

"Yeah. She came down here from New York in January. And we talked. That day you went to New Orleans."

Evelyn felt her whole life pivoting on the axis of this moment, veering toward outer space like a rocket ship whose gyro has tumbled.

"Well, Larocca," she said softly, "I'd say you've got some decisions to make."

He looked off. In his mind's eye, Maria stared back at him, but not from a bed or a dance floor or from the deep joy of their wedding day. Instead, the image that flooded his senses was of her crouched in that filthy alley, hovering over Bruno Kretchmer, and saying, 'I'm. Pregnant.'

He reached for Evelyn's hand.

"I already made them," he said. "Her and me are done."

Their fingers intertwined, her smooth skin warm to his touch, his larger hand engulfing hers.

"Now you," he said, after a moment. "What's your big secret?"

She withdrew her hand and picked up one of his drawing pencils, sensing that they shouldn't be touching when she spoke her peace.

"I . . . um, it's about Buddy."

"Fooshee? Buddy Fooshee?"

She nodded.

Dante felt his pulse quicken. He leaned forward in his chair. Something he hadn't seen in her face before—guilt, memory, melancholy—flitted across her eyes.

"Go ahead, kiddo," he said.

She stared at him and then spoke softly.

"Dante . . . I, well, along with everybody else, really, there was a time when I loved Buddy, and we . . . we, he used to paint me—portraits, sketches, you know, out by the river or up in the barn on a rainy day. . ."

"Can't say I blame him."

Evelyn felt disoriented by all that had gone on that day, disoriented yet compelled by a native honesty to establish a clean slate with this dear, wounded man who had gone through so much in the war and who, in his own way and time had also loved Buddy.

"I . . . I don't know," she said, "how you and I are gonna end up, you know, with each other or not, but . . ."

"I think you do."

"Yes, well, maybe . . . so, anyway, here goes . . ." She drew a deep breath. "Buddy and I were lovers, Dante. Not so very often, really, but some. We were just in high school, of course, and he was a year ahead of me, but . . . but I did love him in the only way that a young girl, young woman, can. That is, totally. I thought he was the one perfect man for me. A crystalline soul-mate or some such stupid thing, and one day I . . . we just sort of gave in to it and I . . ."

"Yeah, that's . . ."

She glanced off. He sat back, looking at the tent floor but seeing Buddy in France.

"He had that same effect on the guys, too. I mean, not like romance or anything, but we all wanted to be his best friend, you know? We thought of him as special . . . like a young, I don't know, god or something."

"It was his eyes," she said, "and his . . ."

He held up his hand.

"Evelyn, you don't owe me this. I don't go in for historical jealousy. You loved him before I knew you—or him. I fought alongside him, and I loved him too. Then he died. End of story."

"Except that we'll both take him with us to the grave, Dante."

He looked hard at her and asked the question that had lodged itself in the forefront of his brain.

"Are you telling me that you and I can't . . . get together because of Buddy?"

"No. I'm not. I'm just telling you that . . . that we share him in some important sense. I wanted you to know that I could love you and love the deep memory of him at the same time—in different ways."

Dante watched her face a long moment, then smiled, shook his head, stood, and stretched, his arms reaching halfway out to the tent walls. Then he reached down, and caressed her yellow hair, hooking a curl over her left ear.

"He called you 'The Thoroughbred,'" he whispered.

She looked up at him.

"What are you talking about?"

"I only just then figured it out," he said. "Stupid, I guess, or maybe I was tryin' not to . . ."

"Dante, what do you . . ."

He sat back down, speaking slowly.

"Close to the German border one afternoon, we had the Krauts on the run, and we were behind the lines, resting on top of the tank—perfect day, not a cloud in the sky, ya' know? We were sitting up there cleaning our sidearms, our pistols, and a buncha G.I.s—single guys—were razzing Buddy and me about being married and about us not going with the French hookers, and all. And after the guys left I asked him . . . I asked Buddy if he would ever step out on his wife. And he sorta laughed, you know how he'd grin up at you out of the tops of his eyes . . ."

She nodded and smiled.

". . . and he said: 'only with the Thoroughbred,' and I said 'what the hell you talkin' about, Thoroughbred'? And he told me just enough about this woman from back home here that—listening to what you've told me—I can see it was you he was talking about. He said you were a pure thoroughbred, and that he was just a cow pony, and that it would never have worked, but that you were really . . . he said you were really something special."

She stared at him, her hands gripped fiercely together.

Dante glanced outside the tent at Sir Plus, then back at her. "I think . . . I think maybe he married Laney to keep from, I don't know, from proposing to you, or something."

Evelyn's eyes swam. She lowered her head, the tears welling up and over, spilling down her cheeks and onto her lap. Then, she let out a sob from deep in her throat, a little broken-hearted grace note of despair.

Dante rose, held her gently by the shoulders and guided her to his cot. He eased her down on it, swung her legs up and let her stretch out, full-length—achieving some sort of latent peace.

Then he sat on the floor next to her and touched her cheek with his fingertips, wiping away the tears, cooing her name. She took his hand in both of hers and kissed it.

"I'm so glad," she whispered, "I'm so glad you came into my life, Dante Larocca."

"That's a ditto, kiddo."

* * *

The next afternoon, the telephone in Evelyn's bedroom rang.

"Hello."

"Miss Curtis?"

"Speaking."

It was Paul Phillips. The name didn't ring a bell.

"I was one of the hopeless jokers who interviewed you for the job at Pan-Am," he said.

Her heart leaped. But which one was he: the ugly One, the Bald One, or the Pretty One?

"Uh, remind me of where you stood on the issue of women in the cockpit."

He laughed.

"Don't worry, I was the tall guy on your left who was arguing we should hire you."

She gripped the phone so hard her hand shook.

"Oh, yes, Paul. So, what's up?"

"Well, I'm calling to apologize for being so delayed in contacting you, but your application really threw us into a sort of tizzy, here."

Did he expect her sympathy?

"Well, desperate measures for desperate times, and all that," she said.

"I guess so. Anyway, I'm calling to say how sorry I am that the brass hats—at the very top of the company—have finally, formally declined to . . . to hire you. They say the world just isn't ready yet to . . ."

She didn't hear the rest of what he said. After making the requisite polite noises, they rang off, and she fell back onto her bed, staring at the ceiling.

* * *

The day following Cohen's death, Dante drove out to Laney Fooshee's. He'd called her that night to tell her, offering to come out then. She'd been silent a long time on the phone, then said, no, that Milo Henderson was there at the moment, and that she and Mama Lou would grieve together. That she'd half-expected this. That David was a wonderful man, but that something in him had been crushed by the war, and she'd come to believe she was not woman enough to fix it.

Through suppressed tears, she thanked Dante. He told her about the note addressed to her, saying he would bring it the next day. Dante never knew what Laney's note said. She didn't tell anyone, neither Mama Lou nor Milo. It too was brief:

Girly-Pearlie—I'm so sorry about this. Please understand it's no one's fault but mine—and the war, I guess. But a lot of guys had it worse than me, and they're making it, on the outside, at least. You may remember that rainy night in my trailer—that wonderful rainy night. I tried to tell you then about earthquakes and aftershocks and all that. Well, I guess the aftershocks won out in the end, those little rumbles that bubble up out of my memory on their own timetable. I can't seem to shake them. Anyway, it's all in the novel. Get Dante to show it to you, maybe. Or, maybe not. I do love you, girl, and wish every happiness for you.

     David

* * *

Evelyn and Tim Fletcher had the long heart-to-heart that had been coming for some time. Both had known it. Both regretted it. He'd been asked to rejoin the doctoral program at the University of Chicago. He'd be leaving in August. She would not be going with him. It was over. After four years of an intense, but much-interrupted courtship, of wonderful afternoons spent riding horses in the country, of long, thoughtful letters, of some good sex and bad sex, and then no sex— they were done.

She wished him all the luck in the world. She hoped he'd somehow, one day get the atomic monkey off his back. He chuckled and said he was working on it. He couldn't tell her that the F.B.I. had finally left him alone—or that they'd even entered his life. He wondered privately about Rangle/Ronchipov. About what had become of that smart, charming spy. About whether he'd made it home to his blond daughter, little Irina.

Tim hugged Evelyn and walked away.

* * *

In early June, a letter came to Dante Larocca. It was from Rachel
Birnbaum at Yale. She had taken the liberty of showing his Dalton
application to her dean, and, on the strength of it—and her forceful
representations on his behalf—she was now authorized to offer him a
position in Yale's 3rd year architecture class. If he was interested, he
should contact her immediately, as they were holding a slot open for
him, and a great many students were queued up for it.

He accepted.

Sir Plus would later find New Haven rainy and chilly.

Rather like Germany.

Evelyn Curtis rethought her response to Betty, Mavis, and Jill's
FEPEX idea of flying parcels around the country overnight. She
decided to give it a shot—but only until she got on as a pilot with a
commercial air line. Meanwhile, she sank $20,000 into their venture,
and her mother, Atlanta, agreed to do the girls' legal work, pro bono.

The day she mailed that $20K cashier's check to her girlfriends,
Evelyn spent the night with Dante in his tent. It was astonishing how
much abuse a stout army cot could bear, although sometime during the
night Dante eased down to the wooden floor and slept next to Sir Plus.
Early next morning, Evelyn awoke first, looked around, remembered
where she was, leaned over, and watched Dante sleeping. Sir Plus
stirred. Dante blinked awake. She reached out and touched his cheek.

"Hello, Brooklyn. Sleep okay?"

"Heyyyy, Bama-Girl. After that? No problem." He studied her face.
"Jeez, you're even pretty in the morning."

She smiled and motioned him to join her on the cot. Snuggling and
whispering, they watched through the tent flap as the sun dappled

Shorty's Beagle Ranch and mist rose on the swimming hole.

"You know," she said, "there's an awful lot I don't know about you."

"Mmmm."

"Like, your parents? I mean are they . . .?"

"Dead. Just before the war. Cancer and a heart attack."

"I'm sorry."

"I was closer to my grandpa. Old country. Artist. Great man. And you? I heard your old man's a big deal . . ."

He felt her stiffen and look away. In doing so, she revealed the pale scar slicing across her cheek.

"My father and I really don't . . . we don't get on so well."

"Mmmm." His finger traced the scar. "Is it because of this?"

She turned to face him, noting his morning whiskers and lovely eyes.

"Yes," she said. I'll tell you about it sometime. His name is Harry. He's a real throw-back, is Harry Curtis."

That August, with Dante and Sir Plus, Evelyn moved to New Haven. She would fly parcels out of Boston, bad weather and all.

Chapter 23
FUTURE-PAST TENSE

Harry Curtis died that Christmas, without being reconciled to his daughter.

The next year, his wife, Atlanta, was nominated to be president of the state bar association, but her candidacy was derailed by a clique of Birmingham lawyers who thought it "inappropriate."

Tim Fletcher and Dante Larocca both proved to be inspired predictors of post-war geo-politics. In Tim's case—just as he'd said to Dr. Feldman—on 29 August, 1949—four years and 23 days after Hiroshima—the Soviets exploded their own atomic bomb, code-named "First Lightning." Its yield was 22 kilotons. Their second, an improved plutonium implosion weapon, detonated on 24 September, 1951, yielding 38 kilotons.

The arms race was on.

The Soviet effort was not, however, aided in any way by Vladimir Ronchipov. Having finally arrived at his mother's Moscow flat quite late in the evening, he was persuaded by her not to awaken his daughter, Irina, but simply to steal a glimpse of her sleeping.

The next morning at dawn, before the child awoke, a knock on the Ronchipovs' door presaged the arrival of four men from the NKVD. They took Vladimir away to Lubyanka Prison. Three days later, following 34 hours of uninterrupted interrogation, and on the orders of Joseph Stalin, Vladimir Ronchipov was murdered by means of a single pistol shot to the back of the neck.

He was 26. He had not held or spoken to his daughter.

As for Dante, his prediction that Ole Gunderson would have his chance to fight for flag and country came true. In 1950, the United States initiated an extended "police action" on the Korean Peninsula. Gunderson, then a partner with a prominent Minneapolis architectural firm, took an immediate leave of absence from his position, joined the Marine Corps, was sent to Korea, and, while leading his men in battle, died from a sniper's round through the eye.

He was 27 and left a pregnant wife and one son behind.

David Cohen's novel—more "abandoned" than "finished"— has not yet found a publisher.

Laney Fooshee married Milo Henderson. They had no children and within six months of their wedding began sleeping in separate bedrooms.

Mama Lou Fooshee died peacefully in 1957, never fully reconciled to the loss of her son.

Laney and Buddy's son, Rafe, grew up and took over the farm. Then, in 1966, at the age of 23, he was drafted into the Army and sent to Vietnam where—on night patrol—he stepped on a booby-trapped grenade, losing a foot and an eye. He returned to Tuscaloosa County and hired Sammy Cleveland's son, Walter, to help him manage the farm until 1972 when he was killed in a tractor accident.

The next year, Walter—with his father's, Sammy's, backing— negotiated with Milo Henderson to purchase, on time, 150 acres of the former Fooshee estate. It wasn't the very best bottom land, but it wasn't bad, either. In fact, it included the great hillside fields where Evelyn almost bought the farm while crop-dusting them in her Stearman bi-plane.

Along with 900 of his shipmates, Vernon Puckett—Shorty & Cleola's beloved son—remains encased inside the USS Arizona at the bottom of Pearl Harbor. Shorty kept promising Cleola he'd take her to Honolulu to pay their respects, but he never found the time—or the will. Now, they're too old.

Neither Karl nor Ben graduated.

Chief Davis did.

Tim Fletcher earned his doctorate in theoretical physics at the University of Chicago in 1948, submitting a brilliant dissertation of only 24 pages. He then embarked on what promised to be a dazzling career in the classroom and laboratory. By 1951—burned out with research and with the burdens of memory—he shifted his efforts to achieving world peace and began working for the United Nations against the further proliferation of nuclear weapons.

Along with Dr. Robert Oppenheimer, he unsuccessfully opposed Edward Teller's efforts to build the thermo-nuclear, so-called Superbomb—a hydrogen-fusion weapon of unimaginable power and ruin. He failed. The U.S. detonated such a weapon in the Pacific at Eniwetok Atoll on 1 November, 1952. The Soviet Union followed suit on 12 August, 1953. Fletcher returned to academia, a subdued man. He never again voted, and he never married.

The fate of Dr. J. Robert Oppenheimer serves as a cautionary tale for any who would speak truth to power. Never one to suffer fools gladly, during the Cold War he was labeled a 'premature antifascist' for his support of the Republicans during the Spanish Civil War and for his early opposition to the Brown Shirts in Germany.

In April, 1954, his security clearance was lifted. He died in 1967.

Rachel Birnbaum retired from the Yale faculty in 1951, having taught Dante in two advanced classes. Free to go where she liked, she traveled, alone, to France and visited the grave of her long-dead fiance. The pain of it devastated her. It was as though he'd expired that morning. She never went back and died quietly near the Battery in Charleston in 1962.

Sidney Greene's wife passed away in 1948 of acute alcohol poisoning. He later married one of his former students but died of an embolism in 1954. Until his death, he continued to oversee the awarding of the Dalton Prize, but he never forgot Dante Larocca.

Maria Larocca did not contest the divorce. Early in 1947 she married Bruno Kretschmer. Six months later she bore the first of their five children. She too never forgot Dante.

Regarding Evelyn Curtis's determination to serve as an airline pilot, the first woman to fly passengers for an American commercial carrier was Emily Warner, hired by Frontier Airlines. The date was January 29, 1973.

FEDEX was founded in 1971.

AFTERWORD

For details regarding the Manhattan Project, I am indebted to the best book ever written on the subject: The Making of the Atomic Bomb, by Richard Rhodes.

The persons and events portrayed in this novel are, with few exceptions, invented. Those exceptions include the fate of Pearl Harbor and Hiroshima, along with that of the ships USS Arizona (BB-39), USS Little (DD-803) and USS Indianapolis (CA-35), and such historical figures as Ralph Graham, Leslie Groves, Robert Oppenheimer, General George S. Patton, Jr., Joseph Stalin, Hudson Strode, Edward Teller, Paul Tibbets, Harry Truman, Emily Warner, and Frank Lloyd Wright.

Sir Plus is based on my Weimaraner, Kate, who, at the age of two ran into the street and was struck by a truck right in front of me. Despite lingering infirmities, she lived to a ripe old age and was once described by my father as "a noble beast."

So was he. He lived to be 97.

George Wolfe graduated from the University of Mississippi and then from the Naval Officer Training Command in Newport RI. He was assigned to a destroyer that was later homeported in Japan for two years.

Aboard ship, Wolfe served as Weapons Department Head and Nuclear Weapons Officer, overseeing a substantial amount of gunfire support for the Army and Marines in Vietnam.

Following a year spent hitchhiking in Europe and the Middle East, Wolfe entered the English graduate program at UNC Chapel Hill, earned a doctorate, and took a position at the University of Alabama, Tuscaloosa, where he taught for many years and received the Burnum Distinguished Faculty Award.

He was instrumental in writing the scripts and securing funding for award winning PBS documentary films on Faulkner, Melville, the G.I. Bill and Marcel Proust.

He is married to the former Suzanne Rau, founding editor of Alabama Heritage Magazine.

This is his first novel.

AFTERSHOCK is his first novel.